FROM HERE *to* REALITY

ALSO BY STEVEN SCHINDLER

From the Block

Sewer Balls

From Here to REALITY

STEVEN SCHINDLER

POCKET BOOKS
New York   London   Toronto   Sydney

POCKET BOOKS, a division of Simon & Schuster, Inc.
1230 Avenue of the Americas, New York, NY 10020

ISBN-13: 978-1-4165-0046-9
ISBN-10:   1-4165-0046-4

First Pocket Books trade paperback edition August 2005

Designed by Elliott Beard

10   9   8   7   6   5   4   3   2   1

POCKET and colophon are registered trademarks of
Simon & Schuster, Inc.

Manufactured in the United States of America

For information regarding special discounts for bulk purchases,
please contact Simon & Schuster Special Sales at 1-800-456-6798 or
business@simonandschuster.com

To Sue—my soul mate. My coach. My inspiration.

ACKNOWLEDGMENTS

MY HEARTFELT THANKS to my publisher, Louise Burke, and my editor, Mitchell Ivers, for their guidance, support, and honest constructive criticism from day one. And most importantly, for the comfort they afforded me by already knowing what a sewer ball is.

FROM HERE to REALITY

Chapter One

AS I PASS A ROAD SIGN informing me that I have just entered Los Angeles County, and see just over the horizon what could be best described as a mushroom cloud of rust, I thought about the many times I almost made a U-ey on the highway and headed back home.

The reports that Los Angeles had become the latest manifestation of hell on earth started coming over the radio about half past Montana. Before last Friday, Rodney King was just another name on the radio news, interspersed with conflagrations in the Mideast, unidentified males found in abandoned South Bronx buildings, octogenarians robbed and raped, and the latest Wall Street gazillionaire opening some haute-nouveau-postmodern-foo-foo-eatery for people desperate to be obscenely seen.

But when the video of Rodney King getting his shins bashed in by teams of cops on a suburban street illuminated by million-candlepower searchlights shining down from police and media helicopters is played over and over and

over, more times than the Zapruder film, it brings to mind one burning question to all thinking New Yorkers such as myself: *How the hell could those cops be so stupid?*

That street scene was lit brighter than a night game at Yankee Stadium, and they continued to whale on his ass with multitudes watching? If they were really that pissed at him for punching a cop in the nuts, or biting his ear off, well, come on! Don't do it in the middle of a Los Angeles street that looks to be wider than most New York highways. Show a little discretion! I mean, you're in Hollywood for chrissakes! Don't you know just about every household in America has a home-video camera with a zoom lens?

Don't get me wrong. Rodney King didn't deserve to be beaten like that. But I mean an unarmed guy, drunk off his ass, trying to take on a dozen cops? To a New Yorker, that's a normal Saturday night in the Blarney Stone.

I'm no expert on the textbook regulations of how to apprehend a 275-pound drunk-driving lunatic, but I would guess maybe five cops tackling a guy and a few kicks in the balls would give you enough time to slap on a pair of cuffs, throw him in a black-and-white, and maybe add a few rabbit punches on the way downtown if you absolutely must. But sheesh!

So when they declared those cops not guilty last Friday, L.A. became a burning, rioting, raging Armageddon with palm trees. To think I packed my 1980 Chrysler Town & Country station wagon with simulated wood siding and drove three thousand miles for this.

I was always the smart one.

The first night of the riots, I stopped in Vegas—the only schmuck in the casino hunched over the bar watching the riots unfold on a small black-and-white TV. The bartender, a short black man named Hercules, was probably pushing seventy, but he looked like he could tap-dance on the face of every guy in the place. He told me he grew up in South Central L.A., right near Florence and Normandie, where the riots started, and he never thought he'd be more ashamed to say he grew up in L.A. after they let those Rodney King–beating cops go—that was until he saw those animals smash Reginald Denny in the face with a brick. "Ain't no good ever come from evil," he would recite whenever there seemed to be a lull in the action on the tube.

As I cruise west on the I-10, entering L.A. AM news-radio range in my K-car wagon, (nicknamed Woody, for the peeling wood-grain Con-Tact paper adorning its side), the news says it appears the riots are finally over in most parts of the city. Although there don't seem to be too many acts of random violence, there is still sporadic looting, having spread as far north as Hollywood, with reports of fires and stores being emptied on Vermont Avenue. Bingo! Guess what exit I have to take to get to my new apartment? Then it hits me: Once I go north on Vermont for about five miles, just past the heart of Hollywood, I have to make a right turn on *Rodney* Drive, my new street.

The sky is a weird shade of mud brown. The air is thick with soot and smoke, and there are ashes descending on my car like snow. This part of Vermont Avenue looks to be very Asian. In fact, I can tell by the lettering on what's left of the burnt-out storefronts that it's the Korean part of town. Pieces of people's lives are wisping through the air in the form of ashes and embers. Furniture, candy wrappers, sneakers, ladies' housecoats, fruit boxes, all up in smoke only to land in the gutter and eventually be swept away, probably by these same shopkeepers, and placed in a trash can for a city sanitation worker to dispose of properly. Law and order will return. But for now I drive up Vermont past the charred shells of mini-malls. Koreans are starting to walk the streets and begin the cleaning up in this part of town.

As I drive a mile or so north, I begin to see the sporadic looting. In a large shopping center on Vermont Avenue, in broad daylight, people are driving into the lot, parking neatly between the lines of painted parking spots, and walking through the broken plate-glass windows of a supermarket, a shoe store, and a tropical fish store. Some people have baby strollers. With babies in them! It's like they're out doing their weekly shopping. There are even a couple of cops directing traffic at the intersection, in full view of this brazen criminal activity, and not doing a thing. These looters don't fall into stereotypical racial patterns, either. In fact, I'd say it's a pretty good chunk of ethnic urban America partaking in this disgusting display of thievery. Blacks, whites, Latinos, Middle Eastern–looking folks. The only ethnic group missing, as far as I can tell, is Asian. But wait! There's a group of Asian teenagers coming out of the tropical fish store toting plastic bags of live fish.

America's melting pot has become Dante's Inferno. I wish I had a video camera for this. And maybe a gun.

Fortunately, the nonchalant L.A. looters haven't made it to Rodney Drive. The stores are all closed, and many of them have plywood boards over the windows or crews installing riot gates. Just a few hundred feet down the palm-tree-lined block is my new home. Hollywood View Court is a modest apartment complex that looks better to me than most places we went on vacation to when I was a kid, like the sagging fire-trap bungalows we used to rent in Rockaway, Queens. I'd classify Hollywood View Court as a typical L.A. apartment building: U-shaped, two-story, with exterior entrances surrounding a common courtyard. Only instead of a weeping willow tree, such as we used to play Chutes and Ladders under in Rockaway, this common area has a large swimming pool surrounded by nice patio furniture and umbrellas.

But now the pool water is a smoky gray, the beach chairs and patio are covered with a layer of soot and ash, and the whole neighborhood smells like the inside of a wood-burning pizza oven.

. . .

I found this place in a day, just over a month ago. I was out here doing a video shoot for my old boss, Karen Marshall, who's now in L.A., having landed a gig as a big kahuna at a major TV network. She promised me if I moved out, she could land me a job. Well, since my flight out from JFK was delayed for three hours due to several deicings, and upon my arrival at LAX it was 78 degrees, I gave it careful consideration. At that time, my writer/producer job at the local TV station in New York was already on thin ice, and I didn't know I was getting ready to fall through into icy-cold, dark waters. The program I worked on wasn't the kind of programming the new owner of the station liked. We were already hearing rumors that syndicated trash TV such as *Busted on Tape*, *In Your Face Hidden Video,* and *Date Bait* were going to replace the weekly show I worked on. That show, *Inside the Apple*, featured reports on the arts, entertainment, and New York neighborhood stories. Out with the old and in with the dreck. My old boss was the first lucky rat to jump ship. But considering I mouthed off in an obscenity-laced tirade at her replacement barely two hours into her tour of duty, calling into question her professionalism, ethics, and choice of perfume, my fate was pretty much sealed. I was the first unlucky person to be let go. And the second person ever escorted out of the building by security. I heard the first guy ever escorted out stabbed somebody.

Karen Marshall more than likely used her patented strategy of sweet talk and passive-aggressive sociopathic bullying to land one of the most revered jobs in Hollywood: TV development. Okay, so it was in the newly coined area of reality programming, but nonetheless, it was a real accomplishment for a college dropout from Utica to be in such an influential position. Now, I know the only way to get anywhere in this town is to have somebody already on the inside, so I figured what the hell. I'm single, have almost ten years of experience in TV, have decent personal hygiene habits, and got removed from my New York TV job at the insistence of an armed security guard—Hollywood seemed like a valid choice. Maybe my only choice.

After an L.A. power lunch with Karen last month, she pretty much assured me she could get me work, and I was sold. She also suggested I head east on Hollywood Boulevard to check out an area for apartments, which she described as the closest thing to New York: an area called Los Feliz. I was amazed at the number of available nice places with swimming pools and palm trees. And, compared to New York, cheap. I found a two-bedroom in three hours for about a third of what a similar-sized apartment would rent for in Manhattan. And the topper is, you get a freaking parking space! Free. The name of the place, painted in script with white lettering on a dark brown piece of wood, was what really sold me: HOLLYWOOD VIEW COURT. I was immediately intrigued, because the prewar building where I grew up in the Bronx had a faded concrete inscription above the entrance: BAILEY VIEW COURT. As a child in that apartment, I would look out my bedroom window and see the world go by as the sun set in the West each evening. Little did I know that one day I'd follow those sunsets, only to discover that the orange glow of the western sky wasn't the sun setting but a city engulfed in flames.

Rodney Drive is eerily quiet. I have to drive through an alley to get to my assigned parking space behind my newly adopted apartment building. Just as I'm ready to make a left turn into the driveway, a van speeding straight toward me in the narrow alley makes a tire-squealing turn directly in front of me, missing me by a foot or so. It careens up the short slope of the driveway, bottoming out in the process, and whips into a parking space in the nearly empty lot. It's a filthy black cargo van with no hubcaps and a huge dent on the front fender, and it's rumbling like it hasn't had a tune-up since it rolled off the assembly line in Flint in the late seventies. It's sitting there with the motor running. I slowly pull into the lot only to realize that he's in space number thirteen, and my preassigned space is number fourteen. I creep into my spot, trying to keep my distance but staying within the painted white line. Just as I kill my engine, the cargo door on the van swings open, just missing my door. From the darkness of the cargo area, I hear an agitated male voice.

"The whole fucking lot is empty, and he's got to park on top of me. Jesus Christ. Dammit!"

Discovering that my neighbor is a raging maniac wasn't exactly the way I hoped to begin my new life in Los Angeles. I can hear more ranting from inside the van, but I can't make out what he's saying. A large box slides into view of the van cargo doorway.

"How the hell am I supposed to get this out? I can't fucking believe this!" a disjointed voice whines from behind the box.

I open my door, careful not to hit his van, and get ready to stand my ground.

"Excuse me," I say in a tone usually reserved for phrases such as *fuck off*. "Is there some kind of problem here?" Knowing full well what the problem is, and that other problems are more than likely to follow.

"How the fuck am I supposed to get this out of here? Huh? Jesus!" the voice says, still in the darkness of the van behind the Zenith TV box. Finally, popping up behind the box, he appears. I can barely make out his severe face, tense with strain. He has absolutely no color, except maybe gray, with thinning, disheveled salt-and-pepper hair, a few strands across his forehead. His eyes are so deep-set I can see barely anything but two dark holes where his eyes should be. Stooped over as he is, he reminds me of some kind of evil troll who has just been disturbed after a two-year nap under a bridge.

"Well, maybe if you'd ask me *nicely*, I could move my car and help with your box," I say without a hint of friendliness.

"Just move your car. I don't need any help."

"That's *nice*? Nope. Not nice. Not nice at all, asshole," I say, slamming my car door shut, which I don't like to do, since every time it's slammed, the simulated wood siding peels off a little bit more. *Asshole* isn't a word I use lightly. I use it only when I'm absolutely positive that the person being addressed as an asshole is one whose ass I can kick. I'm no Hulk, but at five foot nine and 150 pounds, often growing up in the streets, I've learned to swing a tire iron like nobody's business. By the looks of this guy, unless he's hiding a revolver, I've got nothing to be worried about. I've turned and begun to walk away when he jumps out of the van.

"Look. Could you do me a favor and move your car? Please?" he asks, his demeanor switching from ranting shithead to pleading child.

The overcast day adds to his pallor. He stands there, looking down at the ground. He's wearing a black windbreaker that drapes over his sharp, pointy shoulders. He looks to be in his fifties, but if he told me he was seventy, I would believe him. I can't tell if he hasn't shaved or if his face is dirty with ash and soot.

"Will do, *pal*. All you have to do is ask. Nicely." I say the word *pal* as though I'm saying *asshole*.

As soon as I pull out of the space, my nutty neighbor is grappling with the large, cumbersome box. I walk over to the rear of his van, and after witnessing him awkwardly struggle with his cargo, I figure I'll try dropping my harsh attitude to offer help. "Need a hand?"

"No!" he shoots back in a tone that screams to me, *And don't ask me again*.

So much for that. As he's struggling with the box, finally getting it out of the van and onto the ground, I can see that his right hand is missing two fingers, the pinky and the ring finger. Maybe asking if he needed a *hand* wasn't exactly the right way to kiss and make up.

He grips the box, holding it so high he can barely see over it, and swiftly heads for the gate that leads to the apartments. I catch up to him to open the gate, but he doesn't even look at me. He just grunts in my direction, which I believe is the best he can do for a thank-you. When I took the apartment last month, there was an old lady living with her mother in the apartment right next to mine. Lo and behold, he's now fumbling for keys at his front door, standing on a stoop littered with pre-riot trash, balancing the box on his knee, then entering his apartment, which is right next to the old ladies' place. Just two doors over from me.

I walk back to my car, park it in my assigned spot, and remove a small bag with my personal items. I figure I should check in with Harriet, the building manager. I ring her doorbell, and after a little bit too long of a wait, I see a lacy white curtain being moved ever so slightly and a single eyeball peering at me. The curtain is dropped, and I hear light footsteps. Then a mousy voice says, barely above a whisper, "Who's there?"

"It's Johnny Koester. The new tenant in apartment 1A. I just got here."

No response.

So I add, "From New York. We met last month. You rented me the apartment."

I hear some furniture moving, a large clanging sound as though a small pot fell into a large pot, something large being dragged, several locks being undone, and the door opens about two inches, with the chain still engaged. Now I can see a nose, an eye, and half a mouth.

"Can I see some identification, please?"

"Uh, sure," I say as I reach into my small black bag for my wallet. The door closes an inch. "Here. It's my driver's license. From New York," I reassure her as I hand her the license.

"I'm terrible with faces. This doesn't look like you," the half a mouth asks with one eyebrow raised.

"Uh, how's this?" I say, contorting my face to match the awful photo.

"Okay, I'm opening the door," she says as she closes it and undoes the chain. The door quickly swings open, and she shoos me inside.

Harriet is a stoutish middle-aged woman. Her dainty apartment is filled with frilly doily easy-chair armrest protectors and hand-crocheted pink-and-white tissue-box covers. You might expect she'd be more comfortable somewhere like Williamsburg, Virginia, or on the outskirts of Amish country in Pennsylvania, not a few blocks from the bull's-eye of hedonism in Hollywood, U.S.A.

"You picked a peach of a time to move to Los Angeles," she says.

"I noticed. It's pretty quiet now, though," I say, noticing the potpourri of items she has piled in front of the door: a large stuffed chair, a small but solid-looking wooden table, a galvanized steel washtub filled with books, and a shovel.

"Almost everyone headed for the hills. I would have left town, but my friend in Lake Arrowhead is attending a wedding in Las Vegas."

"I was just in Vegas. Why didn't you meet her there?"

She lowers her head and looks up at me as she pulls her glasses low on her nose, saying, "I hate Las Vegas."

"Oh. Well, I'm going to be moving some things into the apartment now. The rest of my stuff will arrive in a week or so. I was just wondering if I needed to sign anything else or . . . anything," I say, stumbling on my words as I notice a large butcher knife on a table behind her.

"Oh, no. I'm just glad that there's a strong young man nearby. I'll feel much safer, being single and all."

"What about the guy a couple of apartments over from mine?" I say, figuring maybe I can get a little bit of background on the jerk.

"You've met Benny?" Harriet asks nervously, as though I've discovered an awful secret. "When did you meet him?"

"He and I had a little orientation in the parking lot a few minutes ago."

"Oh, no," Harriet says, placing her hand over her lips. "Was he coming or going?"

"He was coming. Right at me, in fact. He nearly plowed into me in the alley. Then we got into it when—"

"Well, I'm sure you won't have any problems with him. He's hardly ever around."

"And when he is?"

"And when he is, what?" Harriet asks, tugging on her left earlobe.

"And when he's around, what's he like? Do I need to watch out for this guy? I mean, the last thing I need is some psycho—"

"Oh no, no, no. Benny's fine. He's just, just, a little . . . he keeps to himself. That's all. I've really got to get back to some things. Bye," she says, waving me toward the door.

"Ah, yeah. Thanks."

The door slams shut behind me, and I can hear the furniture being put back into a secured position in front of the door.

My living room looks like a seventies basement rec room. Last month, after I paid my security deposit, I went to a thrift shop and bought three round-back plastic chairs: one lime green, one black, and one red; a dark brown simulated-wood dining room table with imitation mother-of-pearl borders; and a tattered padded chair with leopard-skin-patterned fabric, which will all do fine until my stuff arrives on the moving van. I have a small cassette player/radio I can use for my sounds, and it will do me good not to watch TV for a week or so. Turning on the radio, I scan the dial and find a classical station. I sit my tired butt down in my leopard-skin chair, close my eyes, and after days of driving solo, bad truck stop food, and smelly public toilets, I can finally relax in my own place. The riots and looting seem a million miles away, and a symphony has begun to soothe my monkey mind, when I hear a loud knock at the door.

That must be Harriet. Maybe she wants to be friends and is bringing a tray of home-baked cookies.

I open the door, and there he is. Right on my doorstep. My fucked-up neighbor. He's not smiling. In fact, he looks like trouble. I've seen too many faces like that while spending many days of my adolescence in dark corners of parks, hanging under railroad bridges in the rain, and in apartment building cellars. Now that I can get a good look at him, standing next to the harsh light of an exterior lightbulb by my front door, I can make out what this Benny guy actually is: a junkie. He's standing sheepishly in front of me, holding a much smaller box than he was holding before, but this one is labeled as a Panasonic TV.

"Uh, hi. How ya doin'?" he mumbles.

"What can I do for you?" I ask, trying to sound as pissed off as possible.

"Yeah, listen, want to buy a portable TV? Brand-new. Never been used. Still in the box."

"Actually, no! The last thing I would do is buy a fucking hot TV that some asshole has—"

Before I can complete my sentence, he spins around and feverishly heads straight for the parking-lot gate. He kicks it open and disappears. I hear his car door open and slam shut, the engine start, and tires squeal as he exits onto the street.

I've been in my new abode all of fifteen minutes, only to realize I've got a crazy junkie next-door neighbor who thinks I'm some hick, stupid enough to buy something he just robbed out of a burnt-out storefront. What an asshole!

Hopefully he got the message and he'll never knock on my door again.

Chapter Two

IT'S BEEN OVER A WEEK and my moving van still hasn't arrived. Karen keeps promising she'll have a job for me, but the only possibility so far is on something called *Shocking Hollywood Secrets*, which has me wondering if I should start reloading the Woody. Although the cable-TV hookup is ready, I still don't have a TV, since I didn't want to buy a hot one from my junkie neighbor. So I'll spend my Friday evening relaxing, rereading Kerouac's *On the Road* to compare notes on our journeys across America while listening to John Coltrane's *Giant Steps* on my cassette player with headphones.

On page twelve, Sal (Kerouac) takes the subway to the last stop at 242nd Street to begin his legendary trek across America. Kerouac's first step is whence I just came: my old Bronx neighborhood, 242nd Street and Broadway. I've settled in with a small Flintstones jelly jar bought at the Goodwill, filled with Jack Daniels, when, just above the wailing sax on my head-

phones, I hear a commotion outside. I take off the headphones and hear a woman screaming in a thick accent, "No, no, no! Get away from me, you peeeeg! You goddamn fucking peeeg!"

Never being one to hide under the pillow when there's trouble on the home front, I stick my head out my front door to see, across the pool on the second floor, a very sluttily attired but still strikingly attractive woman with huge breasts barely contained in her skintight red polyester tube top, screaming at a heavyset white guy with a shaved head, dressed in black leather. She's forcefully pushing him out her door. Once he's out, he turns and takes off his dark sunglasses—which is a good idea, since it's midnight—and yells back at her, "You fucking whore. You ain't nothing but a no-good whore." As he turns to walk down the stairs, a jar just misses his skull and splatters on the wall above his head, spraying him with what looks to be . . . bright red borscht!

"Sorry I missed you, you peeg!"

The accent, the borscht . . . she's got to be Russian. And probably as dangerous as Stalin in a bad mood. But my oh my, is she something to behold! Dark red hair that is so straight, it looks like she recently finished ironing it. Rich, red, pouty lips stretched by a clenched jaw. And deep-set eyes with so much black eye makeup it's hard to see her raging eyes at all in the 40-watt patio light. She's wearing black spike heels with fishnet stockings that go from here to Hollywood and Vine.

If I had to lay odds, I'd say she's a very expensive hooker. Not the street variety, but judging by her clientele, the price is up for debate. Mr. Borscht-head slams the front gate shut, wiping the cabbage from his chrome dome as he exits. Once she sees he's gone, she goes inside, comes back out with a roll of paper towels, and begins to clean up the mess. She finishes her job and disappears into her apartment. But a moment later, I hear some soothing classical music, probably Debussy or Brahms, and I'm sure it's coming from her place. Oh well, as Bill Shakespeare said,

"Music soothes the savage breast," right? Well, that's a savage breast I'd like to soothe myself.

I turn to step back into my place and am startled to notice one of my elderly next-door neighbors standing behind her screen door in a darkened living room, staring blankly at me, barely visible through the screen.

"You can set your clock to that," she says softly.

"How's that?" I say with a hand on my front door.

"She moved in about three months ago. Every weekend it's the same. It's impossible to get any sleep. They'll let anyone move in here these days."

Not taking that comment as an insult just yet, I say, "Has anyone tried to do anything about it?"

"That's Harriet the building manager's job," she says icily.

"Well, sometimes you have to take matters into your own hands. Good night," I say, stepping into my apartment.

So much for having a building full of friendly neighbors. Having lived in huge apartment buildings my entire life, I can say that I usually had to deal with assholes only on my own floor. If you live on the first floor and something happens on the sixth floor, you sometimes never even become aware of it. I remember one time an entire apartment was wiped out because of a fire on the top floor, and I didn't hear about it for a week. In this place, you can pretty much tell what everyone's having for breakfast, the way sounds and smells bounce through the courtyard. Now that I think of it, I'm glad my looter neighbor keeps a virtual barricade of dirty, shut windows in front of his apartment.

The rest of the evening was uneventful. I finish up *On the Road* and, following Sal and Dean halfway across America and just like they did many a night, crawl off to sleep in my sleeping bag, hopefully for the last time, as I settle in for a good night's sleep in my new home.

·   ·   ·

I can see the sun is barely up, and some fool is ringing the door-bell like there's a fire. I jump out of bed and swing the front door open, revealing two beefy guys in National Van Lines uniforms.

"You John, er, Coaster?"

"That's pronounced Custer, as in the general," I say, correcting him the way I correct most people who mispronounce my last name like "coaster" instead of the proper way, as in General Custer, who, along with his men, was slaughtered at Little Big Horn in the last real victory the Indians had.

"General? General what?"

"You know, General Custer? Little Big Horn?" I could see from their blank expressions that they were more interested in dumping my stuff and hitting the road than getting an American history lesson. "Never mind. How do we get started here?"

"Sign this, this, and this, then we need a check for the balance and we'll start unloading."

"Great. Let's do it."

Within an hour and a half, old Chester and Bert had placed every item where I directed them to and were on their way to the House of Pies down the block for some breakfast before they made their next stop in Oxnard. I had thought my three bed-rooms of furniture from New York would be too much for my new two-bedroom place, but these rooms are much larger. I even have a dining room off the living room, so there is an open, airy feeling that I've never experienced in my own place. Except for the boxes filled with kitchen stuff, clothing, books, and records, I'm beginning to feel like I really do have a new home.

From my old, favorite living room chair, now in place, I can see the swimming pool and the potted palms through my front screen door when I have my front door open. And, like a vision from the second floor, Miss Russia walks right into my view, wearing a Japanese-style silk kimono and high heels. Just as she unties it, revealing her splendid, slender white body with the outline of her nipples quite visible through her skimpy bikini top, she turns and sweetly says, "Come here, my little Mishka," and a darling little boy about three years old wobbles over to her. She bends down, giving me an even better view of her voluptuous assets, picks up the boy, and begins tenderly kissing him all over his face, neck, bare chest, and belly.

What I wouldn't do to change places with that kid. With the thought of her actions last night, I can see why she behaved like a deranged mama bear. That creep was a threat to her sleeping cub. And everybody knows you never mess with Mama Bear. Especially a Russian one.

Miss Russia spends the next hour or so alternating between swimming with her little Mishka, sunbathing, and playing with him on two chaise longues facing my apartment. As I secretly watch them from the safety of my living room, I think I could get used to this real fast.

But dragging two chaise longues right in front of Mama Bear and Baby Bear, totally blocking my view, are my two elderly neighbors, mother and daughter, wearing plaid terry-cloth robes and rubber bathing caps. When they drop their robes, revealing their powdery, flabby bodies, I think perhaps it's time to start unpacking some of these boxes.

I unpack like a dockworker for a couple of hours and work up quite a sweat. I peek out my front door and see that no one is in the pool area at the moment. So I don my trusty trunks, grab my Bugs Bunny beach towel, and head for the pool. Being a paranoid New Yorker, I know never to leave the front door unlocked. Not even for five seconds. So I lock my front door, drop my towel on a chair, and as I put my toe into the water for the first time, I make an amazing discovery: The pool is heated! I'm used to jumping into the ocean waves of the Atlantic in late May, when the water's so cold it makes your balls jump into your belly and your pecker shrink so small it looks like a soggy Brazil nut. But after the initial shock of icy ocean water, it's always refreshing. A complete rejuvenation of the senses. This pool water feels like one giant warm spot left by a six-year-old. It's so warm, it's like old ladies' bathwater. Oh well, it's wet. So I slowly immerse myself in the tepid water up to my chin and start to feel its calming quality begin to take effect. As I slowly float on my back across the pool, barely moving my arms, staring at the deep blue skies and the puffy white clouds, I feel like I'm in a giant, warm tub, and it's actually quite a nice feeling. Not the shock of most pools I remember diving into as a kid, but a sensual, relaxing, lazy float.

The surrounding apartments seem rather quiet. I hear only soft music emanating from a couple of upstairs windows. Then, suddenly, I hear a loud scraping as if a door is sticking and being pried open. From my floating vantage point, I can see that it's my neighbor, the junkie looter, coming out of his hovel. I haven't seen him in days. He pulls his door shut, and it again makes a loud screeching sound. Then he locks it. He doesn't even glance at the pile of dirty flyers, old phone books, and newspapers littering his doorstep. His skin is almost the same color as it was when the atmosphere was filled with smoke and ash. He has the pallor of a person who is not well, but his features are what my mom would call a good-looking paisan. He has classic Italian features: a curved nose, high cheekbones, a sharp chin, and deep-set dark eyes. But his features are a little too extreme. The high cheekbones and deep eyes, which once probably contributed to his being handsome, are now making him appear to be just another gaunt junkie.

I doubt he knows I'm watching him. My face is the only thing above water, and I haven't made a sound in about ten minutes. There is a gate around the pool, which probably helps camouflage me even more. He turns and looks at my apartment door and begins walking toward it. He opens my screen door and quietly knocks. That knock would be heard only if I were maybe a foot or two away from the door. Definitely not the kind of knock I would hear if I were washing the dishes. I figure I'll just see how long I can remain invisible before something really interesting develops. He pats on my door a couple more times, and then he turns, blocking most of the front door from my view. It's hard to tell exactly what he's doing, but it appears that he's trying the doorknob to see if my door is locked. Nice. Once he realizes it's locked, he makes a beeline for the gate to the parking lot. I hear the sound of his shitty van starting, and then he takes off, bald tires and fan belts squealing.

I climb up the ladder at the deep end of the pool. So much for my relaxing swim. It's not going to be easy to relax from now on, knowing I've got a junkie neighbor casing my joint. I had put aside the thought of buying a gun, but now I think I'll look into it. I don't know what that guy's story is, but if I find his junkie ass rifling through my desk drawers while I'm taking a crap one morning, I want to make sure I give him a little something extra to take to jail with him. Like a slug in the ass.

After a shower, I decide to do a background check into the habits of my mysterious sociopathic neighbor. I figure this is as good a time as any to properly introduce myself to my next-door neighbors, the antique mom-and-daughter act, and get the dope on Benny.

Not wanting to shock them by banging on the door, and half not wanting them to answer, I don't knock too hard. But as soon as my knuckle touches the wood, I hear a stern "Who's there?"

"It's your new next-door neighbor, John Koester."

The draperies on the front window are quickly drawn, and the daughter gives me a quick once-over through the window. The door is yanked open, and I'm immediately struck by the overwhelming odor of assorted powders: talcum powder, sweet-smelling deodorant powder, Ajax.

"Yes, Mr. Koester, how can we help you?" the younger of the two asks me, holding the door half open, revealing her mother sitting in a large chair, wearing white gloves and holding an enormous book.

"Call me Johnny. Now that I'm a little settled in, I thought I'd introduce myself."

"That's lovely of you, Johnny. Come in, won't you?" she asks, her attitude changing from urban paranoia to small-town friendly. "Mother and I were just doing some reading. I'm Rosalynne, and this is my mother, Gertrude," she says, shaking my hand and waving toward her mom, who is cocking her head and pushing an ear forward as though she's trying to focus her hearing on the action. "Mother, this is the new young man who moved in right next door, Johnny Koester."

"Koester? How do you spell that?" Gertrude inquires.

"K-O-E-S-T-E-R," I say.

"That's the German spelling. Not like General Custer. Are you German?"

"Half. The other half is Italian."

"Oh, when I was young, we weren't allowed to have mixed marriages," Gertrude laments. "How old are you?"

"I'm thirty-one."

"You look younger. You need a haircut—"

"Never mind that, Mother. Go back to your book," Rosalynne says as she helps her mother balance the heavy leather-bound book on her lap. "We were just getting ready for tea, would you like a cup?" Rosalynne asks.

"Certainly, thank you."

Rosalynne nods and disappears into the kitchen, leaving me in a chair a few feet from her mother, who manages to turn a page with her white glove after three attempts. Once the page is turned, Gertrude looks over to me and states matter-of-factly,

"Listen to some of these other names used for the Ruddy Duck: Dumpling Duck, Daub Duck, Deaf Duck, Fool Duck, Sleepy Duck, Butter Duck, Bumblebee Coot, Dumb-Bird, Dinky Duck, Paddy-Whack Duck."

"That's fascinating. Those are hilarious . . ." I stop midsentence, because she either can't hear me or doesn't care to hear me, and has gone back to reading her tome.

Rosalynne appears with a large silver tray, complete with three delicately flowered teacups, a matching bowl filled with sugar cubes, and a small silver beaker of cream. She places the tray on the white marble coffee table in front of me and begins pouring. "Help yourself to the cream and sugar. Mother and I have lived in this apartment for over twenty years. We moved here when Father died. We lived up the street in a large house, but after he died, we thought it was just too much. I see you have New York license plates. What part of New York are you from?"

"The city. The Bronx."

"Do they consider the Bronx part of New York City?"

"Oh yeah, we get every bit as many of the murders, muggings, filth, and lunatics as Manhattan does per capita. Only we have more trees."

Rosalynne looks at me with a horrified expression.

"Just kidding. Yes, the Bronx is part of New York City. One of the five boroughs. And the area I come from is indeed very nice, with trees and parks and the Hudson River close by, but it has its share of typical American urban problems. I would've stayed, but I had an employment opportunity here, so I thought I'd give La-La Land a shot."

"La-La Land? Oh dear," Rosalynne chortles, tapping her knee. "Mother, did you hear that?" she says, waving at Gertrude.

"Did I hear what?" Gertrude says, looking like she's none too happy to be taken away from her massive bird-guide encyclopedia of fun facts.

"He called Los Angeles La-La land! Isn't that funny? I have to remember that one! La-La Land," Rosalynne says, before taking the first sip from her good china cup of tea.

"I think it's irreverent." Gertrude scowls. "Los Angeles is one of the world's great cities. It has the largest, most technologically advanced commercial port in the Western Hemisphere."

"Oh, Mother! La-La Land. Ahhh," Rosalynne sighs and happily shakes her head, her cup still at her lips. "And what business are you in?" she asks me.

"Show business. TV," I respond. That usually gets a positive reaction from strangers in a bar, but Rosalynne has a look on her face as though I announced I'm a cat torturer.

"We rarely watch television. Such garbage. A waste of time. What is it you do?"

Not wanting to play up the socially redeeming values of what *Shocking Hollywood Secrets* might hold, I decide to give a brief summary of my last job. "In New York, I worked for a program that aired each evening and highlighted feature news stories, mostly about the arts, entertainment, restaurant reviews, places to shop, interesting weekend getaways, that sort of thing."

"Well, that's not too bad. We like that big fellow with the southern accent who does that kind of thing on public television. I can't remember his name, but he's very handsome and shows you interesting museums and curio shops and such," Rosalynne says, trying her best to forgive me for working in television. "We usually watch the local news on Channel Four and then the national news on public television. But the local news is getting awful. Nothing but sensationalism. And those new programs are just horrid. We saw an advertisement announcing a new program with nothing but Hollywood scandals. Can you imagine such a thing?"

"Yeah, well, ah, I wanted to ask you about the apartment

complex. How do you like living here?" I say, quickly changing the subject.

Rosalynne puts down her teacup and says, "We're moving out the first opportunity we get. This building has gone downhill, terribly. That building manager does nothing! Do you know how many times I've had to complain to the landlord to start heating the pool? The previous building manager made sure it was heated on April first every year. Now you're lucky if it's mid-April. They just began heating it today, you know. And the people moving in! Oh!"

"Like the Russian lady upstairs?" I gently ask.

"Oh my gracious! In the short time she has lived here, the police have been there almost every week! And the class of people you see going up there. One can only imagine what goes on!"

"What about the guy who lives next to you?"

Gertrude immediately looks up and barks, "Don't mention that man in this house!"

"Never mind, Mother," Rosalynne whispers. "That man has lived here for almost ten years. I've never seen him wash or sweep or dust or pick up anything the entire time. I don't know what goes on in there, and I don't want to know. And the police have been to his door on more than one occasion as well. I retire this year, then we're off to Leisure Town in Orange County. A gated retirement community for mature adults, you know. Well, it is getting late. Thank you so much for stopping by. It's nice to know there's a nice young man nearby. The man who was in that apartment before you was a holy terror. In some sort of satanic music group. A disgrace, he was. In fact, if you stand in the parking area and look at the peak of the highest hill straight ahead, that's where he wound up."

"You mean he was . . . found dead up there?"

"No. He bought that huge mansion at the very top when he moved out of here."

"Really? Do you remember the name of the band?"

"Of course not. But Harriet said it has something to do with guns or snakes or something."

"Well, it was a pleasure meeting you, Rosalynne, and your mother. Goodbye, Gertrude."

Rosalynne whispers, "She only hears what she wants to hear when she wants to hear it. Have a pleasant evening, John."

I walk the three steps to my door and enter my comfy new pad. As I turn to lock the door, I notice a small folded note on the floor. The paper is yellow with age and reeks of cigarette smoke. I open it and there, in Catholic-school-style perfect penmanship, written in pencil, is: *Dear Sir, Please knock on my door sometime. I want to tell you something. Your neighbor, one door over— Benny Bennett. Thank you. P.S. Sorry about what happened the other day.*

Benny Bennett. Well, it sounds a little more legitimate than Benny the Ball on *Top Cat*, but not much. I'll bet he has something to tell me. Only I think that's a misprint. I think he meant to write that he wants to *sell* me something. I doubt I'll be knocking on his door anytime soon. But in this place, it will be difficult to avoid him. Unless I start parking on the street and avoid the pool. Nah. I'll just deal with it. Head-on. I wonder if anyone in this building knows anything about purchasing a gun?

Chapter Three

IN HER USUAL passive-aggressive style, Karen waited until the last possible moment to tell me that I really did have a job lined up. She was always one to play her hand close to her vest, but her unreturned phone calls, lame excuses, and general avoidance had me thinking twice about whether she'd keep her end of the bargain. But in her typical Karen way, she called me late last night as if nothing ever happened, told me I would be getting two hundred bucks a day, and gave me the address of the Hollywood production office of *Shocking Hollywood Secrets* where I'm reporting for duty—today. Just like that.

Hollywood is the closest thing to New York. Hollywood Boulevard is the West Coast version of Broadway near Times Square at its sleaziest worst in the '70s. Just like its East Coast counterpart, Hollywood Boulevard is a bizarre juxtaposition of tourists, hookers, artsy types on the way to meetings and rehearsals, junkies, street people, and hustlers. There are cheesy souvenir

stores, porno movie theaters, and tattoo parlors. But amid the sleaze, filth, and squalor, there are also amazing bookstores that sell every screenplay from *Citizen Kane* to *Police Academy 6* and collectible shops that carry vintage posters, for tens of thousands of dollars, that you probably couldn't find anywhere else in the world. There are disgusting convenience stores that cater to bums and crackheads, and a few of the most authentic and grand establishments from old Hollywood that maintain their original luster and glory, such as Musso & Frank's and the Roosevelt Hotel. And on Hollywood Boulevard, just as on Broadway in New York, the human circus transpires on the street while the offices above contain some of the most influential and important businesses in their fields. Above Broadway you'll find offices that rule the music industry and the Broadway theater district. And on Hollywood Boulevard you'll find the companies that dominate the film and television industry. I don't think it's any coincidence, either. The Hollywood industry was founded mostly by New Yorkers in the 1920s and '30s. In fact, if you go to Warner Bros. Studios, which is just a few minutes north of the Hollywood Bowl, you can see the most obvious connection: The studio is laid out in a grid system where the north-south "roads" separating the buildings are called Avenue A, Avenue B, Avenue C, and the east-west roads, 1st Street, 2nd Street, 3rd Street—exactly the same street markers from the Lower East Side of New York where most of the early Jewish producers, writers, directors, and actors grew up.

Just a couple of blocks past the Chinese Theatre—where, for over sixty years, stars have left their footprints, handprints, and, in Jimmy Durante's case, nose print—is the headquarters of the Next Big Thing Entertainment, producers of *Shocking Hollywood Secrets*. I'm a little nervous, for the obvious reasons: new city, new job, questionable program material, but I've got a few extra butterflies biting my stomach lining because my boss is none other than Wendy Valentine. Yes, *that* Wendy Valentine. Star of the short-lived sixties cold war spy comedy *My Daughter the Secret Agent*. It was only on for two seasons, but any boy within a decade of puberty had a thing for Wendy Valentine. And I mean a *thing*! Jeannie, of *I Dream of Jeannie* fame, may have shown her belly, but with the skintight black leather and/or rubber outfits that Wendy's character, Amy Bloom, wore, you didn't need much of an imagination to get a lesson in the female anatomy. When we kids were trolling the basements of our apartment buildings looking for nudie magazines hidden by older teens, we'd occasionally stumble upon those nudist-colony publications with the nipples covered by black rectangles or erased from the picture entirely. I didn't even know that female breasts had nipples until Wendy appeared in that black leather jumpsuit. I must have dry-humped every pillow, sofa cushion, and large plush toy in the house when I was home alone watching. And now the object of my prepubescent lust is the proud owner of the Next Big Thing Entertainment. Little does she know she was the focus of my *first* big thing. I haven't seen her in anything since *My Daughter the Secret Agent*, and my guess is that, in the grand tradition of old stars just fading away, she's a roundish, uglyish reminder of what once was.

I've been told there will be a parking space with my name on it: the true sign that you have arrived in Hollywood. Unfortunately, it says John *Custer*, but it's close enough. The building is not exactly the sort you'd imagine a show business operation would be headquartered in. There's some graffiti on the back wall in the parking lot, and the doorway that leads from the parking lot entrance into the building does have a strong scent of urine. The halls are just industrial green with harsh fluorescent lights. I walk past two dented metal gray doors with press-on letter signs reading A-A COURT REPORTING and MAGIC MAKEUP SUPPLIES, and at the end of the hall a similar sign that reads THE

Next Big Thing Entertainment. I open the heavy steel door, and directly in front of the entrance to the office is a desk so close that the door nearly hits it as it swings open. Sitting at the desk is a female who looks to be about nineteen, putting the finishing touches on her nails as she noisily chews gum with an open mouth. It almost takes away from the fact that she looks like she could be Playmate of the Year. Without taking her eyes off her nail buff job, she says in a high-pitched little-girl voice, "Can I help you?"

"I'm John Koester. I'm the new field producer. I'm supposed to report to Wendy Valentine."

"Oh. Wendy's not here yet. You can take whatever desk you want. Nobody else is here yet."

"Thanks. Any desk?" I ask, surveying the small office with two vacant desks facing each other in front of the window that looks right out onto the Hollywood Boulevard sidewalk, where a bum with a three-shopping-cart train has just parked.

"Yeah. Any desk."

Not having a preference, I choose the desk on the right. The bum has decided to move on. Just as he pulls car number one, he notices me looking at him and gives me the finger. Now I really feel like I'm in New York.

The office furniture and accessories all look brand-new. There's nothing hanging on the walls in the way of art, and there are a coffee machine, coffee, and a watercooler still in their boxes. "Just move in?"

"Yeah," she says, still staring at her nails.

"By the way, what's your name?"

"Tiffany."

"Hi, Tiffany."

"Yeah. Hi."

I sit at my desk in awkward silence, the only sound the crackles and pops of Tiffany's openmouthed gum chewing. I reach into my canvas bag and pull out a copy of the *L.A. Times*, which momentarily distracts Tiffany enough to slip while tending to her nails. She reacts with a disgusted click of her tongue. I gently try to turn to the sports section without causing another manicure malfunction.

The door bursts open, and a woman with hair dyed so black it looks almost blue, wearing jet-black sunglasses, a black leather jacket zipped to the neck, and blue jeans with symmetrical tears in a sort of V-shaped web just above both knees, her arms loaded with two black leather tote bags, a Gucci shopping bag, and an oversize purple leather handbag, blows past without noticing me or, for that matter, Tiffany.

"Tiffany, get Bradley on the line now," she says without turning her head an inch toward Tiffany. "And get your skinny ass in here, pronto. Any messages?"

"Yes. Karen Marshall called three times," Tiffany says, following her into the office.

"Oh, shit!" the woman says as she rushes into her office, plops everything onto her desk, and waits for Tiffany while hovering over the phone.

Tiffany dials and says, "Wendy for Bradley. Hold on, Bradley, I have Wendy," and then she hands Wendy the phone.

"Bradley, I told you I want them that shade of magenta that's on the Japanese screen in the downstairs office. Yes, goddammit! Okay, I want to see samples by three in my office. My *new* fucking office. Yes, yes, yes, goodbye."

She hangs up and whispers something to Tiffany. Tiffany whispers back to her.

"Johnny?" Wendy says meekly as she peeks out her doorway.

"Yup."

"I'll be with you in a moment. Make yourself at home. Tell Tiffany if you need anything. You know, supplies, Rolodex, whatever."

The door closes and, just about thirty seconds later, reopens; this time Tiffany exits. "She can see you now," she says as she continues concentrating on her nails.

I enter Wendy's office, which is about three times the size of the space where Tiffany and I are camped out. She has framed posters on the walls of various French films from, I guess, the thirties, none of which I've ever heard of. My desk clearly came from a secondhand furniture store, whereas hers looks to be from the Donald Trump collection.

"Johnny, I'm very pleased to meet you. I was pissed when Karen first told me she had somebody she wanted to produce the segments for this show, but after I saw your reel, I have to say I was fucking impressed."

Wendy is by no means a roundish or uglyish reminder of a fading star. She is an angular, beautifully groomed, perfectly made-up, sweet-smelling, incredibly fit ballbreaker of a broad with more than a little cosmetic surgery and huge boobs practically leaping out of her low-cut black blouse, demanding immediate attention.

"I'm glad to be here. And it's a pleasure to meet you—"

"Stop right there! Don't even hint that you have some childhood story where you whacked off while you were watching me in that god-awful show when you were starting to grow hair on your balls. Got it? Never."

"Gotcha."

"Now, this job is not going to be easy. You've got shoots from Bumfuck to Palm Springs. Tiffany will help you, and another guy is coming aboard who will be helping you, too. He's an expert in planning this kind of shit. Use the hell out of him. He's young. He can take it. Tiffany's an airhead; don't rely on her for really important stuff." Wendy reaches into her desk drawer and pulls out a large black three-ring binder filled with about two inches of paper divided into sections with multicolored tabs.

"This is your bible. Study it and report back to me what you think. You don't have to sit out there in that dumpy office to do it. Go to the bleachers in Dodger Stadium if that's where you want to read it, but I want a full breakdown tomorrow. How feasible the shoots are. Script concepts, all that shit. Do you have a pager?"

"No."

"Get one."

"Great. Is that it?"

"Yup. That's it," she says, standing up to shake my hand, and once she has my hand, she gives a little extra squeeze, looks me straight in the eye, and says, "Oh. one more thing. Don't fuck up."

"Gotcha."

I take the binder, say goodbye to Tiffany, who still hasn't looked at me directly, and get into the Woody. After all these years of humping my sister's teddy bears in the night, and finally meeting Wendy Valentine, *getting* a woody is, ironically, the furthest thing from my mind.

Once I arrive home and begin studying the binder filled with research, contacts, and the stories I'll be producing, I realize I probably shouldn't have eaten such a large lunch, because I just might lose it. *Shocking Hollywood Secrets* will delve into salacious Hollywood scandals. The first is an exposé on one of the biggest film directors of the 1970s and '80s, who, according to the binder, had sex with his own fourteen-year-old stepdaughter; once he dumped his wife, the girl's mother, he secretly dated the minor until she was eighteen, then quietly dumped her, too, after giving her a huge payout. Other stories involve major Hollywood stars with horrible personal secrets that simply must be exposed! This bit of "journalism" will bring to the program a parade of interviewees to reveal a Hollywood male megastar who seems to prefer prepubescent blond boys picked off the streets of Hollywood rather than the glamour girls he's usually spotted with at award shows and in *People*. Another story reveals that a female movie star who is now enjoying fame and fortune as a "serious" actress got her start when she was a minor in porno, and she bribes her trailer-trash mom into keeping it a secret. And how will we get this menagerie of talking heads to appear on national television and bare their souls? Simple: a signed release form and cash money. I will be provided with envelopes stuffed with cash to pay off this sad collection of humanity whose only claim to fame is that they knew or are related to someone famous. Former friends and distant relatives will take the money and tell America whatever dirt they can dig up from their repressed, alcoholic-soaked memories.

My journey will take me across America and back in a matter of fifteen working days, interviewing enough desperate gold diggers willing to trash Hollywood icons to fill forty-five or so minutes of program time. During those fifteen days, I will be renting rooms in no-name motels on the outskirts of towns—visiting trailer parks, veterans' hospitals, halfway houses, a private eye's office, a lawyer's office in Beverly Hills, and a large gated-estate with an eight-hole golf course in Palm Springs—to hand out envelopes, sit people in front of a camera, and have them spill their guts out. I figure if I'm going to survive this, I'll have to block out the subject matter entirely and approach it merely as another job to plan out, then execute in the most efficient manner possible. God, that sounds like something a Nazi officer would've said during World War II. Oh well.

I begin to map out my trip: which people in which parts of the country, where to stay, which cities to hire freelance video production crews, where to fly into and out of, where to rent cars, and where to hire armed security. In spite of the despicable subject matter of this show, whoever put the three-ring binder together did one hell of a job. All the information is neatly laid out in a masterful game plan. There are many suggestions for pre-production, field production, and postproduction that give evidence of someone with a real grasp on how to put a television program together. And also with an eye for storytelling. In the rundowns for what each interviewee will talk about, there are bullet points next to topics where the interviewer should make every attempt to get the interviewee to cry on camera. It even informs the interviewer that "in certain cases, there should be a predetermined code for the interviewer to loudly tell the camera operator to turn off the camera during a particularly uncomfortable moment during the interview, usually a total emotional breakdown, in which the camera operator pretends to turn off the camera but actually keeps rolling without the knowledge of the interviewee."

Although I find it all reprehensible, it should be as easy as painting a Venus color-by-number. If Wendy Valentine is responsible for this, I have total respect for her as a producer. Well, not total respect. If you also include the part about this type of TV show being the beginning of the fall of Western civilization, culminating with the apocalypse of the Book of Revelations and there being a thousand years of rule on earth by Satan and all that, well, it's not quite my *total* respect, but you know what I mean. It's one hell of a professional job.

I find the research in the production bible both fascinating and troubling. With little or no regard to the original source of the research articles, each subject is painted with a broad brush of sensational accusations. But each of the articles used for references is from a supermarket checkout tabloid, transcripts from trashy entertainment news television shows or an undated newspaper that may have appeared somewhere in print on the planet in the last fifty years. Some of these articles have been culled from the same publications that appear on newsstands with headlines so outlandish and outrageously silly as C-Section Re-

VEALS WOMAN GAVE BIRTH TO SATAN—PHOTOS ON PAGE 13; yet they are included for informational background and as sources for contacting interview subjects. I mean, if they're going to believe this crap, wouldn't it be more interesting to interview the woman who gave birth to Satan?

Also included as research material are transcripts of telephone interviews with subjects willing to spill their guts from the anonymity of their trailer parks and garage apartments but unwilling to appear on camera. Since most professional transcribers carefully report every syllable, these interviews reveal the tenuous thread by which the entire operation is hanging. The only people who can coherently string together more than three words are those who sound like they must be sitting in restraints in a padded room. But as long as they say they saw a celebrity performing some kind of perversion, deviant behavior, or crime, it's good enough for us. I just dread the thought of having to visit these people for an on-camera interview.

If a tenth of the material is true, every one of them should be in jail or at least forced to watch their own movies over and over. Allegations of pedophilia, slavery, bestiality, statutory rape, parental physical abuse, and even murder abound. Now, that's good television! It seemed like only yesterday that late-night television hosts weren't allowed to say the word "pregnant" on the air, and sitcom husbands and wives slept in separate beds. But I guess today's viewing public is dying to see *Shocking Hollywood Secrets*. And believe me, people are dying to give it to them.

I didn't realize that I've spent nearly six hours studying my production bible and have already achieved a pretty good handle on my duties for the next several weeks. I totally forgot to eat and decide it's time to grab a bite at the House of Pies down the street. Not that the food is bad there, but you can just guess that naming the place the House of Pies is an enticing come-on for folks who wouldn't be attracted to a place called House of Sprouts.

I grab a bag of garbage out of the kitchen to drop in the Dumpster in the parking lot and head out. I close my door behind me, and just as I take three steps down the walkway, I hear that unmistakable sound: Benny's door squeaking open. But Benny is nowhere in sight. Then, just as I'm dead even with his door, I hear a voice from behind the screen door, out of the darkness.

"Did you get my note?" Benny asks just loud enough for me to hear.

I stop dead in my tracks, turn to Benny's door, and try to discern a figure behind the dirt and dust-encrusted, still-closed screen door.

"Yeah. I did," I say in a tone of voice I usually reserve for aggressive panhandlers or asshole strangers on a New York street.

There is an awkward silence, then Benny clears his throat and asks with a little more conviction, "Can I stop by later?"

This is a tough one. Do I piss the guy off again and tell him to fuck off, or possibly set myself up for something I may regret later this evening? Screw him.

"I'm busy right now. If I have any time, I'll knock on your door," I say with about as much friendliness as one would have for a half-dozen Jehovah's Witnesses at the front door at seven in the morning on a Sunday after a night of heavy drinking.

"Great. Thanks," Benny says with a hint of optimism, still hidden behind his screen. Then he pushes his front door shut, making that terrible sound again.

Maybe I'm a schmuck for saying I might knock on his door. But I don't owe him anything. The only reason I may actually do it is to see what he's got to offer and figure out if this guy is some kind of total psycho who needs to be dealt with sooner than later. Fortunately, I'm on a month-to-month here, and between Miss Russia on the second floor and Benny the Time Bomb, I might be looking for my second Hollywood bachelor pad quicker than I had hoped.

Pies may be what they're known for, but by the looks of my fellow stool sitters at the counter of the House of Pies, this place knows how to keep their pie-hungry clientele happy until that eight-inch-high lemon meringue pie is plopped in front of them after several thousand calories of comfort food. After a tuna-scoop salad that had at least a mason jar of mayonnaise in it, I passed on the pie but knew I needed a good walk home to get some of the gastric juices flowing before Benny and I had it out beside the pool at Hollywood View Court.

The only other people walking on this pleasantly warm evening are two dog walkers and a bushy-bearded, wild-haired guy carrying a huge backpack with a gamey odor who is either a burglar or a European tourist. In New York, even in lousy weather, everyone walks and is constantly in your face, yet you have no idea who most of the people in your apartment building are. Here, nobody walks even when it's gorgeous out, but I've had more contact with my neighbors in two weeks than I have with my immediate family from Thanksgiving to New Year's Eve.

There's a sweet smell in the air from the lemon blossoms starting to bloom, but that aroma gets obliterated as I pass the open Dumpster in our parking lot. I pause to close the lid on the Dumpster, and as I do, the sound of it prompts Harriet to peek out of her window to see who the culprit could be. She doesn't miss a thing.

I can't tell if there's a light on at Benny's, but I don't think the spotlight from Radio City Music Hall would be visible through those crusty windows. The crash of the Dumpster lid may have also aroused Benny's attention, but just in case, I make sure I close the gate from the parking lot very softly and continue my walk past Benny's dark door practically on tippy-toes. I still haven't decided whether I'm going to knock on his door anytime soon to try and figure out the method to his madness, but after my carb-loaded meal at the House of Pies, I'm more interested in an eight-hour nap than playing Freud with a maniac neighbor.

Suddenly, the sound of Benny's door interrupts the quiet of my sneaky steps.

"Great," Benny says as he steps through his doorway, a brown paper bag in hand. He closes his door and steps down to the walkway. "Let's go."

"Where are we going?" I ask, still stunned at the sight of Benny stepping from the top of his stoop.

"Your place."

It's time for a decision. I could tell Benny to fuck off, probably get into a brief argument that will be continued some other time, or sit down once and for all with him and bring this whole thing to a complete halt once and for all, either in a winner-take-all blowout, or in a civilized discussion at my place where we decide to never bother each other again.

"Oh. Okay," I say, which I immediately regret, asking myself how I could be such an idiot as to give this guy the upper hand.

Benny walks over to my door and waits there for me. Next door, the drapery is pulled open about a half inch, and neighbor Rosalynne's one eye is peering at us.

Oh well.

I open the door, and Benny rushes in with his bag clutched close to his chest before I even have time to switch on the light. Once the light is on, Benny takes a seat in the closest chair, my lime-green plastic thrift-store chair next to the dining room table.

"First of all, I want to apologize for being rude. Secondly, I'm glad you didn't buy that TV off me last week," Benny says hurriedly as he pulls a pack of Lucky cigarettes from his black windbreaker pocket. "Do you mind if I smoke?"

"To tell you the truth, I do mind," I say firmly, letting Benny know he's a guest in my house and he could get thrown out on his ass at any moment.

"No problem, no problem," he says, shoving the pack back into his pocket. Benny appears quite nervous. Not surprisingly, considering the fact that he could be a guy trying to pull a fast one, whatever the hell that might be, on a younger, fitter person.

"Why are you glad I didn't buy it?" I ask, still standing. I learned that riding the subway. If you're suspicious of somebody in your train car, immediately stand up. It's harder to attack somebody standing.

"I needed it. The big TV I bought, the one I was getting out of the van, turned out to be a rip-off."

"Where'd you get it?"

"Well, as we used to say in New York, it fell off the back of a truck. Only thing was, it wasn't even a TV. It was a box filled with bricks. What a schmuck I am. Oh well, serves me right, as the sisters used to say. By the way, what's your name?" Benny asks as he looks me in the eye for the first time since he entered my home.

"Johnny Koester," I say, walking over to him and shaking his hand.

"Oh, like the general," Benny chimes in.

I shake his hand and am immediately shocked to rediscover the fact that he's missing his pinky and ring fingers. The handshake gives me a strange sensation. A feeling I've never had while shaking hands. I'm not sure if I'm hiding my anxiety very well. It's not just the missing fingers that creep me out, but his hand has a sense of deformity that goes beyond the mere physical. Almost as though his hand isn't his.

"I had a feeling you might be from New York. So am I," I say, probably adding a little too much friendliness to my voice. "I'm from the Bronx. How about you?"

"Manhattan. Listen, I've got something I want to show you," he says, trying to change the subject and get down to business.

"Where?"

"In this bag," Benny says flatly.

"No. Where in Manhattan?"

"Downtown. Lower East Side."

"What parish?"

"What?" Benny says with a look of bewilderment.

"What parish? You mentioned sisters before, so you went to Catholic school. What parish?"

"I don't remember. Look, I've got something in here you might be interested—"

"You don't remember your parish?"

"No. I don't. I'm an atheist!" Benny barks.

"Okay. But I'm not buying anything that fell off the back of a truck."

"No, no," Benny says as he reaches into the bag and pulls out a stack of vintage magazines. "I saw your New York plates, and I thought maybe you were a baseball fan. I'm beginning to liquidate some of my collection. These here are every New York Giants yearbook from 1945 to 1957. And about fifty scorecards," he says as he carefully lays out the exquisitely preserved yearbooks and scorecards on the dining room table. "They're in mint condition."

Whatever suspicions I had of Benny being a junkie, a thief, and an all-around scumbag are put aside momentarily as I gaze upon the magnificence of the articles in front of me. I have a few cherished items squirreled away from the days when I worshipped Mickey Mantle and Roger Maris the way girls in my class did John, Paul, George, and Ringo. But none of my mementos look as if they've never been handled by human hands, totally unsullied by the ravages of time.

"Where'd you get them?" I say, trying not to look too interested in the beauties so I won't get overcharged. I'm not about to let him know the sheer delight I'm experiencing merely looking at them, never mind the possibility that I might be able to own them.

"They were my brother's. He died a long time ago. I'm not a fan. I just want to get rid of them now. Are you interested?"

"I guess. How much?"

"These are worth a lot, you know; I'm practically giving them away. A hundred bucks for everything."

"That seems a little steep," I say, knowing that in reality, it's an unbelievable price for a collection of this quality. There are about sixty different pieces, so at the ridiculously low price of two bucks each, that would be $120. I've seen just one going for fifty bucks in collectible stores.

"Let me think about it," I say nonchalantly, trying to hide my greedy glee.

"All right, fifty," Benny says immediately. He now has a desperate look. The look of a man who desperately needs fifty bucks for something, quick.

"Okay. Fifty. Is a check all right?"

"Cash."

"Let me go get it," I say, noticing a look of relief on Benny's face as he begins to put all the stuff into a neat pile.

I grab fifty out of my room, and Benny's standing by the front door, glancing over at his sold goodies.

I hand him the fifty, and as I go to shake his hand, he grabs my hand with both of his and looks me in the eye. "Take care of them, okay?"

"Yeah, okay. Wait a minute. What's going on? Are you sure this is legitimate?"

"Look, I'm sorry for my behavior before. I'm under a lot of pressure. You seem like a good kid. I gotta go," Benny says while walking to the door. "I'm just . . . stressed. Truce," he says, holding his disfigured hand out to me.

I don't know why, but looking into those eyes, I see something more than a stone-cold junkie. There's something oddly intriguing in there. Maybe it's just because I love baseball. And a good deal.

I let him out, and he walks past his door and into the parking lot. I hear the cranking of his engine and the squeal of belts and hoses as he drives away. These baseball items are mint. The last year the Giants played in New York was 1957. It's quite a collection: perfect condition. And the scorecards are immaculate. As I inspect the neat notes on them, the handwriting doesn't look much different from the note he left me. I guess two brothers would have similar handwriting, especially if they had the same nuns whacking their knuckles should they loop their capital *D*'s the wrong way.

As I'm thumbing through the yearbooks, I notice a scorecard stuck inside the 1951 season book. I pull it out to discover that it's a beautifully preserved, penciled-in scorecard from game one of the 1951 World Series, the New York Yankees vs. the New York Giants. And it's one of the most complete scorecards I've ever seen. Every player is listed in tidy box-letter print. Substitutions and pinch hitters are even coded with letters from the alphabet. And several outs are starred, which usually signifies an outstanding play by a fielder. Whenever I keep score, I usually give up in the late innings when too many pitcher changes and double switches make my card a mess of arrows, cross-outs, and ugly pencil erasures. But this gem is worthy of Red Barber. Across the top, written in Catholic-school script, is *Me, Willie, Ralph, and Fr. B., Thursday, Oct. 4th, 1951, World Series Game 1. Final Score: Giants 5, Yankees 1. One down. Three to go!* Out of curiosity, I pick up the 1952 yearbook to see the outcome of that particular series. Although the Giants won two out of the first three, the Yankees went on to win the series, four games to two. Despite the outcome for the Giants, two players emerged from that series who would be at the center of controversy, arguments, and even fistfights in ballparks, bars and living rooms for decades: Mickey Mantle and Willie Mays. To this day, in certain bars in the Bronx and in the Inwood section of Manhattan, brawls can be instigated by trying to prove who was the greatest center fielder in baseball history. I wouldn't try to defend Mickey Mantle at the Polo Grounds Bar in Inwood any more than I would try to sing the praises of Willie Mays at the Yankee Tavern in the Bronx. No matter how much Harlem River water passes under the Willis Avenue Bridge just below Yankee Stadium where the old Polo Grounds once stood, some things will just never be settled and will always ignite controversy, and yes, even violence.

I'm guessing Benny is in his fifties, which would have made him probably ten or twelve in 1951. Which would make sense, having a "Fr. B." present. "Fr. B." more than likely would be a parish priest, rewarding a few altar boys with a weekday outing. Not a bad gift from a parish priest. The thanks we got for being altar boys was a once-a-year bus ride to Lake Hopatcong Amusement Park way the hell out in Jersey, which was the biggest dump of a run-down amusement park and almost an hour and a half away. Even though we had the awesome Palisades Amusement Park right over the George Washington Bridge, and Rye Playland just over the city line in Westchester, I'm sure Lake Hopatcong Amusement Park was a lot cheaper, so Lake Hopatcong it was.

Obviously, the *Me* listed on the scorecard has to be Benny's brother. I'm surprised Benny's name isn't listed as one of the attendees, but I remember when I was a kid, my older brother didn't want to be caught dead with me. Ironic, since Benny's brother is dead. I wonder what his name was, and who Willie and Ralph were. Oh well, there are probably a few more clues in this stack of Giants memorabilia. When I'm through with my own stack of *Shocking Hollywood Secrets* stuff, I'll study Benny's brother's stuff a little more carefully.

Still worn out from carbohydrate overload, I'm thrilled to finally bed down, even though I've been just about setting a record for the most nights bedded down all alone since maybe my freshman year of college. Just as I finally start approaching my dozing zone, I hear a noise that's the last thing one wants to hear just before falling asleep. A balls-to-the-wall, bloodcurdling scream. Right in my courtyard. I jump out of bed, stub my toe on the door to my bedroom, and want to let out a bloodcurdling scream of my own but settle for a litany of *motherfuckercocksuckersonsofbitches* that will have to do. Just like most New Yorkers, I keep a trusty sawed-off baseball bat under my bed, for just such middle-of-the-night emergencies. I grab my trusty half a Louisville slugger and run out my front door barefoot, wearing nothing but boxer shorts and an old torn Kinks T-shirt. Just as I feared, Miss Russia is outside her apartment on the second level, crying and holding her hands to her face. I take a few steps toward her stairway only to discover that something is blocking the way—the bald-headed jerk who was bothering her just last week. He's sprawled out at the bottom of the stairs, but this time his head isn't red with borscht, it's red with blood. He's not moving. I call up to Miss Russia, "Are you okay?"

"Yes. I am. Is he . . . okay?"

Just then the big galoot starts coming to. He reaches up, puts his hand to his head, places the blood-covered hand in front of his face, and mutters, "Is this mine?"

Miss Russia yells at him, "Yes, you fool! Now go home. You are drunk. I called you a taxi. And if you ever come back, I will call police, then kill you."

"No-good bitch," he mumbles as he gets to his feet.

A small dark Middle Eastern man with a mustache that covers his lips enters the front gate from the street, looks at me, and says with a thick Arab accent, "Someone call taxi?"

"I did," yells Miss Russia. "He has lots of money; he will pay. He's a big tipper, too. But be careful, he will think he owns you after big tip."

The bloody fool walks off with the cabbie, and Miss Russia quietly steps back into her apartment. As I turn to go back into my place, I can see Rosalynne staring at me through the space in her drapes. I wave to her and say happily, "Good night, Rosalynne. Say good night to your mom for me, too," and go back to bed. It might be nice to hit the road for a few days.

Nobody in Hollywood starts work at nine. I wound up napping in my Woody for almost an hour until Tiffany showed up at the office at ten. And I certainly needed that nap. In addition to the late-night visit from Benny and Mama Bear throwing the Big Bad Wolf down a flight of stairs, I had to make several visits to the john and, thanks to the House of Pies, drink a bottle of Pepto during the wee-wee hours of the morning. Also, I can hear Rosalynne and her mom boiling tea and banging pots and pans like a Chinese New Year's every morning at about five.

I give Tiffany about five minutes before I follow her in, and instead of barely getting recognized, as I was by her yesterday, I'm invisible today, even though I say good morning to her. Someone must have done her job, because my desk is now outfitted with a phone, calendar, Rolodex, pens, pads, folders, paper clips, the works. I notice that the desk facing mine is similarly furnished with brand-spanking-new items. The front door pushes open, and Wendy rushes in, talking to no one in particular, balancing a Starbucks bag and a distressed black leather bag shaped like a bowling-ball bag.

"Who the fuck pays ten thousand dollars for homeowner's insurance? Fire zone? Nobody ever told me about any fire zone! Shit!" Wendy says as she passes Tiffany and me, adding, "Johnny, come on in, in two minutes. Gotta pee first."

I'm sure to give her more than a couple of minutes before I grab my notes and my bible. I'm amazed that she can find anything in that pile of paper, tapes, phone messages, and Starbucks bags totally covering her desk. She's in the process of clearing a space in the center, I assume, to claim a work area for the day. As she completes it, she looks up at me and forces a tight smile.

"So, Johnny, do we have a show?"

"Absolutely. Amazing."

"Don't bullshit me. What do you think? Does it sizzle or is it shit stew?"

"I think it'll be great," I meekly respond.

Wendy leans over her mound of office mess and taps her two front teeth. "Johnny, see these teeth? They're capped." Next she palms both her breasts, adding, "See these tits? They're fake." She then stretches her lower lip down. "See these lips? Filled with collagen," she slurs while she's holding her lip down. "Okay? I don't want any bullshit in here. I want the truth, no matter how ugly."

Knowing that Karen more than likely put her reputation on the line to get me this gig, I'm not about to blow it now. I'm going to have a hell of an American Express bill next month, after all my moving expenses, so here goes . . .

"Well, I think most of the content is rather repulsive."

Wendy excitedly jumps up from her chair, exclaiming, "Good! Now we're getting somewhere. Now tell me something I don't know. I know it's repulsive. Hence the title, *Shocking Hollywood Secrets*. Will it be a train wreck that I have to pull over and gawk at, or will I just drive by?"

"Definitely gawk. Gawk city."

"Great. Fantastic," she says, sitting back down. "Can we make every story have a beginning, a middle, an end, and at least one all-out crying jag?"

"Definitely. There's plenty to laugh and cry about in this show."

"Good. Listen, Johnny," Wendy says as she gets up from her chair again and walks over to my side of the desk. She clears a corner of the desk and sits close to me, her demeanor much more relaxed. "Karen Marshall and I have a love-hate relationship. She loves me and I hate her. Normally, I wouldn't let a studio exec force anybody on me. But I reluctantly watched the sample reel of your work, and I saw that piece you did on those women in prison. I cried at the end of that, Johnny. And believe me, as you probably figured out by now, I'm not a crier. And I thought, If this guy can hook me and make me cry like that, he can hook and make America cry with the stories we're going to put on TV. None of this is brand-new, Johnny, I know that. But God is in the details. Execution is everything. We can get this sleaze, this depravity, that people eat up every day with those godforsaken tabloids that we all read, and make it look like a goddamn fucking Barbara Walters special with all that soft-filtered video and music and people crying their guts out. And it's your job to do that. Make this the most beautifully shot boatload of shit ever broadcast."

"Wendy, that I can do."

"Then we see eye-to-eye," she says, going back to her seat. "And one more thing: If you ever tell anybody about my tits, you'll find a horse head on your pillow."

"Gotcha."

As I leave Wendy's office, I notice, sitting at the desk opposite mine, a guy wearing a tattered black T-shirt with BLACK FLAG written across it. Judging by the blond peach fuzz on his chin, he could still be in high school. His curly blond hair has a bad case of I-don't-give-a-shit bed head, and he's wearing black shorts that go so far below his knees that, back in grammar school, we would have classified them as clam diggers. On his feet are huge, thick-soled boots, halfheartedly laced. He's sitting there reading one of those comic books they call graphic novels, designed for people unwilling to make the quantum leap to actual books without pictures, wearing a headset connected to a small portable CD player on the desk. And right behind his chair is what appears to be a very expensive mountain bike. I surmise that he's a messenger, sitting there waiting for a pickup, so I just ignore him.

Wendy comes out of her office, carrying an armload of fabric samples, and dumps them on Tiffany's desk, saying, "Have Jose pick these up. Tell him none of them are right and to call me." As she turns to go back to her office, she looks at me and says, "Have you two met?"

"Me and Tiffany?" I respond.

"No. You and River."

"Me and a river?"

Wendy walks over to the guy seated at the desk across from mine and taps him on the shoulder.

"River. This is Johnny. You'll be working together."

River takes off his headset, closes his comic book, looks at me without smiling, and manages to utter, "Hey."

"Hey," I utter back.

Wendy starts back to her office and says over her shoulder, "Johnny, tell River what else you need."

I turn to River, and he's already reopened his comic but hasn't put his headset back on. I figure I better break the ice. "Did you put the production bible together?"

"Me and Wendy."

"Great job!"

"Thanks."

"Did you ever do one before?"

"A few."

"I'm amazed at the cross-referencing and the rundowns and all that, detail stuff."

"I designed the program."

"You designed it yourself?"

"Yeah."

"Well, could you do me a favor?"

"What?" he asks, looking like he's not going to take shit from anybody.

"Could you print out a day-by-day schedule for each city?"

"Does that mean you want to go with the itinerary I mapped out?"

"Yeah. It's awesome."

"Okay. When do you want it?"

"Tomorrow all right?"

"Yeah," he says as he reaches over to his mountain bike and into a bag attached to the rear, pulling out a laptop computer. "I'll have it in an hour if you want."

"No, tomorrow's good. I've got some phone calls to make."

"Is that your ridiculous car in the lot?" River asks, as though he's not being the least bit rude.

"If you mean the 1980 Chrysler Town and Country, which I affectionately refer to as my Woody, then yes, that ridiculous car is mine. Is that okay with you?"

"That thing is a gross polluter, you know."

I think for a moment. What I want to say is *Your mother is a gross polluter, by the looks of you, asshole*, but instead I say, "Well, it has a four-cylinder engine that gets around twenty miles a gallon, I keep it tuned, and just think of the amount of energy it would take to build an entirely new car just for me, and the wasted energy if that car were to be merely deposited into landfill."

"Hmmm. I never thought of it that way."

"Plus, not one tree was harmed in the making of that car. It's a simulated Woody," I say, with a nod and a wink.

Wendy sticks her head out her office door again like an anxious mom. "You two getting along?"

"Just great," I say, looking over to River, who is deep into his laptop, not responding.

"Good. Play nice, River," she says as she goes back inside.

I can't wait for this asshole to ask me for a ride to the airport.

Chapter Four

WELL, IT'S BEEN TWO WEEKS and I haven't conducted one teary-eyed interview at a trailer park. Apparently, there is some kind of *funding* problem at the Next Big Thing Entertainment, and I'm on standby salary, which is enough to keep me from looking for another job but not enough to feel secure about my present financial situation. Still, seventy-five bucks a day for sitting beside my pool is just fine by me.

Except for a couple of brisk entrances and exits to and from his apartment, I've barely seen Benny at all these two weeks. After the initial fire sale of baseball memorabilia, I thought he'd be banging on my door every time he needed to unload another cherished morsel for his next fix. In my two-week company-imposed vacation, I've also managed to introduce myself to Miss Russian Mama Bear herself, who is named Nina, has a three-year-old named Mishka, and always sits on the exact opposite side of the pool from me. She is not shy, however, when it comes to taking off her top and lying on her

stomach for some sun on her back. I never thought it was possible to have a sexual fantasy with a three-year-old boy present, but when she wriggles her body and giggles as he applies suntan lotion to her back, that's all changed. I'm not quite sure what her professional occupation is, but if it has anything to do with wriggling her body and giggling, she's in the right town to make a substantial living.

Today, however, is a little cool, and I'm all by my lonesome by the pool, sitting close enough to my door so I can hear the phone ring in my apartment, which will hopefully mean an immediate $125-a-day pay raise. Across the pool, Harriet the building manager opens her screen door and sticks her head out. "Johnny? Can I see you for a moment, please?" shouting loud enough that everyone in the complex can hear her.

"I'll be right there."

I haven't been to Harriet's since the day I moved in. Our interaction has been mostly her peering through her draperies when I'm at the Dumpster or coming home at an odd hour. With her makeshift barricade of furniture and household items back in their proper positions, Harriet's place is immaculate, as midwestern-doily and hand-crafted-afghans-and-tea-cozies as you can get. And there's a strong aroma of fresh-baked cookies adding to the home ambiance.

"Sit down over here, Johnny," she says, placing a tray of oatmeal cookies on the coffee table in front of me as I sit on her plaid colonial-style sofa with bare dark wood arms. "Would you like some tea?"

"No thanks," I say, trying to contain my enthusiasm for the oatmeal raisin cookies, which have been my favorite since I outgrew Hostess Twinkies after reading the ingredients label.

Harriet takes a seat across from me in a matching plaid easy chair. She sits down in it and immediately grabs the huge dark wood handle on the side and jerks it back, which puts her in a semireclined position. "It's good for my back. Johnny, are you familiar with the woman in apartment 2F? The Russian?"

"Oh, Nina," I say joyfully, with an image of her dropping her robe in front of me, as she has done several times the past few weeks.

"Yes. Her," Harriet says, not at all amused. "Have you noticed what goes on up there?"

"I've heard a couple of arguments. Why?"

"Well, some of us here in Hollywood View Court are sick and tired of the goings-on up there and have decided to do something about it. We want to get a petition to have her evicted."

"Exactly what for?"

"Well, you know," she says, shaking her head as if she's having a small fit.

"I know?"

"Yes, you know. She's a . . ." and at this point Harriet mouths the word *prostitute*.

"Are you sure about that?"

"Yes, we are!"

"And what do you want me to do?"

"Well, you're a man. And we understand you work in the media, and you'd be perfect to write the petition for us, and perhaps even suggest that you might do an exposé on her criminal lifestyle if she doesn't move out."

I put half my cookie back on the plate. There's something especially ugly about a person who seems to bask in a wholesome milieu of good-natured old-fashioned values and then abruptly turns nasty.

"First of all, she has a kid. Second of all, you don't know if she's a prostitute. Third of all, if the people I work for get wind of this, she'll be starring in their next production," I say, standing.

"What exactly does that mean?" Harriet asks as she jerks the chair's wood handle forward with such force, it nearly ejects her into the air. "Are you involved in pornography?"

"No. I'm not. But what you're proposing is obscene."

"I'm very sorry you feel that way, Johnny. We're just trying to protect ourselves."

I can't help but feel sorry for Harriet and the other old ladies in the complex. When they moved to this neighborhood, probably the most menacing living thing was a coyote. Today there are all kinds of human predators posing much greater dangers.

"Harriet, look, if there's anything of real danger in this complex, you can count on me. I'll be there at any time of day for anyone. But let's just see what happens with Nina before we go kicking her out onto the street and maybe thrown in jail, okay?"

Harriet abandoned her defiant stance, dropped her shoulders, and pleaded with her eyes. "Okay. You mean that? We can come to you? Really? You'll be there for us?"

"Yes. And if she is a prostitute and bringing her johns up there, we'll do what we have to do."

"She's going to bring portable toilets up there? For God's sake, why? How disgusting!"

"No, a john is a guy who hires a prostitute."

"Oh. Yes. I heard that on *Phil Donahue,* now that you mention it."

"Don't worry, Harriet. We'll keep an eye on things, and if anything really dangerous is on the horizon, we'll address it at that time, okay?"

"Okay, Johnny. That sounds reasonable. Take the rest of the cookies."

"May I?"

"Sure. I've got lots more in the kitchen, if you'd like."

"No, these on the tray would be great," I say, picking them all up.

"Take the dish. I know where you live."

"Oh, yeah. Thanks," I say as I pick up the tray and wave goodbye.

As I leave her apartment and make the corner around the pool, which goes by the gate that leads to the parking lot, it swings open and Benny walks slowly through. When he lets go of the gate, he immediately grabs his right bicep as if he's in pain.

"Hi, Benny," I say as he shuffles past me. As bad as Benny looked before, in the harsh light of day he looks even worse, with that unmistakably gaunt, vacant look of a junkie in need of a fix. His hair is greasy and flat against his forehead, his eyes even deeper and darker than usual. And there's a dullness to him.

"Hi," Benny says, barely above a whisper.

Dodging junkies is not anything new to me. When you ride the New York subway for a decade or two, it becomes second nature, like changing lanes on the freeway. Not wanting to be rude and just rush past him, which a normal walking pace would seem like next to his stuttering steps, I walk slowly next to him, sharing the walkway to our respective apartments. "Would you like a cookie? Harriet just baked them," I say, holding the tray out close to his face.

"No," he says, weakly motioning to get them away. "I can't think about food right now."

"Sure. Can I help you with anything, Benny?"

"No," he says, trying to inject a little friendliness into his single syllable. "If I need you, I'll let you know, okay?"

"Okay."

Benny opens his screen door, then inserts his key into the door lock. As he pushes, the scrape that usually is a loud squeal is hardly a squeak as he struggles to merely get the door open. I try not to watch but can't help it. Once he's inside, I can hear him strain to push the door closed. He finally does, and I go into my apartment.

I've seen too many junkies suck people into their whirlpool of despair—usually the people closest to them. That's one trip down the drain I don't intend to make.

The message light is flashing on my answering machine. I push the play button, and it's Wendy happily announcing, "It's showtime. Tomorrow. Ten A.M. sharp. Call me."

I grab a paper and pencil, call Wendy, and she fills me in with the good and bad news. Apparently, the funding problems I heard so much about in the past few weeks have affected production quite dramatically. It's no longer an hour show, and we're doing only three segments. The money for travel and production has been cut way back, and I don't know if she's just saying this to keep me on my toes, but my position was almost eliminated. Naturally, she fought to keep me.

The three segments that have titles reflecting the journalistic integrity going into this program are: 1) "The Sleazeball Director"—the director who dated his stepdaughter, dumped his wife, made the daughter get plastic surgery to look like her mother, then dumped the girlfriend/stepdaughter the day after she turned eighteen. 2) "My Family the Trailer Trash"—an in-depth look at the alcoholics, drug addicts, mentally unstable, and criminals hidden away in trailer parks and board-and-care facilities across America, who happen to be kinfolk to some of the most glamorous and highest-paid movie stars in Hollywood. 3) "Super Freak"—one of Hollywood's leading male sex symbols has a thing for prepubescent boys and octogenarian grannies. These titles, of course, will never be used in any official memos or written correspondence, but these are the slugs, i.e., titles, we will be using in-house on an informal basis.

On the upside, due to the budget constraints, I will not be traveling with my angry-young-man protégé, River. It will be a lot of work for me out there in the boonies, on location by myself, but at least I won't have to worry about him slipping me a mickey and murdering me in my sleep because I eat meat and drive an American-made car. He is a sharp kid, though: The revised production bible is now half the size it was and a more concise rundown of my every move for the next twenty-one days, which is another good news/bad news scenario. I'm getting my full-time salary just three weeks instead of four, unless they decide to keep me on at the end of that period. I'm responsible only for going out in the field, supervising a video crew, interviewing the assorted cast of characters and trying to get them to sob on camera, and getting the shots I need of various related locations, such as schools, homes, plastic surgeons' offices, teenage runaway shelters, skid-row flophouses, stately mansions, state prisons, and other flotsam and jetsam left in the wake of America's entertainment darlings. Once I shoot everything, I will hand the tapes over to the show's director, who will edit the stories together and also re-create some of the celebrities' most memorable moments with look-alike actors. Now, that's something even I can't wait to see: *"More powder on Granny's ass, fast! We've got to get the money shot before we go into overtime!"*

My travel plans read like an itinerary for a bankrupt traveling circus: Huntsville, Alabama; Toms River, New Jersey; Utica, New York; and a few other even less desirable locations. But then there's the tony eastern end of Long Island; Santa Barbara, California; Beverly Hills, California; Newport, Rhode Island; and Boca Raton, Florida. It's not too hard to tell where the celebrities are located and where the less fortunate denizens of noncelebritydom reside.

My first two days of shooting will be local, right here in Hollywood, Beverly Hills, and a day trip to Palm Springs. I'll be shooting mostly exteriors of luxury star homes, hospitals, hangouts, etc., plus seedy Hollywood street scenes and a visit to a nearby Hollywood shelter for runaway teens.

Even in Hollywood, the real workers start early. I'm waiting at the office for a video crew to show up at six-thirty A.M. At precisely six-thirty, there's a knock on the office door. I open it and see a six-foot-six-inch black guy in what appears to be a brand-new, or at least just ironed, black golf shirt with a white logo over the left breast featuring a comical Einstein-esque cartoon character with PURE GENIUS VIDEO written underneath.

"You Johnny?" he asks in a bass voice a few octaves lower than Barry White's.

"Yup. I can see you're Pure Genius Video. Love the name."

"Thanks. *You* don't have to be a genius. That's *our* job," he announces, as he has probably ten thousand times before. "My name's Smitty. Let's go out to the truck and get rolling. The earlier we get done, the sooner we go home," he goes on happily as he leads me to the giant, gleaming full-size white cargo van with no writing or logos on the side. "You sit in the back, I'm the navigator." Smitty opens the back door for me.

The inside of the van is the picture of orderliness. I sit in one of the vacant captain's-style chairs and introduce myself to the driver: "I'm Johnny Koester. The new guy."

"Heard all about you. Welcome to Hollywood, Johnny. I'm Joe," the driver says as he throws the van into drive and rapidly takes off. Joe and Smitty are exact opposites; Joe is white, small, and weedy. "Wendy already gave us the rundown of what you're looking for today, so you can relax. Me and Smitty can do this in our sleep."

"You're only doing the one interview today, Johnny?" Smitty asks as he examines a wireless microphone.

"Well, only one at a time in the shelter."

"Okay. So we only need the one microphone."

"Yep."

"Hey, Johnny, let me ask you something," Joe says as he turns quickly onto Hollywood Boulevard going east; I can tell he's watching me in the rearview mirror. "You think Wendy's tits are real?"

I sit in silence. I met these guys thirty seconds ago, and I'm already risking my career by answering wrong.

"Damn, Joe," Smitty says, punching Joe in the arm. "Dude just met us. Don't mind him, Johnny. Wendy does that 'My tits are fake' routine to everybody. She's a sweetheart, though." Smitty chortles a hearty basso profundo. "A real sweetheart."

We zoom down the boulevard and park around the corner from the Chinese Theatre, a hotbed of tourist activity. Smitty and Joe gather their gear in a flash and are ready to roll.

"You want to wait here or come with us while we get some shots of Hollywood touristopia?" Smitty asks with his hand on the open rear door as he decides whether to close it with me inside or not.

"No, I'm coming," I say. I hop out and follow.

There are tourist buses and vans lined up the boulevard, and tourists of every color and shape are pointing cameras and camcorders at everything and anything in the Chinese Theatre courtyard. Handprints, footprints, a wax figure of Rambo, plaques, the marquis, and each other. Just outside the courtyard, some tourists even place their faces on one of the most contaminated surfaces on the planet—the sidewalk on Hollywood Boulevard—so that they can be photographed next to a celebrity's brass star-shaped plaque. But while all this activity is centered in the courtyard of the theater and on the sidewalk immediately in front of it, there's an entirely different scene playing out just beyond the camera lens. On both sides of the theater are trashy souvenir stands, dingy liquor stores, porno shops, and the people who frequent them.

Smitty is discreetly shooting, and Joe holds a stick microphone, pointing it in whatever direction Smitty is directing his lens. I can see that Smitty is shooting not just the obvious multinational tourist hustle and bustle. He's getting shots of the homeless one-legged guy in the wheelchair and panning over to the fat tourists with their bags of video and photographic gear as they chew on a churro and pose the family in front of Rambo. It's obvious that Smitty and Joe know what the hell they're doing.

Just a few storefronts down from the theater courtyard is a large concrete garbage receptacle with what we used to call a bum sitting on top. From behind, it's hard to tell what he's doing there, so I walk around the other side. The guy, who appears to be in his twenties, is sitting with legs crossed over the opening of the receptacle, and he's digging into it, pulling out assorted wrappers, bags, and cups, examining each one closely. If a burger wrapper still has some cheese on it, he licks it off in an exaggerated slobbering mess. Tourists going by slowly in a sightseeing bus stare in horror. Also thinking this is a pathetic sight, I decide to stop into the burger place down the street and get this guy some protein so he doesn't have to forage in a garbage can. I buy a triple decker with everything and walk over to the young bum. He watches me approach from his yogi squat over the garbage.

"I got you something to eat," I tell him as I hold out the white paper bag at arm's length, which gives me an overload of his disgusting body odor.

He scowls at me and says, "What is it?"

Taken aback, I reply, "A triple-decker burger with everything."

He scrunches his nose and lips in a semi-repulsed expression and says, "Does it have onions?"

This I can't believe. "Yes, it has onions."

He begins to stroke his mangy, soot-coated, reddish beard with his dark greasy hands.

Tourists are now looking at me like I'm a jerk, hassling the poor homeless guy. "Look," I say, on the verge of being pissed off, "do you want it or not? If you don't, I'll eat the damn thing."

"Did you get anything to drink? I like to have something to wash it down with," he says as he strokes his dirt-caked neck.

Just then Smitty and Joe come up behind me. I walk over to the garbage can with the picky bum, slam-dunk the bag through his legs and into the garbage can, and say, "If you want it, there it is." I continue past him with tourists gawking at me in shock and Smitty and Joe laughing hysterically.

"Dude, that was classic," Joe says, holding out his hand for a low-five. "Smitty, we should have rolled on that!"

"Nah, nah, nah. Never record the client unless he asks," Smitty says through his deep bass laughter. "Or pays you cash not to."

"What a dick that guy was," I say to them.

"Gee whiz," Joe says, "I'm shocked! You just can't tell by how a person dresses, can you?"

We spend the next hour or so making various stops along Hollywood Boulevard, Sunset Boulevard, and some other Hollywood haunts while Smitty and Joe shoot their asses off. I remain in the van.

After a morning of shooting around the streets of Hollywood, and eating lunch at a fantastic hole-in-the-wall Mexican place that Smitty and Joe seem to frequent every other day, we're scheduled to stop at the first location where I'll conduct my first on-camera interview. We turn off Hollywood Boulevard and go a couple of blocks south and make a left. We park in front of a building that looks like it was once a grand place. The property appears slightly run-down but not dilapidated. It's a large Craftsman-style home with a dark wood trim and a porch that goes around the perimeter. A plaque next to the front door reads SAFE HAVEN.

According to the research in my bible, Safe Haven is a home for runaways. Funded in part by Catholic charities, various state and municipal funds, and private donations, Safe Haven is for teenagers who wind up on the streets of Hollywood, hustling, hooking, and doing whatever it takes to survive. Most are between fifteen and seventeen, and if they're lucky, they have the common sense to stick with the tough-love program that Safe Haven offers.

I'm to meet and interview the person who runs the place, Dr. Joan Archer. Apparently, a priest founded the center in the 1970s, and the facility gained national notoriety and tons of private donations. But everything almost went bust when the good father was caught with his hands in the cookie jar, the cookie jar being the underwear of a fifteen-year-old boy. But Dr. Archer brought the place back from oblivion, rescuing its reputation and the program itself to the benefit of America's forgotten throwaway kids.

Inside the front door is a desk where a sofa might have been in the living room. A young Hispanic guy about twenty, wearing a crisp white shirt buttoned at the neck, is sitting at the desk taking some information from someone on the phone. He hangs up and politely asks, "Can I help you gentlemen?"

With the phone receiver away from his face, I notice that he has three tattoos of teardrops below his left eye and, on the side of his neck, a fading tattoo that reads FROGTOWN in large block letters.

"Yes," I reply, trying to conceal the fact that I find his tattoos quite shocking. "I'm Johnny Koester with the Next Big Thing Entertainment. And this is my video crew."

"Hold on," the receptionist says as he calls Dr. Archer. "The TV crew is here. Yes," he says into the phone and hangs up. "She'll be right out."

A door opens down the hall, and out walks a small woman with long, straight reddish-brown hair flowing well past her shoulders, almost down to her waist. She seems to be wearing jeans, running shoes, and a tight white T-shirt with writing on it. From this distance, with the way she bounces down the hall in her shoes, she could be one of the resident teenage girls. But when she stops in front of me, I can see her Dr. Joan Archer nameplate pinned to her T-shirt, which I now can read as DOC- TORS WITHOUT BORDERS 10K.

I'm immediately struck by the youthful appearance of this woman and her small, tight, wiry frame. Dare I say, I'm knocked out by her sleek beauty. This happens every once in a while out on shoots, and it sometimes can cause problems due to the fact that I haven't had a steady girlfriend in about three years and it's getting to the point where I can't help but put my own hound-dog ways ahead of my journalistic priorities. But heck, this show has no journalistic priorities.

"Are you the person doing the interview?" she curtly asks as she stops four feet in front of me, not even offering a handshake.

"Yes, I am."

"May I speak to you in my office?" she asks as she turns and heads down the hall. Smitty and Joe begin to pick up their cases of gear, and she spins around. "Just you. Alone," she says, stopping Smitty and Joe in their tracks. I follow her down the hall and into her office, which was probably a small dining room at one time.

"Have a seat, Mr.—"

"Koester. You can call me Johnny."

"Mr. Koester, let me tell you that I nearly canceled this interview and Safe Haven's involvement with the program this morning once I found out the title of the program," Dr. Archer says in a rat-a-tat-tat outpouring with both palms down on the desk in front of her.

"I know it's not exactly the title I would have picked, Dr. Archer, but—"

"If it weren't for the work Wendy Valentine does for this center," she says, cutting me off, "and for other extremely worthy causes, I would have canceled—"

"We're just trying to get them in the tent," I say, cutting her off this time.

"Excuse me?" she asks, not pleased by my interruption.

"We're just trying to get them into the tent. You know, tune in. Pay attention. Grab the viewers by the . . . well, you know, grab them. This show will do everything you want it to. It will give your program national exposure, and also expose the sleazeballs who exploit teenage runaways. And it will show kids on the street not only that there are predators out there, but there is someplace for them to go," I rattle off in my own rat-a-tat-tat monologue. "Wendy Valentine knows television. She knows what she's doing."

"You believe that? Or is this a line?" she asks, now studying me carefully.

"I hate the title of the show, too, but I think the concept is great," I say convincingly. I hope.

She takes a deep breath and glances briefly out the window to where two teenage girls share a laugh. "All right," she says. She picks up the phone. "Edgar, tell the crew to come in."

"You won't be sorry. In fact, anytime you want to stop tape, restart, change the way you say something, or whatever, you just let me know and we'll do it any way you want. We want your story to be the story you want to tell," I say, continuing my sales pitch.

As she thinks about my words, the crew gingerly enters the office and begins to set up for the interview. I can see her begin to soften up slightly. The stern, accusatory tone melts away, revealing a gentle, caring quality framed by the beauty that begins in her eyes and radiated outward.

"I probably should wear something else, shouldn't I?" she asks, looking over at Smitty as she unconsciously rubs her hands on her T-shirt just below her breasts, which makes it very clear that her smallish, firm breasts are not hidden in a bra and her nipples are semi-erect.

"That's your call, Johnny," Smitty says as he sets up the light stands.

Dr. Archer turns to me, for the first time with a smile on her face, waiting for my reply, still absentmindedly rubbing her shirt just under her breasts. The outline of her nipples seem to be exactly in two *O*'s of DOCTORS WITHOUT BORDERS, which isn't helping my concentration at all.

"Uh, I think what you're wearing is, uh, just great. But for the interview, you probably want to wear something you might wear to, say, a lunch with some possible donators."

"That's a good way to look at it!" Dr. Archer says. She stands to leave the room. "I'll be right back."

"Hey, Johnny," Joe says as he walks over to me, holding the small microphone that will be clipped somewhere on Dr. Archer, "you want to put the microphone on her? I usually like to stick the wire up under the blouse. I'll let you have the honors if you're buying dinner tonight."

"Am I that obvious?"

"Don't listen to Joe, Johnny," Smitty says as he sets up his lights behind the desk. "Joe thinks everyone's as big a horndog as he is."

I look over to Joe, and he whispers, "Yes. It's obvious."

"Smitty, what's with the tattoos on the kid at the front desk?" I ask Smitty as he carefully focuses the lights and hangs different scrims and filters on them.

"Each one of those teardrops is for a friend or relative who was killed. The Frogtown on the neck, that was his gang. He's trying to have it removed, which is painful and expensive," Smitty says with certainty.

"Frogtown?" I ask, shaking my head. "That doesn't exactly instill fear deep in one's heart."

"Frogtown is a neighborhood over by Dodger Stadium. If you went over there at night, don't worry, there'd be no lack of fear instilled in your heart," Smitty says, even more certain of his words.

"Smitty knows from whence he speaks," Joe adds.

"Amen," Smitty says, exhaling a long sigh.

For the next ten or so minutes, Smitty and Joe glide across the room setting up lights, laying down cable, putting up scrims, filters, reflectors, and colored gels that give the room a warm reddish glow, washing the background with pools of color. I review the research on Safe Haven and Dr. Archer. It's easy to see by the bullet points and suggested questions written up by Wendy and River that a detailed history of Safe Haven is not what we're looking for. Anything that hints of scandal should be pounced on mercilessly.

With the normal room lights out and the blinds closed, the area where Dr. Archer will sit looks dramatic. Shadows and different rich colors blend together, creating an ambience that the room was totally devoid of before Smitty and Joe brought it to life. Suddenly, the door to the room is opened, and because of the bright lights in the outside hall and the mood lighting in the office where we are set up, I can see only the outline of not quite an hourglass but a three-minute egg-timer-shaped, petite woman with hair worn up. As she closes the door and is illuminated by the theatrical lighting, her beauty takes on an otherworldly quality. She is wearing a conservative dark blue pin-striped suit with the hemline not too far above the knee. Her black high heels harden the muscles of her calves, and her long, slender, naked legs reveal the toning of her overall fitness level. The suit jacket is low-cut, and underneath she is wearing an off-white satin blouse. Now, with a bra holding and shaping her breasts underneath, she looks quite busty for such a petite woman. The red filter light is bringing out rich red hues in the hair she has artistically piled on top of her head in a French twist. Her dainty ears are accented with silver hoop earrings. I didn't notice before that she wasn't wearing any makeup, but with just a hint of eye makeup and lipstick, she has created an entire package that would rival any Hollywood star. I look over to Joe, who is now holding up the microphone that will be placed somewhere on her body. He motions to me and mouths, "You do it."

"I guess I sit over here," Dr. Archer says, carefully stepping over some cables and a case. When she does, her skirt rises a few extra inches above her knee, which immediately attracts my attention. Luckily, she doesn't notice.

"Yes, Doc," Smitty says, offering her a hand over the obstacles and into her chair in a most gentlemanly fashion.

"Please just call me Joan. That doctor stuff is in all the official material, but I'm a Ph.D., not an M.D.," she says, sitting in the chair behind her desk and acclimating herself to the interview setting. "Actually, I'm a psychiatric R.N. with a Ph.D. in psychology." She smoothes the front of her suit. "Does this look all right? I wasn't sure if it was too dark."

"Are you kidding? You couldn't have picked anything better. Perfect with the lighting setup we went with," Smitty says, making some final adjustments to the lights on the stands just behind her. "Joe, you want to mike her up now?"

"Sure," Joe says, approaching her with a microphone and a battery pack. "This is the transmitter; just stick this somewhere in the back of your suit. And we'll put this mike on your lapel."

"Well, that was easy," Joan says, smiling. "The last time I did a TV interview, the crew guy insisted he stick a wire up my blouse."

"Yeah, that's an old audio-guy trick," Smitty says, chuckling. "You didn't fall for it, did you?"

"No way. There's nobody more street-smart than a nurse, believe you me," Joan says with an ambiguous half-smile.

Smitty goes behind the camera, which is situated on a tripod right next to my head, and Joe takes his position on a small stool as he puts on headphones and picks up a copy of *Baseball Weekly*.

"Now, do I talk into the camera," Joan says, "or talk to you, er, I'm sorry, I've forgotten your name." She looks right at me.

"Johnny," I say, disappointed that I haven't made much of an impression on her.

"Oh," she says with a hint of excitement in her voice.

I think maybe she's impressed after all.

"That's my cat's name!"

Then again . . . maybe not.

"Okay," I say, getting down to the business at hand. "Look at me, not the camera. Even though I'm asking the questions, my voice will not be on the program. And, like I said, you can stop, start, repeat, whatever you want. But try to keep your answers short and in complete sentences. Okay, are we rolling?"

I hear a click and some whirring, then "Rolling, speed," Smitty whispers.

"Dr. Archer, tell me what kind of person comes to Safe Haven."

"Teenagers from all over the country, and actually the world, come to Safe Haven. Most of them are between thirteen and seventeen, and all of them have either run away from home or an institution, or have been thrown out into the street to fend for themselves."

"And what happens to these kids when they're thrown out or they run away?"

"Usually, they have a little money, so they either hitchhike or take a bus to a large city, such as Los Angeles or New York. Once they get there, they realize their money, no matter how much it was, lasts only a few days or weeks."

"Isn't anyone looking for them?"

"In the majority of cases, no one is looking for them. It's a constant battle. When we're lucky, we get a child, male or female, to enter our program. Our first priority is to convince them to go back to their families. If they refuse, we allow them to live here until we can place them in a safe environment. But it's hard to compete sometimes with the money and the glamour of the rich and famous."

"And what are the survival skills?"

"They steal, sell drugs, prostitute themselves. Female *and* male."

"How did you get involved with Safe Haven?"

"I began my professional career as a psychiatric nurse. My home life . . . wasn't the best of situations . . . let's just leave it at that. I put myself through nursing school with the intention of helping people with mental illness. I'll try and make this short. Working in a county hospital setting, I began to see many young people, by the age of twenty, who were already lost. Whether the reason was home environment, genetics, drugs, financial desperation, whatever, there were scores of young people with their lives ruined, no sense of hope, at a time in their lives when they should have been beginning their lives as adults. The hopelessness I saw in those eyes, day after day, made me realize something had to be done . . ."

At this point in the interview, I'm no longer hearing words or sentences. Her voice becomes a featured instrument in a symphony. I'm still looking at her. Still listening to her every vowel, every consonant and breath. I'm aware of the sounds her lips and tongue make as they form the sounds that become words. But I begin to feel as though I'm absorbing her passion for her work through some other sense besides hearing. She's sharing thoughts about herself that, under ordinary dating circumstances, probably would have taken several movies and a dinner or two. And after several dates with this extraordinary woman, listening to her share her soul, I'm sure I would be doing exactly what I believe I am doing right now: falling for her.

"And . . ." I have no idea how long I've been lost in her story. "You mentioned the rich and famous. Have you heard of any well-known celebrities who have come in contact with these runaways?"

"Can we stop here?" Joan asks, waving her arms.

"Stop tape," I announce to the crew.

"Tape stopped," Smitty says. He touches a button and stands upright, no longer looking at the viewfinder of the video camera.

"I'm not sure I can mention names here. I mean, I know a couple of big Hollywood stars that more than one of our boys has had contact with," Joan says, using her hands more emphatically now that she knows she's not being taped. "I mean, I even had the police check out a telephone number one of our boys had when he showed up wearing an Armani suit after being gone for two days, and the cops confirmed that it was this particular star's phone number."

"Really?" I say, horrified.

"Yes, really."

"Can you tell us who it was?" I carefully ask, hoping not to piss her off.

"Let's just say he has a special place in his, er, *heart* for the very young and the very old. Okay, if you must know, Tucker Kramden is one. There, I said it. We found some information in a resident male minor's pocket. The police checked it out, confirmed it was Kramden, then the boy confessed to it all. I can't say it on-camera, but now you know. We believe there was a large sum of money given to the kid, and that was the end of it, as far as we know. Let's roll tape again, and I'll figure out what I'm going to say."

Joan opens her mouth as though taking a breath to speak again, but stops herself. She then bites her lower lip slightly, and a look of staunch determination comes across her face.

"Roll," I announce again.

"Rolling. Speed," Smitty replies.

Dr. Archer composes herself and says, "I have knowledge of very well-known male Hollywood stars who have had contact with male residents of Safe Haven, but that's all I can reveal at this time." She leans forward and meekly asks, "I'm sorry, is that okay? That's really all I can say right now."

"I think that's fine," I tell her, thinking that in all likelihood, it really is all we need.

We continue the interview for another ten minutes or so. I ask her all the questions on my blue index cards, and she artfully dodges, careful not to divulge anything too specific, but answers each and every question to my satisfaction. Since she has to look at me during her answers, I begin to fantasize that she really does want to spend this much time just talking with me. Me. Not for the television camera, but me. I gaze into her eyes longingly while she continues to speak about rates of recidivism, pregnancy, street violence, and drug use. I watch her moisten her lips between sentences with her tongue, and imagine my own tongue pressing up against hers slowly and sensuously as she discusses funding and the lack thereof. And when she mentions how important it is for teens to practice safe sex, all I can think about is having very unsafe sex with her after I tear off that pin-striped suit, rip open that silk blouse, and begin licking her from head to toe in preparation for hours of mad, passionate animal lovemaking, on top of, behind, over under, back to back, front to front, and upside down . . .

"Is that all there is?" Joan asks after the completion of a long paragraph about government funding. I think.

"Yes, that's all there is. For now. Okay, let's get some shots of the facility," I say to Smitty.

"I hope you have something to work with," Joan says, hiking up her silk shirt in the back to remove her battery pack, which inadvertently pulls her jacket slightly open, revealing the silky outline of her tits while she unclips the microphone from her lapel.

"Uh, yes. I see a lot to work with," I say to her, hoping I don't reveal my animal instincts.

"We're leaving this stuff here while we shoot some other footage," Smitty says, and he and Joe leave Joan and me alone in the room, which still has the dark dramatic lighting illuminating her.

"Um, Dr.—?"

"Call me Joan."

"Yes, Joan. Um, do you think I could call you . . . to just follow up on some of the facts of the interview?"

"Of course," Joan says, bending over in front of me, which allows me to steal yet another covert glimpse. Yup, a silk bra.

Nice. "Here's my card. And I'll write my home number on here if you need me after-hours," she says. Our eyes meet in a different way from how we stared at each other for thirty minutes during the interview. "That is, I know how you TV people work long hours."

"Yes. We do," I say, trying to compute whether this gorgeous, intelligent, caring, sensitive woman just made a pass at me. "Thanks. I'll call you."

"Do," she says, walking to the doorway and flipping on the overhead lights, which brighten the room into an overwhelming bath of ugly green fluorescence.

The crew isn't allowed to shoot any of the minors who were residents, so after a few minutes of getting Edgar at his reception desk and some general shots of the facility, we're back in the truck ready to hit our next location.

"You must be jazzed knowing that she calls her pussy Johnny," Joe says, lighting up a cigarette and pulling out of our parking spot.

"Now, now," Smitty says, punching Joe in the arm quite a bit harder than last time. "Don't mess with the paying customers, Joey boy."

"She was very, ah, pleasant," I say, trying not to make my lust for the good doctor too obvious.

"Did she give you any mixed audibles?" Joe says, while zooming in and out of traffic traveling north on Vine in the heart of Hollywood.

"Mixed audibles?" I ask, keeping both eyes transfixed on the street congestion that Joe is expertly maneuvering through.

"Yeah, you know, like, did she give you any chick clues? They always do that. They give you a mixed signal so that if they change their mind when you follow up on it, they can deny they gave you any kind of come-on," Joe says with his cigarette dangling from his lips, watching me in his rearview mirror.

"Funny you should say that," I say, taking to heart Joe's theory of female ambiguous communications. "She gave me her home number and said I could call her if I had any questions for her during nonbusiness hours."

"Classic mixed audible," Joey wails, gripping the wheel as he jams on the brakes for a red light at Hollywood and Vine. "Perfect! We can't win. Chicks have everything so stacked in their favor. You call her at home and suggest you go out for a cocktail, and she blows you off, saying"—Joe goes into a falsetto voice, imitating a girl—"'Oh, I never intended for that to happen when I told you to call me!' Or if she's in the mood, she says, 'Come on over, my little stud muffin!'"

"Hey, Sally Jesse Raphael, come on, the light's green," Smitty says to Joe, "and just because you've been divorced twice doesn't mean that all women are like your evil ex-wives."

"Oh, Smitty, no, no, no," Joe says, gunning it, "I wouldn't wish my evil ex-wives on my worst enemies. I'll just shut up and drive. But Johnny, she'd be some freakin' catch, lemme tell ya." Joe has a devilish grin as he turns around to look at me.

"Eyes on the road!" Smitty screams, grabbing the wheel with one hand to narrowly miss a city bus that suddenly shot into our lane.

"Oops," Joe says meekly as he takes control again. "I know. Shut up and drive."

The rest of the afternoon is spent shooting exteriors of various mansions in the Hollywood Hills and Beverly Hills, and also some plastic surgeon's offices, a small chapel, and a cliff on Mullholland Drive overlooking the entire Los Angeles basin where the stepdaughter/girlfriend of the famous Hollywood director was rescued from her Porsche dangling off the side after she nearly committed suicide. After we wrap, they drop me off at the office, which fortunately is empty, which means my day is over, too.

I drive home and park my car in my spot. Benny must be home, because his van is sitting there, caked with dirt as usual, and someone has written on the back window CLEAN ME. All seems quiet at the building. A slow cool breeze blows across the pool in the early-evening air, sweet with spring blossoms. No one is at the pool, and the sounds of people having their dinners echo across the courtyard as they settle in for the evening. I hope I don't run into Benny. There are bold junkies and old junkies. But there are no old, bold junkies. That's a deadly combination. I knew more than a few junkies in my old Bronx neighborhood. When I was a kid in the fourth or fifth grade, there was a grown-up who used to sit on the front stoop of his building down by Broadway near the El station on 238th Street. He would sit there all day drinking beer or wine inside a brown paper bag. We thought he was an old man, but looking back on it, I'll bet he was maybe thirty years old. He had carrot-red hair and the face of Ireland across his mug, but even we fourth-graders knew he was a junkie. With his greasy red pompadour, prominent Adam's apple, and bony limbs, he was known as the Red Rooster. He'd scare the shit out of us when we were playing in places only kids usually play, like under bridges, in basements, or behind stairways, and we'd stumble on to him sniffing glue, drinking cough syrup, or shooting up. He'd never chase us. He couldn't. He was too fucked up. But the sight of that skeleton-like red head, flashing his yellow teeth and barking at us, was enough to make any kid run away in horror.

I go around front to grab my mail, and as I turn the corner, there he is.

"Oh, Benny! Shit, you scared the hell out of me," I say, realizing he's starting to look like the Italian version of the Red Rooster.

"Sorry, Johnny. I was hoping I'd catch you. I heard your car pull in. I like that car. Listen, I got something I think you might be interested in."

"Not interested, bye," I say, brushing past Benny, trying to give him the bum's rush. Can't this guy take a hint?

Benny lets me get several steps past him and says, "I got a Willie Mays."

I stopped dead in my tracks. Willie Mays. Not bad.

"Not here, Benny. Okay, let's go into my place."

We turn the corner and go into my apartment. Benny takes the same chair and position he had the last time. He reaches into his bag and retrieves a red, white, and blue box, which I instantly recognize as a box that holds new baseballs. He places the box on the table, carefully opens the lid, and pulls out a baseball covered in protective tissue.

"Can you come over here and look at this?" Benny says, pulling the paper apart to reveal a small portion of the baseball.

I take the few steps over to Benny and get quite close to him to look at the ball. Benny has a strange smell about him. Almost medicinal. I look at the ball, and written on it is *To Dominic— Willie Mays.*

"Where'd you get that? It's perfect. The leather hasn't even aged much," I say, admiring the treasure.

"No one has touched this ball in decades. It was . . . my brother's . . . favorite. But I don't need it. Not even a fan. What will you give me for it?"

"Aw, come on, Benny. I don't know. How do I know it's not a fake?"

"Oh, come on, Johnny. I'm a lot of things, but I'm not a cheat. I've even got a picture of him signing it . . . somewhere. Make me an offer."

"I don't know. Can I see the picture?"

"Absolutely. I've got it somewhere. An offer. Please," Benny says. His pleading eyes are now even more sunken than they seemed just last week.

"Fifty."

"It's yours," Benny says, wrapping up the ball, placing it in the box and back into the bag.

I go into my bedroom, grab another fifty, and give it to Benny, who doesn't look very happy.

"Benny, are you okay?" I ask as he's leaving.

"Yeah. Just peachy," he says, softly closing the door behind him.

I go over and lock the door and look through the peephole to see Benny going to the parking lot. The bag he left behind with the precious autographed ball inside is a wrinkled lump of stiff brown paper. I stretch the bag out, and in red fading ink, I can barely make out the word *Gristedes*, and even more faded below, *Arthur Avenue, Bronx, New York*. Gristedes supermarkets were all over New York City when I was a little kid. But by the seventies, they had all begun to close. And why would Benny have a bag from Arthur Avenue in the Bronx if he's from the Lower East Side of Manhattan? Arthur Avenue is more than just a street. It's the name given to an entire Bronx neighborhood, which is sometimes called Little Italy in the Bronx. I would guess that being from the Lower East Side, Benny would have relatives who lived by Arthur Avenue. The brown bags that his family stored under the sink could have been the bags that aunts and uncles used to bring over jars of tomato sauce or wine or mussels picked off the jetty in Rockaway, and of course, you would never throw away one of those bags without putting it to good use again and again. We used those brown bags for garbage bags, book covers, Halloween masks; we even cut the bottom out of them, taped them above the door, and used them as basketball hoops for rolled-up socks. We never threw much of anything away: rubber bands, string, paper bags, jars, all were stored under the sink for a later job. Not because of any concern for the environment, but simply due to our parents' memories of the Depression and World War II; never waste anything if you don't have to.

I open the Gristedes bag, which I now notice reeks of cigarette smoke. Although there are no tears, the cardboard of the Rawlings baseball box is becoming brittle, and the colors are beginning to fade. I carefully open the lid and am again struck by the smell of cigarette smoke that has permeated the wad of tissue covering the ball. The ball itself is in excellent condition. The leather isn't pure white but slightly off-white, like the color of heavy cream. The bright red stitches are perfect, and there isn't a scuff on it. I doubt anyone ever handled this ball without wearing protective gloves. If you touch a baseball, even with just your fingers, the oils rub off, and in a decade or two, your finger oils will begin to darken the hide.

When I was a kid, the only ball I ever retrieved from a Major League ballpark was at Yankee Stadium during batting practice in the early seventies, when the Yankees were a mere shell of their former glory. The stadium was such a wreck they almost moved to Jersey, until they decided to entirely renovate it in 1974 and 1975. They were lucky to have ten thousand people for a weekend game against other cellar dwellers of the American League, like the Cleveland Indians or the California Angels. During batting practice, Horace Clarke hit a ball to right field that bounced into the stands and rolled around the empty seats. I was the first on the scene and picked it up with the only competition being my two maniac friends, Michael Corsetti and Kevin McCaffrey, who nearly tore off my arm once I had the ball in my hand. We played catch with the ball during the game in our near-empty right field section, and once I got it home, it wound up under a pile of sports equipment jammed in the corner of a closet. When I found it ten or so years later, it was a scuffed-up mess, and the leather had turned a shade of tan similar to a piece of plywood.

It's obvious that Benny's ball was pampered with the utmost of care. I doubt the box was rarely opened, which is an amazing feat, because the ball is probably from the mid-fifties, when

Willie Mays was still with the New York Giants. Benny's brother must have been a very meticulous, conscientious child to keep an item like this under wraps. If I had a ball signed to me by Mickey Mantle, I would be showing it to total strangers waiting for the No. 38 bus. I know I wouldn't have been able to contain my joy and keep it stored away in a box on a shelf for decades. Actually, I think Benny is doing the right thing by selling it. It was his brother, Dominic, who cherished the ball. And if he's dead, it ain't doing nobody any good just sitting there, not being enjoyed by someone. I may not be the world's biggest Willie Mays fan, but that's only because I'm from the Bronx, and any kid born and raised in da Bronx has Yankee pinstripes in his genetic code. But I am a baseball fan and admire Willie Mays as one of the greatest players of all time, regardless of my anti-Giant bias. In the Bronx, only a pain-in-the-ass smart-aleck schmuck would *not* be a Yankees worshipper and root for the Giants. Anyway, I'll bet this ball is worth twice what I paid for it.

I put the ball bag in its box, and then in the Gristedes bag, and place it on an end table in my bedroom. There's no rush in trying to figure out whether I should sell it right away or display it properly.

Being almost eleven P.M., it's a little late for a phone call, but I answer it anyway.

"Hello. Oh, hi, Wendy. Yes, everything went well. Yes, Dr. Archer was fantastic. I left the tapes on your desk, like you said. Well, that was very nice of Dr. Archer to say that. Yes, our call in the morning is six-thirty. No problem. Good night."

Hmmm. So Dr. Archer told Wendy that I made quite an impression on her. Yup. Mixed audible No. 2!

Chapter Five

I WAS HOPING I WOULDN'T see this stretch of the I-10 again for a long time, but at least this morning I'm in a vehicle with a heavy-duty air conditioner that works. Until my trip out to L.A., I had romantic notions about the desert, visions of endless torrid white sand dunes, like in *Lawrence of Arabia*. The reality of the American West is quite different. Oh, it's hotter than hell in the daytime, but at night it can be as cold as standing on the deck of the Staten Island ferry in mid-February. The sand isn't so much sand as it is gravel. You know that quiet sound of walking on the pure white granulated-sugar-type sand on the eastern end of Long Island or in the Caribbean? Well, the California desert is nothing like that. It's more like walking on the gravel dumped in a Christmas-tree lot, and the crunch it makes with each step is bone-jarring. I've heard about the wonders of the desert wildlife, but when I get out to take a piss because the next Shell station is a hundred miles away, the only traces of wildlife I see are the empty beer cans along the side of the road. And as far as scenery, when you've seen a thousand cacti, you've seen them all.

The name Indio, California, conjures up picturesque images of a quaint Indian adobe village, but once we exit the freeway, I can see that quaint is not in the equation. In Palm Springs, the nicest hillside developments are surrounded by lush green gardens and golf courses. Here in Indio, the nicest homes have a better grade of gravel dumped in front of their house. Apparently, we're not going to one of those homes. We've just taken a sharp right turn onto a dirt road, and the only homes we see in the distance have tires on them.

"Who the hell are we interviewing here again?" Joe says, holding the wheel firmly with both hands as the van bumps along the rough road. "This is a hell of a long way to come for one goddamn interview."

"What the hell do you care, Joe?" Smitty says without taking his eyes off the scenery, which he seems to enjoy taking in. "If you don't like new experiences and meeting unusual people, you're in the wrong damn business."

"We're interviewing," I say, opening my bible to the page with the information, "the one and only Beatrice Klettner."

"Beatrice Klettner? Okay. You got me. Who the fuck is Beatrice Klettner?" Joe says. He has a cigarette in his mouth that went out about fifty miles ago.

Reading from my notes I announce, " 'Beatrice Klettner just happens to be a poor, alcoholic, mentally unstable fifty-two-year-old woman with emphysema—' "

"Stop," Joe screams, "you're turning me on!"

" '—who did something very memorable in 1970.' "

"She got out of prison!" Joe yells, while Smitty quietly laughs his ass off.

"No, she gave birth to one Annabelle Klettner, known to millions as America's number one bankable female movie star and known to you as . . ."

"No fucking way. Anna Belle? *The* Anna Belle's mother lives out here in hell's very own slum? You know, the more I work in this business, the more I see what these people are really like, and it makes me very happy to be a—"

Smitty cuts him off: "—a tobacco-addicted, pot-smoking, semialcoholic, twice divorced—"

"All right, all right, shut up, Mr. Perfect," Joe says to Smitty. He opens his window and spits out his cigarette butt, allowing a hot blast of desert air into the van.

"Apparently, Anna Belle ran away from home when she was sweet sixteen and headed for the bright lights of Hollywood, and judging by these pictures of her at that time, I am not surprised that she did quite well for herself in a short amount of time," I say, removing the page with Anna Belle's porno photos and handing them to Smitty and Joe.

"Damn! She was only sixteen in these pictures!" Smitty says, shaking his head. "I didn't even know that sexual position was possible until I was twenty-one."

"If Anna Belle knew we had these pictures, she'd have every lawyer in Beverly Hills on our ass," I say. These shots from her first porno movie are thought to have all been bought up and destroyed.

"Oh my God!" Joe says, hitting a big pothole, not looking where he's going. "She's sixteen in that photo? When I dated sixteen-year-old girls, I thought I was lucky if I felt some baby-fat tit through a zipped-up ski jacket."

"Yeah, well, Beatrice Klettner sits out here quietly keeping her mouth shut about dear Anna Belle. Until now! I hold in my hand an envelope that contains a hundred reasons why Beatrice will appear on national television to tell us about her runaway wild child," I say, holding up an unmarked white No. 10 envelope.

"A hundred bucks?" Joe says, hurt and bewildered by such a paltry payoff. "She's gonna rat on her daughter for a measly hundred clams? Why?"

"It appears that Anna Belle has been neglecting her dear old mom. And after trying to get her into rehab for several years and failing, Anna is now trying the tough-love approach, which includes stopping her monthly shut-up money until she gets some help."

"But still, I mean, a hundred bucks? That's sad," Joe says, feeling Beatrice's pain.

"Okay, Joe. But what if I told you those hundred reasons," I say, doing my best imitation of game show announcer Johnny Olsen, "were not a hundred one-dollar bills but a hundred one-hundred-dollar bills!"

"What? Ten grand? You've got ten grand in there? Shit, I'd sell out my kids for ten grand," Joe says, now agreeing wholeheartedly with Beatrice's choice. "She could live like a queen out here for ten grand."

"Yeah, for six months or six visits to a casino, whatever comes first," Smitty says, shaking his head in disgust.

"There it is. The silver Airstream with the purple awnings," I say, pointing to a dirt driveway on the right.

There's a black Mercedes parked next to a dilapidated Toyota pickup and a newer-model Honda Accord. We park in the driveway and begin to unload the gear in the sweltering dry heat. I walk around the back of the Airstream, which at one time was probably the top-of-the-line model but now is just a dented, dull shell of a trailer home. There's a ramp leading up to the back door, with a large dog taking a siesta right in the middle of it. As I step over it, he looks up at me, thinks for a minute, then goes back to his nap.

I knock on the door, and a man of about forty in a dark green silk shirt, with the chest and armpits soaked through with sweat, greets me. "You're John Coaster," he says, opening the battered screen door.

"That's Koester as in General Custer. Call me Johnny," I say, looking at the tiny, cluttered, stifling room, which will be like a Dutch oven once our lights heat it up.

"I'm Bernie Henchy, Ms. Klettner's attorney. I looked over all the paperwork that Ms. Valentine sent over, and everything seems to be in order. We just need the down payment," he says, attempting to pull the fabric away from his sweaty, furry body. Why is it that the guys with back and chest hair crawling up their necks are usually totally bald, like this guy?

"I'm unaware of the down-payment concept, but I have the cash. I need to present it to Ms. Klettner and have her sign this form," I say, knowing my line, too.

"Another form?" Bernie asks. "I'll have to examine this." He takes it with one hand and uses his other to wave the front of his shirt, hoping for some circulation. "This is fine. It's just a receipt of the ten, um, the agreed-upon amount. I'll go get my client."

He steps to a sliding plastic door, opens it enough for his pudgy body to slip through, and closes it behind him. The living room has been tidied up, but the smell of cigarettes, the fermented wine in the carpets, the cigarette burns on the counters, and the oxygen tank on wheels tell quite a bit about its inhabitant.

The plastic door slides open, and much to my surprise, a very handsome woman appears. It's easy to see where her sex-symbol daughter got her high cheekbones; slender, almost Chinese eyes; and long, sleek body. But it's also clear to see that this is not a well woman, with her skin dried and wrinkled as a stale raisin, and her long fingers shaking slightly as she reaches to shake hands with me.

"I'm Beatrice Klettner. Do I look okay? Peggy has been working on me for hours," Beatrice says, reaching into a drawer for a pack of Camels. "Hope you don't mind that I smoke. I have to. Didn't Peggy do wonders for an old hag like me? She came all the way from Palm Springs to work on me."

Peggy is the kind of rotund gal my mom would always make a point to say how pretty she would be if she weren't such a fat pig.

"Here's my card," Peggy says, timidly handing one to me. "If you ever need hair and makeup in Palm Springs, give me a call."

"Thanks. Beatrice, you look great. And I want you to be comfortable. Once we get started, feel free to stop anytime, compose yourself, rephrase a sentence . . ."

Beatrice jams her cigarette into a large ashtray and begins to cry uncontrollably as she rushes past me and goes through the folding plastic door into the next room. Bernie follows immediately behind. Peggy looks at me and, with both hands on her chin, says, "She's been like that all day. Poor dear. I don't know how she can do this. That no-good daughter of hers. It's just so . . . sad . . ." Peggy starts a crying jag of her own and sits in the creaky La-Z-Boy that takes up most of the living room.

"I think I'll go see how the crew is doing," I say to no one as I walk out the door. Through the screen door, I see Smitty and Joe sitting on their cases.

"We ain't going nowhere until that dog moves," Smitty says.

"Aw, that cute thing? He didn't bother me," I say, opening the door and standing right next to the big mutt.

"Yeah, well, he didn't greet us with a smile," Joe says between drags on his cigarette. "He showed teeth and said the dog equivalent of 'Don't fuck with me, asshole.' "

I bend over and pat the mutt on the head. He looks up at me with soft brown eyes. "Come on, boy, get up. Coming through."

The dog gets up, shakes his butt, walks past Smitty and Joe without making a peep, and lies down in a shady spot next to a rusty old shed.

"What are you, Saint Francis of Assisi or something?" Joe says, and lifts a couple of heavy video bags.

"I've been called a sissy but never Saint Francis of Assisi," I say, holding the screen door for them as they enter the trailer.

Smitty and Joe quietly set up their equipment with quick efficiency as Peggy looks on. The folding plastic door slides open again, and Beatrice enters the room with Bernie in tow.

"I'll be fine now," Beatrice says, lighting another smoke. "Where do you want me?"

Smitty walks from behind his camera, which is already on the tripod. "Okay, honey, you are going to look great. I got you with that pretty picture in the background and a piece of that window looking out onto that beautiful desert landscape, and it's going to look like a commercial for a Palm Springs resort." Smitty leads her by the hand into an old folding chair positioned exactly where he wants it. "Do you have a photo of Anna Belle I could put in the background?"

"Sure. Bernie, get that photo of Annabelle from my nightstand, would you?" Beatrice says, sitting straight in her stiff-backed chair.

Bernie returns with a black-and-white photo of a darling teenage girl dressed in leotards, with evidence of her maturing body bursting through.

"I'll just put this over here," Smitty says, placing the photo on the counter behind Beatrice, then going into position behind the camera.

Joe walks over to Beatrice with the microphone in hand. "Don't mind me, I'm just a sound guy," he says warmly to Beatrice, who giggles as he grabs her hand.

"Okay, let's get started," I say, taking my position next to the camera. "Don't look at the camera. Just look to me as you talk, as if we're having a conversation. Stop anytime you want. Just let me know. Ready?"

"Rolling. Speed," Smitty says, touching a button and leaning in to his viewfinder.

"Let's start at the beginning, Beatrice. What kind of child was Annabelle?"

"Well, she was just the cutest little thing from the day I brought her home from the hospital. A pink little bundle of joy," Beatrice announces happily. "Her father didn't stay around long. Left when she was just three. But I worked, had help from some dear friends. It was tough, but we made do with what we . . . what I . . . she was . . . I . . ." Beatrice's eyes are welling up, and she begins to quietly sob. I can hear the lens right next to my ear zooming in for the kill.

"Do you want to stop, Beatrice?" I say, handing her a box of tissues.

"No, I'm fine. Let's continue," Beatrice says, composing herself nicely. "In junior high, I started to notice Annabelle's grades slipping. And I felt she was running around. You know. Misbehaving with boys. I've got to admit, I was no perfect angel myself during those years. It's hard to be alone, and a woman needs, um, companionship. It can be so lonely out here. You move out here to get away from all the troubles in the city and all the people and whatnot, but when you're out here for a while, you do get that lonely feeling. I was seeing a nice gentleman at the time. He worked construction. But he died in a car crash. He was drunk, they said. He was on the way over here when it happened. I noticed Annabelle changing. We fought for the first time. I found some . . . pills. Birth control. And other pills when she was fifteen. I don't know . . ." Beatrice trails off as she covers her face and weeps into her hands. "Can we stop?"

"Stop tape," I announce.

"Stop tape," Smitty says, dropping his hands from the camera.

"Those days were just so awful," Beatrice says through crocodile tears now running her makeup down her cheeks. "I was a mess. I was drinking a lot, and I was a terrible mother at that time in my life. It was just too much for me, and before I knew it, Annabelle was gone. The last thing she said was that she hated me and would make something of herself and never wanted to see me again." Peggy begins touching up Beatrice's makeup, then gently rubs her shoulders. "Okay, okay, I can go on."

"Start tape," I say to Smitty.

"Rolling, speed," Smitty says, leaning back down to the viewfinder.

"I don't want to talk about all that in the interview. Let me put it this way: Annabelle and I had a falling-out when she was a sophomore in high school. I had a relative in Los Angeles, and Annabelle went to live with her when she was sixteen. She never finished high school but got some modeling work. Next thing I know, I saw her in that movie *End of the Line*. She looked so grown-up from when I last saw her. She was gorgeous."

"So you haven't seen her since she left here?" I ask.

"Just in the movies, like everybody else for the past few years," Beatrice says with a weak smile.

"Has she abandoned you?" I ask, remembering this question from my notes.

"Yes. She has abandoned me. I've had a run of some tough luck, and I've been struggling with some health problems, and I just want her to know that I love her, and I just wish she would, you know, get in touch . . ." Beatrice weeps.

Again I hear the zoom going in for the extreme close-up as she continues to babble and sob.

"I need help. I'm sick. Annabelle, I need you," Beatrice says, crying alone in her folding chair with her young cherubic daughter looking on from a black-and-white photo in the background.

Beatrice isn't the only one in the room who perhaps needs help. I have enough shame for everyone present.

"That's it. Let's break down, Smitty. Get some exteriors and we'll call it a day," I say, rising from my seat and crossing over to Beatrice, who has stopped crying but just sits in her chair with her eyes closed as she very slowly moves her head from side to side as though she's listening to an inner voice. "Beatrice, are you okay?"

"I'm okay. I hope I didn't make too much of a fool of myself. I just hope Annabelle understands I just need a little help."

"I think Annabelle will get the message," I reassure Beatrice, knowing full well that not only will Annabelle get the message, but so will several powerful Beverly Hills lawyers who will probably come down so hard on Beatrice to shut the fuck up that she'll probably never want to hear the name Annabelle again.

I feel like I just led a little lamb to slaughter. Only this slaughter will be nationally televised.

I reach into my bag and pull out the envelope with the money, and Bernie zips out of the other room to intercept it before Beatrice can get a finger on it.

"Beatrice, let's you and me go in the next room and make sure everything is in order," Bernie says, whisking her away.

Smitty and Joe have left the trailer and are outside shooting exteriors, leaving Peggy the makeup lady and me alone. I begin absentmindedly paging through some notes, and I can feel Peggy staring at me.

She clears her throat and says, "I'm sorry to disturb you, but they said that you were going to pay for my services."

"Who did?"

"Well, Bernie said. He said that's standard."

"Oh," I say, knowing that no one told me anything about paying for a makeup and hair person. "Um, well, what is your rate?"

"Well, er, I usually get around twenty-five dollars when I do somebody's wedding or something?"

"Oh, well, here's fifty," I say, reaching into my wallet. "Can you write me an invoice?"

"Absolutely. Can you give me a piece of paper and a pen?" Peggy says joyfully.

"Sure," I say, tearing a page from a spiral notebook and handing her a pen. In New York or Hollywood, this would have been at least three hundred bucks. The people who need the most always seem to get the least.

Bernie and Beatrice come through the folding plastic door with Bernie all smiles and Beatrice looking like she just found out some really bad news.

"Everything's in order here," Bernie says, giving me a release form, which Beatrice has already signed. "Let us know when it's going to be on," he says, shaking my hand gleefully.

Beatrice walks over to me and grabs both my hands. She takes a deep breath and exhales an invisible cloud of cigarette smell and bourbon breath. Her high cheekbones and deep-set eyes no longer mark her beauty but show the outline of her skull. "Please, Johnny, please don't make me look bad," she says, tears filling her eyes.

"I won't let it happen, Beatrice. Don't worry," I say to her, knowing that I have no control whatsoever of what gets used from her interview, yet I have a feeling that I will be able to do something, somehow. I hope.

The ride back to Los Angeles is broken up with a visit to the two huge dinosaurs that are a tourist attraction on the freeway about an hour and a half before L.A. Inside one of the dinos, there's a little museum with some odd exhibits. The displays don't have much to do with dinosaurs. Rather, in a glass case is a pair of rusted antique handcuffs with half a skeleton arm and hand still locked inside. And next to this morbid display, hand-written in pencil on an index card with blue lines, it reads, *Just Desserts in the Desert.*

It's a long day, and by the end of the trip, no one has uttered a word for over an hour. We're finally back in the parking lot at the office, and Smitty hands me the two tapes we shot out in the desert. With a Sharpie, he's making a nicely written label: date, location, tape number of how many were shot, producer, and crew.

"Wow. You really know how to take care of details, Smitty," I say when he finishes the label and hands me the tapes.

"I've got to. I've seen too many shoots ruined by sloppy labels," Smitty says, glancing over to Joe.

"Don't look at me when you say that," Joe says with guilt written all over his face. "I labeled those tapes perfectly. That pussy River didn't have the balls to say he lost the tape, that's all. End of story."

"Johnny, did I say anything about Joe or River? Man, some people are sensitive!" Smitty says, giving me a wink.

"I hope we're getting good stuff on the interviews," I say to Smitty as he closes the van door.

"Oh, I think you'll be surprised how good the interviews are going," Smitty says. Giving me another wink, he hops in the van, starts the engine, and heads for the street. They pause at the curb, and I can hear Joe yelling, "I labeled those fucking tapes! That little shit River, I'm gonna kick his ass one day . . ." They speed onto the boulevard and are gone.

After dropping off the tapes, I'm back in my Woody, headed home.

My message machine is blinking. I think about leaving it until the morning, but decide with a new job and all, I better keep on top of things, so I push Play. "Hi, Johnny, it's me, Karen Marshall. I just heard from Wendy Valentine and wanted to relay to you that she's very, very pleased with your work so far. And I also want to talk with you about another project that you might be interested in. It might be starting up very soon. Call me in the morning around ten-thirty. I have a breakfast meeting. Bye and keep up the good work!"

What is with these breakfast meetings? Instead of picking up a buttered roll and a cup of coffee and eating it at your desk at nine, when most of the planet starts work, these L.A. people show up at some expensive bistro at nine with a showbiz friend, write the whole thing off as a breakfast meeting, and saunter into work at ten-thirty. Nice work, if you can get it.

BEEEEEEP.

A second message?

"Hi, Johnny, this is Joan Archer. You know, from Safe Haven." My heart skips a beat, as I think, Yeah, like I'm gonna forget where I know Joan Archer from. "I know this is a little unusual, but could you give me a call when you get in tonight, as long as it's before midnight. I was wondering if we could have a breakfast meeting tomorrow? Bye."

Wow. Wow, wow, and wow again. I'm not sure if this qualifies as a mixed audible anymore. She called *me*. I mean, it's not like she invited me to a dirty weekend in Santa Barbara, but she did ask me out to a meal. Okay, so it's breakfast, but it's a meal. But let's not start picking out the furniture just yet. It could be just a work-related breakfast meeting. Yeah, that's probably it. It is only eleven-forty-five . . . I'll call.

Damn. Her machine is on. "Hi, this is Johnny Koester, from, er, returning your call—"

Just then I get some kind of weird shock from my phone and almost drop it. I put the receiver back to my ear and hear a faint voice: "Hello, Johnny? Are you there?"

"Yes. Joan?"

"Yes. What happened?" Joan says, obviously having just awakened.

"I got a weird, like, static electricity shock. I'm sorry, you sound like you're in bed, I'll call you in the morning—"

"No. No. It's fine. I just dozed off. I heard your voice and I thought I was dreaming. And when I picked up, I got . . . a shock, too."

"Oh. Really?" I say softly into the phone.

"Really. Listen, where do you live?" Joan asks, still sleepy.

"Los Feliz, near Vermont."

"Do you know where the House of Pies is?" Joan asks. I close my eyes and easily imagine myself lying next to her, with her cat, Johnny, trying to nestle between us.

"Sure. I can walk there. But I already have a breakfast meeting tomorrow."

"Well how about right now?"

"Now?"

"Sure. I feel like a cup of decaf. Can you meet me there in half an hour?" she asks, a little more awake now, sounding like she's getting up from her bed.

"I'll be there in half an hour. Bye."

"Bye," she says softly, hanging up the phone.

Am I dreaming? Is this for real? And what the hell was that shock? It must be the dry night air. Must be.

Then there's a familiar knock on the door.

Shit. Don't tell me. That knock could be only one person. Fucking Benny.

"Benny. What the hell are you doing, it's almost midnight," I say to Benny, who I now notice is standing on my doorstep in a ratty terry-cloth robe barely tied together with a string.

"Can I come in, please, General?"

I can't believe this. I'm letting a middle-aged junkie into my apartment, while I've got the woman of my dreams heading for the counter at the House of Pies to meet me for the cup of decaf I've been waiting for my whole life.

"You've got to help me, General," Benny says, shuffling over to the chair he has already sat in twice, which is more than anyone else in Los Angeles has sat there, much to my dismay.

As many times as I've wanted to punch Benny out or just pretend I don't even know him, the sight of him in that ratty robe, his bony chest dotted with sparse clumps of white chest hair, has finally done me in. As much as I don't trust this guy, I can't turn him away. Not like this. Not even now. Well, maybe I can give it one more shot.

"Look, Benny. I've been helping you out. But it's over. You can get your ass out of here—"

"Johnny. I need help. Please, Johnny. I got nobody. I got nothing. Help me."

Shit. I've never seen a more pathetically sad human being in my life. His eyes are so dark with fear, his skin so gray and without life. "What is it, Benny?" I ask, afraid of what he might answer.

"Do you know anything about needles?"

"Shit, Benny. Why do you ask?"

"Look, I just need some information. Do you know anything, I just need to ask a question, that's all," Benny says, barely able to get the words out. He looks up at me and stares. It's as though all his strength will be used to get the next sentence out. "Johnny, I need some assistance. Somebody who can . . . handle a needle." His voice trails off into sad breathy heaves. His head hangs with his chin on his chest.

Boy, do I feel low. This poor slob is so alone that I'm the only one he can turn to. I just moved in!

"Gee, Benny. I hardly know anybody. Remember? I'm new here."

Then I think of Joan. She's an R.N. Maybe she can do it? That's all I need on a first date, if it even is a date. *Oh hi, Joan, can you pass the half-and-half, and oh, by the way, wanna go back to my place and shoot some guy I barely know full of dope?* But I can't just leave him like this.

"Listen, Benny," I say, bending down to the table where he hangs his head. "I'm going to meet a friend of mine. She's a nurse. I don't know what she'll say, but I'll see what I can do. Okay?"

Benny looks up at me. "Johnny, you're a good guy. Thanks, pal." He uses arms to push himself to his feet. "Knock on my door if you can do it. Thanks. I'll be waiting." He slowly steps across the room and out the door.

This is going to be my most interesting first date ever. And maybe my most interesting last date, too.

The House of Pies is pretty full for midnight. I stealthily take a peek inside, and there she is. She's sitting at the counter sipping a cup of coffee. Her hair is pulled back, and she's wearing an old jean jacket and printed cotton pants that could pass for pajamas. She's holding the coffee cup with both hands, savoring the aroma, then sensuously takes a small sip. I'm nervous as hell. She looks like every woman I always had the hots for in high school, college, and at rock concerts, but always struck out with. Long straight hair, tiny hips, slender and toned to almost being sinewy. She looks so different from the girls I grew up with. Those cute Italian, Irish, and Jewish girls, first- and second-generation ethnic beauties. Joan's Waspy appearance is exotic compared to what I'm used to. And she's petite. Being a smallish guy myself, still fitting into my high school clothes, I like a woman who's not as big as or bigger than I. From the looks of her fitness level, she might be able to kick my ass, but at least I'd put up a good fight.

I walk over to the stool next to her, at the very end, by the entrance to the kitchen, and say, "Is this stool taken?"

"Hello, Johnny," she says, reaching out politely to shake my hand, and as our hands meet, there is a jolt of static electricity. We look each other in the eye and say nothing.

"I'm glad you called," I say, motioning to the white-paper-hatted waitress.

"I'm glad you answered," Joan says, staring at the hot coffee cup just an inch from her lips.

"I'll have a cup of decaf," I tell the waitress. "Have you been here long?" I ask Joan.

"Too long," Joan says with an air of mixed audibleness. "Much too long."

"Sorry I'm late, but—"

"No," she says, chuckling. "I was being existential."

"Gotcha."

The waitress delivers my decaf on a paper doily coaster with an image of an orange coffee cup that appears to have been drawn in the forties.

"I love this coaster," I say, lifting it up for Joan to see.

"I have about a dozen of them. I use them all the time," Joan says cheerfully. "I have this funny feeling. Like I've known you for a long time. Probably because I bared my soul to you in that interview. I mean, it usually takes several dates to delve into the things we got to." She places both of our coasters in the inside pocket of her jean jacket.

"I'm not sure I bared my soul," I say after a long sip of decaf.

"Oh, yes, you did. One can tell a lot about a person by the questions he asks."

"Even if they came out of a production bible?"

"I could tell when you were . . . being you."

"I wish I could."

We gulped our last drops of coffee in tandem, our cups clunking down on the coasterless counter.

"Are you in a relationship?" Joan asks, looking at the empty coffee cup in front of her.

Wow. No mixed audible there. Straight to the heart of the matter. My heart is pounding. It's that moment when guys think that just maybe, maybe, they've got a shot. Oh, it doesn't have to be marriage, or a Caribbean cruise, but at least a shot at something more than just another date that ends with a forced kiss good night, and a trip to the bar to hang out with the guys in the same boat. No soul mate. No love of your life. Just a shot, that's all we ask.

"Not exactly. But I do seem to recall having been. Once or twice, a long time ago in a faraway land known as the Bronx."

"Is that where you're from? I thought I sensed an accent," she says, facing me and smiling.

"And you have no accent?"

"Do I?"

"Midwestern. Mmmm, let's see. Ohio?"

"Very good. Cleveland. What else can you tell about me?"

"You work out a lot. And you have a propensity to love cats named Johnny," I say in true mixed-audible style.

She giggles and waves to the waitress for two more cups of decaf.

"I've been in L.A. for three years, and I am so sick of L.A. guys."

"Well, you can't get much farther from L.A. than the Bronx," I say, holding up my fresh cup of coffee in a toast.

"Maybe not. Would you like to go for a little walk? It's a lovely evening. The air is so sweet with lemon blossoms," Joan says softly, slowly twirling her spoon in her coffee.

Hmmm. Time for a decision. What about Benny? This could be a disaster. How in the world am I going to broach this subject? I'll just see what happens.

"I'd love to." I pick up the checks and throw down a few bucks. "After you," I say, spinning around on my stool. I hold the door for her, and we stroll to the curb. There aren't any cars coming, yet we stand staring at the DON'T WALK sign. "Why don't people jaywalk here?" I ask Joan.

"Because the cops are tough," she says. The light changes and we cross the street.

"Oh, yeah, I forgot," I say, noticing the Rodney Drive street sign and little piles of riot ash still hugging the curb.

We get to the other side of the street, and the air is truly saturated with an intoxicating aroma of sweet blossoms. As we step a few paces down the dark street lined with cozy bungalows and nicely kept apartment buildings, Joan stops in her tracks, turns to me, and says, "I want to get something out of the way, if you don't mind." With that, she leans in to me, closes her eyes, and places a tender, soft kiss on my lips. "There. That's done. No more wondering."

"I'm with you," I say. I turn, tentatively grab her hand and we continue to walk down the pleasant street. I've had women come on to me before, but usually only during last call. And most of the time it's by sloppy-drunk women who need a ride home. I must admit, when one of those lasses planted a big wet kiss on my face in the middle of a white-boy dance to "Brick House," I always felt a desire to do a touchdown dance, knowing that I was about to do what all single guys think about yet rarely get to do with someone they actually want to do it with. Often you both wind up in a strange place, doing strange things with someone you barely know, and in the morning there's a race to see who can escape first, never to be seen again.

But with Joan, I don't feel the need for any tippy-toe dance. I feel a warm tingling all over my body. A lot like a low electrical current flowing through my bones. Then I remember. The static electricity on the phone and when we shook hands. I stop next to a lemon tree in full bloom and face Joan. "Remember when you picked up the phone? Did you say you felt something?"

"I did. Static electricity."

I'm still holding her hand. I reach over with my other hand and stroke the hand I'm holding. "Like when we shook hands at the counter."

I pull her close to me, and instead of a little smooch on the lips, we close our eyes and begin a mad, passionate kiss, right there in the middle of the sidewalk, pulling each other as close as physically possible. Her tongue shoots inside my mouth, and I reciprocate with a full onslaught of French kissing. Every breath

I take through my nostrils is rich with the smell of lemon blossoms and her just-shampooed hair, in an intoxicating rush of pleasure. We stop kissing and stand there, clutching each other, as a short, elderly lady shuffles by walking three Yorkies.

"'If I were any closer, I'd be behind you,'" I say, quoting from a Marx Brothers movie.

"Groucho," she sighs.

I know then and there, this is a keeper.

We walk down the street, still a couple of blocks from where I live. I begin to think about Benny, sitting there. I can't wait much longer to drop this bomb on Joan.

"Joan. This is going to sound so ridiculous. Especially now," I say, squeezing her hand rhythmically.

"Go ahead. Oh, look!" Joan drops my hand and crouches down, facing some shrubs in front of a bungalow. "Do you see him?" She begins to snap her fingers softly.

"See what?"

"The kitty."

"Where?"

She makes short meow sounds, and out of a black bush comes a cute black kitten with white feet. It runs right up to her and meows back, then poses to enjoy Joan's scratches, neck rubs, and full-length back and belly strokes. "Hello, kitty. You be safe now," Joan says. She gives it a gentle push back toward the shrubs.

"Do cats always just come running to you?"

"Usually."

"That's amazing."

"I love cats. What is it you wanted to tell me?" Joan says as we begin to walk again.

"Joan, this is nuts. But I have this neighbor. He's kind of a kook. And, well . . ."

Joan stops and turns to me. "What? Spit it out."

"He needs help with a needle, and I don't mean he's sewing buttons on his shirt."

"A needle? As in syringe?"

"Yes."

"And do we know why he needs help with a needle as in syringe?"

"I'm not one hundred percent sure, but by the looks of him, he could be a junkie."

"Does he look ill?"

"That's an affirmative."

"How do you know he's not just . . . sick?"

"Um, I guess I don't."

"When does he need this help?"

"He said tonight. Now."

"How far away are we?" She grabs my hand and picks up the pace.

"Just a couple of blocks."

"Let's go," Joan says, squeezing my hand in quick rhythmic jolts. "We've got to help him."

How in the world did I get this lucky?

We stop in front of Benny's door, and as usual, it looks like no one has lived there for years. No hint of light behind dirty windows with lopsided blinds and dark drapes closed tight. Piles of old flyers and phone books are still piled on his top step and have even begun to overflow into the small shrubs next to his stairway.

"This is Benny's place," I say to Joan, who is staring in bewilderment at his tattered screen door.

"Someone lives here?" she asks. "You think he's home?"

"He's home," I say. I pull open the screen door and knock on his door. There's no sound from inside, so I knock again harder. After a few moments, we hear a muffled voice.

"Hold on. Hold on. I'll be right there. I'll be right there," Benny says, pulling open his door, which makes a sound like a piece of plywood being dragged across asphalt. "I'm nude, Johnny," Benny confesses through the narrow opening in the door.

"Don't come out nude, Benny. Please. I've had enough excitement this evening," I say. Joan tries to hide her giggles.

"What should I do?" Benny says frantically from behind the door.

"Benny, calm down. Put on some clothes and come over to my apartment with everything," I whisper, knowing my nosy neighbors probably all have their ears hidden behind draperies covering open windows. "My friend and I will be waiting there for you, okay?"

"Okay, great," Benny says slamming his door shut.

"How well do you know this guy?" Joan asks as we take the few steps over to my apartment and enter.

"Not so well. He tried to sell me some riot loot, and it was uphill from there."

"Riot loot? Like what?" Joan says, sitting cross-legged on the floor.

"He tried to sell me a new TV in a box that fell off the back off a truck, but after I decided against it, he discovered it was indeed a new box but filled with bricks."

"Bricks?"

"Yeah, that's an old trick. The thief keeps the TV, then sells the box in a hurry to a sucker who thinks he's going to get something for nothing."

"Nice place." Joan looks around my humble living room, which is dominated entirely by my book and record collections. "Books and music. That's all one needs, really," she says softly, which reminds me that I'm on a first date with a woman, and for the first time in my life, it's bona fide love at first sight. For me, anyway.

KNOCK KNOCK.

I open the door and Benny enters, wearing the old black windbreaker and the baggy khakis that probably used to fit. He's carrying a wrinkled brown paper supermarket bag and half a bottle of wine.

"I thought maybe you and your friend might want a drink," Benny says, placing his bag and the bottle on the dining room table and taking a seat in the same place. "Oh my gosh, I forgot to introduce myself. My name's Benny." He leaps up to shake hands with Joan, but at the same time he reaches for her, his pants fall down to his ankles, revealing legs so bony it brings to mind those awful pictures of concentration camp survivors. Fortunately, his windbreaker covers his crotch and his ass, so he's spared the total humiliation of exposing himself to a beautiful woman he's meeting for the first time. "Oh, shit," Benny says, reaching down with both hands and pulling his pants back up. "I had them loosened because I thought maybe I was going to get a shot in the ass. I'm sorry. Shit. I'm so, so sorry." Benny looks as though his entire world is crumbling and he's not going to be able to handle it.

Joan rises up to meet him, shakes his hand, and with the other rubs him tenderly on his shoulder. "I'm Joan Archer. No need to be embarrassed, Benny. I've seen it before. I'm an R.N. I've seen stuff you wouldn't believe. What happened to your fingers?"

I've wanted to ask Benny that question since I first laid eyes on him, and Joan asks it like it's nothing. She's direct, if nothing else.

"Oh. An accident when I was a kid in my father's butcher shop. It helped my curveball, though," Benny says. He holds up his deformed right hand and flicks his wrist as if throwing a baseball. "Joan, they gave me this stuff and said I could do it myself. But God help me, I just can't. Needles terrify me."

"Back up, Benny. Who gave you this stuff?"

"The doctor, of course. It's my chemo," Benny says with a bewildered look. "Didn't the general tell you?"

"Uh, sorry, Benny. I wasn't sure what the needle thing was all about," I say sheepishly, realizing that all the time I pegged Benny for being a down-and-out junkie, he was suffering from cancer. What a schmuck I am.

"Don't you worry about a thing, Benny," Joan says, her voice rich with compassion. "Johnny, where's your bathroom? I want to wash up a little."

"Right over there."

"I'll be right back." Joan heads down the hall and goes into the bathroom.

"General! Wow! What a doll. What a sweetheart," Benny says, holding his left hand in an A-OK circle. "How long have you known her?"

"Actually, we just met."

"Wow. What a lovely woman," Benny says, probably just a little too loud as Joan returns to the room.

"Okay, Benny, let's see what you've got here." Joan opens his bag. "This looks right," Joan says removing several items from the bag and placing them on the table. "Just stand up, take off your jacket, and reveal a few inches of your butt as you lean over on the table," Joan says, preparing the needle. She places it in a small vial of medicine, withdraws it, then flicks her finger against the syringe a couple of times. "I was voted best needle-giver when we had to stick each other in class for practice." She holds the needle in her right hand, raises her arm high, and, in a very slow and deliberate motion, appears to make the sign of the cross over Benny's rump.

Benny cranes his head around and shrieks, "What the hell are you doing? Why the hell are you making a sign of the cross on my butt?" He jumps up, grabbing his pants, and struggles to pull them up. "Is this some kind of exorcism or some shit or what? I don't want a goddamn Catholic ritual on me or my ass or any-where. I don't want any kind of religious hocus-pocus ritual—"

Joan takes half a step back but stands her ground. Without

raising her voice, she says, "It's okay, Benny. I'm not making a sign of the cross. I'm just marking off the quadrants of your butt to make a target. One this way, then that way, then I aim for where they cross each other. It helps my aim. That's all. I swear. Relax." Joan places her hand on his back, and he returns to his position to receive the shot.

"You're sure?"

"Yes."

"Hit it!" Benny yells.

Joan sticks the needle in, injects the medicine, and takes it out. She then rubs some alcohol on the spot and puts a Band-Aid over it. "There, Benny, that wasn't so bad, was it?"

"Didn't feel a thing," Benny says, pulling up his pants again. "And I've gotta say, I haven't had my pants down in front of such a pretty girl in years."

"Benny, sit down, I'd like to talk to you." Joan moves a chair closer to Benny's. "What is your diagnosis?"

Benny adjusts himself in the chair like a second-grader in the principal's office. "I've got lung cancer. I didn't go to the doctor for a long time."

"How long?"

"A couple of years. I went a few months ago. They said they'd do what they could. I was going in for chemo, then they told me to do it at home if I could. What do you think, Joan? Would you do it for me at least until I can get the hang of it?" Benny asks with the look of a very frightened boy.

"Sure, I'll do it. I'll talk to your doctor as well, if you want."

"Nah. That's okay. But can I tell the General to call you when I need you again?"

"Yes, Benny. That's fine. Any time."

"That's swell, Joan," Benny says, rising from his chair. "Okay, General, thanks. And Joan, you're a champ!" Benny leaves looking much better than he did five minutes ago.

"Joan, that was amazing," I say, still leaning against a wall on the other side of the room. "You don't even know that guy, and you're treating him with such . . . kindness."

"Oh, I don't know. What am I going to do? Say no?" Joan says, walking over to me. "I've got to clean up again." She gives me a peck on the cheek before she goes back into the bathroom.

Yup. That's exactly what 99.9 percent of the planet's population usually does: says no. But Joan strikes me as the kind of individual who wouldn't say no to a person in need or a little kitty with white feet that would enjoy a belly rub. I still have my doubts about Benny. Okay, so he says he's not a junkie. Why have I heard from my nosy neighbors that the cops have been to his place on more than one occasion? And selling off his dead brother's cherished collection is not exactly what you'd expect a decent individual to be doing. And why is he turning to me, a total stranger, for help? He must have some family or friends who can help him. I mean, he's lived in California for decades. I guess Joan doesn't need to know the answers to any of these questions. She sees a person in trouble and tries to help. That's why she has the job she has. Which begs the question, why do I have the job I have?

Joan comes out of the bathroom and sits in the chair Benny was sitting in, where the half bottle of wine he brought remains. "What are you going to do with this?" Joan says, holding the bottle up high.

"Well, do you want a glass?" I ask, approaching her chair from behind. I begin to softly massage her shoulders.

"No. To tell you the truth, I really should be getting back home," she says as she tenderly reaches for my hand and plants a light kiss on my knuckles.

"Can I give you a lift back to the restaurant?" I say, then quickly wonder whether the sight of my 1980 Town & Country Woody will be a turnoff. But then again, if it is a turnoff, then I suppose she isn't Miss Right after all.

"That would be nice. My car is in the lot at the House of Pies," she says, getting up from the chair.

We walk over to my front door and stop. I put my hands on her shoulders and look her dead in the eye. "I just want to make sure this hasn't been a dream. If it is a dream, I never want to wake up," I say, closing my eyes and pulling Joan slowly toward me. I smell her hair, then feel her moist lips pressing against mine. A euphoric rush of blood surges through my brain as I drink in not just what is but what might be. Joan and I fit just right. I gently push her away and open my eyes. A slightly crooked smile beams across her sweet face.

"So, is it a dream?" she asks in a whisper.

I pull her close to me again, and we embrace. "Yes, it is a dream. Don't wake me. Ever," I say, soaking in the moment.

"I won't wake you if you don't wake me," Joan says, her head resting on my shoulder.

"Deal."

We make our way out to the parking lot, and there it is.

"What is that?" Joan says in a loud whisper as she realizes that the Woody is my ride.

"It's my trusty Woody," I say, putting the key in the passenger door and holding it open for her.

"I love it! What a trip! Where'd you get such a treasure? Don't tell me! It must be an heirloom!"

"Yup. Dad's pride and joy is now mine."

"Now, this is style!" Joan says, scooting over the bench seat to be next to me as I get in the driver's side. "Oh, goody! You have a middle lap belt!" she says, buckling up.

I buckle my belt, turn on the ignition, and put my arm around her. I turn to her and say, "Stick with me, kid. I'll take you places," and we begin a soft but passionate kiss.

I drop her off at the House of Pies lot and am immediately impressed by her ride: a Volkswagen Thing.

We embrace one more time, and Joan looks up at me after she sits behind her wheel. "I was just thinking: You've got a Woody and I've got a Thing. Weird."

I can only nod and smile as she starts that noisy four-cylinder engine and chugs down Vermont.

As I lie in my own bed, I start my evening ritual of silently saying my ten Hail Marys each for my parents and can't help but see Joan's smiling face, even as I picture my parents' faces like I always do during prayer, especially during the line "blessed art thou amongst women."

It seems the Hail Mary is about all that remains from my twelve years of Catholic school. After too many bizarre moments with assorted nuns, priests, and brothers over those twelve years, ranging from sociopathic threats from old skinny bonnet-faced nuns to fruity priests talking and waving hands a little too close for comfort, and crazed drunken Irish Christian brothers clobbering me over the head with thick textbooks for minor infractions, I'm amazed I have anything left from religious schooling. But honestly, except for some freaky aberrations from certain people of the cloth, I'm thankful for my Catholic education, which instilled in me a healthy fear of failure and a keen eye for fucked-up authority figures. After my twenty Hail Marys for Mom and Dad, I immediately begin another string of them for Joan, with nothing but thoughts of her peace, health, and happiness. And after I recite the Hail Marys over and over and over until they become a mantra in my head, I imagine Joan lying here next to me and realize that I've never prayed for a girlfriend before. And certainly not after a first date. Maybe I'll get lucky and dream of Joan all night. And okay, one Hail Mary for Benny.

Chapter Six

WENDY VALENTINE CALLS ME at home in the morning and tells me I shouldn't report for duty until I have a conversation with Karen Marshall, ASAP. I guess those two are up to something, but after the past few days, I'm beyond predicting anything. I tried calling Joan first thing at her office, but she was unavailable.

I've already showered, dressed, and had two cups of coffee and am at the ready to head over to Karen's office on the other end of town. It's ten-forty-five, so I figure it's time to get her on the phone, since she must be in the office after her breakfast meeting, which I'll bet was with my boss, Wendy.

"Hello, Johnny. When can you get here? I just walked in," Karen says with a television blasting some blithering laughter from a morning talk show in the background.

"I can be there in twenty minutes."

"Great. Bye," Karen says, abruptly hanging up.

. . .

Just as I'm backing my Woody out of my parking spot, I hear a car at the other end of the lot, trying in vain to turn over. Knowing I'm running late, I think, Perhaps I should just pretend I don't hear it. But instead, I put my car in park and take a short walk over to the late-model Ford Taurus. It's my mysterious Russian neighbor, Nina, with her little boy, Mishka.

"Do you need some help?" I ask, startling Nina as she cranks her engine again.

"Oh. Yes, if you please," she says in her deep Russian accent, which I've become very familiar with due to her late-night activities. "Can you please give me a lift to Sunset Strip?" Mishka, strapped into a chair in the backseat, stares at me blankly.

"Okay, sure. If you can leave now. I have an appointment I have to make," I say, watching Nina reach over her backseat to undo the child safety seat. I can't help but notice her large breasts practically falling out of her low-cut top.

"I can leave immediately," Nina says, dragging the kid through the space between the two front seats and then carrying him on her hip. As I open the front passenger door to my Woody, she says, "May I please sit in back with my Mishka?"

"Sure," I say, opening the back door.

Nina buckles Mishka in and then buckles herself in.

"Where are you going?" I ask, throwing the car into reverse.

"Seven thousand block of Sunset."

"Great. That's on the way to my appointment," I say, watching Nina in my rearview mirror as she grooms Mishka's hair.

Nina doesn't say zilch for blocks, and not wanting to pry into her business any more than I have to, already knowing the company she keeps, I don't say a word, either. We've been driving for a good ten minutes and still not a sound from the backseat when I notice we're at the end of the six thousands on Sunset.

"Where would you like me to drop you off?"

"At beginning of next block, please."

I stop at a red light and look ahead to where she might possibly be going. I see a mini-mall at the corner with a drugstore. A restaurant, a bar, and . . . oh, boy. In the middle of the block is a Sunset landmark: Strip on the Strip, one of L.A.'s most famous all-nude strip clubs.

The light turns green, and as I proceed through the intersection, Nina says, "Please pull into strip mall—I mean, mall of stores."

I pull into the driveway and stop the car. Nina immediately unbuckles both of them and reaches into her purse, pulling out a five-dollar bill. "Please, thank you," she says, waving the fin at me.

"No, no, no, no way. I'm glad to help out. Anytime," I say to Nina, who still holds the bill in the air.

"Are you sure?" she asks, looking shocked that I would turn down her offer. "It's all I have right now."

"No, no. It's my pleasure. Anytime. No tipping allowed."

"Tipping? Oh, yes. No tipping," Nina says as she stashes her fiver and jumps out of the backseat, managing a weak giggle. "Goodbye, and thank you."

"Bye," I say, pulling away and entering the thick flow of traffic on Sunset.

I drive slowly down the block and keep an eye on my side-view mirror. I see Nina and Mishka walk out of the mini-mall and enter Strip on the Strip. Well, another mystery solved. I hear they do a pretty busy lunch crowd in there, featuring a free luncheon buffet. I'm not crazy about strip clubs, unless it's some kind of bachelor party boy's-night-out thing where you're too drunk to notice the vacant, tragic look on the strippers' faces; but the thought of actually eating lunch in a bar with totally nude women shaking their booties over the sneeze guard does not sound appetizing at all. I'm freaked out enough when I find a hair in my salad in a diner where everyone is fully clothed.

Unlike Next Big Thing's production office, Karen's office is in the headquarters of BBX Television, in Century City. Century City isn't a city at all. It's a neighborhood of Los Angeles that has maybe six office buildings, over ten stories tall, just before you get to Beverly Hills. In New York, it would be known as a block. The building has all the accoutrements of a major television network: etched glass signage, dark oak walls, gray-haired white guys in thousand-dollar suits.

"Karen Marshall, please," I tell the receptionist sitting in front of a huge frosted glass wall with the etched network logo in the center. "I'm Johnny Koester."

Two young guys wearing (guess what?) all black leave Karen's office, with her right behind. She looks more like a hostess escorting a couple of diners, with her shock of dyed red hair piled high, a little too much blue eye makeup, and bones creating sharp angles beneath her silk blazer. Her small angular frame and little-Irish-girl freckles are a nice cover for her cutthroat managerial style.

"Johnny, come in! Ciao, Anthony and Charles," Karen says, waving goodbye to her earlier meeting mates.

We sit in our places, Karen behind a huge chrome-and-glass desk, me in an uncomfortable black leather-and-chrome director's chair.

"Johnny, I had a meeting with Wendy this morning," Karen says. She opens a leather folder and examines some papers in it. "And let me say," she continues, head shaking to and fro as if she's going to give me some bad news, "that Wendy thinks you are doing a terrific job." She changes her expression to one of joy, in a silly one-woman good cop/bad cop display.

"That's nice of Wendy to say that."

"Not just nice, Johnny, it's marvelous," she says with dramatic seriousness. "And we've got some good news for you."

Oh, boy. Here it comes.

"We want to put you on an additional project," she exclaims as if she's just announced that I've won the Powerball lottery.

"Hey, that's great," I say with all the enthusiasm I can muster in my suspicious state of mind. "What exactly is it?"

"Wendy and I have a new show that will air several weeks after *Shocking Hollywood Secrets*, and we want you to start working on it!"

"In the middle of working on this show, you want me to work on another show?"

"Yes. Now, we know you might be working just a little harder, so we're going to look into additional compensation."

"Okay, and when will you look into that?"

Karen looks taken aback. "As soon as we can, Johnny. But right now it's more important to see if you're on board so we can get started." This means *Shut up, you ungrateful schmuck, we'll talk about money when and if I'm good and ready.*

"What's the title of this program?" I say, bracing myself for the worst.

"Drumroll, please." Karen starts to beat her leather file folder as if it's a drum. "*Psychic CrimeBusters!*" she says as though she's just discovered a cure for cancer.

It is the worst.

"Wow," I say, trying desperately to contain my disdain. "Very original. Amazing. What is it, in a nutshell?"

Karen rises from her desk and pulls out of her leather folder a couple of napkins with writing on them. "It's real crimes that have been solved by real psychics. Wendy has all the research done. These cases are unbelievable! Wait until you read about them. Everyone in the country will be talking about this! Listen, a woman finds a kidnapped child by looking at photographs of him, and by holding his toys, and by actually looking through his eyes in the photograph, she sees street signs, which lead to his rescue. It's all true!"

"Wow," I repeat. "When do I start?"

"I hope you already have," Karen says, holding her hand out to me as if to say, *Shake my hand and it's a done deal.*

I hesitate. In that split second, I think about telling Joan of my new show, and I'm already embarrassed. But what the hell. Nobody else is offering me work, so I reach out, show some teeth, and say, "Count me in," as we shake hands, sealing the deal.

"I'll call Wendy to tell her you're on board, and by the time you get to the office, she'll have some things for you to start going over," Karen says, sitting back down in her elaborate black leather chair with such a large headrest it looks like a dentist's chair. "I'm very excited, Johnny. I've got some calls to make, bye." She has the phone receiver already in hand.

"Yeah, I'm excited, too," I lie as I leave.

Wendy wasn't at the office by the time I drove over there, but there was a production bible for *Psychic CrimeBusters* already sitting on my desk, with a note from Wendy suggesting I take it home to study, which I was happy to do.

Its rundown makes even *Shocking Hollywood Secrets* look like Peabody Award–winning stuff. Some of the research is ripped from the usual supermarket tabloids, but most of the facts are garnered from newsletters and tiny photocopied magazines, known as zines, that cater to wackos who believe some guy whose day job is hypnotizing women to enlarge their breasts but whose real calling in life is solving crimes with his psychic abilities. The show will feature "proven" psychic crimebusters who supposedly solve crimes by aiding police with their psychic abilities. Incredibly, one of the psychics is a dog. In an amazing tale of canine psychic power, a farmer is in his barn about fifty yards from a house where his thirteen-year-old son sits with the family dog, watching television. A piece of heavy equipment that the farmer was lifting with a winch falls on top of him, crushing his legs and pinning him to the ground. The boy doesn't hear anything, but the dog starts acting as if something is wrong. He runs to the window facing the barn and whines, whimpers, and barks. The boy ignores him for a few minutes, but the dog continues to get more agitated. The boy begins to ask the dog what's wrong, then eventually opens the door. The dog leads him to his dad, pinned beneath the heavy machinery. The kid calls 911, the dad is saved, and the dog is a psychic hero. Yeah, right. You don't think a dog, which obviously has far better hearing than a human, could have heard his master crying for help, now, do you? Nah. It must be a psychic dog!

The other story outlined in the production bible has quite a bit more going for it. First of all, the psychic is a human. Good start! According to the research, a woman of Fresno, California, who was interviewed in *Psychic Power* magazine, helped a mother rescue her son from a kidnapper—supposedly by holding the boy's personal items, such as toys and articles of clothing—and, after staring at photographs of the boy, was able to see through his eyes, eventually naming the street where he was being held captive and even the name of a church. There is also a small item clipped from a Sacramento newspaper actually stating that a boy was indeed rescued in Oklahoma after an abduction and returned to his mother in California. Not bad. I'll have to look into this one.

Uh-oh. That could be only one person's knock on the door. Benny. I'm sure that after last night he's going to be stopping by quite often, knowing this is where he'll get his treatments. I guess I could pretend I'm asleep or in the shower . . . no. He'll just keep knocking. It's better to talk to him for a minute and get rid of him.

I walk over to the door, brace myself for the encounter with the poor soul, and open it.

"Joan! I thought you were Benny!"

"Do I look that bad without makeup?" Joan kids, looking gorgeous despite the fact that she is sweaty from head to toe and wearing running shorts and a sports-bra-styled top. "I was running in the park and thought I'd take a chance and see if you were in," she says, huffing and puffing lightly. "Can I have a drink of water?" She gives me a moist peck on the cheek. How come if a man sweats, he smells like a septic tank is backing up? I swear, Joan smells delicious. In fact, *smell* is the wrong word. She is fragrant. Like the inside of a greenhouse in the spring. Earthy yet sweet.

"How far are you running today?" I ask, going to the fridge for some ice water.

"Ten," Joan says, taking the frosty glass from me and rubbing it across her forehead.

"Blocks?"

"No, silly. Miles. But I've got to get home. I have a meeting this afternoon." She rubs the glass on her upper arms, then across the upper part of her chest, just above her bra top.

"Can I help you with that?" I say coyly.

"No, not now," Joan says as she downs a hearty drink of water in just a few gulps. Still standing, she sets the glass down on the table and sidles up next to me. "I hope I don't reek?"

"You? Reek? Yeah, like the inside of a flower shop," I say softly as we caress.

"I just wanted to see you," Joan says, her face still glistening with sweat. "For a moment."

"Yeah. That's what life is all about. Moments. Like these," as we begin a soft make-out session.

"I think I should go. Or I might wind up missing that meeting," Joan says, inching away. "I'm meeting a guy from the LAPD Hollywood division. I think our movie-star friend is working the streets again."

"Tucker Kramden? You're kidding me."

"I wish I were, but we're not sure yet," she says, punctuated by a quick kiss on the cheek. "I want to run back to my place, shower, and get over to Safe Haven."

"You can shower here if you want," I say with a broad grin across my face.

"Not today," Joan says.

"What about tonight?"

"I can't tonight. I'm going to the gym to work out with some friends," she says, and opens the door to reveal Benny standing on my front step.

"Hello, General, hello, Joanie," Benny says, looking as chipper as he has looked in a while. "Joanie, I thought I heard you. Do you think you could come over tonight for a . . . session?"

"Uh, well," Joan stalls, looking at me with an expression that says, *Gee, I feel stupid*, "Okay, Benny."

"What time?" Benny says, beaming at his good fortune.

"Eight?" Joan asks, still watching me sorrowfully.

"Eight it is! See you tonight, guys!" Benny says, turning around and heading straight for the parking lot with a slight bounce in his step.

I look to Joan, and she shrugs as if to say, *What else could I do?*

"So I guess I'll see you at eight," I say as Joan runs by the mailboxes out onto the sidewalk.

She turns around, throws me a kiss, and says, "Eight and don't be late!"

She has perfect running form. Head and neck tall and strong. Legs perfectly aligned. Tiny waistline with strong back muscles flexing under her sports bra as she runs down the street. Running looks like a hobby I can get used to in a heartbeat.

Thoughts of Joan come to a cold-shower halt as soon as I get back to my production bible. The psychic who solved this kidnapping case sounds amazing. But before I get too excited, I want to meet her. Having watched a few too many late-night public-access programs on cable, I'm well aware of how some of these wackos come off on-camera.

Wendy wants me to get rolling on *Psychic CrimeBusters* to start booking interviews and planning reenactments for the director to shoot. First I'll have to schedule a meeting with Wendy and this kidnapping psychic. I sure hope I don't have to fly the psychic dog in for a meeting.

A messenger has finally delivered about a dozen *Psychic Power* magazines to the office for me to pore over. It doesn't take me long to realize that a binder full of these could just as well be a manual for a graduate psychiatry course. The pages are loaded with story after story of visions, voices, and victims of seemingly inexplicable phenomena. Our psychic detective lady, Angelyne, appears more than once with an amazing tale of how she solved a crime with her uncanny psychic abilities. The editor wouldn't divulge Angelyne's phone number for "obvious security reasons," but she did say that she would contact her and give her my phone number at the office. Lo and behold, about ten minutes after I hang up with *Psychic Power* magazine, Angelyne Zboinski is on the line.

"Hello, Johnny Koester with *Psychic CrimeBusters* here. Ms. Zboinski? Did I say that right?" I say.

"Call me Angelyne," a soft, childlike voice says.

"Yes, Angelyne, we read the article about you in *Psychic Power* magazine, and we are thinking about doing a story on you for our television program."

"Is this being taped?" she whispers.

"The show? Yes, it's taped."

"No. This phone call. Is it being taped?" she whispers even more softly.

"No, it isn't."

"Are you . . . sure?"

"Positive."

"I'm being followed, and I have reason to believe that my

phone is tapped. I've uncovered a story that will expose an international child slavery ring that involves politicians from all over the country."

Oh, boy. Here we go. I think about hanging up but figure I really should try and get her in here for an interview, so Wendy can see firsthand what we're dealing with.

"Would it be possible for you to come in for an informal meeting? We'll pay your expenses."

"Can I fly?"

"Certainly."

"Can I drive and keep the money it would have cost you for the airfare? I don't fly."

"I'll have to check into that, Angelyne. Can you hold on?"

"Yes, I'll hold."

I press the hold button and rush over to Wendy's closed office door. I give a quick knock.

"Wendy, we need to talk about this psychic detective lady," I shout into the door. Now that my ear is just inches from the door, I can hear some weird sounds coming from the office.

"Right this second?" Wendy asks, her voice muffled to the point that I can barely hear her through the door.

"Sorry. Yup."

"All right, come in."

Her office is illuminated by about a dozen candles surrounding a massage table. Wendy is facedown with a white sheet barely covering her ass. A dark-skinned woman wearing a white jumpsuit and turban is leaning over her legs and twirling acupuncture needles, which number in the dozens.

"What's that noise coming out of the speakers?" I ask. "It sounds like somebody rubbing the top of a glass."

"Bingo," Wendy says, her face aimed at the floor on the other end of the massage table. "It's called sacred singing bowls. What's up?"

Trying not to notice the needles being inserted into the bottommost part of Wendy's butt cheeks, I say, "Angelyne wants to be paid for coming down for the meeting. She wants to drive from Fresno and keep the airfare we would have spent." The acupuncturist sticks another needle in Wendy's ass, a little higher, causing a little more of a distraction for me.

"Shit. Everybody's got an angle," Wendy says, her needles wiggling as she speaks. "Tell her we'll give her three hundred if she drives, but we're not paying for a hotel or meals."

"Gotcha," I say as Wendy gets another needle stuck into her fully exposed left buttock.

"Ow! Watch it, Venus! I'm not a goddamn voodoo doll! Let me know what she says."

I rush to my desk, pick up the phone, and hope Angelyne is still there. "Angelyne?"

"Yes."

"Our budget only has three hundred dollars allotted for pre-interview expenses."

"Oh, that would be great. I'll be there tomorrow at ten."

"Wow. Okay. Tomorrow at ten. Great. And bring any related documentation you have."

"Such as?"

"Newspaper clippings, police reports, testimonials, that sort of thing."

"I'm not sure if I can do that. You know, in case I'm stopped."

"Okay. But try and bring what you can. See you tomorrow."

"Bye-bye," she says, barely audible.

I knock on Wendy's door again. Chants are coming from behind the door.

"Come in."

Venus holds what appears to be a lit cigar just inches from Wendy's ass.

"So is she coming?" Wendy asks.

"Yeah, tomorrow at ten," I say, staring at Venus and her cigar. "Can I ask a stupid question?"

"Go ahead," Wendy sighs.

"Why do you have a cigar over your butt?"

"That's not a cigar, it's a moxa. It's Chinese medicine. Venus is heating my needles."

"Oh, is that what they call it now."

"Very funny. See you at ten," Wendy says, waving me out of the room.

Benny is not one to be tardy. At precisely seven-fifty-nine P.M. there's a knock on my door. Benny is standing there looking as worn as his wrinkled brown paper bag.

"Is Joan here yet?" Benny says, trying his best to sound enthusiastic.

"No, she's running a little late, Benny. Have a seat. Can I get you something to drink?" I say as Benny takes off his windbreaker, revealing his bony arms exposed by a short-sleeved dress shirt. "Or maybe a snack?"

"Nah. Can't eat. No appetite," Benny says, removing medical items from his bag, neatly placing them on the dining room table, then taking his place in his favorite chair. "Do you mind if I just wait here for her?"

"Not at all. Nothing to eat or drink?"

"No, thanks."

"Do you mind if I put on some music?" I say, knowing exactly what I want to play for him. Since Benny's an Italian from New York, I'm sure a little Sinatra will pick him up.

"I don't care," Benny says flatly, fiddling with his wrinkled brown bag.

I put on *Sinatra at the Sands* with Count Basie, which always cheers up my mom because Sinatra's patter between songs is filled with ad-libbed jokes and audience put-downs. Not to mention that it's probably Sinatra's best live recording ever. As soon as the announcer on the LP does his intro to Sinatra, Benny's head snaps around. "Oh, shit. Not that dago!"

"What?"

"I can't stand that wop. Please, anything but that. It's like fingernails on a blackboard. Don't you have any Tony Bennett?" Benny asks with conviction.

"Sure. Yeah. I got Tony Bennett," I say as I take the needle off the Sinatra LP and reach for my Tony Bennett albums. "You know, Bennett worships Sinatra. Isn't that good enough for you?"

"Come on. That's just paisan-to-paisan shit. If Tony didn't say that, he'd get thrown off a Hoboken pier into the Hudson wearing a concrete tuxedo. Bennett's my guy. He's the man! Sinatra's just for people who don't know any better. They follow like sheep. Give me Tony!" Benny says with more enthusiasm in his voice than I thought he could muster. "See if you got him singing my favorite, 'I'm Always Chasing Rainbows.'"

"Yeah, that's on *I Left My Heart in San Francisco*," I say, knowing the song very well. It's a man's lament over being a failure, not knowing whether to blame the world for his sorrow, or himself. "It's a beautiful song."

"You bet your bottom dollar it is. It's based on a melody from Chopin, you know," Benny says emphatically.

"Really. You know your Tony Bennett, don't you, Benny?" I say, putting the song on.

Benny closes his eyes and begins to mouth the words to the haunting song, not paying any attention to my question. "Ooh, that's stupendous. Haven't heard that in months. My damn record player's on the fritz," he says after a few lines.

With the music playing, Benny seems about as relaxed as I've seen him in the weeks I've known him. He looks almost like he has some color in his face, and his wrinkles are for once in the shape of smile lines and happy crow's-feet instead of tragic clown lines. He's also slowly rubbing the part of his right hand where his two missing fingers would be. Although Benny had me wondering if I should keep a loaded handgun handy when he was first making his appearances, now I have a genuine curiosity about who the hell this guy is. Why has he turned to me for money and his medicine? Doesn't he have anyone else in the world? Why have the cops been to his place? What the hell parish is he from? And what really happened to those fingers?

"Benny. Where did you say you were from?"

"New York. I told you," Benny says, trying to concentrate on Tony.

"Where in New York, exactly?"

"Uh, we moved around a lot. Manhattan, Queens, the Bronx, you know, all over," he says, trying to shut me up.

"Where'd you graduate from grammar school?"

I think where you graduated from grammar school defines where you grew up more than anything else. Mostly because that's where you were when you were going through puberty. And puberty is when things really get interesting in the classroom and on the street. Hormones start crashing through bodies, injecting brains with new urges and impulses you couldn't even imagine just a few months before. I remember my best friend Michael Freehill's mom scolding a couple of us seventh-grade boys for teasing Michael's cute little sister, Ann Marie, and her friend Mary Jane, telling us how we'd regret our taunts. I had no idea what she was talking about until that summer, when I noticed the bumps in Ann Marie's and Mary Jane's bathing suit tops getting bigger, and having to stay in the deep water longer because the bump in my bathing suit was getting bigger and harder. I also noticed that I wanted to punch Junior Flynn in the nose because he was making Ann Marie and Mary Jane laugh with his Jerry Lewis imitation. Little did I know that I was jealous. The eighth grade is where fistfights get real and kisses turn into makeout sessions. Harmless pranks become vandalism, a sip of beer on New Year's Eve becomes Friday- and Saturday-night binge drinking. One minute you're trick-or-treating with Casper the Friendly Ghost masks, and the next minute you and your friends are egging commuters on the No. 38 bus and setting a storage shed on fire behind a supermarket.

"Grammar school? Why?"

"No real reason. I'd just like to know."

"Uh, it was, uh, Immaculate Conception," Benny says, struggling to remember.

"On Fourteenth Street? My cousins went there!" I say happily, thinking this will prompt some reminiscing. "When did you graduate?"

"I didn't actually graduate. Uh, I got kicked out," Benny says, obviously still trying to avoid my probing.

"For what?"

"Jesus Christ, General! What's the fucking difference, huh? Give it a rest, will ya?" Benny says, pissed, bringing to mind my first impressions of him.

I've never met a New Yorker who didn't want to immediately start telling me every minor detail of his or her childhood. Stories about the craziest kid on the block, who maybe stole a horse from a stable and rode it down the block. Or how many sewers he could hit a Spaldeen in stickball. Whether they're from Brooklyn, the Bronx, Queens, Staten Island, or Manhattan, fellow New Yorkers have an immediate bond. Even if they were little rich kids who grew up on Park Avenue, by the time they got to be teenagers, they were hanging out in parks with their crazy friends just like every other kid in the city.

"Benny, all I'm doing is making conversation. You don't have to have a fucking conniption over it, all right?" I say, giving it back to Benny. "Don't be so defensive. I'm not a freakin' cop."

Benny begins rubbing his right hand where his two fingers aren't. "Look, General. I know. I just don't like talking about the past, that's all. I got kicked out of grammar school. It was one of many I got kicked out of, including public school. And what do you think, you're the first New Yorker I met out here who thinks that every guy who took the same IRT train is a long-lost cousin? I ain't got no long-lost cousins. No brothers, sisters, uncles, aunts, nothing. Okay?"

"Okay."

The Tony Bennett album ends with Tony singing his classic "The Best Is Yet to Come" in stark contrast to the fatalistic sentiment in "I'm Always Chasing Rainbows." As soon as the needle lifts off the record, Benny's head seems to drop a little. His face seems grayer.

"You don't like Sinatra much, huh, Benny?"

"I'm not a fucking sheep," Benny blurts out.

"What's that supposed to mean?"

"Just because you're Italian and you're from New York, you have to worship Sinatra." Benny energetically rises out of his chair. "That's bullshit. Fuck Sinatra. And fuck the Yankees, too. Jesus Christ, all I ever hear is Sinatra this, the Yankees that. 'The chairman of the board,'" Benny says, now mimicking a sissy, "'the most storied franchise in the history of sports.' Ruth, DiMaggio, Gehrig, Mantle." Benny points at me, striking a forceful pose. "Well, fuck them. Fuck all of 'em. I'm not a fucking sheep."

Benny looks worn out. Like he just used up a week's worth of energy on his tirade.

"I thought you didn't care about baseball, Benny."

Benny sits back in his chair, exhausted and confused. "Huh? Why do you say that?"

"Well, considering you just sold me some of your brother's prized baseball memorabilia, I thought you couldn't care less about baseball."

"That's right, I don't," Benny says, rubbing his forehead as if he just got walloped with a migraine.

"For somebody who doesn't care about baseball, those were pretty heated words of hatred for the Yankees."

"Nah. That's nothing. I just don't care, that's all. Listen, what time is it? When is Joan going to get here? I'm starting to feel sick. Weak. Any idea? You got any coffee?"

"Coffee? Sure. Leaded or unleaded?" I say, walking over to Benny and giving the back of his chair a love tap.

"Leaded."

As I begin rooting around for the coffee stuff, Benny sticks his head in my kitchenette. "Do you mind if I look through your records?" he asks meekly.

"Knock yourself out, Benny. How do you like your coffee?"

"I like my coffee like I like my women—dark and sweet," Benny says heading into the living room.

I'm curious to see what he thinks of my music. My record collection varies from every Beatles record to Béla Bartók. From the Stones to Sunnyland Slim. From pornographic blues recordings from the twenties to speeches by Franklin D. Roosevelt. From Allen Ginsberg poems about his penis to Jack Benny radio programs. From Rosselini to the Rutles. From Duke Ellington in the twenties to Miles Davis in the eighties. And Sinatra. Lots of Sinatra. With plenty of my other favorite performers: Louis Jordan, Louie Prima, Bing Crosby, and, yes, Tony Bennett.

"Go ahead and put something on if you'd like, Benny," I shout as my teakettle begins to whistle.

Benny doesn't respond, so I continue my coffeemaking by pouring the boiling water into my French coffee press.

The phonograph needle drags across an entire side of an album at full volume.

"Sorry!" Benny shouts.

I can hear the needle lifted and placed in the groove of a record.

But instead of hearing a stylish intro to a Tony Bennett song, I catch the strange sounds of an extremely old, scratchy record I forgot I even owned. "illy-say, illy-bay, had an uppy-pay . . ." I remember that record as being one of those small yellow records, a little smaller than a 45, but it plays at 33⅓. I've had that record since I was a child. I haven't even seen it in years. It must have been stuck inside another album jacket or something.

I press down on the coffee, trapping the grounds on the bottom, and pour two dark, rich cups of French roast coffee. I use a Three Stooges mug, and I'm giving Benny his coffee in a mug with a sign from the Yankee Stadium elevated subway station. I bring the coffees out on a small tray with a little milk and some sugar on the side, and see Benny sitting on the floor in the middle of the living room, facing the speakers with his back to me.

"How the hell did you find that, Benny?" I ask, placing the tray on the dining room table.

Benny doesn't respond. I'm surprised he was able to cross his legs in that position, considering his overall weakened state.

I walk across the room to see Benny sitting there with his eyes closed and crocodile tears streaming down his face. I've seen a lot of sad things in my life: my mom crying at her younger brother's wake; my dog with my pet turtle's bloody carcass hanging from his jaws. But this is right up there as one of the saddest.

The song ends, and the needle automatically lifts off the scratched yellow vinyl with the simple black label. Benny immediately opens his eyes, wipes the tears away and tries to get up. "Can you give me a hand here, General?" he says, holding his deformed hand out to me.

I pull Benny up, and he groans with pain. He composes himself as he wipes a few more tears from his face.

"I could use a cup of joe," Benny says as he sits down in his favorite spot. "General, is this my cup?" He points at the Yankee

Stadium subway sign on the side of the mug. "What the hell are you trying to do to me here?"

"Do you want my mug?"

"No, I'll drink from it. But your weasely manipulation has not gone unnoticed. Cheers." Benny takes a sip. "Oh. Needs sugar." He puts the mug down and dumps in several spoonfuls of sugar. He takes another sip, then smacks his lips. "Now, that's good coffee. Dark, sweet, strong. That's how I like my women," he repeats, in case I already forgot.

I take a couple of sips of coffee and let a few moments of silence pass as Benny and I savor our java.

"You've heard that song before, Benny?"

"What song?"

"What song? 'The Star-Spangled Banner'! The song you were just sitting in the middle of my floor weeping over."

Benny takes a long, loud sip of coffee. "I had something in my eye. My mother used to sing me that song."

"My mother used to sing it to me, too," I say, thinking this could be a starting point to figuring out what makes him tick. Or what made him tick.

"A lot of mothers sang that song to their kids. No big deal."

"Did your mom work with your dad in the butcher store?"

"Who told you about the butcher store?" Benny barks.

"You did. You told Joan last night about how you lost your fingers."

"Oh yeah," Benny says before slurping another mouthful. "Yeah. We all worked in the store. Me, my brother, Mom and Dad."

"Where was it again?" I ask, hoping Benny might think he told us last night and reveal it to me.

"Uh, like I said, downtown. Lower East Side. Just below, er, Fourteenth Street. Are you sure Joan is coming? Isn't it after eight?"

"Just after. What avenue?"

"Ah, I think it was in Little Italy. It was a long time ago, General. A long, long time ago. A time I don't like to think about," Benny says, staring into his cup. He slowly lifts his head and looks into my eyes. "I'm not a good bullshitter, General. I just don't like to talk about those days, okay?"

There's a soft knock.

"Must be Joan," I say, setting my mug down and going over to the door.

"Hi, Johnny," Joan says with a half-smile across her lovely face, immediately reminding me that I'm crazy about her. She gives me a quick kiss on the lips and heads for Benny. "I'm sorry I'm late, Benny, I had some business to take care of at the office."

"No problem, sweetheart," Benny says, gathering up his energy.

"Want to do it right away?" Joan asks Benny from across the table.

"Oh, honey, you don't know how long it's been since a beautiful girl asked me to drop my drawers like that," Benny says as he unbuckles his pants.

I was a little worried that Joan may take Benny's crude New York humor the wrong way, but she's laughing out loud, just like I am.

Joan begins going through Benny's meds. "Oh, I'm sure there were quite a few pretty girls taken by your charm," she says sexily as she sticks a needle in a small medicine jar.

"General, how the hell did you get so lucky?" Benny says. He stands and lowers his pants just a little too unashamedly.

"Don't ask me. Clean living, I guess."

Joan walks over with the needle in one hand and an alcohol swab in the other. Like she did the first time, she makes what appears to be the sign of the cross over his butt.

"No! Don't!" Benny yells, jumping up, pulling his pants up. "It's a trick. You two are trying to brainwash me!"

"Benny, is your brain up your ass?" I shout.

"Benny, I told you last night, it helps my aim. Remember?"

Joan says. She slowly re-creates the move, punctuated with the needle stabbing at the imaginary center.

"Oh yeah. The target," Benny says meekly, then turns and drops his drawers. "Hit it."

I turn my eyes away as she begins to inject him.

"Oh, baby, you make it delicious!" Benny says, sounding like he's actually enjoying himself.

"Don't get carried away there, tiger, or I'll give you a dull needle next time."

"Yes, Nurse Ratchett," Benny says as Joan withdraws the needle. He then hitches up his pants, buckles his belt, and gives a hearty salute. "May I stand at ease, General?"

"At ease," I tell Benny as Joan puts away the meds. "And take more coffee, if you'd like."

"No thanks. I'll leave you two lovebirds alone," Benny says, picking up his things and heading for the door. "I'll stop in tomorrow for coffee before you leave for work, okay, General?"

I didn't know how to answer. Coffee with Benny before work? I wish I could see Joan this often.

"Uh, okay. See ya, Benny."

Benny gives another salute and leaves.

"He likes you, Johnny," Joan says, taking me by the hand and leading me over to the couch. "So do I," she says, pushing my shoulders back so I'm on my sofa lying down. She begins to lie on top of me.

"I think Benny likes me," I say as Joan shimmies her way up and puts her face just an inch or so above mine. "But he could be just using me. And maybe that goes for you, too," I say, stroking the side of Joan's smooth, soft face with the back of my fingers. "I hope Benny's not using me. You, on the other hand . . . feel free to use away . . ." I reach up to kiss her lips so slowly, so tenderly. Just before our lips touch, I say, "Make it delicious."

My mind is swirling with a joy I don't think I've ever experienced as Joan undulates on top of me while we passionately kiss and caress. I'm trying to control my desire and not be too forward. I try to resist grabbing her breasts under her loose top, or rubbing her ass with both hands, but once her thigh starts pushing into my now-hard crotch, well, so much for trying to control myself.

I open my eyes at the precise moment Joan opens hers, and we're the only two people on Rodney Drive, in Los Angeles, in the state of California; in fact, at this moment, we're the only two people on the planet.

"Joan?"

"Yes."

"Do you know that song Frank Sinatra sang with Nancy?"

" 'Something Stupid'?"

"Yup. I remember I was a kid in about sixth grade, sitting at the counter in Snooky's candy store when that song came out. I was having an egg cream with my friend Buddy, and that song came on the jukebox. So of course, me and Buddy were talking about how we didn't understand what that song was about, and Josie, the Italian lady who ran the place with an iron fist, turned around from her hamburger grill and said, 'You'll understand that song soon enough!' "

I can see from the look in Joan's eyes that she knows what I'm about to say. I go on, "That song. I'm afraid I'm going to say something stupid right now."

"Go ahead," Joan says, stroking my five o'clock shadow.

"I love you," I whisper, probably trembling, knowing that telling a woman I love her after barely knowing her a week could be disastrous. I've never said anything so stupid so soon in my life.

"That's the most unstupid thing I've ever heard," Joan says as she closes her eyes, turns her head, and places it on my chest.

As I begin to silently stroke her long hair down her back, I know she's right. This is right. I wait for Joan's response. Because there's nothing stupider than telling someone you love her and not getting the reply you were hoping for. I wait. And wait. And wait. But no reply.

"Want to hear some music?" I ask, feeling her heartbeat against my chest.

"Put on some Sinatra."

I get up, go right for *Songs for Young Lovers*, which has that classic album cover with Frank leaning up against a lamppost in the dark, put it on the turntable, and we immediately get back into our position.

Joan looks at me, snuggles as tight as is humanly possible when Sinatra starts to sing, and says, "We sure do fit."

"We sure do."

We don't say a word for the entire side of Sinatra, yet I feel like I'm learning all I long to know about this beautiful woman who stumbled into my life by some kind of osmosis. And all because of a trashy TV show, which the mere mention of is cause for embarrassment. I'm just soaking in her good vibrations, trying to send mine back to her with every touch of her skin, kiss of her lips, and silent glance. I thought I knew love before. Now I know. I just hope she can say she loves me.

"Do you think you want to spend the night here?"

"Ummmmmm . . ."

"No pressure," I say. "Just because Sinatra's on and the lights are low and we fit together like two spoons in the kitchen drawer, and I blurted out that I love you, that's no reason to rush into anything."

"I never rush. I'll stay. After the album," Joan says, her eyes still closed, her head nestled on my shoulder.

We listen to the album, then move to the bedroom with the lights off, our eyes used to the darkness. She removes her clothes slowly and places them neatly on the chair, while I watch her silhouetted against the closed venetian blinds that leak just a little of the streetlights. I remove my clothes on the other side of the bed, and we crawl under the sheets and immediately find that every contour, every joint, every muscle seems to fit perfectly together as we snuggle, caress, and even squirm joyfully together. The kisses get longer as I discover the sweet wonderful smells and tastes of her toned, firm, exquisitely feminine body. I'm out of my mind with ecstasy as we hold back no longer and enjoy each other like only two lovers can. Completely and unselfishly. Her lovemaking is a perfect expression of the sensitive, caring, beautiful woman I already knew she was. The one I knew I wanted to be with for the rest of my life.

Did I think that? Yes, I did. But I'm not going to say something *that* stupid. Yet.

I've had first-sex sessions when, immediately following orgasm, the first instinct is to escape like a criminal at the scene of a crime. But after this, our first intense mutual explosion of fiery sex and love, I have no desire for anything else in the world but to feel Joan next to me. Every sense of my being is absorbing her every molecule as we silently lie together entwined in each other's bodies. I'm not thinking about yesterday, or tomorrow, but only of this pure moment. The only brief moment that could be interpreted as awkward was when I had to search for a condom through some unpacked boxes piled in a closet. Apparently, my naked bony butt sticking out of a closet door is quite a funny sight.

As I rest my head on her stomach, even the sound of belly bubbles is a cause for joy. Every little mole, tiny wild hair, or scar is a new discovery that brings me a smile and sense of comfort. There isn't enough of Joan than I can get right now.

"Benny seemed a little disturbed when I arrived," Joan says.

"He was really nutty before you arrived."

"How so?"

"I started asking him where in New York he was from, and he was cracking like a pickpocket being interrogated by Joe Friday.

Then a few minutes later, he's sitting in a pool of his tears listening to an old recording of 'illy-say illy-bay.' "

" 'illy-say illy-bay'?" Joan says as she sits straight up, knocking my head off, making her breasts jiggle in a delightful manner. "Oh, I haven't thought about that for ages! You have that? Can we listen to it?" She bounces on the bed and smacks the sheets.

"Yes, yes. Don't worry. It's in the living room," I say, getting off the bed. I take Joan by the hand, and we walk naked into the living room. "Whoops!" I say, noticing the living room curtains are wide open and cars are going down the street just outside my first-floor window. I go over to the curtains and close them.

Joan is belly down, naked on the floor with her elbows propping up her chin, facing the stereo. Her cute, tight butt bounces as she kicks her feet. "I haven't heard this since I was three or four."

"You were probably wearing the same outfit and in the same pose," I say, putting the record on the turntable. "I wouldn't be surprised if we were the only three people in Los Angeles who have a psychic connection because of 'illy-say illy-bay.'" I sidle up next to Joan on the floor.

Joan starts singing along to the silly words. That's it. I am so in love right now, I could get my brains blown out by a howitzer and I'd die happy, right here in this room.

In the distance, I hear the unmistakable squeal of Benny's fan belts as he starts his car and pulls out of the parking lot.

Chapter Seven

THIS MORNING'S MEETING with our star psychic detective is so important that Wendy has to cancel a session with her aromatherapist. Angelyne is already an hour late, and she hasn't called in once since we set this whole thing up.

I'm sitting in Wendy's office reading *Baseball Weekly* while Wendy whines nonstop on the phone about everything from paying ten grand a year for homeowner's insurance, to the unacceptable haircut her shih tzu had yesterday. I'm more concerned with the four of five prognosticators who have picked the Yankees to finish in third place this year, and the fifth predicts fourth. It's going to be a long season.

Tiffany sticks her head in the doorway with a befuddled look on her usually blank face. "Angelyne is here. Should I send her in?" she asks cautiously.

"Gotta go. Send her in!" Wendy says, slamming down the phone. "This better be good."

We both look at the office doorway in anticipation of Angelyne. And here she is. The word

frumpy was created for people like Angelyne. Despite the fact that it's probably 78 degrees today, she is wearing a tweed coat that would do nicely on a January afternoon in Chicago. Her hair is cut in a blunt pageboy style, and if she paid more than five bucks for it, she was ripped off. It's a good thing that Wendy told her meals weren't included in her payment, because she just might have busted our budget. Angelyne is anything but angelic in appearance. She has on large rectangular glasses that Charles Nelson Reilly made famous in the seventies on *Match Game*. She's not particularly old, not particularly young. She has the look of someone whom you can't imagine young.

She is carrying a large cardboard file holder overflowing with papers. On the front is a white label, and written in large black letters is TOP SECRET.

"You must be Angelyne," Wendy says graciously. "Please come in. I'm Wendy Valentine, and this is our producer, Johnny Koester. Have a seat, won't you?"

Angelyne shuffles in with a weak smile and sits. I have a feeling I'm going to reek of her cheap perfume for several days, judging by the overwhelming presence of it permeating the room.

"Hello, Angelyne. We talked on the phone. Thanks so much for making the trip," I say, shaking her flaccid hand.

"We're very excited about your story, Angelyne," Wendy says as she rises from her chair and begins pacing. "We've researched you, and I must say we are fascinated by this case in Fresno when you were instrumental in rescuing the child. Where's that story, Johnny?"

I reach into my file and pull out the article from *Psychic Power*, handing it to Wendy.

"Very, very impressive," Wendy says, holding up the article.

"You're Wendy Valentine from *My Daughter the Secret Agent*?" Angelyne says in her childlike voice. "I used to watch that when I was just a little, tiny kid. I loved you in that show."

"Yes, I'm sure you did, sweetheart. Now, tell us about how you went about solving this kidnapping," Wendy says, sitting back down in her chair.

"Well, I was contacted by a lady who lived near me."

"That's this Mary Pacheco in the article?" Wendy asks.

"Yes, that's her. She had heard that I was a psychic, and she came to me. She knew somebody I did a reading for. I didn't charge her anything."

"I'm sure you didn't, darling, go on."

"Well, Mary was all distraught. Her seven-year-old son had been abducted. She didn't know what to do. So she came to me. And I told her to bring me several personal items that her son owned and some recent pictures of the boy."

"Right, right," Wendy says, running her long purple fingernails along the article. "It says that here. She gave you a toy truck, a shirt, and two pictures."

"Yes. That is correct. We had several sessions. You can't do this type of thing in one session. I didn't charge her anything."

"Got it. Continue," Wendy says, on the verge of getting her story.

"Well, the first time, I held the toy truck and I rubbed one of the pictures, and I began to see things." Angelyne closes her eyes as if she's going into a trance. "I saw a freeway. A long freeway. I was in the front seat of a truck, looking out on the passenger's side. But I could barely see over the dashboard."

"Right, right! Like a little kid would have trouble seeing over it! This would make a fantastic re-creation. Write that down," Wendy says, getting up again, glancing at the article, and stabbing her finger in the air at me.

"The next session, I held the shirt and rubbed one of the pictures again. I began to hear sounds. Children playing, like in a classroom or something."

"Yes, yes, go on, go on. Do you mind if I smoke?" Wendy says, hardly able to contain her excitement.

Angelyne and I both shake our heads, no problem.

"Then the third time, it was the hardest. I almost had a seizure," Angelyne says, opening her eyes and looking at us to make sure we understand the severity of her state at the time. "I had all of the objects, and I was rubbing them and licking them."

"Licking them?" Wendy says, taking the cigarette out of her mouth.

"Yes, I find that gets me focused."

Wendy puts her cigarette out in the ashtray.

"I was licking them, and I saw signs. One was a street sign: Cannon Place. Another was a church sign: St. Stephen's. But I saw them from down low."

"Like a child would, right, Angelyne? So you saw through the boy's eyes and heard through his ears, isn't that right? Isn't that how you located the child?"

"Yes, it is the truth," Angelyne says emphatically.

Wendy looks at me with *I told you so* across her face. I'm surprised she doesn't stick her tongue out at me. "It has it all right here. Mary Pacheco, the child's name, the town, the detective who got the boy back once he was provided with the information of his location. Angelyne, you are amazing!"

"Thank you. But I have another story for you. It involves child slavery, a police chief, a governor, and a United States senator. I'm being followed and my phone is being tapped. I have all the information in these files, can I show you?"

"No, please, uh, Angelyne. One story at a time, okay? Maybe if we go to series," Wendy tells her, obviously not wanting to get involved in this one. "You've done a splendid job. Thanks so much for coming." Wendy walks over and gives her the bum's rush. "We'll be getting back to you real soon. You left Johnny your number, right?"

"Oh yes," Angelyne says as she holds up her files. "But can't I show you what I have in my files? It will blow the lid off the child slavery problem."

"Next time, Angelyne. Thanks so much. We'll call you. Tiffany, please show Angelyne out," Wendy says, shoving her out the door, closing it right behind her. Wendy spins around and glares at me. "I don't care if it's bullshit or not. If we can get these other people on-camera to confirm what she's claiming, this will be awesome. Fantastic! Get on it right away!"

"Okay. I'll call the mother and the detective and take it from there. It would be great to get the kid on-camera."

"Oh, yes, it would. I have another appointment on the way over," Wendy says. She sits at her desk and picks up her phone.

"I'm on it," I say, going to my desk to begin checking on this story. Unfortunately, the only phone number I have is Angelyne's. I don't have even an address for Mary Pacheco.

I call Fresno information and get the operator. "Can I have a number for Mary Pacheco, please?"

"I'm sorry, no Mary Pacheco listed in Fresno."

"How many Pachecos are there?"

"Many."

"Just give me the first three, then."

"I'm sorry, I can't do that. You must have a name."

"Oh, all right. Give me Jose, Juan, and . . . Bob Pacheco," I tell her, using the first names that pop into my mind.

The operator gives me the numbers, and I figure I'm in for a long afternoon of calling Pachecos trying to track Mary and her kidnapped kid. I dial Jose's number, and a woman answers.

"Hello, is Mary Pacheco there?"

"Speaking."

"The Mary Pacheco . . . who knows Angelyne Zboinski?"

"Yes, how can I help you?"

I can't believe it. This is probably going to be the only true psychic moment anyone will experience during the entire production.

"Well, Angelyne was just here, and she was telling us about when your son was abducted and how she helped you."

"Oh yes! Angelyne was marvelous! So supportive! I don't know if I would have made it without her."

"So Angelyne did help you?"

"Oh, yes. Immensely. She is such a wonderful, caring human being."

"Can I ask you exactly how you got your son back?"

"How I got my son back?"

"Yes."

"Why, my ex-husband called me."

"And how did that help get your son back?"

"Well, duh, he's the one who took him."

"Your son was abducted by your ex-husband? I assume he's the boy's father?"

There was a long pause, after which I expected another, even louder duh.

"Yes," she says. Thankfully.

"So your husband took your son? Then what happened?"

"He took him to where he had moved, in Kansas, where he's from, and after a few days he called me to apologize."

"Apologize?"

"Yes, he felt terrible. My little boy wouldn't stop crying. My ex-husband knew what he was doing was wrong, so he called and told me where to pick Billy up. He couldn't take any more time off from work, so he said I should go and pick Billy up at St. Stephen's School. I went with the detective, and we got Billy and came home."

"Why did the detective accompany you?"

"He's my boyfriend."

"Oh. What exactly did Angelyne do?"

"Do? I'm not sure I know what you mean."

"Well, without trying to embarrass anyone, did Angelyne have anything to do with locating your missing son?"

"No. Not at all. She was a wonderful person, though. Telling me to hang in there and giving me great emotional support."

"How do you know Angelyne?"

"She lives by me. Everybody knows her. Are you a reporter? I told all this to a reporter already."

"No, I'm with a TV show, and I'm doing research on missing children."

"Well, if I can do anything else, let me know. I hope I've been helpful."

"Oh yeah. Indeed. Very helpful. I'll call you if I have any other questions. Bye."

I hang up the phone and can't help but laugh out loud, which, amazingly, is enough to get Tiffany's head out of the *National Enquirer* to look at me with disdain.

"Tiffany, could you buzz Wendy and see if I can meet with her for a minute?" I politely ask.

Tiffany sighs and buzzes her. "You can go in," she says without looking at me.

Upon entering Wendy's office, I can see she's involved in another heated phone conversation.

"I don't give a shit if the pope made an appointment yesterday. I've been a client for ten years, and half of Malibu goes to you because of me. Okay. Fine. I'll be there at eight," Wendy says, hanging up the phone and motioning for me to sit down. "Tell me some good news."

"Well, the psychic dog is looking really good."

"Oh no. Don't tell me. Angelyne?"

"Yup. I just dug up the kidnapped kid's mother, and she spilled the beans."

"How bad is it?"

"Bad. Remember the part about Angelyne saying she saw through the kid's eyes and heard through his ears and saw the signs on the church?"

"Didn't happen?"

"Didn't happen. Want to know how the mom found out where the kid was?"

"That detective solved it?"

"The abductor was the kid's father, the mom's ex, and he called her and told her where to pick the kid up. The detective is her boyfriend."

"Dammit. Dammit dammit dammit. Okay. It's okay. We still do the story."

"We do?"

"It's the best one we could find," Wendy says, shooting daggers at me with her eyes. "We do the story, and just like everything else, we leave out the parts we don't need and use the stuff they *actually* say, just the way those sleazy morons at the magazine did it. And who's gonna bitch, anyway? Nobody."

"Yeah, but it's total bullshit."

"What's your point?"

"I guess I don't have one."

"We interview Angelyne. Get her story. Shoot the whole re-creation with the kid being kidnapped, the mom turning to Angelyne and doing the hooey reading with the pictures and the kid's toy truck and all that—"

"And all we need the mother to say on-camera is 'Angelyne was terrific'—cut!" I chime in, joining the scam.

"Exactly! Tell River to start booking it. Oh, you're from New York, right, Johnny?"

"Yup."

"We've got another story for you."

"Which show?"

"*Psychic CrimeBusters*. We've got a guy who calls himself the psychic stockbroker. He predicts stock buys for a real brokerage house on Wall Street, and of course, once I told him the name of our show, he swore he could solve a missing-person case somewhere in the city. He has a new case going right now. We're almost there with it, but you'll probably be going there next week, is that okay?"

"Wow. Sure. I just moved here, but it would be nice to get back there."

"Tell River to start booking that, too. And tell Tiffany I want the name of that tattoo artist she knows on Sunset."

"Got it."

A trip back to New York already? That will be strange. If I stop in on anyone, they probably won't even realize that I've left. I think a trip back will do me good. But the thought of leaving Joan, even for a couple of days, has me missing her already. I don't think I've ever had it this bad for a woman. Oh, there were a couple of girls in college whom I thought I could never live without because they did things to me on the first date that I had only read about in *Penthouse* Forum letters, but once I found out that was kind of a hobby for them, those relationships didn't last too long. Not that any guy would object to being used sexually, but having the girl you're banging talking on the phone while you're actually banging her, and having her plan her next rendezvous as soon as she's done with you, doesn't do much for your ego.

River is jumping on both projects, so I can head back home and start doing some research from there. And since Joan is coming over again tonight to give Benny his next shot, I better clean up a little. Women hate unmade beds.

As I drive past my building, I see a marshal's squad car parked in front. Turning into the lot, I notice Benny's van in his space, with the CLEAN ME still clearly visible on its filthy back window. I park my car, and upon entering the gate to our courtyard, I see the two men in green uniforms exiting Benny's door and walking toward the main exit to the street where their car is parked.

I can't imagine why Benny has marshals on his tail. I'm not even sure what marshals do. I think they have something to do with people who have already had their cases adjudicated, and making sure they adhere to whatever conditions the court decided. I'm not even going to begin to guess what Benny might have done. But if it involves fencing stolen goods, I wouldn't be surprised.

I give the marshals a few moments to get in their car and take off before I venture past Benny's door. And right on cue, just as I pass his doorway, I hear the familiar sound of his door scraping open.

"General," Benny whispers from behind the screen door that obscures him entirely, "can I stop by?"

Benny sounds very weak. Raspy with strain.

"Sure, Benny. Give me about ten minutes, all right?" I say to Benny's door.

His door slowly scrapes closed.

I go into my apartment, hoping to catch at least five minutes of relaxation while listening to some soothing music, like maybe Django Reinhardt's Quintet of the Hot Club of France, and give Joan a call. I haven't had time to dump the change out of my pocket, and I'll bet that's Benny already at my door.

Yup. Benny slowly walks past me without saying a word and takes his seat by the table. *Disheveled* is a word I would use to describe Benny if he didn't look so far beyond it. He looks lost, forsaken, deathly ill. Pathetic.

He puts both elbows on the table, and his head collapses into has hands. His back arches forward as if his spine can't support his head and neck.

"Benny, are you okay? Can I get you something?"

Except for his exceptionally heavy breathing, Benny sits in silence. It sounds as if he's pushing every breath through a water-filled lung. His inhalations are extended, almost like gasps for air.

"Did you see them?" Benny mutters.

"Who?"

"Don't bullshit me," he says, too tired to raise his head.

"Yeah. I saw them. What's going on?"

"I can't fight it any longer. I'm too weak. I'm behind on child support. My ex-wife's sucking the life out of me. I try. I really try. My ex-partner lets me work when I can, delivering tapes and stuff. I sell what I can. But I just don't think I can do it anymore."

Benny lifts his head from his hands, and as he straightens his spine, I hear little cracking sounds. He flinches and turns to me. "If I don't come up with the dough, I go to jail. I don't know, maybe I should just . . ." His voice trails off as his head drops forward.

"You've got a kid?"

"I haven't seen him since he was two. He and his mother, Satan incarnate, live out in Barstow in a methamphetamine lab on wheels. She and her biker boyfriend need my money to feed and clothe the kid so they can spend all their welfare checks on drugs and Indian bingo."

"You deliver tapes?"

"When I can. I used to work in the film and video business."

"Really? As what."

"Aw, shit, General. Fuck films. Peep show stuff. Porno movie theater crap, you know, like *Close Encounters of the Slutty Kind*, or *When Harry Banged Sally*. We used to own theaters all over the country: Times Square, Hollywood Boulevard, State Street in Chicago, the Combat Zone in Boston. But home video killed us. We had to start distributing it all ourself. I used to produce, direct, edit. My partner bought me out when things got tough. I stashed some money away, and he lets me deliver whenever I want. Keeps me on the books and pays my medical insurance. If it wasn't for that medical insurance, I'd really be up a creek without a paddle. But it's getting tough to pay rent, eat, buy gas, and keep my ex in crank and bingo chips. You must really think I'm a scumbag, huh?"

"Why, because of what you did for a living? Believe me, I'm doing pretty much the same."

"General! You're in porn?" Benny exclaims delightedly.

"Nah. TV that's just a notch or two above. It's called reality television."

"Oh! Like *COPS*! I love that show. Ever notice how no matter whether they're shooting in Miami or Anchorage, the crooks never have shirts on?"

"So how far are you from going to jail?"

"Well, if I play my cards right, I can avoid it." Benny gets up out of his chair, walks across the living room, and stares out the window facing the street. "You shoulda seen me. I lived up there on Mulholland. At night I had a view with the whole of Los Angeles laid out in front of me, sparkling like diamonds. A pool, hot tub, sauna, Corvette convertible, and chicks. Oh, man, there were chicks everywhere I looked. Then it hit me like a fucking brick shit house. Those goddamn Japs." Benny turns to me with a look of disgust on his face. "Betamax. Those damn Betamax machines. We thought they were a joke at first. We called them masturBetamax machines because you could watch porno at home. Then they took off with those VDHS or whatever the hell you call them, video machines, and we started losing theaters faster than the Cubs lost baseball games." He turns to the window again as a limo passes by. "I had it all. I lost it all. And now look at me." Benny holds up his three-fingered hand in front of his face and examines it as though he has never seen it before. "I got even less than that."

I don't have any soothing words for Benny. What can I say, *Don't worry, Benny, you'll be just fine*? I'd be a fool to think I could say something that would ease his pain in any way. "Want to hear some music?" I ask.

"Yeah. Got any more Tony Bennett? How about 'Rags to Riches'?" Benny wanders back to his usual chair.

"Yeah, I think I got it here somewhere," I say as I fumble through my *B* section. "Got it."

"That's a great tune," Benny says, closing his eyes. I can still hear the heaviness in his voice and his breathing, but he seems more comfortable. "Nineteen fifty-three. Number one hit." The needle hits the groove. "You know how many number one hits Sinatra had in 1953?"

"Ah, one?" I guess.

"Zero. Zilch. Nothing. I'll never forget the look on those kids' faces when it hit number one. This was before rock took over in the early fifties. Everybody thought Sinatra was it. Parents, kids, teachers. I was the only one who backed Tony B. I rubbed it in their faces but good. That was a good year. But fifty-four was even better. Yup, 1954. The catch."

"The catch?"

"Sure. Mays's over-the-shoulder catch of Vic Wertz. Saved the game," Benny says with his eyes still closed, as if he's watching a highlight film in his head. "I only wish it could have been against the Yankees instead of Cleveland, but winning four straight was sweet. The icing on the cake. I got the fellas good on that one."

I know something is up with Benny. He just told me that he doesn't care about baseball, yet he's reminiscing as if it were the only joy in his past.

"That must have been something. I think I remember reading that the Indians were favored in that series."

"That was the beauty of it. Willie's catch was game one. He turned the series around. And the rest, as they say, is history," Benny says, eyes still shut, savoring his words.

"Did you get to any of the games?"

"Yup. Game one," Benny says with a large grin.

Remembering the scorecard I found tucked inside the yearbook that Benny sold me, I recalled a name. "Did Father B. take you?"

Benny shot up out of the chair, his eyes wild and wide open. "What did you say? Who told you that?"

"What? What are you talking about?"

"Who the fuck mentioned that name? Who? Tell me!" Benny says, transforming his raspy, breathy voice into a Linda Blair-as-Satan voice.

"Calm down, Benny—"

"Don't tell me to calm down, how the fuck do you know that name? Tell me!" Benny says, standing too close to me as I sit on my couch. Benny has mustered up as much strength and intimidation as possible, to appear threatening. But in his weakened state, it's almost comical to think he actually imagines himself as some kind of violent force to be reckoned with. I also notice that Benny is nervously flicking his right thumb against the part of his hand where his fingers are missing.

"Benny, take it easy. Let me show you. Relax. Sit," I say to him in a voice as calm as if I'm asking a two-year-old to hand over a loaded gun. I go into my bedroom and return with the scorecard from the 1951 series that had the inscription *Me, Willie, Ralph, and Fr. B., Thursday, Oct. 4th, 1951.* Benny is sitting on the sofa, and as I start to hand the scorecard to him, he begins to tremble. Not just his hands but his whole body. He takes the scorecard from me and places it on his lap. Now only his hands are shaking. He takes the two fingers on his right hand and ever so lightly rubs the inscription. As he does so, I notice a single tear dropping down his right cheek.

"Can I have this, General?" Benny says, still staring at the inscription. "I'll refund your money, if you want."

"No, Benny, it's yours. Take it."

"I couldn't find this for years. I didn't really want to find it," Benny says, wiping the tear away.

"What I don't get, Benny," I say, sitting next to him on the couch, "is the names."

"Uh, well, er, ah, um, I was the only one who knew how to keep score," Benny says unconvincingly.

"But you said your brother's name was Dominic. That's who the Willie Mays ball was signed to."

"Uh, well, yeah. Er, that's right. His name is Dominic, but Willie is his nickname," Benny says, struggling to speak coherently.

"Willie a nickname for Dominic?"

"Yeah, so what?"

"And who are Ralph and Father B.?"

"I can't, General," Benny says, shaking his head frantically. He looks at me, sizing me up. I can see the wheels spinning. "Okay. Me is me. Willie is my brother, also known as Dominic. Ralph was my . . ." Benny begins to shake again. He sticks the two fingers on his deformed right hand in his mouth and bites on them. Hard. "Ralph was my best friend. And Father B., well, he's a priest who used to take us places. But he's dead. He died a long time ago."

"Your brother and Father B. are both dead?"

"Yes."

"And what about Ralph?"

"He's dead, too!" Benny yells in anger.

I stare blankly at Benny, trying not to show any hostility in return.

"It's hard for me, General. I'm going to take this, okay?" Benny says, rising with the scorecard in hand. "Can I still come back for my treatment with Joan later?" he asks softly, staring at the scorecard.

"Sure. Absolutely," I say.

Benny quickly grabs the front door and opens it. "I'll see ya later," Benny says, closing the door behind him.

If I didn't have any words of comfort for Benny before this outburst, I sure as hell don't have any now.

It's already half past eight, and neither Benny nor Joan has arrived. Joan called to tell me she would be about a half hour late and offered to bring over some takeout. But it's highly unusual for Benny to be this late. Having the extra half hour has already given me time to set the table with some nice dishes, silverware, and even candlelight. If all goes according to plan, Joan can stick Benny with his meds, and he can be out of here in just a few minutes, leaving Joan and me to a night of food and whatever other pleasantries may come our way.

A knock on the door startles me. "Who is it?" I say to the still-closed door.

"Delivery," Joan says from the other side.

I open the door to see her standing there holding several bags. "Where would you like me to put this, buddy?" Joan says with a sexy smile.

"Anywhere. Do you accept tips?" I ask, taking the load from her.

"Whatever you can afford," Joan says just behind me.

I put down the goodies and turn around to Joan. "How's this?" I ask as I plant a short kiss on her lips.

"That will do for now. Is Benny here?"

"No. That's unlike him," I say, starting to unpack the salads and plastic utensils. "Maybe he changed his mind. Maybe we should just get started, and if he shows up, he shows up."

Joan hugs me from behind. I can smell her fragrance and am immediately reminded of our euphoric lovemaking the night before. "I think maybe we should check on him, Johnny. He is sick."

I turn to Joan. I look into her eyes and see only the absolute love she has for others. Not the love that I hope and pray she has for me, but the love she already has for this strange, sick man next door. "Okay. Let's check on him."

"I knew you'd say that," Joan says, punctuating it with a kiss.

I lock the door behind us and take the few short steps over to Benny's. His stoop is still a mess of dirty, faded flyers and ad handouts.

"Have you been inside before?" Joan whispers.

"Nope. This should be interesting."

"Let's hope not too interesting."

I open the screen door and knock firmly three times. No reply. I knock three more times.

And from behind the door, I hear a faint voice: "Hold on. Hold on." Then I hear a small crash. "Shit. Ow. Damn it to hell. I'll be right there."

Joan and I look at each other and shrug in unison as if to say, *Well, here it goes.*

Benny's door creaks open. "I'm nude!"

"We've seen it before, Benny," Joan says. "Can we come in?"

I'm shocked that Joan has offered to go in Benny's hovel. This woman has moxie. She looks to me and whispers, "Believe me, I've been in much worse situations than this."

"I'm nude!" Benny reiterates.

"Put on a robe. And then let us in?"

"Let you in?" Benny says, shocked.

I whisper to Joan, "Let us in?," also shocked.

"Yes. Yes," Joan says to both of us.

Benny closes his door.

"You can tell a lot about someone by seeing the environment they live in," Joan says to me, grabbing my hand.

"I sure am glad I made the bed today," I say.

The door scrapes open once again, and Benny stands there in a tattered old robe. "The place is a little messy, but come on in."

Messy? World War II was a slight inconvenience. The universe is kind of big. From the moment we take one step into Benny's apartment, it's clear that he has a problem with housekeeping. The place is extremely dark due to the fact there seems to be one lamp with a forty-watt bulb sitting on the floor at the rear of the room. There is an aisle created between mounds of newspapers, pizza boxes, magazines, and loose papers. All I can think of is that two doors over from my apartment is an absolute fire hazard, and it makes me very nervous. We make our way through the maze in the living room toward the back, where a space has been created for his dinette set. The table is a mountain of junk: a car battery oozing acid, broken jumper cables, four or five radios in different states of disrepair, and a rusty old manual typewriter are the prominent objects, surrounded by real junk.

"Let me clear this off a little," Benny says, lifting a few things off the table and placing them on the floor. He then moves three chairs into position next to the clear corner.

"Benny, how long has the place been like this?" I ask, trying to hide my disbelief.

"Awhile, I guess. I'm not a good housekeeper."

The apartment has the look and feel of a place that was given up on long ago. Things appear to have been left in their place to decompose. What was once a plant is now a dry stalk of some kind, sitting in a pot of sand in the corner. At the back of the living room, a window doesn't quite close properly, and a branch from a tree is growing about two feet into the room through a two-inch opening.

"When were you going to get around to trimming this tree?" I ask Benny, who has gone into the kitchen and is frantically trying to tidy up. Joan shoots a stare at me, letting me know in no uncertain terms that I should not be joking about this. I immediately understand that she is right.

Joan takes a step over to the entry of Benny's kitchenette, where he is filling the sink with water and dishwashing liquid, covering whatever dishes happen to be in there. "Is there anything you'd like us to help you with, Benny? It would only take a little while to get rid of whatever you don't want."

Benny is throwing more dishes, glasses, and coffee mugs into the two kitchen sink basins, where they disappear under the bubbles. "Nah. Nah. I need most of this stuff. I've been saving it. I'm going to read all those magazines. And books, too."

"You just let Johnny know if you want to get rid of anything, and we'll both help you," Joan says calmly.

She is so amazing. My first reaction is to joke about whatever is in front of me. Joan is always way ahead of me. While I'm thinking of a good line, she has already analyzed the situation and anticipated what might happen after words are spoken. She doesn't blurt out a dumb remark but figures out how to help solve a problem.

"I might take you up on that, Joan. And Johnny. I could use maybe a little help to clear out some of this junk," Benny says, dumping more dishwashing detergent into the nearly overflowing sink. "In fact, Johnny, could you maybe help me get rid of some of these boxes in here?"

"Sure, Benny," I say, entering his kitchenette. I'm immediately shocked at the sight in front of me. An entire wall, from floor to ceiling, is piled high with pizza boxes. "You mean these boxes?"

"Yeah, could you? They're blocking the window," Benny says sheepishly as he washes the dishes.

"No problem," I say. I pick up a tower of empty pizza boxes and slowly turn around. Joan is standing in the doorway with a coy, approving smile. She gives me a big thumbs-up and, stupidly, I try to return it, dropping my tower of boxes all over the kitchen, spilling whatever crumbs and waxed paper were inside. "Oops," I say to Benny, who is looking at me like I'm the biggest idiot in the world. "Joan, could you go into my kitchen closet and get my little mini vacuum with the hose?" I ask as I throw her the keys to my apartment. Joan catches them and tries not to giggle out loud as she heads back to my place.

"That's why I don't touch some of this old stuff. It's been here so long I'm afraid that if I mess with it, it will just make matters worse," Benny says, staring at the mess of boxes and crumbs around his feet.

"Nothing a little elbow grease couldn't cure, as my old man used to say," I announce to Benny, in the same tone of voice I remember my dad bellowing at me, as I begin to pick up the boxes and stack them on the floor again. A couple have fallen between the sink and the refrigerator and, I believe, even behind the refrigerator. I can barely stick my head between the wall and the refrigerator to get back there; I have to move the old Frigidaire a few inches to reach them. As I stick my head in the narrow space to see what the box is hung up on, I can see, amid the ballpoint pens, rubber bands, and old laundry lists, a photograph standing on edge against the wall. I reach as far as I can and am just barely able to grab hold of the picture. Once I have it in my hand and can take a look at it, I glance over to Benny, who is still concentrating on the dishes. The photo is a group shot of three boys and a priest in front of a store on a city street. I turn the photo over and see that there is writing and a date. I know I shouldn't do this, but I stick the picture in my back pocket for a later examination. In this mess, it will be easy to tell Benny I found it anywhere in the apartment.

"I'm back," Joan declares, with the small vacuum in hand. "Johnny, you just worry about the boxes, and I'll start cleaning up the little bits with this."

Benny looks happy as he watches Joan on her knees vacuuming. But as I pass her, I see that part of her butt is showing, which is the cause for the look of glee on Benny's face. "Watch it,

Benny," I say as I give him a slight elbow in the ribs, almost dropping the boxes again.

"Watch it? Yes sir, General!" Benny says joyfully, with a thumbs-up on his deformed right hand.

I dump ninety-seven pizza boxes from the kitchen alone. There are still a few dozen in the living room. And we never even get a look at Benny's bedroom, which is probably a good thing. It's hard for Joan to find a clean area to administer Benny's shot in the ass, but she manages. We work for an hour straight, and we make only a little dent in the filth and clutter of Benny's lair.

Back in the relative cleanliness of my place, I feel like I've got a thick film of dirt on me.

I bring Joan a glass of seltzer. She takes a small sip and looks at me as if she has a funny taste in her mouth. "I think I need a shower," she says.

"Me, too. I feel like I've been hunting for sewer balls."

"Eeewww, what is that?" Joan asks, contorting her face into a disgusted expression.

"A sewer ball is a ball that's down a sewer, and you don't have money for a new ball, because you're a kid, so you have your friend lower you down into the sewer by the ankles, with a bent coat hanger in hand, and you fish the ball out of the sewer so you can play with it."

"You did that?"

"Sure. I was the lightest kid."

"Did you at least clean it off first?"

"Of course. Whaddyah think we were, gross or something?"

"Speaking of gross," Joan says, taking another sip of seltzer, "what about that shower?"

"If you're inviting, I'm accepting."

"I'm inviting," Joan says, placing her glass on the coffee table. She gets up and grabs me by the hand, leading me to the bathroom.

Thank God I cleaned the bathroom yesterday. Even the towels are clean.

You really know you're crazy about someone when you want bright lights on while disrobing. I like a bright bathroom, so I have a couple of hundred-watt bulbs in the fixture over the sink. Joan begins to take her top off. I'm afraid I'm going to be embarrassed when I drop my drawers. I take off my shirt and wait a moment for Joan to take off her pants before I drop mine. She takes hers off, then her panties, steps into the tub, and turns on the water.

"You like it really hot or just hot?" Joan asks as I take off my underwear.

"Uh, just hot," I say, stepping into the shower with an erection already.

"Oh my goodness!" Joan says, noticing it immediately. "You don't waste any time, do you?"

"I'm sorry," I say softly.

"Don't be," Joan says as she turns to me with the hot water blasting her from behind and splashing onto me.

"You just drive me wild," I say, looking at the water dripping down the front of her face, onto her breasts, and running down her legs.

"Come here," Joan says, closing her eyes and pulling me toward her.

The water is hot, and with the shower door closed, the space is quickly filling with steam. We are so perfectly sized for each other. We caress and begin to rub each other's backs and butts while we kiss softly. Joan grabs the soap and begins to lather our bodies. Everything about her—her touch, her kiss, even the way she rubs the shampoo in her hair—just oozes of sensuality. There's a calmness to her that makes me feel more comfortable, even in here, than I have ever felt with a woman. Joan puts shampoo in my hair and begins to rub her hands through it. I didn't think it was possible to feel this sexy, this aroused, this sensuous, and not actually have an orgasm. But the way Joan touches me has me imagining I'm in some sensuous Botticelli oil painting, not in some Hollywood Boulevard porno movie.

After the shower, Joan takes the time to towel me dry with a loving wave of her hand.

"I'd rather not put on the clothes I was wearing before," Joan says, standing there stark naked with her hair wrapped in a towel turban.

"I prefer you just as you are," I say as I embrace her.

"Johnny," Joan says in a voice that frightens me. I've heard that voice before from naked women. It's the voice when they have some bad news to give you, like *I know we just screwed, but I'm not interested in a relationship,* or *I know I just banged your brains out, but I don't really love you . . .*

"What is it, Joan?" I say, bracing for the worst as I inch backward.

"I really can't spend the night. I've got an extremely early start tomorrow," Joan says matter-of-factly as she touches my lips with the index finger of her right hand.

"That's okay," I say relieved.

"Timing is everything," Joan says as we embrace and kiss. Her body is so pure and clean. Not wet but moist.

"I'll get you something to put on," I say as I leave the bathroom.

Joan would look fantastic in anything. But seeing her in my old Cardinal O'Brien High School sweatshirt and a pair of cross-country O'Brien sweatpants gives me a special thrill. We heated up our takeout and are sitting on the couch, listening to the sweet lyrical violin of Stephane Grappelli while we eat.

"Wait! I just remembered something," I say, putting down my paper container of food and heading for the bathroom. I forgot all about the photo I found in Benny's kitchen. I retrieve it from my pants pocket to show Joan. "Look, I found this behind Benny's refrigerator. I didn't get a chance to tell you, but he was acting the strangest ever today before you got here. He was being just quietly weird about his past, then he totally freaked when I mentioned this Father B."

"Father B.? Is that his father?" Joan says as she takes a sip of green tea.

"No. *Father* as in *priest*. It was written on a scorecard from the fifties. And when I mentioned it, he just went ballistic. When I reached for a pizza box behind the refrigerator, I found this photo."

I hold the photo out for both of us to examine. It's a black-and-white photo, probably from the fifties. It has that old-fashioned white border with the scalloped edges. The oldest boy looks about sixteen, the one who resembles Benny appears maybe twelve, and the one who just has to be Benny's younger brother looks to be five or six. Benny and the little boy have big grins on their faces, but the older boy standing next to the blond priest isn't smiling at all. In fact, he looks like he's about to receive a vaccination. The priest and the boys are standing in front of a storefront. You can see only half the writing on the window. It looks like ETTO, and underneath is written SH.

"It says something on the back," I say as I turn the photograph over: *Dominic Benedetto, William Benedetto, Ralph Bonifazio, and Father Biselli, Oct. 1953.*

"That older boy has to be Benny. But his name is Bennett, isn't it?" Joan asks while enjoying the last bite of her veggie spring roll.

"Yes, and he told me his brother's name is Dominic. I should say, his deceased brother's name is Dominic."

"He said he had a dead brother named Dominic?" Joan asks.

"Yeah, and a dead friend named Ralphie. And the priest was dead, too," I say, dipping a shrimp in some hot-and-sour sauce.

"He says everybody's dead? That's quite a coincidence."

"You got that right. Something's fishy. Hey, wait a minute. The writing on the front of that store. The SH is the end of FISH—"

"And the ETTO is the end of Benedetto. Benny's real last name," Joan chimes in, proud of her Benedetto's Fish revelation.

"Oh, this is too much. Guess whose real last name is Benedetto?"

"Who?"

"Tony freakin' Bennett. And remember when you asked him how he lost his fingers and he said he lost them in an accident in his parents' butcher store? Maybe it was a grinder in a fish store."

"Why would he lie . . . so weakly?"

"Good question."

Chapter Eight

IT'S PITCH-BLACK, five A.M., and I can barely fit my bony butt in the van with all the boxes of gear that Smitty and Joe have piled in here for our trip to the airport. We're meeting the psychic stockbroker this afternoon at a Wall Street brokerage. There are still a few holes in his story, but according to Wendy and River, he's going to provide us with a psychic reading that supposedly will lead the authorities to a child who has been missing for a month or so and has been making headlines in New York on a daily basis. I think the jerk is merely using this, and us, to gain publicity for himself, and yeah, what else is new? We're just as guilty as he is. Apparently, the psychic is working with some credible law enforcement personnel, so hopefully, there will be some legitimacy to this whole thing.

I hated to say goodbye to Joan last night. Since we gave each other electric shocks the first time we touched, we've hardly been apart. I'm not surprised that Joan has agreed to administer Benny's meds while I'm gone. To simplify things, she is going to use my apartment for the procedure, rather than risk being buried alive under a pile of pizza boxes in Benny's place. Just for curiosity's sake, I've brought along the picture of Benny and the gang in front of the fish store. If I have a little downtime, which is extremely unlikely on these road trips, maybe I can do a little research and find out exactly where this shop was, and maybe take a picture of me and the crew in front and give it to Benny as a memento.

Joe has already ascertained the life stories of several of the female flight attendants, as he's been chatting them up nonstop since we stepped foot on the plane. Smitty has been reading a thick tome by Carl Sagan and putting it down only to eat, drink, or go to the restroom. I've been mostly going over our itinerary for our New York shoot, planning ways to save time by scheduling shoots in close proximity, trying to figure out how I can possibly get away to visit the old neighborhood and surprise the guys at the Place, the corner bar.

We're making the ideal approach into New York: down the Hudson River with a bird's-eye view of Manhattan, and hanging a left at the World Trade Center. From there you travel along the southern part of Brooklyn, Queens, and over the Rockaway Peninsula, former home of Rockaways Playland. In fact, I can see the empty lot where Playland stood until a few years ago, when it was razed to make way for . . . an empty lot.

We'll be landing at JFK at the height of the afternoon rush hour, and then we're scheduled to meet our psychic stockbroker at six P.M. It should be tough making it on time, but he's already told us he'll wait for us if we're late.

Wall Street after six P.M. is like a ghost town. Joe must've smoked three packs of cigarettes on the way from the airport, cursing New York drivers and their "shitty New York attitudes" every bumper-to-bumper inch of the way. Smitty and Joe drop me in front of the grand old fifty-story building that has seen better days. Here we are to meet Milo Spivak, aka the psychic stockbroker and occasional missing-person finder. The elevator is the kind that probably used to have an operator, but now a visitor must slide open the grating himself and close it properly, too, to get to a floor. On the twenty-third floor is Floody and Tabar Brokerage, where Milo has an office. Floody and Tabar isn't exactly Merrill Lynch, but it is a large, professionally equipped office with a few guys in suits still manning the phones and staring at computer screens. One of them looks up at me. "Can I help you?"

"I'm here to interview Milo Spivak."

"Oh, great! Nice to meet you," says the amiable middle-aged man with a youthful flock of salt-and-pepper hair hanging in his face. "You must be with *Psychic CrimeBusters*."

"Yes. That's right," I say, shaking his hand.

"Come with me. I'm Kurt Floody. Managing partner. Milo's a trip, let me tell you," he says, leading me down a hall.

"So, you really think he's on to something with this psychic stockbroker thing?"

"I got him on a retainer, if that means anything to you," he says as he stops in front of a doorway and motions for me to enter.

Milo is a diminutive man with very, very dark hair. It's more like the color of black shoe polish than Clairol No. 22 chestnut brown. His bushy eyebrows and perfectly manicured goatee are the same shade of deep, dark black. It's a good thing that Milo is skinny, or he wouldn't be able to sit behind his desk, which somehow is crammed into this room that must have been a slop-sink closet at one time. Milo has about a six-inch space to squeeze through so he can come around to shake my hand. There's no window and not enough room for Floody to stand in there with us, so he stands in the hallway with the door open while Milo and I stand a little too close to each other. I'm already aware of the fact that he had a healthy dose of garlic with his most recent meal.

"I'm Johnny Koester. It's a pleasure to meet you, Mr. Spivak," I say, backing off as much as possible without joining Floody in the hall.

"Call me Milo. Pleasure to meet you. Is the office okay for filming the interview?" Milo says, stroking his magician's black beard.

"That's up to my cameraman; he'll be here in a minute. It might be a little tight, but he works magic," I say, noticing that there's a tarnished brass plaque on the wall for MAGICIAN OF THE YEAR LOCAL 22 1959. "We'd like to interview you as well, Mr. Floody. Is that okay? We'll shoot that in your office."

"Sure, whatever you need," Floody says, smoking a cigarette and placing the ashes in his cupped hand. "Milo is a trip, lemme tell ya. Oh, we got company," he says as he makes way for Smitty and Joe pushing their gear on a small dolly.

"This isn't where we're shooting, is it?" Joe says with a look of disbelief. "Hey, could I bum a smoke, pal, I'm dying."

Floody gives him a cigarette and a light, and Joe seems to relax a little with his first drag.

"We can make this work," Smitty says, putting down his gear. Joe immediately begins to unload and set up lights on stands. "We'll move the desk out a little, hang a backlight off that pipe up there, bounce some soft colors, and it'll be easy to manipulate the look we want," Smitty goes on calmly, eyeballing the situation. "Is there another interview?"

"Yes. With Mr. Floody."

"Joe, you go set up that office with Mr. Floody, and I'll set up here, and we'll bang these out," Smitty says as he pulls the desk away from the back wall and then starts to hang some lights off a pipe near the ceiling. Milo and I stand in the hallway and watch.

"So tell me about this missing child, Milo. I'm out in L.A., so I don't really know that much about it," I say to Milo, trying to ascertain how much he knows.

"Oh, yes!" Milo says as if he just remembered that the whole reason we flew three thousand miles was the missing-kid story and that he was going to try to find her. "Yes. I've been working with an investigator close to the case. I have some good readings, which I'll share with you. I want to show you something."

Milo sneaks past Smitty, who is taking up pretty much the entire office with his large frame, and reaches into the bottom drawer of his desk. He pulls out a dusty crystal ball on a bronze stand. "I was thinking of gazing into this when I'm doing my reading, and thinking that perhaps you could have the cameraman zoom into the ball and do that blurry effect and then cut in pictures of the girl with smoke and harp music and everything like that."

Smitty is trying very hard not to bust a gut laughing.

"Uh, that's very interesting, Milo," I say, hoping upon hope that this guy isn't as nuts as Angelyne. "But that's a little old-fashioned for us. We like to present things in a more . . . contemporary manner."

"Yes! Very good! I like that! Contemporary!" Milo says, holding his crystal ball with one hand and stroking his beard with the other. I have a feeling the shoe polish will start rubbing off if he doesn't stop pulling on it.

"Who is this investigator you're working with? Is he a cop?"

"No, he's not exactly a cop. He's a private eye. You know. A real hard-boiled dick. Like Philip Marlowe, you know."

"He's a private investigator?" I say, trying to conceal my utter skepticism. "Who hired him to investigate this? The family?"

"Not exactly. You see, he's more of a freelance private eye. But he has good contacts in the police department. He can get information to them in a flash!"

"Fine. We'll worry about that later. I'm going to interview you for general background, then we're going to have you do a reading. What do you need for that?"

"Oh, you mean props! Yes, well, besides this?" Milo says, holding up the crystal ball and dusting it off with his flower-print tie. "This is all I really have with me. I don't use my turban here at the brokerage. It rattles some of the investors."

"That's all right. We'll just keep it simple."

"I know! I can use a map. Rub the map, look for hot spots, then if I get a hot reading, you know, then we can go with that!"

"Do you have a map, Milo?"

"Uh, no, not here."

"I've got the map from the rental car company," Smitty says, pointing to one of his bags.

"Fine. We'll use that," I say, reaching into the bag and pulling it out. "How close are you to being set, Smitty?"

"I'm done. All I have to do is set up the camera on the tripod and focus the lights a little. In fact, Milo, will you sit down here for me?"

Milo gets behind his desk and takes a seat. Smitty has used pools of red light and shadows, and if Milo held a pitchfork and had a couple of horns on his head, the scene would be complete. Joe arrives and gives Smitty the thumbs-up as he picks up a microphone and mikes Milo. I take my position next to the camera.

"Now, just talk to me, don't look at the camera. If you want to stop tape, just say so. We'll start out with general background on you. Now, Milo, tell me how you started out."

"Well, as you know, I'm known as the psychic stockbroker. But originally, I was known as the psychic upholsterer. People would come into my shop, and I'd immediately tell them all kinds of things about themselves from my psychic impressions of them. And then one thing led to another, and I'd be giving everyone readings. No charge, only donations."

"And how did that lead to you being the psychic stockbroker?"

"Well, I was doing a big job for Mr. Floody at his Park Avenue apartment—"

"What kind of job?"

"Oh, you know, new springs, stuffing, imported fabrics—"

"Upholstery."

"Yes, I was doing a huge reupholstering job. Three lovely rooms. And one thing led to another, and I did some readings for Mr. Floody and Mrs. Floody and their dog—"

"You did a reading for their dog?"

"Oh, yes! That's what really sold them on my talents. They asked me to find out what was wrong with their dog, and I told them he needed an operation. They took him to the vet, and the vet saved his life."

"What did the dog have?"

"A bad tooth. That can lead to serious liver and kidney damage. They removed it just in time. Then Mr. Floody asked me if I wanted to get into the stock market and he put me on retainer, gave me this office, and here I am. On national television!"

"Tell me about this missing child."

"Yes, well, this child has been missing. It's in all the papers and all over the TV news. I've had some strong, strong impressions. And I'm just about ready to offer my help. In fact, I have this map." Milo reaches across the desk and grabs the map.

"Not yet, Milo," I say, stopping him cold.

"Not yet? Okay. What do you want me to do now?"

"Tell me more about why you got involved trying to find this child."

"Yes, this child has been missing, and I have a very, very strong impression about where this child is."

"Tell me those impressions."

"Now?"

"Okay, now."

"I'm going to give you some impressions. First I have to go into what I call a trance." Milo leans back in his chair, flares his nostrils, closes his eyes, and begins to breathe heavily through his nose. After about ten inhalations and exhalations, he begins to speak in a much deeper tone of voice. "Yes, I see water. I definitely see water. And I see trees. Trees. And not too far away, I see something, I'm not sure, wait, yes, I see either railroad tracks or maybe a road, yes, a road. With a train going by or maybe trucks on the road. Yes, I'm certain of it." Milo pops his eyes open and goes back to his normal voice. "Now you've got that. Water. Trees and either train tracks or a road. You've got to give me those when they find the kid. If she's found and I've hit on two or three of those, you've got to release that to the press as a psychic hit."

"Yeah. Okay. A hit. Now let's do the map thing," I say to Milo, pushing it over to his side of the desk.

"Where was this kid from?"

"Shirley, Long Island," I say. "Can you find that?"

"Uh, give me a minute . . . Yes. Here it is. Now I'm going to give you some psychic impressions. You can film these." Milo goes back into his trance with his flared nostrils and heavy breathing. He begins to rotate his head in a circle and opens his eyes just slightly. He begins rubbing the map near Shirley. He moves his finger from Shirley down to the ocean and rubs hard on the map. He then goes back to Shirley and moves his finger up to the Long Island Sound. He then moves his finger along the Long Island Expressway toward Manhattan, going through Nassau County, Queens, Brooklyn, and into Manhattan before he rubs along the eastern side of Manhattan Island. He drops his head as if all that traveling plumb wore him out.

He lifts his head and opens his eyes. "How was that?"

"Great. You get all that, Smitty?"

"Got it. Stopping tape. Cut lights," Smitty says, turning off his camera and beginning to strike the set.

Milo leans across the desk. "You've got to give me those hits if they come true. I had some real hot stuff going there on that map. Could you feel it?"

"Yeah. I felt it, Milo," I say as I take the map from him and put it back in Smitty's bag.

"Do you want me to do a reading for you on the stock market? Free, of course."

"No donation?" Joe says as he removes Milo's microphone.

"No. No donation."

"Nah. I'd rather invest my money in something with a little better odds, like at a craps table," Joe says, stuffing the mike into a case. "We're all set up in the other office for Mr. Floody."

"Let's go," Smitty says, grabbing his camera, tripod, and a couple of bags. "Lead the way, Milo."

"Uh, let's see. Oh yes, I believe his office is this way," Milo says, leading us down the hall.

"Fucking psychic can't even find his boss's office," Joe whispers in my ear.

Mr. Floody is sitting behind his desk going over some files. His office is certainly no slop-sink room: spacious and nothing but the finest furniture, oak paneling, and trim throughout.

"Check out that sofa," Floody says. "Milo did that. Gorgeous, isn't it?"

Joe leans over to me and whispers, "I wonder how much of a donation he got for doing that."

I say to Floody, "I'll sit right here, next to the camera. Just talk to me; don't look at the camera. So, tell me, how does Milo give you information on the stock market?"

"I don't want to know nothing. All I know is he gives me information and I use it. I use meteorologists, I use geographic engineers, I use economists, I use political consultants, and I use Milo. I don't want to know nothing. If I think about what he does, it makes me crazy. But I use him. And nobody does upholstery like him. He's an artist."

"Okay, that's all we need."

Joe and Smitty look at me like *That's it?*

"I've got everything I need. Smitty and Joe, why don't you have Milo and Mr. Floody show you around and get some shots of the place. Computers, charts, books, stuff like that. Can I use this phone to call L.A., Mr. Floody?"

"Just dial nine."

"Thanks."

Joe and Floody light up a couple of smokes, and the four of them head down the hall together. It's about six in L.A. I want to catch Joan at her office.

"Johnny, I'm glad you called," she says when she comes on the line.

"Is everything okay?"

"It's Benny. I went over to your place around four to see if I could maybe do Benny early, and he was being taken away on a gurney. He was semiconscious. I'm going over to the hospital in a little while to see how he is."

"Shit! Joan, are you sure?"

"He needs someone, Johnny."

"Okay. You are an angel," I say to Joan as softly as one can talk on a phone and still be heard.

"You're *my* angel," Joan says even more softly. "How's the shoot? How's New York?"

"The shoot is nutty. I haven't seen New York yet. Can you page me when you see Benny?"

"I'll page you right after I see him."

"I miss you."

"I miss you, too. Hurry home."

The foursome come back into the office, all chatty with Joe and Floody, smoking up a storm. Joe's asking Milo to show him some card tricks, and Smitty's asking Floody for some stock tips. All I can think about is poor Benny, all alone in an emergency room, and the fact that Joan will probably be the first thing he sees when he opens his eyes. Lucky guy.

I've never stayed in a hotel in New York before. Having lived in the city my whole life, why would I? Now that my parents have retired way out on the eastern end of Long Island, at least a two-hour drive away from Manhattan, I'm not sure when I'll free up to visit them. A visit to the old neighborhood in the Bronx will have to wait, too. It's strange merely being a tourist and looking north from my midtown hotel room and seeing the Bronx looming in the distance.

I'm meeting Smitty and Joe for dinner. They've never been to New York with a real New Yorker, so they want me to show them some off-the-beaten-path places. Let's see how far off the beaten path they really want to go. Tomorrow we're scheduled to take Milo Spivak out to Shirley to get some footage of him getting his psychic impressions from areas close to where the girl was abducted. Wendy and River are still trying to get the parents and the police to cooperate with us and appear on-camera. Hey, I guess any national publicity might help, even if it's in the form of something as ridiculous as *Psychic CrimeBusters*.

Why does the phone always ring when I'm on the toilet?

"Hello?"

"We're down in front with the van whenever you're ready," Smitty says hurriedly on the phone. "Don't be long, I've already had to grease the doorman with ten bucks."

"Be down in a flash."

As I stand alone in the elevator going down to the lobby, I ponder a rule of thumb: You can always tell how big a hick somebody is by whether or not he comments on the elevator ride. The car stops on the seventeenth floor, and a relatively sophisticated-looking, well-dressed young yuppie couple gets on. They could both be lawyers in a large metropolitan city. The male presses the *L* button, even though it's already illuminated, and once the car drops and hits a steady speed, he turns to his female companion and says, "Boy, I wonder how many g's that was?" She giggles. Hicks!

Smitty and Joe are sitting on a sofa not far from the main entrance. Joe has what looks to be a tumbler of whiskey in his hand. Smitty is reading the *New York Times*.

"You guys ready?" I ask.

"Let's go before I gotta give this guy in the monkey suit another ten," Joe says. He and Smitty lead me out to the van parked next to the front door.

We take our usual places: Joe drives, Smitty takes shotgun, and I'm in the back.

"So what do you have cooked up for us in the Big Apple there, Mr. New York?" Joe asks, lighting a cigarette and pulling out of the parking lot into midtown traffic.

"Well, how about we eat in Little Italy?" I say.

"Yeah, Umberto's Clam House, where they whacked Joey Gallo," Joe says enthusiastically.

"Sounds good to me," Smitty agrees.

"Pass Sixth Avenue here," I say, pointing to the street ahead.

"The sign says Avenue of the Americas," Joe says.

"Just another trick New Yorkers play on tourists," I tell him.

Joe does a great job of following directions, and we're in Little Italy before we know it. We decide against Umberto's Clam House, just in case there are any other unfinished whacks waiting to be discharged this evening. Smitty and Joe think Puglia's looks like a fun place to soak in some Italian culture, since a three-hundred-pound woman can be seen through the front window, singing with an accordion. We park a few blocks away and pass some of the landmarks of the legendary neighborhood: social clubs, with their doors wide open, where old Italian men drink wine and play cards on folding chairs and table. The butcher shops, lambs and goats hanging in the windows, with fur still intact on gutted bodies. And old fat Italian ladies sitting on front stoops dressed in black from head to toe, including their black babushkas.

As we stroll past a live poultry store, I notice a butcher shop with the name Benedetto's on the front window and the lights still on. I stop for a moment, wondering, could this possibly be any connection to Benny? Benedetto is a pretty common Italian name. I even had a priest in high school with the name. And although the photo was probably of a fish store, Benny did say his folks had a butcher store in lower Manhattan, which is where we are.

"Could you guys hold on a minute? I just want to ask this guy a question about an old friend of mine."

"Hey, cool," Joe says. "A real New York experience. Maybe this guy's like a Mafia butcher, and he's grinding up some rival mafioso in the back."

"Joe, just relax for a minute," I say as I knock on the front window.

A thin, thirtyish man with a thick mustache, still wearing a bloody apron, looks at us. He picks up a huge cleaver, also still bloody, and comes toward the front window. "We're closed," he announces, a cleaver clenched at his side.

"Can I ask you a question? About an old friend. A Benedetto."

He looks at us, obviously trying to judge whether or not we're trouble, and finally walks across his sawdust floor to the front door. He opens the door, ringing the bells attached to the top, about six inches with his booted foot securely behind it and his cleaver clearly visible. "There's a lot of Benedettos in New York," he says, still suspicious.

"Do you know a Benny or Dominic or Willie Benedetto?"

"You guys cops?" he asks, moving the cleaver behind his back.

"No. We're actually in New York from L.A., shooting for a TV show, and I'm trying to look up some people related to a friend of mine there."

"What show?"

"Oh, it's not on the air yet. It's called, er, *CrimeBusters*," I say with hesitation, leaving out the stupid *psychic* part of the title.

"Yeah, well, those Benedettos, I don't know them. Never heard of them," he says emphatically. "Are they in trouble?"

"No, no. Just, er, ah, a friend is sick and he's trying to get in touch with them."

"Yeah, well, no relation," he says, removing his foot from the door. "You might want to try a fish store up in the Bronx, on Arthur Avenue. That might be Benedetto's, too. Bye," he says, closing the door in a sharp punctuation to his statement, clanging the bells hard.

"Thanks!" I shout so he can hear me through the glass as he walks back to the rear of the store.

"What was that all about?" Smitty says as we continue on our way.

"Shit. This is getting interesting. Some real Mafia intrigue over here," Joe says, lighting another smoke.

"Nah, just a little inquiry regarding a friend who might be dying. I'm just trying to see if he's got any relatives who care anymore."

At Puglia's, we walk past the three-hundred-pound lady and take our seats at a long common table. The guy sitting next to me is digging his fork into an actual cooked goat's head. Joe's and

Smitty's eyes are as wide as antipasto plates as they gawk at it. Which reminds me: I've got to pick some brains on Arthur Avenue. Why would Benny tell me he was from lower Manhattan if he's really from the Bronx? I never knew anybody from the Bronx, Queens, or Brooklyn who would claim they were from Manhattan, even if they lived there for years. The only people who say they're from Manhattan when they aren't are usually from Jersey, upstate New York, or some other godforsaken place they're too embarrassed to fess up to.

Back at the hotel, I notice there's a message on my phone. It's Wendy, telling me that she's gotten another bad report from the network, and Karen Marshall says that our budget's being cut back on *Psychic CrimeBusters*, too. In her kvetching—after she's done bitching about the network and Karen, and the fact that her Ferrari broke down on the 405 again—Wendy also says something that shakes me to the core—she begins warning me not to go into any overtime with the crew, and to come back a day early. She actually yells, "They better not find that damn kid and ruin our story!" That's a hell of a thought to run through my brain as I lay my head on my cushy pillow, close my eyes, and say my Hail Marys.

The phone scares the hell out of me. I look at the clock next to my bed and see it's after two A.M. Realizing that it's only after eleven on the West Coast, I quickly pick up, hoping it's Joan.

"I'm sorry to call so late, but I just got back from the hospital," Joan says, sounding exhausted.

"Joan, there couldn't be a time when you called that wouldn't be the right time. What happened? How's Benny?"

"He's got pneumonia, but the doctors think they can handle it in a few days. That's the good news."

"That's good news?"

"Yes. Johnny, Benny is in really bad shape. I pulled a doctor aside. His cancer is everywhere. Lungs, brain, lymph nodes, liver, he doesn't have much time left."

"How long?"

"They don't know, but if it was this week, they wouldn't be surprised. It could be a week or two months, but not much more."

"Shit. I feel terrible. Does Benny know?"

"Yeah, he knows; the doctor told me so. But Benny pretends everything is going to be fine. He said next week he's going to take you and me to his favorite restaurant in Malibu to thank us. It's so sad, Johnny . . ." Joan's voice trails off.

"God, I wish I were there with you, Joan."

"I wish you were, too. Johnny, Benny asked me to ask you to get him something from the Bronx."

"Really?"

"But I think he must have been delirious, because it makes no sense."

"What is it?"

"He says he wants you to make sure you buy it on Arthur Avenue."

"I'm all ears."

"Johnny, it makes no sense."

"Let's hear it."

"He wants an extra munchkin kit."

"What?"

"That's what he said. His voice was very soft and raspy, but that's what he said. An extra munchkin kit."

"Extra munchkin? And he said to get it on Arthur Avenue? Extra munchkin? Extra munchkin. Shit! *Extreme Unction*. That's it."

"What."

"It's not extra munchkin. It's Extreme Unction. They sound almost the same, it's just that the *extreme* is Latin, and the pronunciation is *extrem*."

"What in hell is it?"

"That's just the point. It's to keep you from going to hell. It's a shrine that's usually hung on the wall. A couple of my aunts had them in their bedrooms. It's an ornate wooden box with a picture of Jesus or Mary, and there's sort of a hidden compartment that contains all the items needed for last rites."

"I know what that is."

"Yeah. It's got beeswax candles, holy water, holy oil, six balls of cotton, crumbled bread or salt, a crucifix, preferably made of wood from the olive garden at Gethsemani where Christ wept."

"Are you serious?"

"Dead serious."

"How do you know all that?"

"I was an altar boy. The last generation of Latin-speaking altar boys, I may add."

"Oh, and he also wanted a crucifix to hang around his neck, but he asked me to get that for him."

"That's strange. Benny recoils like Dracula from any mention of religion."

"That's what happens. I see it all the time. Many people facing death find God. Or hope to."

"Oh, yeah. You must see that in your work all the time," I say, remembering that in her work as a psychologist and as a nurse she must often deal with people facing their own demise.

"I've got to get some sleep."

"Me, too. I miss you, Joan. And thanks. For everything."

"Good night. I miss you, too. Dream a little dream for me," Joan whispers.

"I will," I say as I hang up the phone.

That's certainly as puzzling as it is sad. Benny knows he's on the way out, and he's asking for an item that most modern Catholics don't even know anything about. Extreme unction is one of the seven sacraments of the Roman Catholic Church and one of those old-world traditions usually maintained by only first-generation European immigrants. My mother's older sisters kept the extreme unction shrines on display after their husbands died, and they began preparing for their own deaths first by wearing only black every day when at home. It was a strange sight to go into the bedroom to put our coats on the bed, as we always did in the winter, and see the extreme unction shrine just hanging over the bed, waiting to be put to use. It was almost as weird as when one of my aunts had her own name put on the gravestone after her husband died, minus the date of death. That was an unnerving sight for a ten year old as he watched his uncle being lowered into the ground, his wife looking as though she was ready to jump in with him.

I shower and shave, and I'm ready to meet Smitty, Joe, and Milo in the lobby for our drive to Long Island, where Milo will attempt to channel some psychic impressions on location to go with his on-camera psychic reading.

First stop is on the north shore of Long Island, just above Shirley, so Milo can walk along the shore in one of his "trances" while holding a photo of the lost girl on his forehead. Thinking this could be just a little bit melodramatic, I ask Milo to merely hold the photo in his hand and occasionally glance at it. I'm glad he didn't bring his turban. After about a half hour on the north shore, we head to the south shore along the beautiful Atlantic coastline. Milo does pretty much the same thing: walk, look at the photo, look up in the sky, hold up his finger in discovery, walk a few paces, stop, look at the photo, etc., etc., etc. It looks hokey as hell, but it will probably cut together okay.

Before heading to the Long Island Rail Road tracks to do the same thing there, we take a break at Howard Johnson's for a quick cup of coffee and a pee. I figure I should call the home office to get my latest marching orders. Wendy is excited to tell me that River has set up an interview tomorrow with the missing girl's mom at her house in Shirley. The desperate mother said any publicity would be good and added that she wouldn't even mind using a psychic. Wendy also says she had to lay off River due to budget cuts. Oh well.

Milo is thrilled that we're involving him even more with the story, and he puts even more effort into his reading at the railroad tracks by quivering and jerking his head while in his trance.

We set our time to pick up Milo tomorrow and drop him off at his home in Astoria, Queens. For someone who claims to be a psychic stockbroker, you'd think he'd live in a Park Avenue penthouse instead of a row house on Astoria Boulevard. Since it's almost dinnertime, I figure Smitty and Joe will be up for a trip to the only real Little Italy left in New York: Arthur Avenue, Bronx, New York.

Arthur Avenue is the name of an area of the Bronx right next to the world-famous Bronx Zoo. Unlike Manhattan's Little Italy, which has become a touristy parody of itself, Arthur Avenue is still the real deal. In the seventies, when the rest of New York was falling prey to the worst kind of street crime in its history, Arthur Avenue was kept safe only because of grassroots vigilantism backed by local mobsters. If you messed with anybody on Arthur Avenue, Belmont, 187th Street, or any of the streets considered part of Little Italy, you received instant justice and more than likely were never heard from again. There were legendary tales of captured muggers turned into chum and dumped off a motorboat near City Island. Arthur Avenue also has some of the finest mom-and-pop Italian restaurants this side of the Coliseum in Rome.

I convince Smitty and Joe that it's safe to park anywhere and walk around the neighborhood before we decide where we want to eat. The smells range from repulsive, like walking behind the fresh-kill poultry shop, to deliriously delicious, as in walking past any of the many Italian bakeries. First stop is the Arthur

Avenue municipal market. From the outside, it looks like the entrance to the motor pool on an army base. No signs except a tiny plaque with the simple engraving ARTHUR AVENUE MARKET. But once you step through the front door, you're immediately immersed in the sounds, sights, and smells of an authentic Italian marketplace. The giant warehouse-type space has a concrete floor with a layer of fresh sawdust on top. Even the concrete floor is ancient, to judge by the size of the large pebbles used to mix the cement. The different establishments are set up on old wooden stands constructed with rough two-by-fours painted green. Some are overflowing with fresh fruits, vegetables, flowers, nuts, herbs, and spices. Others are stocked high with Italian cookware, olive oil, and even underwear and socks. Along the perimeter are the most permanent vendors: bakeries, butchers, fish stands, and pizzerias. The owners hawk their goods loudly and aren't shy about yelling at shoppers who squeeze the tomatoes a little too hard or look like they might be getting ready to stick a few garlic cloves in their pocket. The butcher shop has on display a bizarre array of animal parts, giving it an aura of dark mystery: goat heads stripped of their skin, huge trays of brains, giant cow tongues lined up neatly in a row, and baby lambs gutted but still with their furry white coats and cute faces intact.

"You grew up around here?" Joe says as he eyeballs a tray of hearts.

"Not too far away, though in a different neighborhood entirely. But because my mom's Italian, we spent a lot of time over here," I say to Joe, who is bent over, taking a closer look at the tray of gluttonous organs on display.

"What's tripe?" he asks me.

"It's the stomach lining of oxen," I tell him.

"My mom bought all this same stuff in South Central," Smitty says as we pass a large display case filled with freshly killed ducks. "She told us it was soul food."

"It is soul food. It's food for the soul of peasants all over the world. It's how poor families fed their families by using the parts of the animals the rich folks didn't want," I say, watching Joe light a cigarette and shake his head.

"I grew up eating ham on buttered Wonder bread," Joe says. "No wonder you guys are so whacked."

Dusk is beginning to fall on Arthur Avenue, and some of the stores, like the bakeries, are beginning to close up shop. The restaurants are lighting their neon signs and putting the daily specials on easels or chalkboards in the windows. As Joe and Smitty stop to pick up a few things at a newsstand, I notice that down the block is a religious-article store. *The* religious-article store on Arthur Avenue where Benny wants me to buy the extra munchkin kit.

"I'll be in that store where the guy is closing his awning," I say to them. Smitty gets out the *New York Times*, and Joe opens the latest *Penthouse* to the centerfold.

The store looks as though it has been in business since the building was built, and it is definitely prewar. A short, stocky old man with thick glasses and the map of Italy across his face is cranking an awning shut.

"Are you the proprietor here, sir?" I say to the man as he wrestles with the long, odd-shaped crank.

"Yeah. You need something in particular?" he asks, giving the rusty rod an extra jerk.

"Do you have any of those extreme unction shrines?"

The man turns to me like I just told him I was interested in buying a Cadillac for cash. "Yes sir, step right this way," he joyfully proclaims as he bows and motions for me to step through his front door. "We don't have much of a demand for those anymore, but I always keep a few in stock," he says, moving a cardboard display loaded with cheap tin medallions of St. Christopher, the Blessed Mother, and Jesus blocking a cupboard door. He slides open the door, and hanging there in a row are three extreme unction shrines. Each one is about two feet high, about a foot wide, and look to be six inches deep. They also sport a two-dimensional statue behind decorative glass. The one on the left is a copy of Michelangelo's *Pietà*; the one in the middle is Christ with his heart exposed; and the one on the right is Mary and Joseph with the baby Jesus. On the front is a small door on the lower six inches, each with a scene of the Last Supper. "These are all handmade in Italy. They come fully equipped," the man says as he opens a small cabinet door on the bottom of the shrine, revealing all the essential items needed to conduct the last rites. "We have the holy water and holy oil for sale, too. And the cross is made from the wood of the olive trees in Gethsemani. You can't even get these anymore. They were made by a certain order of nuns in northern Italy, but they switched over to making wine. More profit," he says softly, including me in some inside information.

"Are they all the same price?"

"Yup. Two hundred twenty-five dollars each."

"Wow. Two-twenty-five? That's a lot of money."

"Yeah, but look at all you get. The sculpture in the box alone is worth a hundred. You buy this stuff separately, and see what it adds up to. Let me show you something," he says, opening a drawer behind the counter and pulling out a black velvet box. "See this crucifix? It's the exact same one as in the shrine. Made from the olive-tree wood in Gethsemani and everything. Seventy-nine bucks. See what I'm talking about? I tell you what. You seem like a nice kid," he says, just as Joe and Smitty walk in front of the store's window and wave to me. "Are those your buddies?"

"Yeah. Actually, we're part of a TV crew. We're in town from L.A."

"Hey! No kidding. You know, we get a lot of Hollywood stars around here. Scorsese, he comes around here a lot. They shoot movies around here all the time. De Niro I see all the time. What show is it?"

Not wanting to sound like the total loser that I am, I decide to cheat it just a little bit again. "It's a show called *CrimeBusters*. You know, like *COPS*."

"I like that show, *COPS*. Catch them crooks. That's good. You gonna take this back to L.A., or is it for somebody here in the Bronx?"

"It's for a friend in L.A., unfortunately."

It just occurs to me that this guy has probably been here as a shopkeeper since the Depression, and if Benedetto's Fish Store ever existed, he'll probably know about it.

"Have you ever heard of a fish store around here called Benedetto's?"

"Are you kidding? Sure. They were right around the block, on 187th, until maybe the seventies. They must've been there for forty years. Sure, I knew them pretty good. In fact, one of the kids still lives around here. Look down the block," he says, taking me over to the front window, where Smitty and Joe are looking on in wonder, and points down the street. "See that bar down there, across the street? It's called Tony D's Lounge. You'll probably find him in there."

"Really. Um, did he have an older brother?"

"Oh, yeah. Poor kid. Died years ago. I don't remember how, but it was something tragic. So can I wrap one of these up for you? You know, if I ship it to you, you don't have to pay sales tax. And I tell you what—I'll knock off ten bucks because you seem like a nice kid."

"Okay. Yeah. Good idea. Ship it, then."

"Which one?"

"I'll take the one with Jesus exposing his heart."

"Yeah, that's beautiful, that one is. I tell you what, I'll throw in the holy water and the holy oil, too. Just fill this out, give me your credit card, and we're good to go."

It takes only a few minutes to finalize the deal, and Smitty and Joe are ready to chow down. But before we go into the Half Moon for our dinner, I've one more stop to make: Tony D's Lounge.

From the outside, Tony D's looks pleasant enough. Clean white brick exterior with a black awning above a darkly tinted window in front, featuring a red neon sign that reads COCKTAILS. The front door is painted black with a diamond-shaped window. There's a sign right under it that reads 21 AND OVER. DRESS CODE ENFORCED.

"How could a place like this have a dress code?" Joe asks after we witness a chubby, bald, middle-aged guy wearing shorts and flip-flops entering the establishment.

"That's just to let you know that you'll get thrown out on your ass if they don't like your looks," I tell Smitty and Joe, who have decided to wait outside while I go in to look for Benny's brother or at least somebody who has heard of Benny.

Obviously, if Benny told me his brother was dead, something awful must have happened between them. I know a couple of my uncles didn't talk to each other for twenty years after an incident, though no one can even remember exactly what happened. And when one uncle was on his deathbed, the first person he asked for was his estranged brother. I think Benny's brother would want to know if his only brother is about to die.

"You guys stand over there, so that you're visible through the window, and give me exactly fifteen minutes," I tell Joe and Smitty, pointing to a parking meter in front of the window.

"I feel like I'm in a Scorsese movie," Joe says, laughing.

"Let's hope it doesn't turn into a scene out of *Goodfellas*," Smitty says solemnly.

"If I'm not out in fifteen minutes, come inside, see if I'm stuffed in a toilet, check the Dumpster in back, then call 911," I say, only half kidding.

"Johnny, don't you worry," Joe says with mock seriousness. "If you're not out in fifteen minutes, Smitty will take care of everything. I'll stay here and keep a lookout."

"Thanks," Smitty and I say in unison.

The place is almost pitch-black. Most of the light comes from a jukebox on the wall opposite the bar. Frank Sinatra is singing "My Way." The bartender, a young Italian guy with greased-back jet-black hair and a black shirt-jac with silver trim, shoots me a look, then looks out the window. No doubt he notices Smitty and Joe hanging out by the parking meter. There are about seven or eight men at the bar, all at least twenty years older than the bartender. I take a seat at the end of the bar, with four bar stools between me and the rest of the patrons. The local news is on the television hanging from the ceiling with the sound off.

"What'll ya have?" the bartender asks, wiping his hands with a small white towel.

"Just a Bud," I say, putting a ten-dollar bill on the bar.

The bartender grabs a longneck, places a coaster with both the Yankees and a Bud logo on it in front of me, and puts down the bottle.

"Two bucks," he says as he takes my ten. He doesn't ring it up on the register but gives me my change and puts it next to my bottle. I'm no fool. That way they don't report as much income on their taxes. But he must be the owner or the owner's kid, because only an extremely trusted employee would have the authority to do such a thing.

I take a sip from my bottle and notice the rest of the patrons down the bar from me: a few in nice clothes, like they just got off work on Wall Street, and the rest in jeans and sweatshirts or those fancy velour jogging suits; one guy wearing shorts. There's a lot of laughter, ball-breaking, and cursing, just like a bar in my old neighborhood in the late afternoon. There are a couple of guys who could be Benny's younger brother. The guy I'm leaning toward resembles Benny the most in size and stature. He's in his forties, with a devilish goatee and a dark greasy ponytail that goes halfway down his back. Even though the guy looks like he's just over 150 pounds, his arms have unusually large muscles, with veins protruding like a weight lifter's. He has a tumbler of whiskey in front of him, and he seems to be the alpha dog of the bunch. I can tell by the group laughter after he speaks that his loud curses and funny put-downs make him the center of attention.

I motion for the bartender. He comes over and takes a peek at Smitty and Joe hanging outside before giving me his undivided attention.

"I'm looking for a guy. I've never met him, but he's a brother of a friend of mine out in L.A.," I say politely.

"Who are you? And who are those guys outside?" the bartender asks bluntly.

"I'm sorry. My name's Johnny Koester. Those two guys work with me on a TV show."

"Like what TV show?"

"It's, er, called *CrimeBusters*."

"Oh yeah? How come I never seen it?"

"It'll be on in a couple of months. It's a new show."

"So who you looking for?"

"His name is Benedetto."

The bartender's poker face doesn't give me a clue as to whether he's ever heard of a Benedetto. He looks at me, looks at Smitty and Joe through the window, and says, "Doesn't ring a bell. But I'll ask around." He walks back to the regular crew and starts whispering and nodding in my direction.

I'd be lying if I said I wasn't a little nervous. Okay, a lot nervous. But I just take a few more sips and listen to Frank singing "Summer Wind," trying to look like I don't give a shit what happens. Suddenly, the guy with the long greasy ponytail and well-defined arms pushes out his stool and begins to take a walk toward me. Now I'm way beyond nervous and approaching scared shitless. He's got the look of someone who knows how to instill fear in a stranger. He has Benny's deep-set eyes, tattoos on his arms, and a look that tells me he likes the ladies and the ladies like him.

"You looking for Benedetto?" he asks me directly, from about two feet away, with both of his hands stuck in the small of his back, which pushes out his chest.

"Yeah. If I'm right, I think I have some information this Benedetto might want to have," I say, quickly realizing this sounds way too much like a Scorsese film.

"Who exactly do you know, and who exactly are you looking for?"

"I have a neighbor in Los Angeles. His name is Benny Bennett. But I think his real name is Dominic Benedetto. And he has a brother named Willie. His family used to own a fish store around here. He used to hang with a priest named Father B."

The guy begins to clench his jaw, and a vein pops out in his neck, but he maintains his deadpan expression. "So, big fucking deal. You know somebody. What is it you want?"

"Are you his brother?" I ask loudly, thinking I'm on to something.

"Keep your voice down!" he says, sidling up next to me. He take a seat. "What do you want?"

"I want to tell Benny's brother something."

"Just say it. Go ahead. But say it really softly."

"Benny is dying. He's only got a little while to go. He's got cancer. It's advanced. Everywhere. I hate to tell you this, but he's selling off your Giants stuff. That is, if you're his brother. I mean, I think I'm the only one he's selling it to, but I'll give it back to you if you want. Look," I say as I pull out my personal business card, "here's my name and address. You can call me. I'll be back there in a couple of days."

He discreetly takes my card and shoves it in his front pocket. He's looking down at the bar and says quietly, "Does he have any distinguishing characteristics?"

"He's missing a couple of fingers on his right hand."

"Did he tell you how he lost them?"

"Just that it was an accident in the store."

He looks up at me and shouts, "My fucking brother's been dead for thirty years," and as he screams it, everybody in the bar looks over at us. He then pulls up the sleeve of his shirt, revealing two tattoos. The one on top is the Yankees' top-hat logo, and just under it, written in flamboyant script, is *Dominic B. 1940-1962 R.I.P.* I stare at both tattoos in shock as he pushes his sleeve back down. He leans in to me, puts his hand on my chest, and I expect the worst. But instead of making a crazed threat, he whispers to me almost affectionately, "And I ain't never been no fuckin' Giants fan. Only an obstinate, bullheaded son of a bitch would be a Giants fan in this neighborhood. And only a stubborn little prick would pick Tony Bennett over Francis Albert."

He takes his hand off my chest and goes back to his gang, where he is met with silence, and I get the message that my fifteen minutes are up and I better get my ass out of here.

"Thanks," I say to the bartender, leaving eight bucks next to my glass. "See you next time."

I head out the door, feeling their stares on the back of my neck, and walk past Joe and Smitty. "Come on, let's get out of here."

"Shit, am I going to get shot?" Joe asks as they follow me across the street, cutting through traffic.

"Not if you keep moving," I say, jumping onto the sidewalk.

They follow me to the Half Moon, and we manage to have a nice meal once I fill them in on everything I can tell them about me, Benny, Joan, and the boys at Tony D's. I tell them almost every detail, except for the fact that I gave that guy my card with my home address and phone number. I don't want them to know how stupid I really am.

Chapter Nine

I CAN HARDLY SLEEP all night. Besides being in a strange bed, and for the first time in my life a stranger in my own city, the thought of presenting Milo as a psychic crimebuster who may be able to assist this helpless mother willing to try anything, no matter how hopeless, has me tossing and turning until just before my travel alarm clock begins chirping. Not to mention that I'm actually going to have to interview this poor woman, who's facing the death of her own child every waking moment.

We pick up Milo in Astoria and hit the Long Island Expressway for our hour or so trip. I'm surprised Wendy was able to book this interview. But I'll bet it came down to Wendy playing her "You might remember me from my show *My Daughter the Secret Agent*" card, as she is wont to do when required.

"Hey, are we going to visit Laverne, too?" Joe asks as we approach the exit for Shirley on the LIE.

"Ooh, that's funny! Laverne and Shirley! That's funny!" Milo says between chuckles.

Kimmie Tambini was abducted in front of an empty lot across the street from her house on Orloff Avenue in Shirley, where she lived with her mother, Cathy, and her nine-month-old baby brother. Cathy is a single mom, and her ex-husband has already been cleared of having anything to do with the kidnapping. There's a dirty red vintage 1975 Monte Carlo in the driveway and a black van parked in front of the home. It must be a law enforcement vehicle.

I tell the guys to stay in our van while I go knock on the door. A man in a black windbreaker with an FBI patch on the front and a walkie-talkie in hand answers. He's a large man with a bushy mustache that hangs down almost to his bottom lip.

"How can I help you?" the FBI agent asks.

"I'm Johnny Koester with *Psychic CrimeBusters*," I grudgingly reply.

"Come in," he says coldly as he closes the door behind me and leads me into the kitchen.

A young female FBI agent, also in an FBI black windbreaker, is assisting a woman I assume is Cathy, feeding a crying toddler in a high chair; the tray is a mess of pureed fruits and vegetables. Despite the piercing cries from the boy, he appears to be a welcome distraction to the two females.

"Cathy, this is Johnny Koester, the gentleman from the TV show," the male agent says.

Cathy doesn't get up but gives me a wave and a weak smile as she tries to dump a few more splotches of food into the kid's mouth. "Thanks for coming. I'll be through in a minute," she says, sneaking a spoonful of orange stuff through his lips, then wiping her hands on a towel. "I asked around, and Susan and Eric here told me that as long as I'm careful about what I say, any media publicity could help. Even, er, ah—"

"I know, even *Psychic CrimeBusters*," I add.

"Yes, well, you know. What would you like to do?"

That's a good question. I don't have much prepared, and I feel like an intrusive moron bothering this terrified woman for the sake of our stupid TV show.

"Well, I'd like to interview you. Here in the kitchen is fine. Just the normal questions. How it happened, your reaction. And, er, any message you might have for Kimmie or the kidnapper—"

Cathy immediately bursts into tears and is aided by Susan, the female FBI agent, who embraces her like a family member.

"I should tell you right now," says Eric, the male agent, "we'll guide you about what to ask and what not to ask. And we'll also help Cathy with her answers. You should also know about some other procedures. See that phone?" He points to a black phone sitting on some kind of black box that has several long wires protruding from it, leading out a door into another room. "That phone is hot. Every call that comes in here is evidentiary. It's being recorded and instantly traced. Anytime that phone rings, you are to stop what you're doing, be quiet, and let us take over. Got it?"

"Got it. Can I go get my crew? Oh, wait, I almost forgot. We have a, er, psychic who is going to do some kind of reading, with Cathy or without her, whatever works, and see if he can get any psychic impressions that might aid in the case. Is that okay, Cathy?" I ask, noticing the look of bewilderment on the faces of both agents.

"Well, I guess. It couldn't hurt, could it, Eric?" she asks him.

"Let me just say that as a professional detective of sorts, I rely on hunches. If you want to call those hunches psychic impressions, fine. The more brains we got working on this thing, the better. We've get to get that little girl home, no matter what it takes."

"Yes, it's fine. I'll do it," Cathy agrees.

"Great, I'll go get the guys," I say, with Eric following me through the house and out to the van.

Milo is standing next to the van, reading Joe's palm. Smitty is sitting on a case reading *The Wall Street Journal*. It looks like the gear is ready to be moved into the house for the shoot.

"This is FBI agent . . ." I pause, realizing I didn't know his full name.

"Agent Eric Monahan. I only ask that you adhere to any instructions I or my partner, Agent Levine, give you. Let's go inside."

"Should I come in, too?" Milo asks, his hand raised as if he's attempting to get the teacher's attention.

"And who are you?"

"I'm the psychic."

"Yes. You, too. Maybe you should lead the way, being the psychic and all," Agent Monahan says.

Joe and Smitty grab their gear, trying not to laugh out loud, and we all follow Milo and the agent into the kitchen. The baby has been put in his crib for a nap, and Cathy is tidying up the mess he left behind.

"Looks like we should shoot from behind the table this way, considering the angle the sun is moving across that window," Smitty says, already setting up his tripod and lights, with Joe's assistance.

I notice that Milo has a large crucifix around his neck, which he definitely did not have before. I discreetly approach him and ask, "Isn't that a little over-the-top?"

"Oh, this?" Milo asks, surprised. "I find it helps a little in the credibility department."

"Fine. But I'm going to ask Cathy if she minds whether you wear it when you're doing your reading."

"No problem."

Cathy is about as calm as a woman trying to deal with a kidnapped child can be. She is sitting at the kitchen table with a small mirror, applying some makeup, while Susan is brushing her hair.

"We did lots of interviews when it first happened," Cathy says as she puts on lipstick, "but after a few days, they stopped coming. I can't believe it's almost two weeks now . . ." She begins to cry again.

"Come on now, Cathy. You just put your makeup on. You'll ruin it," Susan says, comforting her.

"I'll try to make this as simple as possible," I say, with Smitty and Joe in position and Cathy already with her microphone attached. "First we'll do a short interview. Just the basics. Milo, can you come over here?" He's borrowed Smitty's *Wall Street Journal*, probably checking out his latest stock predictions.

"Yes," Milo says, putting down the paper. "Milo Spivak," he announces to Cathy, shaking her hand. "I'm a psychic reader and professional stockbroker," he continues, probably trying to add to his credibility. "We'll talk," Milo whispers to her as he backs away.

"If you're up for it, Milo will sit with you. We can do it here, and he'll try to conduct a psychic reading to see if he can receive any impressions," I say.

"That's fine. Anything that might help. Anything, dear God. I'm okay."

"First, if you could state your name and spell it for me."

BRRRRRIIINNNNGGGG.

Everyone freezes and stares at the phone. The hotline.

"Nobody says a word. Susan, you go monitor in the other room. I'll stay here with Cathy. Cathy, pick up on three," Agent Monahan commands loudly, holding up his fingers. "One, two, three!"

Cathy takes a deep breath and picks up the phone. "Hello? What! Oh. Yes. Yes. Oh my God! Yes! Oh my God! They got her! She's alive! She's alive! Oh my God! Thank you, God! Thank you, God! Thank you, God!" Cathy is ecstatic, crying, jumping up and down. Agent Monahan grabs the phone from her.

"Go . . . Yes . . . What's her status? Ambulance? We'll be there in five. Over, " he says, hanging up.

I look over to Smitty, who has taken the camera off the tripod and is shooting everything off his shoulder.

"They've got her," Monahan says, trying to contain his emotions, despite the water welling up in his eyes. "A retarded church custodian had her hidden under a stairway. She appears healthy and unmolested. She's going to the hospital for examination."

Susan and Cathy are embracing and crying, with huge smiles on their faces. Smitty is shooting them with Milo in the background, his arms folded and a satisfied look on his face.

"Okay, guys," Agent Monahan says. "You'll have to leave. We're going to the hospital for the reunion. No cameras. Call us later for further inquiries."

We grab all the gear as quickly as we can and rush out the door. Smitty continues to shoot their every move until their van speeds off.

"Fuckin' Milo," Joe says, his arms full of cables, microphones, and lighting equipment. "You solved that one in a hurry."

"The Lord works in mysterious ways," Milo says. He holds his crucifix up high for all to see, and then kisses it.

"Did you get all that, Smitty?" I ask, knowing already that he must have come through.

"Everything. The phone call, reactions, tears, laughter, even Milo acting like he called God on his hotline to get her rescued."

The ride back to the hotel was quick and relaxed. We were all still flying high, having seen a mother go from the depths of despair, not knowing if her child was dead or alive, to the exultation of hearing the best news imaginable. I just hope Wendy thinks of it in the same terms. The kid was found, and according to Wendy, that was the one thing she was worried about. Welcome to Hollyweird.

I'm shocked. Wendy acts thrilled when I call her. According to her, Milo *did* solve the kidnapping. She *was* found when he arrived on the scene. We don't even have to lie! A simple re-creation will make that clear to America's viewing public. And the fact that we have the actual happy ending on-camera, with Mom jumping for joy at the actual moment of discovery, or, as Wendy calls it, the money shot—every news organization in the country offers Wendy cash for the use of footage of Cathy getting the call, so Wendy couldn't be more pleased. Plus, one of the conditions of usage is a lower-third on-screen super, with the words *Footage—Psychic CrimeBusters—BBX TV*; you can't buy publicity like that.

We take Milo out to dinner at the hotel restaurant and give him cab fare back to Astoria, although for about two seconds, he pretends he doesn't want it. Smitty asks him for some stock tips and, after Milo leaves, Smitty says he's out of his mind. Joe writes down every word he said. I can't wait to get back to my room and call Joan.

I tell her all the news about Benny's brother and finding the girl, and she tells me that Benny will be out of the hospital in a day or so, but all I can think about is how I can't wait to be next to her. Thank God, she feels the same way. We're getting an early morning flight back to L.A.

After two hours stuck in traffic on the way to JFK, then sitting on the runway for a half hour, then flying cross-country and waiting another half hour for our gear to come off the baggage carousel, I think I'll visit Joan at Safe Haven before stopping at home. She says it's okay, even though I'm jet-lagged out.

This is my first trip to Safe Haven since we became an item. The same kid is at the reception desk, and the tattoo on his neck is almost completely gone, as are the tattooed tears on his face, although the places where they once were are inflamed. He buzzes Joan on the phone, and she immediately emerges around a corner down the hall. She probably has another meeting today, because she's in her business attire. Seeing her all dolled up like some yuppie female exec being featured in *Forbes* throws me for a loop. Can this be the woman I'm madly in love with? From this distance, she looks like the kind of woman I used to sneer at on the subway in college. But as she gets closer, I can see those smiling eyes, her perfectly crooked smile, her long hair slightly blowing in the breeze her quick walk creates, and how her perky breasts bounce even under a pin-striped blazer.

"Hello, Mr. Koester," she says, stopping several feet in front of me while sticking out her hand for a handshake, which throws me into a momentary panic attack. Imagine if I felt this way about Joan and that was the only way she greeted me.

"Hello, Dr. Archer."

"Come this way," Joan says as she spins on the balls of her feet, which pumps her calves into sharp muscular mode. We enter her office, and Joan closes the door, backing up against it. "Hi," she says softly.

"You know," I say, inching toward her, "I don't think I ever kissed anyone wearing a pin-striped suit before. Unless you count an uncle at a funeral."

We kiss tenderly, making sure no one is able to hear our passion.

"How long were you gone?" Joan asks. We're still embracing. "A month? The spring?"

I sigh. "It felt like that to me, too."

"I have a meeting with the board of directors in a little while," Joan says. She smoothes her suit after we separate.

"Any news on Benny?"

"Yes. Benny's not well. He's coming home tonight. In fact, he wanted me to ask a favor of you—"

"Not tonight. My head's going to explode if I don't get to spend some time with you."

"I know. But of course, I told him you'd be there. Here's the info," Joan says. She hands me a piece of paper and puts her arms around my neck. "And if it's not too late, call me as you're leaving the hospital, and maybe I can meet you back at your place." Joan closes her eyes, and our lips barely touch, putting me in a state of pure ecstasy.

"How could I say no after that presentation?"

Joan opens the door and says loudly, "Thanks for coming by, Mr. Koester. Hope to see you again soon."

"Likewise, I'm sure," I say as I turn and head down the hall.

As I pass the receptionist, he says with a wink and a smile, "Thanks for coming. She'll be in a good mood now."

I'm glad today is considered a travel day and I don't have to go into the office. Once I took a nap, unpacked my bags, took a shower, grabbed a quick bite, and did laundry, it was already seven P.M. I figured if Benny was going to come home earlier, he would have called me. But it's time to call him to arrange his homecoming from the hospital.

"Benny Bennett, please."

A voice so weak I can hardly hear it comes across the line. "Who's this?"

"Benny, is that you? It's Johnny. Johnny Koester."

"Oh, General," Benny says with a little more strength and clarity. "Can you come get me?"

"When?"

"Now, I hope."

"I can be there in forty-five minutes."

"Call me when you get here. Don't bother coming to my room. Bye," Benny says, quickly dropping the phone into the cradle.

It takes a long time to find a parking spot in the garage at the hospital. And it's pretty far away. I figure I'll park, get Benny into the lobby, and then pull the car in front. I walk into the lobby, which is busy with activity. I notice a house phone on a far wall by the elevator and head for it. As I'm walking through the sea of humanity in the big-city hospital lobby, I see an old, thin man sitting in a stuffed chair with his eyes closed and mouth open. He has stubble on his face, and his bags are next to his feet. If it weren't for that black windbreaker, I don't think I would have recognized Benny at all. I've been gone less than a week, and Benny looks like he aged ten years.

I walk over to the chair and say, "Who won the World Series in 1962?"

Without opening his eyes, Benny says, "What, are you trying to kill me? Yankees beat the Giants in seven." He opens his eyes, which have sunk even deeper into their sockets. "You got the car?"

"It's in the lot."

"Let's go," Benny says, beginning a slow rise out of the chair.

"It's pretty far, Benny."

"That's okay. I'd rather walk to Poughkeepsie than sit here another five minutes."

It looks to me like just getting out of the chair has worn Benny out. I take his two old bags, one a canvas gym bag and the other a canvas sack from a grocery store, and walk alongside him through the doors to the parking garage. I can hear Benny breathing. He doesn't say a word, just shuffles along into the elevator and up the concrete ramp to my Woody.

"My old man had a real Woody," Benny says as I put his bags in the back. "Used to make deliveries with it. I bagged a few chicks in the back of that thing, too. How about you?"

"Me? Oh, well, a couple. But nothing this decade," I say, starting the car.

Benny blankly stares out the front window, and every once in a while mentions a sign or a store as we drive by. I can hear the mucus rattling around in his lungs when he clears his throat. He explains, "It's just a little frog."

It's almost nine o'clock by the time we arrive back at the apartment building. I help Benny to his front door, which has a few more take-out menus and phone books added to the pile.

"Could I come over in a few minutes?" Benny says with his key in his door.

"Well, Joan might come over—"

"Great! I'll be there," Benny says with as much conviction as he's had all night. Pushing the door as it scrapes along his floor seems to take all his strength.

"Okay. See ya later, Benny."

I'm afraid it might be too late for Joan. I know she's had a long day. But I want to see her so bad, I'll drive over there just to tuck her in if she wants. So I call her.

"Joan, is it too late?"

"Not for you, Johnny."

My heart soars. I remember so many women whom I thought I was crazy about. I was so bad at taking hints. They'd make up all kinds of excuses not to see me . . . dance class, dentist, relatives visiting, studying, too depressed, not feeling right, on and on and on. What a moron I was. Yet when it's the right person, anytime is the right time.

"Can you come over?" I ask.

"I don't know, Johnny. I have a big day tomorrow, and it's already late, and—"

"I understand. I'll tell Benny you can't make it."

"Okay. I'll come over. I have something for him. He might need it tonight. Bye."

Once again, Joan reminds me why I love her.

Benny must have mental telepathy. Two minutes after I've hung up with Joan, he's knocking on my door and sitting in his usual chair. This time, however, there's something missing: his brown paper bag. The fact that it's missing tells it all. The doctors must have decided to stop Benny's chemo.

Without his bag to fiddle with, Benny sits idly at the table, his hands palms down in front of him, eyes closed and head slightly forward. "Did Joan say anything about having picked up the, ah, thing I asked her to get?"

"She did say she wanted to bring you something."

Benny didn't respond.

"I'll put on some music."

"Not Sinatra," Benny squawks.

"Not Sinatra. I'll put Tony Bennett on."

"Good choice."

KNOCK KNOCK.

Benny's head whips around and points toward the door as if I may not realize that someone is there. I let Joan in, and she gives me a quick peck on the cheek as she reaches into the front pocket of her Cleveland Indians hooded sweatshirt. "I've got something for you, Benny."

Benny turns his body around in the chair to face her, an action that appears to be painful for him. "Joan, you're an angel."

Joan opens a small Ziploc bag and takes out a gold chain with a small crucifix. "I went to a store called Lighthouse Religious Articles. When I asked for a chain and a crucifix, she gave me the dirtiest look and said, 'No, you'd have to go to a Catholic store for that. We don't carry those,' as if I had asked for a satanic pentagram or something. Is this what you wanted, Benny?" Joan holds it out to him.

Benny holds his palm out just under the crucifix, and Joan lowers it toward his hand. Benny abruptly pulls his hand away, and the crucifix lands on the floor.

"I can't. I can't," Benny laments, staring at the cross on the rug.

Joan looks to me and makes a sad face, as though she is going to cry. I try not to make one of those faces, because I'm afraid I might.

Joan reaches down and picks it up. "Let me put it on for you," she says as she takes the chain and goes behind him.

"No. Don't," Benny says firmly. "Just give it to me. In the box. I'll put it on when the time is right. You hold it for me here. I'll ask you for it when I'm ready. Thanks," Benny says, then motions for Joan to get closer for a whisper. Joan whispers something back and takes the small box from Benny.

"So, Johnny, tell me, how was New York?" Benny asks nervously.

Joan crosses the room and stands beside me with her arm around my waist. She coaxes me over to the sofa as Tony Bennett sings softly in the background.

"It was weird. Oh, and we, er, stopped in Little Italy," I tell Benny, trying to gauge his reaction. "We went to Little Italy downtown and then up to Arthur Avenue. I got it, Benny."

A terrified expression comes across his face, which, in turn, makes Joan take notice.

"Got what?" Benny says, playing dumb.

"From the religious supply store, Benny," I say, not forcing the issue.

"Oh. Yeah," Benny says meekly.

"I did some talking to some of the shopkeepers." Joan squeezes my hand ferociously, wanting to know what's going on. "Do you remember a place called Tony D's Lounge?"

"I think I've got to be going," Benny says, standing and obviously beginning to panic.

Joan gets up and heads for him. "Benny, what's wrong, are you okay? Johnny, what are you doing?" she says with an accusatory look.

"Nothing. I'm sorry. Benny, look . . . I've got to tell you something."

Both Benny and Joan look at me like I'm the lord high executioner. Joan looks at Benny as if to say *Your call.*

Benny sits back down and glowers at me. "What? Tell me."

I get up and walk over to Joan, who is standing behind Benny's chair. "I talked to the guy in the store on Arthur Avenue. He told me . . . about your brother."

"What? That he died thirty years ago? Is that it?" Benny says nervously.

"No, Benny. That he hangs out in Tony D's. And he was there."

Benny's head drops so low, his chin touches his chest. He shakes his head slowly. Joan tenderly massages his neck. "How did he look?"

"He looks good, Benny. Wiry. He was hanging out with a bunch of guys, having a good time. I told him . . . about you."

"What? What did you say. Who heard you?" Benny says, extremely agitated.

I lower my voice to just above a whisper. "I told him you weren't well, Benny. I told him you were sick."

"What did he say?" Benny asks, his face a quivering muscle of nervous energy.

"It was strange. At first he asked a few questions, real softly so only I could hear. Then he said real loud, so the whole bar could hear, that . . ." I just couldn't say it.

"Say it, General," Benny says, with a knowing, confident look on his face.

"He said you had been dead for thirty years. He shouted it. Then yelled something about how only an obstinate prick would hate Sinatra and the Yankees, and then he showed me his tattoos."

"Tattoos? What tattoos?" Benny asks, halting Joan's massage.

"He had a few. But he pulled up the sleeve of his shirt to show me two of them. One was a Yankee top-hat logo. And the other said *Dominic B. 1940-1962 R.I.P.*"

"That asshole," Benny whimpers. He grabs both of Joan's hands on his shoulders, lowers his head, and begins a long steady sob. "I wish I could see him," Benny says in the middle of a whimper, "one . . . last . . . time . . ."

"Why don't you, Benny?" Joan asks, leaning down next to his face.

"Are you kidding? If I ain't dead, I'm dead! And probably Willie, too!"

Joan gives me a bewildered look.

"Benny, I gave Willie my card."

Benny comes to. He stops crying and quickly rises up out of his chair, surprising Joan with the speed of his movement.

"He knows where you live? Did you say I lived next door?" Benny asks, a maniacal look on his face.

"Uh, yeah."

"Oh, shit, General. I don't know. I might have to move. What if somebody finds out? Shit, I'm fuckin' dead meat."

"Don't worry, Benny. Nobody's coming after you."

"And how the fuck do you know, General?" Benny says as he walks to the door.

I have no answer.

Benny looks at us, shakes his head, and storms out.

"Johnny, sit right down and tell me what the hell is going on," Joan barks, taking the needle off the record.

"I don't know, Joan. But here's what I think. Benny did something. Or he saw something. So in order to keep breathing, he says he's dead, moves to California, changes his name, and never has anything to do with his past again."

"Come on. That kind of stuff only happens in the movies. That's pure Hollywood."

"Nope, that's pure Bronx. It happens all the time. Guy gets too deep into a bookie or a drug deal, or gets the wrong girl pregnant, and if he's lucky, he still gets to breathe somewhere faraway. If he's unlucky, he's down in the basement taking an acid bath."

"That's a lie," Joan says, obviously hoping I'll confess that's all it is.

"It isn't."

"Really?"

"Really. So Benny's been on the lam for thirty years. And now he's freaking out that I blew his cover. Which I did."

"How bad?"

"Well, the guy in the religious store and every guy in Tony D's know that I said that a Benedetto is alive and living in Los Angeles, and I think his brother might want to get in touch with him. The word is out. Fuck!"

"What?"

"I told them I worked for a show like *COPS*, called *Crime-Busters*."

"Oops."

"So now they think there's some kind of investigation, I'll bet."

"We better tell Benny."

"No. Not yet. Let's see how this plays out. In the meantime, did I tell you how much I missed you?" I say as I snuggle into Joan's armpit.

"Not now, Johnny," Joan says in a tone that scares me. A tone that tells me to stop. But I don't. I look up at her soft brown eyes. I take a chance on a head turn, but I'm going for a kiss. It works. We kiss, and I forget all about Benny and Milo and kidnappings and dead lambs in the meat case. All I can think about is getting so close to Joan that I want to become part of her.

"Let's go in the bedroom," I whisper.

"I don't know. This whole thing has put me in a bad mood," Joan says, stroking my hand. "Oh, all right."

We each make a pit stop in the bathroom before hitting the sack, and then we nestle nude under the sheets. Joan and I are both worn. I can see in the way Joan touches Benny and even the way she touches a stray cat that she has a pure nurturing quality that just exudes humanity. A quality that I don't happen upon often. Perhaps because of my upbringing on the streets. Our family was poor, but so was everybody else on the block, and nobody seemed to either mind or be aware of it. Babysitters? Sorry. From the time you were old enough to understand that you weren't supposed to walk out into traffic, which was about four and a half, you were outside making choices about what was right and wrong. And you soon realized that some kids were just bad. They were bad when they were four and evil by the time they were fourteen. Evil is everywhere, and you better be able to get away from it fast, even if it means kicking it in the balls first for a head start. I'm slow to trust anyone, but if someone proves themselves to be a friend, well, that's it. It's do or die together.

This is the first time I've been nude with Joan that I don't immediately have an erection. That could easily change with the mere suggestion of arousal on Joan's part, but right now, having Joan next to me like this is the most important thing in the world. I'd be the loneliest person on the planet if not for her companionship.

Joan readjusts her butt, and that suggestion of arousal is just a millimeter away. I'm behind her, and with the light leaking in between the blinds, I can admire the muscular tone and utterly feminine curve of her back. She has the body of a teenager and the wisdom of an Eskimo elder. I have my arms wrapped around her tight, with my hands on either side of her breasts. I swear, she seems to be purring as she inhales and exhales. I can feel her breath filling her lungs, and I imagine my air and blood mixing with hers as we lie here in silence.

"When will you get the extra munchkin kit?" Joan asks, clasping my hands with hers.

"I would think in a day or two."

"That could be tricky. Giving it to Benny."

"Maybe you should present it to him. He really likes you," I say softly in Joan's ear, wanting to tell her how much I really like her. Love her. "Joan?"

"Yes."

"I'm going to say something stupid again."

"Not now, Johnny. I need to get some sleep."

I push back from Joan a couple of inches and begin to turn her toward me. She has absolutely no makeup on, not a stitch of clothing, and she's partially illuminated by the pinkish mercury vapor streetlamp outside my window. I've never seen a more beautiful woman in my life.

"Okay" I say, crushed.

Joan takes her hand and brushes the back of it against my face. She looks me in the eye from four inches away. She's so close my vision is slightly blurry, adding to the otherworldly beauty of the moment. Joan parts her lips, and I see a small thread of spit connecting them and then coming apart. She closes her mouth again and closes her eyes as if she's in deep prayerful thought. Her eyes open, and she whispers, "Good night," then she closes her eyes, turns away from me, and gets into a comfortable sleeping position.

Garbage trucks make a racket first thing in the morning no matter where you live in the industrialized world, but five-thirty does seem extreme. Somehow Joan and I slept with arms and legs wrapped around each other all night long without waking up once. The sun is just coming up, and the streetlamp light has been replaced by streaks of early-morning sunshine that sparkles across Joan's body as it filters through the trees outside my window.

"Good morning," Joan says, still snuggling next to me with her eyes closed.

"Cock-a-doodle-doo," I say.

"Don't get any more ideas. I've got to go home and change before I can go into the office."

"What? All I said was cock-a-doodle-doo."

"Yeah, well, I remember that old joke from grade school."

"What's that?" I ask innocently.

"You know, 'What's the difference between a rooster and a whore? One says cock-a-doodle-doo, and the other says—'"

And we both say, "'Any cock'll do!'"

"I'm shocked at you, Joan! Such filth coming from those gorgeous lips," I say as I plant a morning kiss on her.

"That's nice. But I've got to go," Joan says, hopping out of bed. I pretend to still have my eyes closed as I watch her get dressed.

"No peeking!"

"Damn! Busted again."

Joan throws on her things and is ready to walk out the door.

"Let me walk you out," I say as I pull on shorts and a T-shirt and walk toward the door. We walk down the street hand in hand, toward her Thing. "What about the extra munchkin kit? Who's going to give it to him?"

"I think you should, Johnny. It will mean a lot to him," Joan says as she gives me a lovely kiss on the cheek.

"Okay. You're the psychologist," I say as Joan starts that god-awful-sounding VW engine.

"When's my next session? Of therapy, I mean?"

"We'll see. I'll have to check my schedule," Joan says as she pulls out of the spot and throws me a kiss.

I watch as she drives her bucket of bolts down Rodney Drive. She disappears when she makes a right onto Vermont. I'm standing in the middle of the street barefoot, unshaven, on a chilly Hollywood morning. I just hope the next time we're naked and in bed together, I get more than a "good night" and a polite kiss.

Chapter Ten

I HATE MEETINGS. And this is the one I've been dreading for days. Karen Marshall is coming over to Wendy's office, and we're going over the progress of *Shocking Hollywood Secrets* and *Psychic CrimeBusters*. Also attending the meeting will be the show's producer/writer/ director, Skip Darby. Skip used to be one of Hollywood's top young directors, having written and directed one of the highest-grossing independent movies of 1979, *Images of Death,* a slasher movie that mixed footage of actual blood-and-guts-drenched car-crash scenes, slaughtering of animals, and bullet-riddled bodies with a typically bad B-movie rip-off of every teen slice-and-dice movie made in the seventies. The fact that he's heading up our two shows illustrates how far he's fallen down the Hollywood food chain. I haven't heard anything about him since he was in the newspapers a couple of years ago, after he was caught in a car on a Hollywood side street with a transvestite hooker giving him a blow job. Apparently, that's what kicked his career into high gear again.

Wendy has her tits in full battle position: sticking about as far up and out of her black leather top as might be legal on the Strand at Venice Beach. Karen is wearing her idea of a power outfit, a red business suit with a frilly off-white blouse. Skip looks like he just crawled out from changing his oil: dirty jeans, a stained black T-shirt with the words NO! FUCK YOU! written in small white letters across the front, and a pair of Nikes that a skid-row thrift store would refuse to sell. I can tell that each of the three main characters thinks he or she is the smartest person in the room.

I take my place at the table and wait for the fun to start. Small talk about that morning's gossip in the trades and which young starlet is screwing which middle-aged director gives way to a long pause in conversation and a shuffling of papers. Wendy makes the loudest noise when she bangs her three-ring binder on the table, which gives her the floor.

"Just let me say, Karen, that Skip and I really appreciate you and BBX standing behind us with your support and encouragement in these two cutting-edge, risk-taking programs that I believe can and will make the industry take notice of this exciting new trend in reality television," Wendy says with all the authority of a seasoned politician addressing her biggest cash-cow donor.

Karen soaks it up, smoothes her ruffles, places both hands on her pile of papers, and responds, "I'm happy to report that BBX is thrilled by our progress and is anxious to move forward so we can all benefit from these breakthrough programs. It's clear to BBX that we've all been thinking outside the box, addressing core issues, keeping our eyes on the ball, and raising the bar." Karen is apparently pleased that she managed to string together so many clichés in one meaningless sentence. "No other network would have the courage to stand behind these shows."

"Puh-leeze! Courage? Try chutzpah," Skip says, slouched back in his chair, arms folded tight across his chest, waiting for a reaction from the table, which doesn't come. "What is this, the fucking debate team tryouts?" He reaches down, pulls a beat-up leather schoolbag-type briefcase from under the table and lays it flat in front of him. He pulls out assorted papers, ranging from loose-leaf pages to napkins, and arranges them in front of him in some kind of geometric order. After he lays everything out—it spreads from one end of the large table to the other—he leans forward, stretching his fleshy, hairy arms as far apart as possible, places his hands on the table, and bellows, "Let's cut to the chase. We're fucked."

"Goddammit, Skip," Wendy blasts across the table, jerking forward, which almost makes her tits flop out.

"No, Wendy! Let him finish," Karen seethes.

Now, this is the Karen I know. While Wendy uses riveted leather and torpedo tits as her battle gear, Karen's strategy of donning Catholic schoolgirl–type outfits as camouflage is much more effective. Most Hollywood players don't expect a big-haired, bad-dye-jobbed, freckle-faced female adorned in a June Cleaver blazer to be as ornery as a wolverine caught in a leg trap.

"I want to hear this straight from Skip Darby," Karen continues. "I mean, no one has heard much from him since, oh, let's see . . . the seventies! Unless you count the Hollywood division police blotter."

"Wendy!" Skip says in mock horror. "You didn't tell me the Bozo's anorexic evil twin sister was the studio executive in charge of production!"

Karen uncoils like a cobra. "Shut your yap, you unwashed, washed-up—"

"People!" Wendy screams, pounding her fist on the table, making the fat on her bare biceps jiggle. "Can't we all just get along? That's it! Skip, what is the problem? Please explain why you think we are *fucked*, as you so elegantly stated."

"Maybe because the first show airs in three weeks, and we need more money or we won't have a show," Skip says calmly, as though he hasn't been viciously insulted.

I sense by Karen's silence, and the smug look on her face, that her assault has ignited this situation according to plan.

"Skip, this is the first I've heard of this. We haven't even seen a rough cut yet. Why wasn't I told before now?" Wendy asks through clenched teeth.

"You didn't need to know until now, that's why. Now, can we put the past behind us and move forward?" Skip says soothingly. "Look, Wendy, do you know how many executive producers of feature films that I've directed never got to see a thing until I was damn well ready to show them something?" Skip grasps the edge of the table, restraining himself.

"Oh, let me guess. None? Could that be it? Well, I'm not an executive producer of a slasher film that's being cut by slave girls in Sri Lanka. This is a fucking network prime-time special," Wendy says, her chest heaving rhythmically over her leather top.

"Skip," Karen says softly, patting her open production bible, "you know the network is supposed to see the segments three weeks out." She runs her finger along the clause on the page.

"You'll get your damn screening. Stop hounding me!" Skip blasts, pounding the table once.

Wendy doesn't react to his current tantrum and puts on a sweet face. "What do you want, Skip?"

"I need ten grand more for the psychic show. I want to do a half-day on location." He pulls a detailed production schedule from his flotsam and jetsam and pushes it toward Wendy. "I need fifteen grand more for the *Secrets* show. It's all in here." Skip holds up several more pages torn from a spiral notebook.

"We're already over budget, aren't we, Karen?" Wendy says, examining the papers.

Karen is shaking her head in disgust. "We're lucky if we can get five grand."

"I need at least five grand *each*," Skip deadpans, calling their bluff.

"I'll see what I can do," Karen says.

"Get me the money, and I can show you something in two days," Skip whispers as if they're his last words.

"I think I can do that," Karen says, closing her binder while beaming a satisfied smile.

Once Skip hears that, he's a different person, telling humorous stories about the moronic actors who are doing a wonderful job only because he tricks them into doing what he wants. And how only he could take the garbage he has to work with and turn it into something slick enough for network television. Everybody's suddenly best friends, and they're all so thrilled to be working together.

Thank God, nobody asks me anything. I'm afraid I might slip and tell the truth.

As the meeting breaks up, I happen to be walking out with Skip right behind me. He tugs on my arm, pulling me aside outside Wendy's office. "You're the kid who's doing the shoots and the interviews?"

"Yes, I am. I hope they're okay," I say, inching back just a little from his intrusive stance.

"Yeah. They're good. But take some advice from me. The crazier you look and act, the more money you get."

"Uh, thanks," I say. He opens the front door and walks over to a red Maserati sitting in a red zone directly in front of the office.

Finally, some advice I can use!

As I pull into my parking place at the apartment, it appears that Benny hasn't moved his car in days. I haven't seen him since last night, but I'm reluctant to knock on his door. Judging by his reaction after I told him I spilled the beans on him in Tony D's, he'll probably try and flush himself down the toilet. But his health has deteriorated so much, I'm afraid to just ignore him. When Joan comes over later, we can go over there and maybe clean up his place a little more.

There's a yellow note on my front door from UPS, saying that a package was dropped off with my next-door neighbors, the two old ladies. I haven't seen much of them lately, but I'll bet they've been keeping a close eye on the comings and goings of me, Joan, and Benny. I noticed their car was in their space, so they must be home. I knock on the door, and it quickly opens.

"Oh, yes. We have a package for you. It's a little heavy. Would you mind stepping inside and retrieving it?" Rosalynne says, opening the door for me.

"Thanks so much, Rosalynne. I haven't seen you lately. I've been busy," I say as I pick up the large cardboard box.

"I can see how busy you have been. We're moving, Mother and I," she says with an air of haughtiness.

"Oh, I'm sorry to hear that."

"Yes. The building has just gone too far downhill," Rosalynne says as if she's smelling something putrid.

"Yeah, well, there are still some good people here," I say as I step onto my own stoop.

Rosalynne closes her door without replying.

"Thanks again," I say to her door.

I get a razor blade from the kitchen drawer and begin to open the box. It's wrapped nicely. I remove the packing material and pull out the extra munchkin kit. Luckily, there hasn't been any damage. It really is a thing of beauty. Too bad every time you look at it, all you think about is death. The wood is dark mahogany. The faux sculpture behind the glass is pure white with soft flowing curves, except for Christ's exposed heart, which is blood red. I open the latch on the compartment door to see the cotton, crucifix, candles, silver candleholders, and two cruets, one marked HOLY WATER and the other HOLY OIL. I put the packing material back in the cardboard box and place the extreme unction shrine on the table next to the spot where Benny usually sits.

Even though it's brand-new, it has the smell of a musty antique. The dark wood looks as though it's been sitting in a storage room for a century or so. And the crucifix . . . well, if it's what it purports to be, which is made from wood in the olive garden where Christ wept as he pondered his fate just before he was crucified, the wood could be several centuries old. But I have my doubts about the authenticity of the Gethsemani wood. If every crucifix were actually made from those olive trees, the garden would have to be the size of an Alaskan forest and the olive trees as big as redwoods.

I can imagine how freaked Benny is now, thinking that the wrong people back home know he has surfaced again. I probably blabbed a little too much to the bartender, who I'm sure let everybody and his bookie in on the news about the resurrection of Dominic Benedetto and the fact that I work for a crime TV show.

I figure now's as good a time as any to present Benny with his last rites kit, and since I'm the one who might have accelerated the implementation of the device, it's more than apropos for me to give it to him.

To avoid the nosy neighbors getting a glimpse of it, I put it back in the box and walk over to Benny's.

I feel awkward standing in front of his door with this large box in broad daylight as people pass me coming home from work. Benny is taking his sweet time, and then the door jerks open. Little by little, scraping on the floor, as usual.

Despite the fact that it's daytime, the apartment is quite dark, and I can barely see Benny, since my eyes haven't adjusted to the darkness.

"Come in," Benny says in a monotone as he backs up.

I step inside and close the door. I put down the box on the floor in front of me. Benny has walked backward as far as he can. He has something heavy in his hand that makes his arm stretch straight down along his side. I can't make out what it is.

"Benny. I think you know what I have here—"

Suddenly, Benny collapses like one of those little puppets on a pedestal with a disk underneath, and when you push the disk up, the puppet buckles at every joint. Luckily, Benny is close to the wall, and his head and body just kind of slide down. Whatever is in his hand makes a loud thud as it hits the floor.

"Benny! Jesus! Benny, are you all right?" I ask as I rush to him, attempting to right his head and straighten him out. I look over, and just beyond Benny's reach, there it is: a gun. It's a big one, too. Looks like a cannon. Maybe a .357. We're lucky it didn't go off when it fell, or Rosalynne and Gertrude would have a SWAT team in here in no time. I go into the kitchenette, where there is an empty bottle of Dewar's next to the sink. I take a not exactly sterile dish towel and run some cold water on it. I rinse a glass that reeks of whiskey and fill it with cold water.

Bending over, I start to rub Benny's face and forehead with the wet towel. "Benny! Benny! Are you all right?"

Benny begins to stir and tries to talk but only mumbles instead.

I put the glass of water to his lips, but he doesn't respond.

"Benny! Benny! Dominic!"

His eyes shoot open, and his hands knock the glass out of my hand, spilling the water over both of us.

"Mom. Mom," Benny says, trying to shout.

"It's Johnny, Dominic. The general," I say loudly.

"Fuck," Benny says, holding his head with both hands. "What happened?"

"You fainted, Benny. Fortunately, you were against the wall and didn't crack your head wide open. Are you drunk?"

"No. No. Not anymore. Just hungover. Where's my piece?"

"It's right here, Benny," I say, holding the gun. "What are you doing with it?"

"Ah, it's, my, uh, protection, that's all. Just in case."

"Are you sure, Benny?"

I know it could have just as easily been Benny getting ready to do himself in. It would have made an awful mess for someone, but with that bazooka, it would have been quick.

"Of course I'm sure. Help me up, would ya?"

I grab Benny's arm, and I'm shocked to feel it's nothing more than bare bones, with absolutely no muscle or meat at all. Benny winces in pain as I use the wall to raise him up and then lead him over to a chair.

"I feel like I got run over by a garbage truck," Benny says, still woozy.

"Where does the gun go?"

"I keep it in the kitchen drawer, right next to the sink," Benny says, pointing.

"I'll put it back there. Is it loaded?"

"Fuckin' A it's loaded. I ain't gonna *scare* the bastards to death with it. That takes bullets."

I put the gun in the drawer and notice an ammo box with bullets spilling over. "What bastards are those, Benny?"

"I don't know yet, but I got a pretty good idea. There's something fishy going on around here. I've been seeing . . . people . . . and things. Something is up, and when I go down, I'm taking them with me."

"Benny, I'm not sure I should be hearing all this. You know, in case I'm called to testify, if you get my drift."

"Fuck it. This one will be an open-and-shut case, don't you worry about it. I know there's something going on. What's in the box?"

We both look over to the cardboard box sitting by the front door, next to a stack of newspapers and magazines.

"Oh, that," I say. "It's the . . . thing . . . you wanted from the religious articles store on Arthur Avenue. Remember that?"

"Yeah. Arthur Avenue. A piece of Arthur Avenue right there. Right back where I started."

Benny seems to levitate out of his chair and float across the room to the ordinary brown box adorned with nothing more than a shipping label and FRAGILE HANDLE WITH CARE printed on the sides. The room is still quite dark, but my eyes have now adjusted to the light level, which is basically whatever sunlight sneaks through the dirty windows, tattered orange drapes, and broken venetian blinds. The light filtering through the drapes has a quality not unlike that passing through dark stained glass. Benny stands over the cardboard box, drops his head with his eyes closed, and folds his hands in front of him. Much the same body language Catholic high school students have when they attend Mass but won't commit to a pew and only stand in the back of the church for the minimum amount of time, which would constitute having attended, in case a parent or teacher might ask. Benny's lips are moving slightly, as if he is praying. His lips stop moving, and he stands there silently for what seems like a minute. He looks over to me as if he's waiting for a cue. I remember being an altar boy in the second grade. We were always teamed up at first with older boys who would show us the ropes: when to kneel, stand, sit, get the water. Being rookies, we of course didn't ring the bells or pour the wine; that was for the older, more experienced altar boys.

"Should I open it?" Benny asks, still looking over at me with his hands neatly joined.

"I think so."

Benny slowly drops to both knees, grunting as he tries to find a painless part of his kneecaps to support his bony body. He carefully pulls back each flap of the box and bends them back, leaving a square pit of darkness in the center. Benny rubs his hands together, which reminds me of the way a priest washes his hands with water poured from a cruet by an altar boy. Benny wipes his palms on the front of his shirt, and as he pushes his arms forward, his hands are trembling. He places them palms down over the dark square where the shrine sits, and then reaches down into the box.

The wooden box is not light, weighing about seven pounds, and as Benny grasps it, I can see he is sensing its weight, unsure whether he'll be able to pull it out unassisted, in his kneeling position. The strain spreads from his arms to his shoulders and neck and across his face as he begins to lift the shrine out. He uses the top of the box for leverage as he finally pulls it up and places it in front of him. A glint of orange light slashes across the statue of Jesus behind the glass and stays for a couple of seconds on his red heart.

"This is something else. Beautiful. My mom had one of these in the bedroom. I didn't even know what it was until I was in high school. It was just one of those things a kid sees and doesn't think about or question. It was just there. And I wasn't even there when she got to use it," Benny says, clutching the shrine to his breast in a solemn embrace. "I missed my mom's death. And my father's. I couldn't go back." He turns to me. "Because I had my own death to deal with."

I guess it's time to start asking Benny questions again. "What do you mean by that?"

"I was dead. I had to be. I couldn't go to their funerals. If I did that, too many people could get hurt. Including my kid brother, Willie. Back then I didn't care. I wanted out. I hated everything around me. The thought of moving to California and starting over was the greatest thing I could imagine. I wanted to bury Dominic Benedetto. So I did." Benny tries to raise himself up from his knees while holding the shrine, and he almost falls over.

I grab his arm and help him stand up. "Did you change your name legally?"

"Had to. Started over. They told me as long as I shut my mouth, I wouldn't get hurt. And neither would my brother. That's what did it. The mention of my brother, those motherfuckers. And I knew they weren't bullshitting. I'd seen guys get it who didn't listen. I listened. I shut up. And never went back," Benny says as he shuffles over to a chair, sits, and stands the shrine on the table right in front of him. "This is really a nice one. Does it have all the extra stuff?" He opens the compartment door, revealing the cotton, the crucifix, candles, and the cruets. "Oh, yeah. Nice."

"What about Willie? Didn't he wonder? Didn't he try to look you up?"

"Nah. He couldn't. All he knew was I was on the lam. He probably thought I did something awful, and he didn't want to risk giving me up."

"Did you?"

"What?"

"Do something awful?"

Benny covers his face with his hands. The hand with the two missing fingers is prominent from my angle. "I didn't do something awful. I had awful things done to me. And I saw something awful done to somebody else," he says from between his hands, as if he's hiding behind a mask. "Please, General. Don't ever ask me about it. It's the past. What's done is done . . ."

"*Macbeth*," I say.

"What about *Macbeth*?" Benny asks.

"You know, Shakespeare? The play in which every evil deed generates another more dastardly evil?"

"Don't go intellectual on me *now*, General. Look, I want to hang this up next to my bed, but it's a mess in there, and I don't want you to see it. Plus, I don't have a hammer and nail. Give me a chance to clean up a little, and come back tonight and we'll put it up in there. Bring Joan, too. Would you?"

"Sure, Benny. Or should I call you Dominic?"

"Dominic is dead, General. Really dead."

"What about the gun? I don't like you with that gun, Benny."

"Don't worry about that. It's staying right there."

"Benny, I'm worried, you know, you might do something—"

"I ain't doing nothing stupid. Suicide's a mortal sin, General. You should know that. And I didn't get this shrine so I should wind up down there."

"Yeah. You're right, Benny. See ya later," I say, hoping to placate him as he sits staring at his shrine standing upright on the dinette table, surrounded by a bowl of cereal, orange juice containers, assorted dirty dishes and glasses, newspapers, magazines, and a lamp made of an old seltzer bottle like the kind the Three Stooges spritzed at one another. I remain at the door and open it slightly, which makes that loud noise and startles me almost as much as the fact that I'm leaving Benny with a loaded gun in a kitchen drawer. Benny doesn't turn as the daylight fills the room. He sits and stares at what I'm sure he hopes will be his stairway to heaven.

One of the advantages of living in this area is the close proximity to Griffith Park, a six-thousand-acre city park resplendent with hiking and bridle trails that zigzag across mountains and valleys. There's also the famous Griffith Observatory, the L.A. Zoo, two full-size golf courses, the Gene Autry Museum of Western Heritage, and even a vintage carousel that, like many of L.A.'s inhabitants, was transplanted here from back east. In fact, I read somewhere that when Babe Ruth found out he was sold by the Boston Red Sox to the New York Yankees, he was playing a round of golf on the Griffith Park links.

A ride through Griffith Park can be a joy, especially on a weekday, when it's not too crowded. Unlike most public parks in New York, roads go through most areas of the park, reminiscent of a drive in the country, complete with majestic vistas around every bend, and red-tailed hawks circling above.

Joan tells me this is where she does her running, which I hope to soon adopt as my own form of regular exercise in order to spend even more time with her. So I decide to put on sneakers and shorts. I've tried running before, but back in New York, it's mostly a fair-weather activity. Here, it's most definitely a year-round affair.

As I pull into the park, there's a stop sign about a hundred yards in. As soon as I stop at the sign, a woman appears in the open window on the passenger side. She's about sixty-five years old; has long gray hair and wears a T-shirt with a large-eyed kitten on the front. She's wearing oversize thick glasses, and except for the tape holding them together above her nose, she looks well groomed. She is carrying a supersize cup with a cover and a straw, and asks, "Can you give me a lift, please?" with her head completely inside the interior of my station wagon. "Please. I live in a trailer in the first stable outside the park. I got left over here, and my ride is gone. Please? Don't make me walk, fella, please?"

This is one of those moments for split decisions. No one would be the wiser if I just stepped on the gas and left her standing at the sign, waiting for the next car to come along. But in the moment of trying to decide, I thought of why I was in the park in the first place: to run, so that I can be closer to Joan. And being closer to Joan means being more in tune with her outlook on life, which tells me that Joan most certainly would open her heart and the door of the Woody to offer this poor old lady a ride.

"Okay, come on—" Before I can complete my sentence, she whips the door open and plops down on the seat next to me. I proceed through the intersection, and she's sitting quietly sipping her soda for about three seconds, then she explodes, "I told that motherfucker not to leave me there, that cocksucker son-of-a-bitch bastard. Who the fuck does he think he is? Hitting me there," at which point she raises her pink T-shirt with the kitten on the front, exposing her pendulous withered breasts, and begins to pound herself on the chest. "Hard! Hard! Hard! He hit me hard right here! That bastard!" she yells, throwing both arms up in the air and spilling the soda, which turns out to be cola, all over the interior of my car, including the dashboard and the headliner. Looking in my rearview mirror to make sure no one is behind me, I jam on the brakes.

"Last stop, Grandma!" I announce as I reach across her and open the door.

"But it's only just outside the park," she pleads, with an innocent look plastered across her face.

"Out. Now."

"Okay. Sorry about the drink," she says as she exits the car, closing the door softly behind her.

I came close to leaving rubber, which in this vehicle is nearly impossible. Maybe I'll start running tomorrow.

Back at the apartment, Joan has left me a message telling me that, yes, she will be stopping by this evening, and that she's hoping we can take Benny out to dinner. So that leaves me with two immediate tasks: getting my apartment tidied up, and warning Benny that he's going out into the world tonight.

It's been only a little while since I left Benny alone with his monument to his own death. I'm reluctant to knock on his door, in case he's still in a heightened emotional state. I would be, too. And in light of Benny's aversion—if not outright hatred—toward all things religious, it's rather amazing to witness him embracing religious icons from the past. Being a lapsed Catholic myself, I often wonder how my Catholicism will change once I discover that the end is near and I'm staring at death's door. But in my case, I have no hatred of religion, or for that matter, Catholicism. I just have a problem with the institutional and ritualistic aspects of the religion. My spirituality remains. I pray to Jesus and even to Mary as I recite my silent mantra of Hail Marys each evening. I can imagine latching on to Catholic rituals in my time of imminent death. The irony with Benny is, now that his cancer has eaten away his flesh, the more he looks like Nosferatu, the more he seems to desire the religion of his youth.

It's a beautiful spring afternoon. With my front door open, I can see Nina and her kid out by the pool, lazing in the late-afternoon sun. I haven't seen that biker puke come back again. Maybe a little borscht over the head is the right recipe for keeping jerks away. As I open my screen door to head over to Benny's, Nina turns and looks in my direction. She then tells her boy something in Russian and walks over to the fence toward me.

"Excuse me, Johnny," she says, her bikinied body glistening in body oil. "May I ask a favor of you?"

I take the extra two steps and stand on the other side of the fence from Nina. I'm trying very, very hard not to look at her breasts, which are vying for my attention.

"Hello, Nina. Yes, how may I help you?"

"My car is again broken. Could perhaps you give me ride this evening to work? My friend cannot drive me at last minute, and I hate to pay taxi."

"I'd like to give you a lift, but I do have plans," I say apologetically.

Nina takes a deep breath, which seems to inflate her breasts even more, and lets out a huge, sad sigh.

"Well," I say, catching myself staring at her boobs a second too long, "if you can go at around eight o'clock, my girlfriend and I would be happy to drop you off. Is it back, er, in the same area I dropped you off last time?"

"Yes, please."

"I'll knock on your door around eight."

"Thank you, Johnny. You a good guy," Nina says with a warm smile as she turns and sashays back to Mishka, sitting on the chaise longue coloring.

I push a new phone book away from Benny's front door and knock three times. Benny immediately opens the door about an inch.

"Hey, I was watching you there, General, you little devil. That's one white Russian that won't give you a hangover," Benny says from behind the dark one-inch space of his door.

"That's how rumors get started, Benny. I'm doing her a little favor tonight and—"

"And she's doing you a big one, huh?"

"Joan and I would like to take you to dinner tonight, Benny. Is that okay?"

"Sure. What time?"

"Be ready a little before eight. And we're dropping Nina off at work on the way."

"Nina. The white Russian?"

"Yes, Benny. So be ready, and when we get back, we'll help you around your house if you'd like."

"That's my goal in life right now. Being ready. See you then."

Just then Nina shouts over to me from the stairway as she goes up to her apartment, "Thanks, Johnny! See you at eight." The sound of Nina's voice prompts Benny to open his door enough to stick his head out and get a good look at her. Just as she starts to wave, her young son, whom she is balancing on her hip, grabs hold of the strap on her bikini top and pulls it down, revealing one of her breasts. She giggles and immediately pulls the strap back up as she steps inside her apartment.

"Wow. That's the best show I've had since the Orpheum burlesque house closed down. I'm looking forward to that ride tonight. You must have one understanding girlfriend. Bye-bye," Benny says, shutting his door. I hope he's right.

A knock on the door at seven-thirty means Joan has arrived. She's wearing a black T-shirt, a jean jacket with colorful flowered embroidery on the pockets, black karate pants, and black running shoes, which sounds terribly informal, but Joan has a way of making any outfit look upscale. And dead sexy. She takes one step inside my doorway, and before we speak a syllable, we are kissing passionately. After a few moments of making out, Joan rests her head on my shoulder and says softly, "I had such a bad day at work. A young girl who was with us for a few days last month was found dead. Hanged herself in an abandoned building. So sad. She was a beauty. I had to call her parents and tell them. Sometimes it's just too sad."

Joan's hair is like silk. She is quietly breathing long sighs as I stroke her long hair. If I could only will her strength and happiness right now.

"Are you sure you want to do this tonight? Haven't you been through too much already today? I can just tell Benny we'll do it another time," I say.

Joan looks up at me with a crooked smile. "You never know. There may not be another time. I'm fine. Wasn't there something else we were supposed to do tonight with Benny?" She crosses the room and sits on the living room sofa.

I follow her over and sit next to her. "Tonight's the night for the extra munchkin kit. Benny is anxious to get it up on the wall in his bedroom. He's busy tidying up so we can do it after dinner."

"You presented it to him this afternoon?"

"Yeah. It was heavy. He was reeling. And revealing."

"How?"

"He started telling me how Dominic was dead, how he has been on the lam in L.A. for thirty years, and even missed both his parents' funerals."

"Did he tell you why?"

"He said something to the effect that he had terrible things done to him and saw something terrible done to someone else. And to never bring it up again."

"That is heavy. What do you think?"

"I'm trying not to. But I have a feeling it's all part of his new-born religious fervor, and it just might resurrect some things from his past that he's been suppressing for all these years."

"The truth has a way of revealing itself, in spite of the darkness that tries to cover it up."

"Did anyone ever tell you that you're beautiful when you're metaphysical?"

"Not in this lifetime," Joan says, pushing me back so she's on top of me as we again play kissy-face.

"Oh, by the way," I say midkiss, "I offered a neighbor a lift on the way to the restaurant tonight."

"Oh, the old elderly woman next door?" Joan asks with a tender smile.

"Ah, not exactly. Have I told you about Nina?"

Joan's smile disappears, and her head tilts to the side with her eyebrows raised, as if she is anticipating an interesting moment. "No. But do tell!" she says, now sitting stiffly upright with arms folded across her breasts.

"Nina is the neighbor who has had a few run-ins with some biker dude, and Harriet the building manager wants to have her evicted."

"Oh, you're painting a lovely picture. Continue."

"I gave her a lift one day. To her . . . job."

"Which is?"

"I believe she is a . . . er, an . . . exotic dancer."

"And have you seen her, *er* . . . performance?" Joan says, sitting even more rigidly.

"No. Just dropped her off. And her kid."

"She has a child?" Joan asks. Her arms drop, and her body language transforms from defensive scorn to utter sympathy. "She's a stripper with a child. That's a rough one. Do you think she's a junkie or a prostitute?"

"I doubt she's a junkie. I have to admit, I've seen almost every square inch of her body when she sunbathes in her bikini." I can see Joan lapsing back into jealous-lover mode and immediately add, "I can't help but see her. She's right there in front of everyone with her kid a few times a week. She looks, er, healthy, to say the least. She could be a hooker, though. So?"

"So what?"

"Can we give her a lift?"

"Of course," Joan says sweetly.

As I head into the bedroom to grab my car keys, I feel an even deeper sense of love for Joan now that she's revealed she has a jealous side. The mere thought that Joan may find it upsetting that I would look at another woman both surprises me and gives me a sense of comfort. Joan? A bit jealous? Wow. Who woulda thunk it?

"Let's get Benny," I say to Joan. I take her hand, give her a kiss on the knuckles, and head for my front door.

"And don't think for a minute we're going to catch Nina at work this evening!" Joan says, kidding around as she waves a fist in the air.

"I know we won't. But Benny's a big boy," I say, closing the door behind us.

Outside of Benny's doorway, I can hear the movement of boxes and furniture and even see traces of light coming through his window. "Sounds like Benny is actually cleaning up in there," I say to Joan, who's standing on the bottom step. I knock hard on his door.

From behind the door, I hear Benny saying, "Who's there?"

"It's Johnny and Joan."

"Hold on a minute."

There's more commotion behind the door, with things being moved to and fro. Then Benny's door scrapes open a few inches.

"Benny, why don't you just look through the peephole and see who it is?"

"That thing hasn't worked for years. Hi, Joan. I'm really glad to see you."

"I'm glad to see you, too, Benny," Joan says, smiling.

"Let's go," I add.

"Okay. One more minute," Benny says, leaving his door open a crack, then returning a few seconds later. He comes out and pulls his door shut, locks it, then turns to face us. His hair is combed neatly and obviously has some kind of hair tonic on it. He's wearing a crisp clean shirt with the top button fastened, which exaggerates how thin his neck has become. Benny seems to be shrinking. His teeth look grayer and too large for his face. His cheeks are so high and sharp that the skin seems to be concave.

"I feel pretty good tonight. I'm actually hungry," Benny says as he puts his arm around Joan.

"You look great, Benny," Joan says.

"Benny, I told Nina we'd give her a lift on the way to the restaurant. I'll go get her and meet you guys at the car," I say, handing Joan the keys to the Woody. She and Benny slowly walk off together, Benny's arm still around Joan's shoulders.

I knock on Nina's door, and she swings it open before I can knock a second time. She is wearing a full-length red coat made of an iridescent material that goes almost to her ankles. She is carrying a garment bag and is wearing what my mom used to call a babushka over her hair, which is piled high on her head.

"Oh, thank you so much. You are on time. Can we go now?"

"Yes. My friends are waiting for us in my car."

Nina's high heels clomp behind me, echoing through the courtyard. Just as we walk past Harriet's apartment, she appears with a kitchen garbage can.

"Hello, Johnny. Hello, Nina. Have a nice time," Harriet says coldly.

"Yes. Good evening to you, too, Harriet," I say as we pass her. Nina is silent.

Joan and Benny are already in the Woody. I walk Nina to the passenger side, where Joan is in the front seat. "Joan, this is Nina."

Joan sticks her hand out the window and shakes Nina's free hand. "It's nice to meet you, Nina," she says warmly.

"It's so good of you to help me this evening. I hope I am not an imposition," Nina says as I open the rear door for her.

"No. Not at all. We're glad to help you," Joan says, helping Nina with her garment bag.

"I don't know if you've met our neighbor, Benny," I say. Benny turns to face her. The harsh dome light illuminates his face as he puts on a huge smile, which unfortunately gives him a ghoulish appearance in his current emaciated state. I can see that Nina is taken aback for a moment, then she offers her hand. Benny shakes with his right hand, which of course is missing the two fingers, and I witness Nina's realization of that fact.

"Yes, I have . . . seen you, Benny. You live across from me," Nina says.

"I hope you haven't been spying on me while I walk around. Sometimes I'm nude," Benny jokes.

"You, too?" Nina responds gleefully.

Joan is wonderful. In just a few blocks, she makes Nina feel like she's among friends and not just some hooker out to show off her tits for pervs in a bar. I don't know if Nina realizes it, but Joan is even hinting that she can help her get out of a situation, if there is a situation that needs to be gotten out of. I don't think Benny even realizes what Joan is doing. He's just sitting there quietly ogling Nina in the dark.

We drop off Nina, and she scurries into the side entrance of the club. Joan even discreetly slips her a business card.

As we drive away heading for our agreed-upon place to eat—Barney's Beanery, a lively restaurant with a roadhouse atmosphere—Benny taps me on the shoulder and says, "Hey, General, I think she was checking me out."

I agree that perhaps she was, and I glance over to Joan, knowing that the only looks Nina gave Benny were confusion and pity. The mind is a wonderful thing. Benny saw what we saw, and yet in his mind, he saw a flirtatious woman checking him out.

Throughout dinner, Benny seems to have trouble with his food. It's too hot, too spicy, too tough, too fatty, too bland, too cold. He looks as if his teeth are hurting whenever he chews. A strained look comes over his face whenever he swallows. Joan and I attempt to keep the conversation going, trying to avoid talk of medication, hospitals, illness, and pain. But Benny's appearance and mannerisms are a testament to the fact that he will soon die.

After Benny manages to finish most of his meal, he makes an effort to be jovial. Upon first obtaining Joan's approval to do so, he tells some ribald tales of life in the porn biz. Actually, most of the tales are devoid of sexual exploits, concentrating on the wheelings and dealings of Mob-type backers and sleazeball suckers willing to pay the bills just to be able to hang around the sets.

I sense Joan is tolerating Benny's stories, but barely. I try my best to steer him away from his subject matter and bring things I think he and I can talk about, like baseball or the Bronx. But both subjects seem to sour Benny's stomach, and we're soon back in the Woody, heading home to nail above his bed the last item he will ever use on this earth.

Chapter Eleven

ON FIRST GLANCE, it's obvious Benny has tried to clean up his apartment. The stacks of newspapers have been cut at least in half. The filth of the kitchen is gone, although it is still cluttered with just-cleaned plates, bowls, pots, and pans. Benny has even cleared a corner of his living room, which reveals a vintage seventies plaid sofa with enough room for Joan and me to sit on.

"I've got some sodas," Benny says proudly, pointing to the kitchen.

"No, thanks. I'm still too stuffed," I say, with Joan agreeing.

Benny walks to the bedroom door, which is down a short hallway. The door is closed, and Benny stands facing it for a moment. He then turns to face us. "Do you have the hammer and nails, General?"

"Shoot. I left them on my kitchen table. I'll be right back. Do you want to come with me, Joan?"

"No, I'll just wait here."

I bound out his door and into mine and in a flash am back with the hammer and a handful of nails of varying sizes. As I enter Benny's, the two of them are sitting on the couch, and Benny is quietly weeping. Joan has a hand on his shoulder and is rubbing it.

"Is everything okay? Are we sure we want to do this tonight?" I ask.

Benny takes a moment to lift his head and rub his sleeve across his nose. "Yeah. We should do it tonight. Let's go."

With help from Joan, Benny gets up from his seated position and leads us to his closed bedroom door. Joan and I stand behind him, me with the nails in one hand and the hammer in the other. Benny turns the doorknob and pushes the door open. The room is rather large but is cluttered with boxes, dressers piled high with more boxes, and a king-size bed that takes up most of the center of the room. There's a battle of two competing smells: dirty laundry and recently sprayed "outdoor fresh" air freshener. A two-bulbed light fixture with one bulb burned out hangs over the bed. The walls are painted a crimson red. The only thing on the walls is a black-and-white photo of Willie Mays in a New York Giants uniform, which, from this distance, appears to be auto-graphed. On our side of the bed is the cardboard box that contains the last rites shrine.

The reflection of the light off the dark red walls casts an eerie glow across our faces. We stand awkwardly next to his bed, trying not to notice the box containing the extreme unction kit.

"Do you want me to take it out of the box?" Benny asks slowly.

"I'll do it," I say, approaching the box. "Where do you want it?"

"I'd like it on this side of the bed, since there's already some-thing hanging on the other side," Benny says.

"Is that picture of Willie Mays signed?" I ask Benny.

"Yeah. But not to me," Benny responds quietly.

"Can I take a look at it?"

"Yeah."

I walk around the bed and read the inscription: *To Father B.—Willie Mays.* I remember the Father B. inscription on the World Series program and on the back of the photo I found behind Benny's refrigerator. "You were pretty close to this Father B., huh, Benny?"

"Close? Yeah. Too close," Benny says with a hint of anger in his voice.

"How's that?"

"Let's just put this up, okay?"

I walk back around the bed and place the hammer and nails on the gold terry-cloth bedspread. I lift the shrine out of the box and hold it up against the wall. "Is this okay? Right here?" I ask Benny and Joan.

"I'd like it lower so I can see it when I'm lying in bed," Benny says, pointing to an area on the wall almost level with his pillow.

"Sure, Benny. Joan, would you set it on the bed?"

Joan takes the shrine from me and gently places it on the bed. I center the nail on the wall. As I strike it once with the hammer, Benny winces. I look at the shrine lying on the bed, where Benny just might breathe his last breath, and I notice for the first time that the statue of Jesus behind the glass has two tiny red dots on its open palms, obviously the wounds from the crucifixion. We were taught, as kids in Catholic grammar school, that Christ suffered and died for our sins so we might have eternal life in heaven. But mortal sin would damn us to eternal pain and suffering in hell. Benny's head jerks back slightly each time I hit the nail. I remember Sister Annunciata suggesting we prick our fingers with a pin until we got a drop of blood, and then, as we felt the pain, to imagine the pain Jesus felt as He was being nailed to the cross. It takes only three whacks of the hammer to drive the nail in.

"Joan, would you put it on the nail, please?" Benny asks with his eyes closed.

Joan silently takes the shrine off the bed and hangs it from the nail.

"Is it up?" Benny asks, still with eyes closed.

"Yes," Joan whispers.

Benny opens his eyes and stares at it. His lips are moving as if he's talking to himself. He closes his eyes, hits himself lightly over his heart three times, then makes the sign of the cross and kisses his finger upon completing it. "Do you still have the crucifix, Joan?"

"Yes, it's in my bag," Joan says, reaching into her purse. "I've been keeping it with me." She holds the small box in the palm of her hand and opens it.

"I should do this," Benny says softly. He reaches for it with his right hand and holds it up with the chain around his third finger, highlighting his two missing digits. "Well, there it is. I just hope it works," he says, putting the cross around his neck. "Let's go back to the living room."

The three of us sit shoulder to shoulder on the sofa, with Joan in the middle. At least a minute goes by, and no one has uttered a word. But it's not an awkward silence. It's as if we're recovering from what has just transpired.

"Benny? Who is Father B.?" Joan asks, turning her head to Benny.

Benny rises up by pushing with both arms against the arm-rest. "I can't, Joan. I told the General I just can't go back there. Not yet."

"Then when, Benny?" Joan says, looking at Benny, who has moved to the kitchen door.

"I'll know when," Benny says, stepping into the kitchen. He comes back out a moment later with a can of ginger ale. "Are you sure you don't want a soda?"

I stand up and reach for Joan's hand. "We should be going, Benny. Can we help you with anything else?"

Benny takes a small sip from the can. "I think I'm being watched."

"By who?" I ask.

"I don't know. I just got this feeling. I think somebody's checking me out. Casing me. Don't forget, General, what went down back in the old neighborhood," Benny says, shaking his soda can. Some spills out. "Those guys don't mess around. It might be coming down. You gotta watch out for me, General. I wouldn't be in this fix if you hadn't spilled the beans on me."

"Benny, come on," I say, trying not to reveal how pissed I am that he's accusing me.

"Guys. This isn't helping," Joan says, cutting us both off. "Johnny, keep an eye out for Benny. Benny, if anything seems suspicious, call Johnny or me right away. Or 911. There's no sense in blaming anyone at this point."

"You're right. It's too late for blaming. Too late for blaming," Benny says as he sinks back into the sofa. "Good night. Thanks for everything, guys. I'm sorry, General," Benny says, holding out his right hand.

"Me, too," I say, shaking his three-fingered hand. As I look to the left, I can just see through Benny's bedroom door to the shrine on one side and the picture of Willie Mays on the other, signed to Father B.

Back in my kitchen, Joan roots around in a cabinet. "Don't you have any herbal tea?"

"I thought all tea was from herbs," I say, digging through some albums, hoping to find the right mood after our religious ritual at Benny's.

"I mean green tea."

"Here it is!" I announce as I stumble upon an old Hoagy Carmichael LP.

"You have herbal tea in there?" Joan asks, still looking through my kitchen cabinets.

"No. Hoagy Carmichael," I say as I put the needle on the faux Chinese piano introduction to "Hong Kong Blues." "I have Chinese music. But no Chinese tea."

"Yes, you do," Joan says, poking her head out of the kitchen, dangling two tea bags. "I found a Chinese take-out bag at the bottom of a cabinet. I'll boil some water," she says.

I prefer Hoagy Carmichael's versions of his songs to the many wonderful interpretations. Hoagy was an amazing songwriter whose works were made famous by the elite singers of the thirties and forties, such as Frank Sinatra, Ella Fitzgerald, and Nat King Cole. But somehow, Hoagy's reedy voice and quirky phrasing gives him a contemporary sound. He's funny, dreamily romantic, and poignant. And I can't think of a better song to sit and sip tea with the woman you love than "Stardust," which will be playing at just about the time Joan serves tea.

Joan glides barefoot across the carpet with two small flowered teacups I forgot I even had.

"Where'd you find those?" I say, sitting on the sofa as Joan hands me my tea and takes her seat directly in front of me on the floor.

"They were in a box under the sink," Joan says, holding the warm tea under her nose, inhaling the aroma.

I spread my legs so that Joan can lean back against the front of the sofa between them. "Take your shoes off!" she says, playfully smacking my running shoes and then untying them.

"Okay, but you asked for it," I say, kicking off both shoes. "Do they reek?"

"No, they don't reek."

"Are you sure?"

"I'd tell you if they did."

Yup. She would. That's Joan. To the point. Direct. No bull-shit.

I take my first sip of tea. As the music enters Joan's ears, it seems to filter through her spine; she becomes even more relaxed, soft, at ease. Her head leans to the right and touches my knee. I place my teacup on the end table and begin to massage her neck as Hoagy sings one of the most beautiful songs ever written. Without even seeing the look on Joan's face, I can feel her very soul being cradled by "Stardust."

"I love this song. I've never heard this version," Joan says, rubbing my leg gently.

"This is the man himself. Hoagy Carmichael."

"I love his voice."

"Me, too."

Joan and I sit for three or so minutes, not speaking and barely touching. The lyrics and the music, combined with the warm tea, are a welcome tonic after our evening with Benny.

The song ends, and a more upbeat tune begins. Joan stands to join me on the sofa.

"When you went to get the nails and hammer, Benny told me he was sorry for everything. I felt like he was confessing. You know, like a confession with a priest."

"Did he say what he was sorry for?"

"No. Just that he was sorry. I think Benny is reviewing his life. There's a theory that when you die, you experience all the pain and suffering you caused during your lifetime. I think maybe Benny, subconsciously, is fearing that."

"That's what extreme unction is all about. It's your opportunity to make your peace with God before you die, and to hope for the best."

"And is that supposed to just wipe the slate clean, even if you've been evil your whole life?"

"That's supposed to be the forgiving nature of Christ. But I believe there's a difference between forgiving and justice."

Joan takes a long sip of tea. In that moment, I realized this is a conversation that you don't have with just anyone. It's one of those discussions when principles and convictions are laid bare, with the risk of rejection. Or worse yet, when the other party doesn't have a clue what you're talking about.

"I agree," Joan says into her teacup.

"Benny has a gun."

"Oh my God. How do you know?"

"I saw him with it," I say calmly, playing down the episode.

"And what happened to it?"

"I told him I didn't want him doing anything stupid with it, and he said he wouldn't. It's in his kitchen drawer. He feels he needs it for protection. You heard him, he thinks some goons from his past are going to come after him."

"Why?"

"Joan, you've got to understand. Benny may have seen something awful."

"Be specific. What are you saying?"

"He could have seen something like a rape or murder or who knows what, and that's why he had to go on the lam. And if the guy or guys involved are now upstanding citizens, and they think a stupid TV show like *CrimeBusters* is going to uncover something, you don't know what they might do."

"After thirty years?"

"It seems plausible to Benny. I think that says it all."

The thought of Benny alone in his cluttered apartment with a gun in his kitchen puts Joan and me back in a somber mood. We hug, listen to music, finish our tea. But when I close my eyes, visions of poor Benny cowering next to his extra munchkin kit make me feel very helpless. And I sense, as lovers do, that Joan is feeling the same way.

"I think I should go home tonight," Joan says softly.

"I'll walk you to your car."

Joan and I walk hand in hand to her Thing. She starts that rattletrap and looks at me with an expression that tells me we're both in a tough spot. "Keep an eye on Benny."

"Yeah. Good night."

Joan blows me a kiss and rumbles off.

On the way to the office, I don't think once about the crucial production meeting I'm about to dive into. Nor did I sleep very well, thinking any clanging of the Dumpster lid was Benny blowing his brains out. But work is work, and once I open the office door, the world of make-believe becomes real.

I haven't seen a frame of anything I've shot yet, even though I know that the first deadline for the network to approve rough cuts of *Shocking Hollywood Secrets* segments is just two days away. Skip is looking even grungier than he did the other day, so he's probably trying to appear more intimidating, knowing that his work will soon be screened and scrutinized. He's sitting on the edge of Tiffany's desk with one of his dirty Reeboks actually touching the edge of Tiffany's chair, which doesn't seem to faze her in the least. In fact, she's smiling and giggling and paying more attention to him than she has given me the whole time I've been sitting just a few feet from her.

The front door pushes open, and Wendy bursts in, shih tzu in her arms.

"Watch it, Tiffany, Skip may have you starring in his next snuff film. Skip, come into my office, I'm late for a vet appointment," Wendy says without pausing.

Skip removes his foot from Tiffany's chair, pivots away from her, and follows Wendy without a trace of a farewell to Tiffany, who watches him disappear into Wendy's office. Once he closes the door behind him, she takes a bottle of Windex from a drawer and begins wetting down everything that Skip and his Reeboks may have touched. She then takes a handful of tissues and begins wiping.

From behind Wendy's closed door, I can barely hear muffled bits of loud conversation and things being slammed down. The only sounds I can translate with any certainty, because Skip is shouting them loud enough, are *no, bullshit,* and *fuck it.*

The office door opens, and Skip appears, a large smile on his face, waving amiably to Wendy. "No problem, sweetie, just call me when you can. Ciao!" He walks past Tiffany and me, ignoring us both, and leaves.

"Johnny, can you come in here?" Wendy shouts.

I gather my notes and walk over to her office, where I suspect she and I will be screening segments without Skip. But much to my surprise, Wendy is holding her dog on her desk, with a plastic tube in her mouth.

"Johnny, would you hold Rosebud while I put this salve on her butt?" she mumbles.

"Uh, sure," I say as I take hold of the dog on the desk. Wendy removes the tube from her teeth, squirts a fingerful of ointment on her index finger, and rubs it on the dog's ass. And I mean right on his ass. "Are we screening the segments without Skip?" I ask.

"I won't have time. I'm already late for the vet. Rosebud needs her anal glands expressed."

"Any chance I could see them?"

"Why in God's name would you want to watch anal glands being expressed?"

"I mean the segments. Can I watch them at home tonight? Particularly the segment on the sleazeball actor—the one with Dr. Archer. Would it be possible for me to see a cut before it's presented to the network?"

"Why?" Wendy asks as she brushes Rosebud.

"Um, I just know that it's the closest to being done, and I have no idea how the re-creations or the interviews are coming off."

"Any other reason?"

"Uh, no."

Wendy points to a VHS tape in a pile on top of her TV set. "There it is. Going to the network tomorrow. In fact, the whole show is going tomorrow. Host wraps, bumpers, everything. This is just one story, but you'll get the idea." She swoops up Rosebud and rushes away.

I grab the tape and walk over to my desk. I sit down and see Wendy waiting for an opening in traffic at the end of the driveway with Rosebud standing on her lap and licking her face. Once Wendy zips down the boulevard, Tiffany picks up her purse, heads for the door, and announces, "I'm going to lunch. Lock the door if you leave." It's ten-thirty in the morning.

I look at the VHS tape sitting on my desk and can't help but wonder. It's a strange feeling knowing that the moment Joan and I first met is forever documented in a television program that will air across America. I just hope it's not *too* shocking.

Back at home, I'm tempted to pop the tape in, but I think I'd rather experience it for the first time with Joan. That's the way I feel about most things these days. It brings back memories of being in grade school, when I couldn't wait to tell my mom about winning a spelling bee or winning a game with an amazing hook shot over Gerard Pierce, who was the best basketball player in our class. Once you become a teenager and start drinking beer with your friends on the seesaws in the park, those little triumphs of daily living are more than likely shared with your buddies, rather than your parents. But now I want to share everything with Joan. And if she can't be with me, I want to call her on the phone and tell her all about it. So tonight we'll have dinner at my place, maybe a cocktail, and pop in the tape.

One of the great things about having an Italian mother is learning how to cook Italian food. It's easy to concoct a nice Italian meal without meat, since Joan is a vegetarian. I usually make marinara sauce on Sundays, when it becomes an all-day affair, as it always was growing up. Start the sauce early, turn it off, but leave it on the stove when you go to church. Stop at the bakery for some Italian bread, then turn the sauce back on. Once it's warm, you put some of it in a bowl and *spoonze* your bread in it. You spend the next hour or so with the marinara simmering, filling the entire house with its sweet aroma; then you start pan-frying the freshly rolled meatballs, and boiling huge pots of water for the macs. We never called it pasta. It was either spaghetti or macs, short for macaroni. It didn't matter what shape they were. They could be rotini or ziti or penne, but to us, it was macs. The only different aspects this evening will be no meatballs and no church.

I've told Joan to park at the front of the building so she won't accidentally bump into Benny, which would undoubtedly lead to dinner for three. She seemed just as excited to view the tape as I am, and for the same reasons. Even though only Joan will be on-camera, we talked on the phone about how cool it would be to see if there was a little twinkle in her eye as she talked to me for the very first time.

I've timed the meal perfectly. The sauce is done, and the water is just coming to full boil. The oven is warm, and the smell of the garlic bread, I'm sure, is wafting out my screen door onto the patio. It's dark out, and I have some red candles strategically placed on the dinette table, in the kitchen, by the sofa, and two unlit ones next to my bed, which I hope to have burning soon after our planned activities.

"Ooh, it smells fantastic in here!" Joan says through the screen door.

"Hey, whaddya expect? SpaghettiOs?" I say as I open the screen door for her, closing it and the wooden door behind her.

"It's nice out. Don't you want to leave the door open?" Joan says. She puts down a small overnight bag and gives me a soft kiss on the cheek.

"I don't want to attract a crowd, if you know what I mean."

"Do you think Benny's okay?"

"Benny's fine. If we have any leftovers, they're his. Tonight it's just you and me," I say, holding Joan's shoulders, looking her in the eyes. "The macs'll be ready in a few minutes." I scoot into the kitchen.

Joan sits at the dinette table in Benny's chair. I've already set the table and even put out a fifties-style tablecloth with colorful fruits and vegetables adorning the edges.

"When do you want to look at the tape? Before or after dinner?" she asks.

"Definitely after," I say, stirring the macs. "It'll be a nice way to top off the evening."

"I hope so. I'm a little nervous."

"Nah. Don't be nervous. You looked and sounded great that day. I mean, I fell in love with you!"

Joan smiles, but I can tell there's more on her mind than that. "I'm just worried a little about what I said and how Safe Haven comes off. This could be very big for us. We've had an off year for fund-raising, and this national TV exposure could, well . . ."

"Could what?" I ask, putting down my red-and-white kitchen towel and giving her my full attention.

"Could make or break us."

"Haven't you ever heard the saying there's no such thing as bad publicity? You're giving Safe Haven national exposure. Plus, Wendy wouldn't screw you."

The lack of a response from Joan has me just a smidgen concerned.

"She wouldn't, would she?" I ask, hoping Joan will reassure me.

"I don't think so. But I'm nervous," Joan says, looking at me with what could be fear.

I pick up the pot of macs and pour them into a colander in the sink. I strain them well and place them in a large bowl. I take a couple of ladles of marinara sauce and thoroughly stir it in.

"Joan, I don't want us getting agita over this and ruining our meal. How about we look at the tape first, then eat. Maybe we can enjoy our meal a little bit better."

"Will it keep?"

"Absolutely. It's good for the pasta to sit for a few minutes in the sauce. Plus, the tape's only like ten minutes long. It's just one segment."

"That's all?"

"That's it," I say, standing behind her and gently stroking the back of her neck.

"Let's watch it now," Joan says.

I put a plate over the bowl of macs, turn off the oven and the stove, and head to the TV, where I shove the tape into the VHS machine. I turn around, and Joan is sitting on the sofa with her palms on top of her thighs and her knees together, like a girl nervously sitting in a folding chair at her first high school dance. In reality, I'm terrified and trying not to show it. I've invested quite a bit of myself in this first project since I landed in La-La Land. Sometimes that first door you pass through puts you on a path that you never intended. And as new doors open, it gets more difficult to get back to where you started.

"All right, here goes," I say as I press Play and back up slowly until I'm sitting next to Joan on the couch.

A loud blast screams out of the speakers, with color bars on the screen. I lunge for the remote to turn down the volume.

"That was a shocker," I say, putting the remote down.

On the screen is written, *Shocking Hollywood Secrets Directed by Skip Darby Executive Producer Wendy Valentine "Sex Secrets."*

"Here goes nothing," I say as my palms begin to go all clammy.

The writing fades to black, and then stereotypical porno sound-track music kicks in, dripping with wah-wah guitars and tha-dumping bass lines. The scene fades up on the heart of a sleazy stretch of Hollywood Boulevard when the sun is down and the hookers are out. The first scenes are actual footage of hookers, drug dealers, transvestites, junkies, bums, maniacs, and an occasional out-of-place tourist with a look of horror on his face.

"These scenes were shot by the crew you met."

"I'm glad I washed my hands afterward," Joan says, not amused.

There are fast cuts to the music, showing close-ups of needles in the gutter, flashes of bare flesh behind lace, bloodied faces, and other graphic images of life on Hollywood Boulevard after dark. Then a long black limo pulls into the frame. Obvious to me is that this is a re-creation.

"This is what the director shot. He's interspersing it with real footage," I tell Joan.

"Isn't that deceptive?"

"Oh yeah."

The camera is now at a low angle behind what appears to be a teenage girl wearing very short shorts. The limo pulls in front of her, and the black-tinted window opens just enough to show a man's face in the shadows of the backseat. The man asks if the kid needs a lift. The camera cuts to the side, revealing that it was not a teenage girl being propositioned, but a boy who looks to be well under eighteen years old.

A deep male voice begins, "Not far from the glamour and glitz of the Hollywood studios, scenes play out almost every night with some of Hollywood's biggest stars. But not on a soundstage. It's the streets of Hollywood, where long black limos troll the boulevard looking for fresh young faces. And usually those faces are the faces of young boys far from home . . ."

The scene then cuts to an exterior shot of Safe Haven at night.

"Oh, shit," Joan says. "Something tells me I'm about to be mortified."

"You and me both."

"But those lost children of the streets do have a safe haven where they will be protected from the super-rich celebrity sexual predators . . ."

"Oh God!" Joan is leaning forward with her jaw practically in her lap. She appears in the video at her desk, talking on the phone. She looks fantastic and totally professional as she takes notes, flips through some papers, and takes care of two telephone calls at once.

"Dr. Joan Archer is an angel of the night. An angel who saves and protects the fallen angels of the dark Hollywood nights. She runs Safe Haven, which truly is a safe haven, even though they are outmoneyed and outsmarted by some of Hollywood's richest and most powerful men in their quest for disposable sex . . ."

Joan gasps as her close-up appears in the interview setting.

"You look great!" I say.

"Shhh."

Joan's image is beautiful. Outstanding lighting, camera composition, perfect hair and makeup. She begins to speak: "It's a constant battle. When we're lucky, we get a child, male or female, to enter our program. Our first priority is to convince them to go back to their families. But if they refuse, we allow them to live here until we can place them in a safe environment."

The video then shows several teenage boys jumping into limos and fancy sports cars on Hollywood streets, obviously set-up shots by the director.

"Oh, shit," Joan moans. "I think I just saw one of our kids from Safe Haven get into the limo. Don't tell me you used kids from Safe Haven as extras."

"Not me. I swear," I answer, fearing that those idiots did use the kids as extras.

Joan's voice continues under these images. "But it's hard to compete sometimes with the money and the glamour of the rich and famous." Joan's face once again is in a close-up. "Tucker Kramden is one. We found some information in a resident male minor's pocket. The police checked it out, confirmed it was Kramden, then the boy confessed to it all."

Joan bolts out of her chair like fifty thousand volts just shot through her seat cushion. "Stop it! Stop it!"

I leap to the tape player and start pushing until I finally hit the Off button.

"You bastard! You lying bastard! You told me the camera was off! Oh my God, I'll be ruined! I'll be sued. You son of a bitch!" Joan screams as she grabs her overnight bag and runs to the door. She is trembling. "How could you? I'm . . . I . . . You! You are a liar. A scheming liar."

Am I? Maybe she's right. Maybe I was just deluding myself into thinking that this program would resemble anything other than pure, unadulterated, lying sleaze. Am I that stupid? Joan is standing not two feet away from me, and I know she is already gone. Perhaps forever.

"Joan, I don't know what to say. They . . . tricked me."

"How could I have been so stupid? I should have known," Joan says, her chest heaving. She turns and leaves, slamming the screen door behind her.

I follow Joan, slamming my door shut, not even bothering to lock it. Joan is running down the street at full speed. "Joan wait, please!" I yell as I gain on her. She gets to her car, and I reach her just as she jumps in.

"Joan, please. I swear to God almighty, I had no idea the camera was running. You think I'd let them do that?"

Joan has tears of rage running down her cheeks. "That's what hurts. Yes, I do." She then actually gets the Thing to peel out and speed away.

I am so screwed. I can't believe this. Smitty fucked me big-time. So did Joe and Wendy and Skip. Smitty shot Joan speaking when she and I both told him to stop shooting, and then those assholes used it in the piece. I can still see Joan at the end of the block, waiting at a red light. The light turns green and she drives off. I'm still standing in the street watching her lights as they disappear in the distance. "Fuck me!" I scream at the top of my lungs.

I hear a window opening in a nearby apartment, and a female voice says firmly, "Go fuck yourself somewhere else, asshole."

Not only is the video segment a disgrace as far as production and content are concerned—which will send my career down the toilet—I've just ruined the best relationship that ever happened to me. I have no idea if Joan can ever trust me again. But I have to try.

As I amble onto the sidewalk, dazed, not knowing my next move, I come to the realization that in a crisis situation such as this, one normally consults a close friend for solace and advice. Suddenly, I realize that here in L.A., I don't have anyone. Looks like without Joan, it's just me and . . . Benny. But not tonight.

The lemon blossoms are still sweet in the night air, but I flash on the sour taste of the lemon as I open the unlocked door of my apartment. I listen intently for any sound of a possible intruder who may have entered while I was gone. I half expect Benny to be sitting on the couch. Actually, maybe I even hope he'll be there. But nothing. Just the sound of an empty apartment.

Chapter Twelve

I DON'T BOTHER taking a pee before bed or even brushing my teeth. Despite the fact that all the lights are out, the room seems bright. There's hardly any traffic on the street outside, but it's still too noisy for sleep. I'm lying on my back and staring at the ceiling, waiting for a sleepy feeling. I try to imagine favorite peaceful memories, but my brain will play back only the scene of Joan and me watching the video and the ensuing freakout, over and over and over, with super slow-mo and arrows and close-ups magnifying my towering blunder like Mookie Wilson's roller going through Bill Buckner's legs in the '86 World Series. What kills me more than anything is knowing my biggest fuckup was trusting Smitty, Joe, and Wendy.

With a cup of sleepy-time tea in hand, I open the front door and look through the screen door out toward the pool patio. It's especially dark, because the submerged pool lights have turned off. There's not a light on in any of the apartments. I wonder if Joan is sleeping. I wonder if her video replay of the evening is the same as mine. How could it be any different? No matter which camera angle you look at, Buckner should have caught that ball. I should have known better.

Joan trusted me. She trusted Benny. And, I guess, now I trust Benny. I know more about him than I do about most of my relatives and old friends. In fact, there's no other person on the planet who could understand how devastating a loss it will be to lose Joan, except Benny. When Joan touches Benny, whether she's giving a little rub to an aching muscle or administering his meds, Benny reacts like she truly is a healer. And I agree. I quietly leave my apartment, making sure the screen door doesn't make a squeak, and walk to Benny's. It's hard to tell if he's up, but I knock anyway.

Benny comes to his door and is barely able to pull it open.

"Can I come in, Benny?"

"Uh, okay, but I'm nude. Come in," Benny says, turning and heading for his bedroom. I am shocked to see Benny's skeletal frame shuffling in the darkness like a figure in a haunted house.

I shove Benny's door closed. I dare not venture too far in the darkness from where I'm standing, for fear I may stumble into a tower of newspapers. Benny switches on the light in his bedroom, and I can just see the last rites shrine next to his bed with the bottom compartment open and two unlit candles in their holders. Benny is now wearing his ratty terry-cloth robe and slippers. There's enough light from the bedroom to illuminate my path over to the dining table near the kitchen.

"What's with you, General?" Benny asks. "Want a soda or something?"

"A ginger ale, if you got it."

"Got it," Benny says, popping into the kitchen, turning on the light, and returning to the table with a can of ginger ale. He sits in the chair next to me. The dining area is dark, with the only light sources being the overspill from the kitchen and the little bit coming from Benny's bedroom. The harsh fluorescent kitchen light cuts deep shadows into Benny's face, neck, and hands. He seems to be losing weight by the hour. "What's wrong, General?"

"It's Joan . . ."

"Shit! Is she okay?"

"Yes, she's fine. I'm fucked. I don't think she'll ever talk to me again."

"Ah, that's a bunch of baloney. So you had a fight. Everybody has fights."

"Nah, Benny. I really screwed up."

"You didn't bang Nina, did you?" Benny asks with total disgust.

"No!"

"I mean, I'd give the rest of my fingers to bone Nina, but you better not be fooling around on Joan, General."

"No, it's worse. I interviewed Joan at her job for this sleazy TV show I'm working on. You know, that's how we met. Anyway, we've got a video crew, and I tell the crew to turn off the camera for a minute while Joan gathers her thoughts. The crew tells me they turned off the camera, and Joan mentions some things that she never would have mentioned on-camera for public knowledge."

"Yeah, so what's wrong with that?"

"What's wrong is that the cameraman didn't turn off the camera, and they used Joan's confidential statement mentioning a famous movie star's habit of prowling for young boys on Hollywood streets."

"A guy movie star?"

"Yeah."

"Oh, boy, that's bad. Real bad. Back in the porno biz, we made some big bucks just burning films that actors made during some hungry times, once they started to make it big. And that was hetero porno. If a story like this gets out, there will be some pissed-off big shots."

"I mean, forget the fact that Joan despises me right now. She could be in danger, if she outs one of Hollywood's biggest male movie stars as a pedophile on national television."

"You're in a pickle, kid. But what's more important to you right now: your relationship with Joan or this schmuck being outed on TV?"

"If something I did causes Joan harm, I don't know what I'll do."

"Good. Your heart's in the right place. You've got to go see Joan and tell her. Come on, let's go," Benny says, slowly standing.

"Are you nuts? It's four in the morning."

"So what? She's up, just like you."

"I can't. What good will it do?"

"Just show her your heart's in the right place, that's all. I know you love Joan. But try and understand what she means to me, General," Benny says, sitting back down. He glances over to the kitchen, then turns back to me. He licks his lips, which barely even makes them moist. I think Benny was looking at the drawer where he keeps his gun, but I can't be certain. "Joan saved my life, Johnny. I don't know, but when she touched me, I just felt like I wasn't sick. Like I was getting better. I knew, and I know, I'm dying. I know that. But somehow Joan made me live with that. And get ready for it. You've got to see Joan. We'll go together." Benny gets up again.

"Now? You and me?" I ask, shocked at Benny's sudden resolve.

"You bet your ass. Let's go. I'll change," Benny says as he heads back to his bedroom.

I sit, downing the rest of my ginger ale. I try to look a half hour into the future and imagine Joan's reaction to Benny and me appearing on her doorstep in the middle of the night. I can't conjure up a thing. If I were Joan, I don't think I would ever talk to me again. I'm sure glad Joan isn't me.

The drive to Joan's is quiet. Benny and I don't discuss strategies or preplan any sort of agenda to lay on her. I have no idea what we're going to do there or what I'll say. Or if she'll even open her door.

Joan lives in a small Hollywood bungalow on a leafy side street off Hillhurst Avenue, only a few minutes from where Benny and I live. Her small front yard is overflowing with beautiful blossoming flowers. You can actually smell the aroma from her garden as you're driving down the block. There is a small front porch, and I know that it's difficult to hear the front bell from her bedroom.

Benny is standing next to me in his long raincoat, pajama bottoms, and slippers. I ring her bell once, and soon see the hall light comes on through the small rectangular stained-glass window in the front door. The drapes in the living room are pulled back quickly so that Joan can see who's at her door. Much to my surprise, the door opens.

"Come in," Joan says, not at all pleased. "To what do I owe this honor in the middle of the night?" she asks harshly. It's a tone of voice I've never heard from her before.

I feel like the stranger Joan thinks I now am. I don't know what to say.

"Joan, Johnny wants to talk to you," Benny whispers.

Joan's defensive stance seems to immediately melt away. She looks at Benny, who has placed his three-fingered hand on my left shoulder. He's squeezing my shoulder slightly, his three fingers giving me strength.

I open my mouth, not knowing what will come out. "Joan. I didn't know they would do such a thing. I would never do anything to harm you in any way. Ever. I won't let it hurt you. I wouldn't blame you if you never forgave me, but I'll do everything within my power to fix it, from this moment until that program is scheduled to air the day after tomorrow."

Joan is looking at me with a neutral expression. She is processing my words. "How can I believe you now? After what you've done to me?" she asks, not angry, not bitter. It's as if she's more stunned than anything else.

The idea that Joan thinks I could intentionally do something so awful makes me feel so low, so small, so lost.

"Joan, I would never knowingly harm you. I hope you can one day forgive me."

Joan takes a step toward me, then stops. She glances over my shoulder at Benny, who gives my shoulder an extra squeeze. I feel like he's a ventriloquist and I'm his dummy.

"Joan. I love you so much. I want nothing but good things for you always. I will do anything to protect you, always. Please forgive me. Please . . ."

I stop midsentence and stand there like a mannequin with my eyes closed. I'm afraid to look. I feel Benny's hand drop from my shoulder and another hand replace it. I can smell Joan now, so she must be just in front of me. I open my eyes, and she's standing in front of me.

"I can't. Please . . . go," she says.

I can't speak another word. My heart sinks into my sneakers. I can't look at her. Benny turns me around, pointing me toward my car. Joan closes the door ever so slowly, so that the sound of the door touching the frame and the clicking of the lock snapping shut are several seconds apart.

It takes a couple of minutes for my bleary eyes to clear enough to see through the windshield. Benny sits silently beside me on the bench seat with his elbow sticking out the window. I wonder if this is the last time I'll drive home from Joan's house.

And I wonder how many more times Benny will sit in a car with his elbow out the window.

Back in our parking lot, Benny shuffles along behind me. I wait for him at his front stoop and make sure he doesn't have a problem getting up the steps or through his doorway. Just before he disappears through the door, he turns to me and shakes his head. "Women need time, General. She'll come around. I guarantee it."

"Thanks, Benny. I'll take you up on that guarantee."

I go home and lie in bed as the sky lightens and the traffic noise increases. I need a plan. I need to find a way to convince the producers to cut Joan's libelous statements from the piece. And to get Joan to forgive me, trust me, love me, and yes, somehow, marry me. Now, that really sounds like something stupid.

Even though I haven't had a drop of alcohol in days, I feel hungover this morning. I don't know how long I've slept. Maybe less than an hour. I have that buzzy, shaky, jittery feeling in my bones from not enough REM sleep And not enough REM sleep means not enough time for my subconscious to figure out a solution to my dilemma while sawing wood. So it's up to my conscious mind to come up with some answers. But my conscious mind hasn't been too reliable lately.

First on my list is Smitty. I trusted him implicitly as a professional who was looking out for my butt, and it was his deceit that has caused all this. Despite the fact that he could probably kick my ass, even naked with both hands tied behind his back, I'm going to give him a little what-for, face-to-face. Maybe a little alcohol would do me good. Nah.

The drive to Smitty and Joe's office is almost as nerve-racking as the ride to Joan's last night. But getting my ass handed to me by one very large dude will be a welcome outcome if it will make everything right for Joan and me again.

.   .   .

"I work with Wendy Valentine. I'm here to see Smitty," I tell the middle-aged woman sitting at the reception desk.

She smiles pleasantly and points me to Smitty's office, just behind her desk. "Just go right in."

Smitty is sitting at a drafting table with parts of a camera lens in front of him. He's surprised to see me but looks pleased nonetheless. "Johnny, how ya doing? What brings you over here?"

"Can I close the door, Smitty?"

"Go right ahead. What's up? Everything okay?"

I close the door and stare at it for a moment, hoping that in those three or four seconds, I can gather enough courage to verbally kick Smitty's ass. I turn around, digging deep into my Bronx street smarts. "You fucked me, Smitty. You fucked me good."

Smitty gently places the lens on the desk with a perplexed look dropping from north to south across his face. "Johnny, I suggest you take a step back, take a deep breath—"

"You fucked me!" I shoot back.

"Take a deep breath, Johnny!"

The suggestion to take a deep breath works. Especially since it comes in the form of a basso profundo command.

Smitty looks cool, calm, and collected as he walks around his drafting table and sits on a stool facing me. He folds his arms across his chest in silence and shakes his head slowly. He appears to be going through his mental files, searching for the root cause of my implosion, and finally comes up empty. "What are you talking about?"

It's ridiculous of me to confront Smitty like this. He's about the only person I've met since I've been out here who I could project to be a friend. Except for Joan.

"Smitty, man, I am screwed. You remember Dr. Archer from Safe Haven?"

"Sure. Beautiful, smart woman. How could I forget?"

"Well, since then she and I have developed a serious relationship."

"Serious serious?"

"Serious serious. You know, I obtained a copy of the piece with her interview, and we both had our minds blown when—"

Smitty's arms drop as though he's a puppet and the strings were cut. "Oh shit. Damn. The stop-camera command, right?"

"How could you do that?" I ask, biting the inside of my mouth to stop my lip from trembling.

Smitty rises from the stool and approaches me. He puts his huge hand on my shoulder. The weight of it pushes my shoulder down an inch or two. "Johnny, are you kidding me? It's even in the production bible. That's the oldest trick in the book. We always do that. I'm sorry. Really sorry. I thought you knew."

"Oops," I say as Smitty turns and sits behind his desk, motioning for me to sit on the stool in front of his drafting table. "So now Joan is going to be on national television saying Tucker Kramden is a street-hustling pedophile."

"Johnny, I don't get involved in this political intrigue and maneuvering. I do my job. Wendy tells me what to do, and I do it. She pays the bills on time, and we deliver what she wants. Clear and simple."

"I screwed up big-time. You're right, Smitty. It does say that in the bible. I should have known."

"Sorry, Johnny. That's showbiz," Smitty says. He gets up and reaches across the table to shake my hand, which almost disappears in his hand. "Sorry, man. One thing, though."

"I'm all ears."

"Did Joan sign a release form?"

"Yes."

"Where is it?"

"I handed it in with the rest of the paperwork."

"Now, you didn't hear this from me, but if you got that release form, the original, and destroyed it, Joan could deny them use of her interview. Sometimes you gotta do what you gotta do."

"Hmmm. Thanks, Smitty," I say, juggling concepts of right and wrong in my percolating gray matter.

"Good luck," Smitty says, smiling broadly.

I think we already are friends.

As I drive from Smitty's, it all starts to come together. I have the keys to the office. It is before nine A.M.. I can take a peek around and see what I can find before everyone starts moseying in after ten. If I'm caught, well, that's the end of my career with Wendy, Skip, and whoever the hell else gets wind of my royal fuckup. But it's worth a shot at saving face for Joan.

Just as I thought, it's 8:33 A.M., and not a soul on the premises. I know that once I use my code on the alarm, they can instantly trace who entered the office surreptitiously. That will probably lead to other crimes and misdemeanors, but it's the time for action.

First thing is to rifle through Tiffany's desk. It's as empty as her head. But her top drawer contains the key to Wendy's office . . . Here it is. Once I'm in there, it'll be pretty hard to bullshit my way out of a jam if I'm caught red-handed.

I insert the key in Wendy's door and slowly open it. I turn on the light, step inside, and make my way toward the point of no return. I know which filing cabinet contains the show files because I've seen Wendy go in it during meetings. Shit. It's locked. Hmmm. I know she keeps some keys in her stash box. Yup. I open the file drawer, and there, labeled clear as day, is a file marked RELEASE FORMS. Got it. I tear it into fours and shove it in my pocket. Now it's time to cover my tracks and figure out a way to—

"What the fuck is going on here?" Wendy screams from the doorway.

I'm stunned. The file drawer is still open, and I'm standing here with a key in my hand.

"Uh, I'm doing some filing?"

"You better have a good line fast, or I'm calling the cops," Wendy says, gripping her key ring, which has one of those black bars women use for self-defense and a leather pouch that un-doubtedly contains pepper spray.

In an adrenaline-fueled breath, I spurt, "All right. I confess. I was taking back a release form. Dr. Joan Archer's release form. It's already destroyed, so you'll have to take her out of the piece. I can't believe you would use something after a person requests the camera to be turned off—"

"Oh, when the hell did you fall off the turnip cart?" Wendy says as she plops her bag and keys on the desk. "We're not doing fucking *60 Minutes* here, for chrissakes. This is entertainment. We do whatever the hell we want to make a story."

"Even if it means ruining the career of—"

"Of who? Some fucking pedophile? That asshole deserves to be outed!" Wendy says indignantly.

"No. Of a woman who—"

"Who what? What? Who?"

"Whom I love."

"Oh, shit. Joan? You and Joan? No wonder. Well, all's fair in love and war, I guess. She's a hell of a person."

"And you were going to hang her out to dry?"

"Relax, relax. First of all, Einstein, what you saw wasn't the actual finished segment. The network never would have let that go. I never would have let it go, either. The part of the interview when she stated emphatically that Tucker Kramden was Holly-wood's most rich and famous pedophile, that wouldn't ever make air. Ever. That's called the bargaining chip. They need to have something to take out, so you put in something you know they'll take out, and it distracts them from the stuff they don't like. But I would've loved to see the faces of the corporate wonks in that screening session when Tucker Kramden's name popped up. Joan wasn't going to be hung out to dry, and your problem is solved. Now, if only I had problems as minor as yours," Wendy says as she sinks into her chair. She reaches into a bottom drawer, pulls out a half-empty bottle of Jack Daniel's, and pours herself a tumbler. "Want a taste?"

"No, I never drink before breakfast. What's *your* problem?" I say, taking a seat across from Wendy, who is brooding as she sips the whiskey.

"The reason I'm here at this ungodly hour is I'm expecting a call. A very important call that actually involves you and me and Joan and even Tiffany, for chrissakes," she says, dumping the rest of the sour mash down her gullet.

"How? What's going on? Something about *Shocking Hollywood Secrets*?"

The phone starts to ring, and in a split second, Wendy has picked it up before a single ring can be completed.

"What happened?" she says immediately. "No. No. You're kidding. She said that? They can't! They couldn't! They're not supposed to!" Each declaration is louder than the one preceding it. She's standing, pushing the receiver hard into her mouth. "They did? Okay. Okay. Okay ..." Her voice trails off; she's absorbed defeat of some kind. She hangs up and whispers, "Mother!"

"As in *fucker*?" I ask, grasping the arms of my chair tightly in preparation for her next outburst.

"Worse. As in my fucking mother," Wendy seethes as she pours another tumbler of Old No. 7.

"Your mother? What does she have to do with this?"

"Oh, right. You're new in town. My mother practically owns BBX," she says, sipping.

"I did not know that."

"So, of course, after every other studio honcho at BBX signed off on the thing, the last gatekeeper to piss on the fire hydrant is guess who? My own mother!" Wendy puts down her glass and leans completely across the desk, coming at me, whiskey breath through morning mouth, and tits hanging low, scraping across the desktop. "*Shocking Hollywood Secrets* is dead. Not airing. Done."

"It's supposed to air in two days."

"Not anymore. Because Mom doesn't approve! And then there's the matter of, oh, about a million bucks down the toilet. And, my little freelance-segment producer friend, it looks like your old pal Karen Marshall is out on her ass over at BBX-TV."

"What?"

"Seems Karen didn't keep certain people on board with our little exercise in video vigilantism!" Wendy screams, and bangs her glass so hard on the desktop that it splashes bourbon all over.

"It's . . . not airing," I whisper.

"No, it's not airing! My father practically owned the god-damn network. After he died, my mom has occasionally kept tabs on what's going on. And when she saw it, she flipped. She said if this was the kind of rubbish the network was producing, then we're in the wrong business." Wendy takes another sip from the glass. "And she's right. It is all trash. So's every other new show that gets any attention. Plus, with all the lawsuits the show would cause, it just wasn't worth the risk. It's not airing. So go tell Joan everything is all right in your little world. While mine is turning to shit."

"I'm sorry, Wendy."

"Here's to sorrow," Wendy says as she gulps the rest of her drink. "By the way, did you ever hear of Nostradamus?"

"Yeah, he's that guy from the Middle Ages who supposedly predicted Hitler, Kennedy getting shot, the Mets winning the World Series in 1969—"

"You got it. Well, read up on him, because in a couple of weeks, you're going to *be* him."

"Define *be him*."

"We've got another show coming up called *Nostradamus: The New Shocking Revelations*. So you're going to be making them up. Don't worry. This one will air."

I hold my hand up to my ear with the index finger and pinky pointing out, illustrating that I'll call her. She holds up her empty glass in a toast. I guess that means we have a deal. Just as I'm leaving the office, my beeper goes off, displaying Joan's work number. Joan! Calling me. Thank God. I immediately pick up a phone and dial. "Joan. It's me. Hi."

"Johnny. It's Benny," she whispers, "a cop just called here. Benny's been taken to the emergency room. Cedars-Sinai. I'm hung up right now, but I'll meet you over there as soon as I can."

"Okay. Joan, I have news about your interview."

"I can't talk now. Tell me later. Bye," she says, obviously dealing with her own emergency at Safe Haven.

Cedars-Sinai is a huge hospital complex on the west side of L.A. I wind my way from the parking lot through the halls and lobbies and pedestrian bridges and find the emergency room. I wait in line and ask for Benny Bennett. The woman behind the counter tells me he's seeing a doctor, and I can go through the door and poke around to see if he's still waiting there.

I try to discreetly peek behind the curtains separating the beds with assorted weekday-morning emergency room visitors. It's not as extreme as the weekend middle-of-the-night variety of emergencies, but harried nevertheless. I poke behind a curtain, and there he is. Benny is laid out on a bed with a white sheet up to his chin. His eyes are closed, and he is as still as a corpse, which of course is the first thing that crosses my mind, sending me into a panic. I try to calm myself as I stand just outside his curtained cubicle. Maybe he is dead. What should I do? Who is his next of kin? Maybe the hospital knows from a form he filled out. I've never seen a dead body before. I take a couple of baby steps closer to the head of the bed, where Benny's skull protrudes from the white sheet. I'd say Benny is as white as a sheet, but next to the sheet, he is gray. His lips are slightly parted, and I can't sense any breathing coming from either his nose or his lips, or by the expansion of his chest. I inch a little closer to put my hand near his mouth and feel if he is breathing. Suddenly, his eyes pop open wide, and he speaks.

"Name the manager of the Giants the last time they won the World Series."

"Shit, Benny. You scared the bejesus out of me."

"Can you name him?"

"Damn. Give me a hint."

"Not a *nice guy.*"

"*Nice guys finish last*: Leo Durocher. How are you, Benny?"

"Not so good. I'll spare you the gory details, but when I was on the toilet, I had some problems, felt dizzy, fell down, and managed to call 911. I could only remember Safe Haven and told the cops to call Joan there. Is she coming over?"

"Yes. Did they say what's wrong with you?"

"Yeah. Cancer."

"I mean, can they do anything for you?"

"Oh, they already gave me some glucose injections and some other stuff. I'm actually feeling a little better. Hey, here she is!" Benny says with surprising gusto, looking past me. "Joan! You came!"

"I got here as soon as I could."

Joan looks beautiful. She must have had an important meeting, because she's in one of those *I've got a meeting* suits.

"Hello, Joan," I say, not reaching out to touch or kiss her for the first time since the day we met. I want to blurt out how sorry

I am, how I'll do anything to gain her forgiveness. Our eyes meet for a split second, and in that moment, that nanosecond I sense something that tells me we still have a chance.

Joan stops at the foot of Benny's bed. "Are you okay, Benny?"

"Yeah. Had a little scare. But you two together makes me feel a lot better. General, any news on the show? You know what I mean?"

"Uh, the show. Yeah."

"Johnny, I don't think we should be talking about this when Benny's here—"

"Are you kidding? I feel fine. Come on, I want to know what happened, too."

"Do you really want to know?" I ask Joan, remaining on neutral footing, not encroaching an inch into her space.

"No. I mean, Johnny, I don't care. I believe you. I know it wasn't your fault. I know I'll—we'll—get through it."

"You forgive me?" I ask in total shock.

Joan nods.

I rush to her and we embrace, quietly and gently.

"That's nice. That's real nice," Benny says, managing a broad smile.

I say, "Joan. I don't know what to say. What an idiot I am! And it's not even airing. The stupid show isn't airing. And you weren't even going to be nailing—er, naming—anyone anyway. We viewed the wrong piece."

"It's not airing? Are you kidding? Why?" Joan asks gleefully.

"Apparently, Wendy's mom has a sense of dignity. Amazing, huh?"

"You got paid, though, right, General?" Benny asks.

"Oh yeah. The check's cleared."

An older black female nurse enters our joyful cubicle and looks surprised. "Mr. Bennett, you sure are looking much better."

"I feel a lot better, too."

"Doctor says you can go if you'd like."

"Then let's go!" Benny says, rising from his white sheet fully clothed, even still wearing his jacket and shoes. The three of us look at Benny in disbelief. "I was cold! What?"

Joan and I make plans to see each other that evening as Benny and I head for the Woody. During the ride home, Benny's energy seems to dissipate with every block. By the time I've pulled into my parking space, I have to jump out to assist him. He lifts his knees one at a time to move them from the front of the passenger seat to the side, and then has to be practically lifted out of the car.

"Are you sure you're okay, Benny? I can take you right back there if you want. I don't have anything to do today."

Benny grunts as he grabs the frame of the open car door and hoists himself up with my help. "No. I'm fine. Peachy. I feel like forty bucks."

We start a shuffle to the walkway leading to our apartments. It's a beautiful day, and the sounds and smells of the apartments with open windows and doors are blending into a pleasant mixture. People seem to be putting more plants in front of their doors and on their stoops: hibiscus, birds-of-paradise, miniature fruit trees, and many types of palms growing in Mexican terracotta pots and even Tupperware. We stop in front of Benny's three-stepped stoop. He looks down at the pile of dusty dirty flyers, newspapers, take-out menus, and phone books and lets out a deep sigh. "You wanna help me clean up the stoop?"

"Good idea, Benny. You go inside, and I'll be over in a minute with some garbage bags and cleaning stuff."

Benny smiles weakly and labors up the three small steps to push his front door open. As I turn to head over to my place, I notice Nina coming out of her apartment on the second floor, directly across from Benny's. She doesn't notice me, and just before she closes the door, I can see her planting a kiss on someone in her apartment. Unless her kid grew to adult size overnight, she's got a man in there. Good for her. I just hope it isn't some biker asshole like the other one.

I grab a few garbage bags, some Windex, and a roll of paper towels from under my kitchen sink and notice the red message light blinking. I push the button, hoping it isn't work. Not yet, please!

"Greetings, Johnny!"

It's Wendy, sounding awfully cheery for someone who just had a program canceled before it even aired.

"We decided that we're going to have a wrap party tonight, in spite of the show getting shitcanned. It's at the Chateau Marmont, you know, where Belushi died, eight o'clock, and bring a guest. If you dare. Ta-ta!"

I was hoping for a quiet evening with Joan, to heal some wounds and offer some more mea culpas, but Wendy has already offered me a job making up stuff that Nostradamus might have said. If Joan wants to go, I'll go. If she doesn't, we won't.

I knock on Benny's door, and he opens it quickly, as if his hand was already on the doorknob.

"Come in."

"I thought we were going to clean up the stoop?"

"Come in."

I step inside Benny's nearly dark apartment, and he closes the door behind me but doesn't step away.

"Are we going to just stand here in the dark and bond, or what?" I ask Benny, who is silhouetted by a streak of light sneaking through a back window.

"I think I'm being watched."

"Why do you think that?"

"I just feel it. Something is wrong. I didn't say anything coming back from the hospital, but I thought we were being followed. Did you see that late-model black Lincoln behind us on Sunset? I was watching him in the side-view mirror."

"Benny, every other freakin' car in L.A. is a late-model black Lincoln. Those are all private-car-service vehicles. They're all over the place."

"This one was following us all the way to just a few blocks from here. And when we pulled onto Rodney, I saw the car coming around the block from the other direction and pass us just as we pulled into the driveway."

My eyes are adjusting to the darkness of the room, but I can barely see Benny's eyes in their deep sockets.

"Then there's Nina," Benny says as he grabs my arm.

"What about Nina?"

"She's got somebody in there, and I think he's watching me."

"Benny, if Nina has somebody in there, I think he's got a lot more to be preoccupied with than watching you."

"I'm telling you, something ain't right. I can smell it."

"Look, Benny, I know what you're thinking. But nobody's coming after you. Unless you've skipped some more child-support payments—then somebody will definitely be coming for you, and you'll know it right away."

"I've been on time. I swear!"

"All right, then. Don't worry. Nobody's coming after you."

"I wish I could feel as certain as you do."

"Let's clean up the stoop, all right?"

"All right already."

In about ten minutes, Benny's front steps are cleaned up, and I've even placed a couple of potted pink pansies on his top step; Joan had put them by my door. I Windex his front windows, which takes about half a roll of paper towels, since the first few sprays and wipes are like mud. But now everything looks spic-and-span.

"Hey, Benny. Now this place looks like somebody actually lives here."

"Let's see how long that lasts," Benny says sardonically.

In light of the circumstances surrounding her participation in a television show that was too sleazy to see air, Joan isn't thrilled about going to the wrap party but agrees to join me, since Wendy offered me more work. Also, Wendy has always been a supporter of Safe Haven.

When I think of the term *bungalow,* I see a ramshackle summer place by the ocean in an urban resort community like Rockaway Beach, New York, constructed with fortified cardboard and linoleum jammed together like cans on a grocery shelf. This Hollywood-style bungalow on the grounds of the Chateau Marmont is more like a small house in Southampton, complete with servants. There's a living room larger than my entire apartment; caterers are buzzing around with trays of drinks, dark gooey stuff on crackers, and shrimp the size of small lobsters. There must be fifty revelers at this bash, and scanning the crowd, I don't see one familiar face. Since no one greeted us at the entrance, Joan and I just meander slowly through the crowd holding hands and smiling that silly smile one uses at these kinds of perfunctory affairs.

"Johnny and Joan!" an invisible Wendy shouts from the crowd. Suddenly, between two young waifs dressed in black lace dresses, strategically torn near private parts, Wendy appears with a drink in her hand and half a colossal shrimp protruding from her mouth like a big pink fleshy cigar. She's wearing some kind of gauze wrap that is supposed to be a dress. Her nipples are clearly visible. "I still can't believe you two are an item!" she says, shrimp still in her mouth. Once she finishes her exclamation, she seems to inhale the shrimp. "Joan, I heard about your scare over the interview. Sometimes Johnny needs to slow down."

"Yeah, before I go saying something stupid," I say.

"That's what happens when you try deception instead of honesty," Joan says, discreetly squeezing my hand.

"Yeah, well, did he tell you that I caught him rifling through my file cabinet?" Wendy says, adjusting her boobs.

"Uh, no," Joan says, looking at me with a *This I gotta hear* expression.

"So here I am going into the office early, believe it or not, and there in my office is Double-O Johnny here, looking like the cat that swallowed the canary. Turns out he was risking life, limb, and career to steal your release form, Joan, and destroy it so you could deny permission for use of your interview."

Joan's face is quizzical, as if she's both outraged and delighted to hear this.

"And to tell you the truth, I was ready to come down hard on him, until I found out love was involved. For a guy to risk his only meal ticket in town because of love? That's my kind of guy," Wendy says with a wink. "I've got to go break some balls on the other side of the room. See ya." She disappears into the sea of Hollywood trendoids.

"Were you going to tell me about that?" Joan asks through a crooked smile.

"Oh, probably not until I could throw it in your face after our first argument."

Joan shoots me a devilish look.

"I mean our second argument," I sheepishly add.

"Let's see if there's any place remotely isolated around here," Joan suggests as she leads me through the throngs.

We pass the main food table, which looks like an idol to gluttony: giant towers of red meat and shrimp with bowls of caviar and creamed vegetables. But judging by the looks of most of the gaunt semi-Goth partygoers, I think most of the servers will be taking the lion's share of this spread home to their families.

There's a pair of French doors at the far end of the room, and Joan and I glide toward them. We try peering through the windowpanes to see what's behind them, but they are tinted quite dark. I open the door, revealing a lovely garden with a fountain and dim lights strung across the small slate patio. There is a wooden bench next to the small bubbling fountain.

"This will do," Joan says, leading me to the bench.

We sit down, still holding hands. I can hear some traffic not far from the garden wall, but with the French doors closed and the water bubbling in the fountain, it's easy to imagine we're far from the maddening crowd. The tiny strings of Christmas-style lights hung over the patio give the garden a soft but festive mood. Joan taps me on the knee and points to the action behind the French doors: Wendy holds court with a circle of sycophants, making huge hand gestures to emphasize some showbiz story that enthralls her onlookers.

"I love the weather here, but not much else," Joan says, watching the party take off without us. "But there are a lot of people in pain in this town. People need help, especially people drawn to the bright lights."

"I wasn't going to mention it, but this is the bungalow where Belushi died."

"Case in point," Joan says as she gently pats my hand.

Chapter Thirteen

THE AIRDATE FOR *Shocking Hollywood Secrets* comes and goes with nary a notice anywhere. No hew and cry from the media, lamenting the loss of such an important piece of journalism. No boycotts from any associations or groups or societies or public interest consortiums because an important voice has been silenced. In fact, I'll bet there are quite a few sighs of relief, from Malibu to Long Island, that the checks cleared and the program didn't. And to think the network can absorb such a loss without a second thought. But I'll bet it's better to eat a million bucks than to be socked with multimillion-dollar lawsuits from the scumbags who were to be exposed in our little slice of trash TV. And who am I to complain? I got my couple of thousand bucks out of it, with more to come. And I never would have met Joan if not for the show. Then again, I have a feeling that Joan and I would have met somehow, somewhere, sometime, and the result would have been the same.

For the past two days, Benny has been carrying small boxes to the Dumpster. I offered to help, but he refused. He said he had too much garbage to go through first, but once he got a little more organized, Joan and I could come over for a grand dumping-in-the-Dumpster soiree. What has me a little worried is that Benny hasn't been knocking on my door to hang out for a few minutes like he normally does, or even stopping by to see if Joan is coming over. I can understand why he's not eager to hang with me, but he's always anxious for his Joan fix. In fact, I'm desperately in need of a Joan fix of my own, but she's at a three-day teen-runaway conference in Las Vegas. I guess Sodom and Gomorrah were all booked up.

I've noticed something else strange about Benny. Whenever he walks to the Dumpster, he seems to be staring up at Nina's door. And sometimes he doesn't come back the most direct way, which is walking through the main courtyard; he walks all the way around the outside of the building and comes back through the main entrance at the front of the building. In Benny's weakened condition, that's no small feat.

Joan has told me that when people get to this point in an illness, it's not unusual to become delusional and even paranoid. And in light of what Benny has revealed to us about his past, he has plenty to build upon for a good paranoiac episode. Which reminds me—Benny's gun. In the period of time from when I first discovered that Benny was *armed*, he has achieved the status of *dangerous* as well. I think it's time to help him with a little housekeeping, and perhaps to assist him with removing some unnecessary items from his apartment. Like a .357 Magnum.

I don't want to arouse Benny's suspicion by appearing too eager to gain entrance into his place, but the way he's deteriorating, it's obvious that time is of the essence. I hate to even think like this, but given the amount of time he has to live, I'm not worried that he might blow his own brains out, except for the space deep in my mind reserved for maintaining subconscious fears regarding the violations of Roman Catholic doctrine, damning a soul who takes his own life to the fires of hell for all eternity. But if Benny has some kind of paranoid episode, he could snap and maybe start shooting his cannon, despite Catholic canon, at some innocent victims. Like Nina, or Harriet, or who knows? Maybe even me or, God forbid, Joan.

It's about eight P.M., and I haven't seen Benny since he dumped a box at around six. It might be a good excuse to knock on his door and see if he wants some food, since I'm going to the pizza place anyway. Then I can easily find an excuse to go into the kitchen and sneak the gun out.

KNOCK KNOCK KNOCK.

"Yeah? Who is it?" Benny asks, with mock toughness from behind the door. It's sad to say, but the only thing about Benny that would frighten anyone is his gaunt, discolored, emaciated appearance.

"It's me, Benny. Johnny."

Benny jerks the door open in one-inch increments, until there's enough room for me to see his lips and nose.

"Hey, General. Oooh, I'm beat. So tired. Is Joan back?"

"No, still in Vegas. Listen, Benny, I'm going down to Hard Times Pizza to get some pizza and salad. I'll bring you back some, too, okay?"

"Gee, I don't know. I'm not really hungry now. I think I'm going to take a nap."

"How about after your nap?"

"Aw, it'll be late."

"So I can wait. Look, it's eight now. I'll get the pizza, and at nine-thirty or ten, I'll knock on your door. If you're hungry, I'll come in and we'll have a slice or two. Okay?"

"Oh, well, okay. Around ten. You're a good guy, Johnny. But Joan's a lot prettier," Benny says, taking extra breaths, worn out from our brief conversation.

"See ya, Benny."

Benny struggles to push the door closed. At this point, it could be a matter of days for him. I hope Joan is around when the going gets rough. I think Benny would feel much better with her close by. And Lord knows, so would I.

With Joan coming back in a couple of days, I decide to kill some time by attacking the funk in my bathroom. If it were just me, I wouldn't bother about stained porcelain and grout, but exposing Joan to it embarrasses the hell out of me, which might be why Benny has also been doing some housecleaning. There aren't many things in life as humbling as cleaning bathroom filth. The initial repulsion to sticking one's hand into a stained toilet with a sponge or even a brush must be repressed. If you allow the fear of the most disgusting by-products of human-animal behavior to prevent you from cleaning up, you'll soon find yourself in a world of shit.

For L.A., Hard Times Pizza isn't too bad. It's on a street that has enough foot traffic to support selling pizza by the slice, a prerequisite for any decent pizza place. Foot traffic is the only way a pizza place can have enough turnover to provide fresh slices. There's nothing worse than stale pizza sitting under heat lamps, or worse yet, sitting on a counter for hours on end. Well, I guess, there is something worse: getting pizza from a franchise joint. I don't get the name: Hard Times? I can't think of a pizza place in New York that doesn't have an Italian-themed name, unless it's a name connected to a street or neighborhood. The two guys behind the counter are olive-skinned, like an Italian might be, but their facial features call to mind a map of Mexico rather than Italy. Then again, looks can be deceiving.

"Are you guys Italian?" I ask the stout, middle-aged man, who has a mustache thicker than a two-inch paintbrush. He's spreading the marinara sauce over a perfectly round, flattened palette of pizza dough with the bottom of a ladle.

"Italian? No! Mexican!" he answers, his voice full of pride.

"The pizza here is just like New York Italian pizza," I say as he spreads the bright white shredded mozzarella over the bloodred sauce.

"Never been to New York. And I hate the Yankees! Go Dodgers!" he shouts, smiling wide, only his bottom teeth exposed from under his bushy mustache. "But the guy who taught me to make pizza, he was from Brooklyn. Flatbush. Original home of the Dodgers!"

Now it all makes sense. I collect my pizza box and brown paper bags of salads, napkins, and utensils; pay my bill; and hop in the Woody. I decide to give Benny a little extra time, and sit in my parking spot for a while, listening to Bronx native Vin Scully doing the Dodgers game. Hearing Scully's Bronx accent announcing *bawl fawh!* and saying a recently called-up minor-leaguer might be here only for *a cup of cawfee,* mixed with the aroma of pizza filtered through a cardboard box, washes me in a sense of comfort and familiarity. Scully is amazing. Of course, I grew up hating him, not just because he's been the Dodgers announcer since the 1940s, but as the symbol of a franchise that abandoned the most blindly dedicated fans in the world for Los Angeles. Still, listening to him do a game is like listening to a poet, historian, and Dutch uncle all rolled into one. Who else could notice a pitcher's large hands as he grips a ball, and recall a quote from Pee Wee Reese from fifty years ago, saying that Gil Hodges's hands were so big, the only reason he wore a glove is because it was in the rule book. Vin takes things from long ago and makes them seem connected to what we're seeing now.

But another former Bronxite is about to put an end to my sense of calm as I plot my way into his kitchen to remove a weapon. I kill more time listening to the Dodgers and puttering around my kitchen. At eleven-thirty, I take my warmed-up pizza and everything else and head for Benny's stoop.

After I knock firmly, the door scrapes open all the way, and Benny is standing there in his chinos and a plaid shirt with his hair plastered down. He has a broad grin on his face, which unfortunately gives him the appearance of Lon Chaney in *Phantom of the Opera*.

"Perfect timing!" Benny says, waving me in.

He has finally made some headway in his battle against his years of pack-ratting. Except for one prominent four-foot pile of papers, the towers of trash have shrunk considerably, and the dinette set could almost be called tidy.

"You're really doing a nice job, Benny," I say as I place the food on the table and begin to unpack the goodies.

"I figure in a couple of days, this place will look decent," Benny says, sitting at the table and watching as I lay out the plastic utensils, napkins, pizza, and salads. "Wow. What a feast! I actually feel hungry. Where's Joan again?"

"Joan's at a conference in Vegas for teens in trouble."

"They couldn't have picked a better place for teens in trouble than Vegas. That's like a proving ground for them."

"Dig in," I announce to Benny. I fold my slice in half and bite off the pointy end.

Benny may have said he was hungry, but to judge by the way he's eating, he could be a kid sitting before a plate of nothing but brussels sprouts and liver. He takes tiny bites of the pizza, plays with his salad, and barely makes a dent in anything as he silently pretends to enjoy the food by moving his fork from pizza to salad to pizza to salad in rapid succession, without swallowing a thing. When he does manage to put something in his mouth, it looks like it pains him to do so. But after about a half hour, Benny manages to down a slice of pizza and about a third of his salad. We don't speak a word for that entire half hour. I don't think Benny has the energy to talk and eat at the same time. In that same time, however, I manage to eat four slices of pizza, my entire salad, drink three beers, and feel like I've swallowed a phone book.

"You made short work of that, General," Benny says as he dabs his thin lips with a paper napkin.

"I guess I was a lot hungrier than I realized."

"I used to be able to eat like you. I wish I still could. I wish I still wanted to," Benny says, his voice trailing off.

I've heard that cancer has its own metabolism, consuming whatever it needs from the cells surrounding it. It reminds me of a Three Stooges episode in which Moe orders breakfast by asking for burnt toast and a rotten egg. The waiter asks why, and Moe replies, "I got a tapeworm, and it's good enough for him!" Perhaps similar thinking is behind a cancer victim's lack of appetite.

"Benny, I feel like I'm going to explode. Do you mind if I lie down on your couch?"

"Go ahead, General. I just cleaned up over there. You can relax all you want. I'll throw some of this stuff out," Benny says, gathering some of the empty plates and plastic containers and placing them in bags.

As I move over to Benny's couch, I take a few steps down the hall to peek into his bedroom. The extreme unction shrine is open, and the candles on the shelf appear to be burned about halfway down. A pillow on the floor in front of the shrine has indentations exactly where two knees would make a mark. Benny is definitely getting his house in order.

I turn on the television and start watching a documentary on PBS. They're presenting exquisite aerial footage of glaciers and frozen tundras with accompanying music but no narration whatsoever. In a matter of minutes, the beauty of the sterile, icy-white landscapes and hypnotically calm music, along with my bursting gut of pizza and beer, begins to lull me into a twilight zone of dreamy half-sleep. The score of the documentary is the kind of *New Age* schlock you hear in the dentist's office or through speakers in a shop selling crystals, with the desired effect, of course, being to prime the subconscious mind to accept a high-speed diamond-tipped drill going through an aching molar, or to believe that rocks have magic powers. In my semi-conscious state, what began as visualizing my scheme for sneaking into Benny's kitchen to retrieve the gun transforms into a full-blown dream as I fall deeper into an involuntary doze . . .

I levitated off the sofa and began floating up until I was against the ceiling . . . I pushed against the cottage-cheese ceiling as if I were doing a breaststroke and headed for the bedroom . . . Benny was kneeling on the pillow in front of the shrine . . . he didn't see me as I floated silently above him . . . his hands were folded together in prayer . . . he opened his hands, revealing a stigmata on each palm . . . the phenomenon of a person bleeding from wounds in the same places Christ's wounds were after he was taken down from the cross . . . with blood trickling out, he reached into his left palm and retrieved a small silver object—a bullet . . . he then pulled a bullet out of his right palm . . . with a bullet in each hand, he reached up and touched the scarlet heart of Jesus on his shrine . . . then he held the shiny bullets—in his good hand, between his thumb and index finger, and in his deformed hand, between his thumb and pinky . . . he then slowly began to push the bullets into both of his eyes . . . then suddenly . . .

Yuck! I'm awakened by one of those disgustingly awful wet belches, when your mouth gets a blast of bile and acid stomach juices. My eyes shoot open, but I can hardly see a thing in the pitch-black darkness. The television is off, and there's only a dim light coming from Benny's bedroom, which I can see through the slightly open door. I assume he's in there sleeping. I have no idea how long I was asleep—ten minutes? two hours? I don't want to turn on any lights and risk waking Benny, so I feel my way to the bathroom. I turn on the faucet and begin to rinse my mouth with water to try and get rid of the sickening pizza-and-beer-belch taste. It isn't quite doing the trick, so I search for some mouthwash. I stoop down and look in the cabinet under Benny's bathroom sink, which is not a good idea. I'm already feeling a little nauseated, and the underworld of Benny's bathroom sink is not a place for refuge. The cabinet includes a plunger, a funked-up toilet brush, soiled rags and sponges, jars filled with Lord knows what, and to top it all off, a mousetrap with a fossilized mouse still ensnared. I begin to feel woozy. I gag and slam the cabinet door shut. Shit. I hope that didn't wake Benny. I stand and listen intently. I think I hear something, but not from his bedroom. I take a step closer to the closed bathroom window that leads to the side alley of the building, and I think I hear voices. In fact, I can faintly hear someone . . . crying?

Probably for security reasons, and certainly not for sanitary reasons, a nail is stuck in a drilled hole just above the frame of the window. I can probably remove the nail and open the window, but I'm afraid I'll be heard and noticed if I do. Could it be Benny out there? I run to his darkened bedroom and switch on the light. Benny's not here. There aren't any other windows that face the alley, so it's worth the risk. I pull the nail out of the hole and try to raise the window. It won't budge. A knife or screwdriver would help. I go into the kitchen to retrieve one, and as I open Benny's top kitchen drawer, I make a dreaded realiza-tion: The gun is gone. The box of shells is still there, but the gun is nowhere in sight. A horrible thought crosses my mind—what if Benny is involved in a situation in the alley and he has the gun on him? It's not too far of a leap of faith to think that some bizarre scenario in an alley, in the middle of the night, could lead to shots being fired. I grab a screwdriver and head back to the bath-room. I slowly jam the blade of the screwdriver under the window frame, and a jiggle breaks the dried paint seal, allowing me to quietly open the window about a half inch, just enough to get a view of what's transpiring in the alley.

I have to put my head all the way to the left side of the window to look to the right, where the voices seem to be coming from. Is it Benny? Is he alone? I shift even farther to the left and recognize Benny's black windbreaker. He's standing, leaning forward, slowly rocking over something or someone, in the darkness of the dim, litter-strewn alley. His arms seem to be folded in front of him, his head dropped forward. Then another figure emerges from Benny's shadow: a diminutive, white-haired, frail man covering his face with both hands, only his eyes exposed. I can see a crooked aluminum cane at his feet and Benny's head slowly shaking *no, no, no*. The old man takes his hands down from his face, revealing wrinkled white skin streaming with tears. He reaches his right hand to Benny's shoulder, and Benny grabs it firmly with his three-fingered right hand, then pushes it down and releases it. The old man pulls out a handkerchief and begins wiping the tears from his face.

Believing that Benny has the gun, I don't think it's a good idea to head back to my apartment and wait for the shooting to begin. I decide to wait this out and see if I can possibly help to avoid a bloodbath. Benny steps back from the old man and points toward the end of the alley. "Let's go inside," he says through thick phlegm.

I haven't a clue what this could be about. Could Benny be involved in a gay relationship? I guess. But why the hell would he be with the guy in the alley out back? Maybe he's an old lover and Benny's embarrassed. I could probably sneak out, but something tells me that I better stick around. In case of what? I don't know. This could backfire, but I quickly grab a pencil and a piece of scrap paper sitting next to Benny's phone and write a short note: *Benny—Went home to sleep. Later, da General.* I place the note on the kitchen table and began an urgent inventory of possible places to hide in Benny's apartment. Under his bed? In the shower? In the closet? How about behind the four-foot-high stack of newspapers and magazines in the living room? That sounds good. I can easily duck behind it, and if Benny and his companion come back to the apartment and head for his bed, I can easily slip out the door. If they go somewhere else, I'll go back to my place, eat a few Tums, and call it a night.

The front door slowly opens. From my vantage point next to the pile of newspapers, I can see Benny poking his head in.

"Let me just check on something first," he says quietly.

From behind the tower of paper, I sneak a peek at Benny as he discovers I'm no longer sleeping on the couch. He then goes into the kitchen, finds my note, switches on the kitchen light, goes back to the front door, and opens it all the way.

"Come on in. My friend isn't here," Benny says as a black-and-white figure enters the room. The living room is still rather dark, with the only light coming from the kitchen and Benny's bedroom down the hall, which helps my cover. The other guy is an ancient man, humped over like he has osteoporosis, and shuffling with a cane. I can just make out the details of his face: bulbous nose, waxy skin speckled with dark liver spots. His neck, head, and arms tremble as he slowly meanders to the sofa where I was sleeping until just minutes ago. He has the look of a forgotten soul, someone you see wheeled out onto the front veranda of a nursing home until the next meal is ready.

A creepy, disgusting feeling comes over me, and it's not the pizza this time. What if they actually are old lovers? I mean, Benny has more secrets than a CIA bureau chief, and they just might start, you know, doing something . . . sexual . . . right here in the living room. This other guy is old as dirt, and Benny's not exactly signing any long-term contracts, but who knows what they might try to pull off here. Hmmm. Bad choice of words, that. Being a few feet away from two dried-up humans attempting to engage in some kind of sex act is an experience I'd rather not be privy to, especially in my semi-woozy state.

Benny sits on the couch just a little bit over from the old man, and an eerie shadow slices across their faces. Craning from behind the newspapers, I can see them both sitting there, staring straight ahead, neither one making a move. They could be two strangers sitting on a bench in a subway station. After a moment, the old man raises his hand, which is trembling terribly, and reaches inside his jacket. He pulls out some kind of scarf and places it around his shoulders.

My mind is reeling. A purple satin scarf with gold fringes? That could be only one thing: a priest's shawl. And precisely the type of accessory a priest would put around his neck while conducting a confession. But why? Here? Now? Could he actually be a priest? But then what was with the scene in the alley? And why here, late at night, with this strange old cleric not wearing a collar?

Benny continues to look forward, as if he's pretending he doesn't see what his fellow couch sitter has just done. "What's that?" he asks, barely able to get the words out.

"You know what it is, Dominic. You know that's why I'm here. I've made my confession. Now you must make yours," the old man says in his raspy, tired voice, smoothing the wrinkles on the purple satin cloth.

"Father B., I don't know, I just don't know," Benny says, standing up and stroking his couple of days' worth of gray whiskers.

Father fucking B. *The* Father fucking B. The priest in the photo who was with Benny and his brother, Willie. The Father B. Benny can't talk about. I struggle to shake the fuzziness from my brain. It's time to focus. This is Father B. The priest Benny can't stand to look at in a faded photo, or have someone merely mention, and here he is in the flesh? On Benny's couch? In the middle of the night? To give confession? What in hell is this?

Benny is a couple of steps in front of Father B. "Even if I wanted to do this, what makes you think *you* can still do this? How can you still give sacraments? You were kicked out! You were in goddamn prison!" Benny begins to pace nervously in the darkened room, coming just inches from where I'm hiding behind a stack of papers and magazines.

"They can take away the cloth of a priest, Dominic, but once a priest, always a priest." The old man holds up the index finger and thumb of his right hand. "And these fingers are forever consecrated."

Benny whips around and glares at the old priest. "And what about these fingers, Father B.? These fingers I don't have aren't fucking consecrated! What about them?" Benny holds up his right hand, the hand missing two fingers. "You know it's your goddamn fault. Fucking Ralphie! That goddamn son of a bitch. You let him do it. You fuckin' let him do it!" Benny is seething. His words emanate from his thin, tight lips in controlled, fiery bursts. Not screams.

"I tried to stop him. I tried, Dominic. I didn't know he would go to those extremes," Father B. says weakly. "I couldn't control him."

"There's the fucking understatement of the century. You couldn't control him. What a joke. You created him. In your likeness. Your monstrous fucking likeness."

The old priest closes his eyes and begins sobbing pathetically. He's barely audible as he whimpers, "It wasn't me, Dominic. I had no idea Ralphie was going to do that to you. He wouldn't obey me."

"You were there! You were in the kitchen. You saw him put my hand in the grinder! You knew it!"

The old priest is worn and out of breath. "I didn't know. He said he was just going to frighten you. I didn't think he'd really do it. Just to . . . make sure no one would ever . . . tell. Just to . . . frighten you. That's all. I swear to God."

"Don't you dare swear to God. Take that off," Benny says, pulling the shawl from the old man's neck and throwing it in his face. "You know, ever since then—ever since that day at the altar boy outing, when Ralphie . . . did that to poor little Louie . . . whenever I remember that my two fingers are missing, I remember. You know, when you lose a part of yourself, like two fingers, you get used to it. You forget you ever had two fingers. But sometime during the day, just about every day, you shake hands with somebody for the first time, or you pay for something at a store, or a little kid points at your hand to his mother, and you remember those fingers are missing. You remember *why* those fingers are missing. And I see a face. Every time. Little Louie." Benny strains to breathe, like a fish on a beach gasping for air. "That poor kid. When they finally dragged him out of the lake and laid him down on that dirty gray sand. And everybody knew he was dead. And I knew who killed him." Benny slowly sits back on the couch, right next to Father B. "How could you? Poor little Louie. After seeing what you made Ralphie do to Louie . . . to drown that poor kid . . . I just knew . . . I thought . . . I had to . . . I knew Dominic had to die, too. And Benny was born—"

"I didn't do that to Louie," Father B. says emphatically.

Benny jumps back up so fast, he almost loses his balance. "Stop playing fucking games! Yes, you did! You made Ralphie kill Louie to protect you. And you killed all of us. You and your goddamn sex games. Games? What a joke! You killed Louie. You killed me that day, too. We were kids! Fucking just little . . . kids. I saw Ralphie holding Louie under the raft in the lake. I was the only one who saw it. But you killed Louie! And don't you ever forget it!"

"I paid for my sins," Father B. says sternly.

"Don't you fucking tell me you paid for your sins. You destroyed us! For what? So you could get your rocks off by jacking off little kids. I know you were kicked out of the priesthood and spent twelve years in jail. So fucking what? That's nothing! You're going to burn in hell! You know that? And I'm going to make sure it's sooner rather than later!" Benny rushes into the kitchen. I can hear him opening the kitchen drawer, rumbling through the odds and ends. "Oh, shit! Shit." He shuffles back into the room with a glass of water in his hand. "Just as well. I'm not ready to die yet anyway. You're lucky, Father B. I usually keep a gun in there. But I dumped it yesterday. Totally forgot about it. I guess it's your lucky day." Benny sits back down on the sofa.

"What do you mean? A gun? You were going to—" Father B. mumbles.

"Yeah, big fucking deal. I was going to kill you, then myself. But I'm too tired. And thirsty. And fucking disgusted," Benny says in defeat. "What's the difference? Look at us. How long do we have—days, weeks? All I know is before the next World Series victory parade, we'll both be worm food. And one or both of us will be trying to outrun white-hot pitchforks." Benny looks over at Father B. "Hopefully just one of us."

Father B. looks at his watch. "Oh. Dominic. I have to ask you something. It's very important. Oh dear, I'm late."

"Late? Late for what?" Benny says, perplexed.

There's a soft knock at the door.

"Oh, that's probably Johnny," Benny says, going over to the front door.

I consider jumping up and revealing my presence, but I don't want to freak Benny out any more than he already is.

"Who's there?" Benny says as he pulls open the door.

"Pizza," a male voice declares.

"Pizza? Johnny, this is no time for—" The door reveals a large, fat man in his fifties. He's wearing a short black jacket, black pants, and a black turtleneck.

My mind is racing. What the hell is going on here?

Benny takes one look at the guy, gasps like he's seen a ghost, and drops the glass of water on the carpet. "No. Fucking no. Oh my God, no," Benny says as if he's in a trance. Not shouting. Just talking to himself.

"Don't worry, Dominic," Father B. says. "Ralphie just wants to talk to you."

"I knew it. I fucking knew it. Set up again by Father B. Ralphie found me. After all these years, Ralphie finally found me," Benny says, still trancelike.

"I just want to talk, Dominic," Ralphie says. "Sit down. You, me and Father B. Just like old times. But real quiet."

Benny looks like a zombie as he sits, staring at Ralphie. Father B. seems ready to crumble like a burnt charcoal briquette.

"We have a lot of catching up to do, Dominic. I haven't seen you since you ... well, died." Ralphie chuckles. "But I've been living. Did you know I was a judge? A freaking judge, Dominic. And three kids. Ivy Leaguers, each one. Did you know any of that, Dominic?" Ralph walks into the darkness and stands in front of the two pathetic souls on the couch. "I knew Father B. would get to you. I knew you'd let him in your apartment. I knew he'd get to you before you got to me, Dominic. Too bad you couldn't just leave well enough alone. You opened the can of worms again. And the old fag priest who taught us everything—taught us how to jerk off into a red silk scarf when we were altar boys—brings us back together. You liked that, didn't you, Father B.? And then you'd take that scarf soaked with altar-boy jizz and jerk yourself off in front of us. And when that wasn't enough, you started blowing us. It was a secret. Our secret society. Don't tell. Don't ever tell," Ralph says, his voice fading into the darkness.

It's all too clear now. The revelations blurted out from three ghosts is more than I thought possible. Lurking here behind this pile of papers, the realization that I set all this into motion sickens me. Obviously, Judge Ralphie thought a show called *CrimeBusters* was reopening a cold murder file. They do it all the time. And here we are, at Hollywood View Court, with fucking Judge Ralphie.

"You could've just left well enough alone, Dominic," Ralph says, kneeling on one knee next to Benny. "You had your new name, your new city, your new life."

"What about my new fingers?" Benny asks, holding up his misshapen hand.

"Two fucking fingers. Big deal. I could've taken your head!" Ralph says, inching toward Benny. "You'd rather I took your head? Ungrateful bastard. It shut you up, right? But I should've known you'd squeal eventually. Double-dimin' me to some shit TV show. Schmuck."

"I should've squealed then. Maybe I would've gotten my head taken off, and maybe I would've had a life," Benny says clearly, right into Ralph's face.

I'm pretty much out of options. Maybe I should sit here with my eyes closed and wait this little drama out, whatever the hell it's all about. But it's getting a bit too heavy and mysterious for me. So I figure if I just stand and introduce myself, it will put an end to the dysfunctional family reunion. What's the worst that could happen? So, here goes . . .

"All right, no more of this bullshit," I announce as I stand and emerge from the shadows.

"Johnny, oh, no, Johnny!" Benny says, his voice dripping with dread.

Ralphie turns toward me and pulls from the inside of his jacket a dark object with a glint.

"Fuck me," I say so only I can hear it. The reason for the *Fuck me* is that Ralphie has just reached into his jacket and pulled out a gun. And having seen more than my share of *Man from U.N.C.L.E.*s, I'm certain it is fitted with a silencer. Ralphie looks at me and jerks the gun in my direction.

"Who the hell are you?" Judge Ralphie demands in a voice he probably uses quite a bit while presiding on his bench.

"Um. A neighbor. I just came over to borrow a cup of sugar. I think I'll come back another time—"

"Sit on the couch, schmuck," he says, showing his teeth in anger and waving the gun to head me over to the sofa. "This is fucked. First of all, nobody says a word or everybody's dead," he goes on, beginning to appear nervous and agitated. I can see his wheels spinning. "You really fucked this up, neighbor." He reaches inside his jacket and pulls out a plastic bag containing something else heavy and dark. Yup, another gun. "This was going to be a nice clean homicide-murder. An old fag priest gets out of jail, kills the old altar boy he used to abuse, then kills himself. Nice and easy. Only now it's got to be a double homicide-suicide. Well, the cops'll have to figure this one out for themselves."

I've heard the term about hair standing up, and I think if I looked in a mirror, that would be the do I'd have right now. I have to pull my sphincter tight, or my BVDs would be loading up with pizza and beer. As dark as the room already is, black spots start to appear in my field of vision. It's the opposite of seeing stars, like when you get punched in the face; black blobs appear to be hovering everywhere I look.

"Wait! Why?" I say in a stage whisper.

"Shut up! Because I'm not going to let something that happened forty years ago ruin my life now. Not after all these years," Judge Ralphie seethes.

"I won't tell, I won't tell, I swear. Kill me. Don't kill Johnny, Ralphie," Benny pleads.

"Until now only you and Father B. knew I killed that other squealer. It was a breeze. A kid gets found under a raft in a lake, drowned. Nobody knew. Except for Father B. and you, Dominic. Because you were the only other kid in the water. And now, with this gun that has Father B.'s prints all over it"—the judge pulls the gun out of its plastic bag—"and this suicide note Father B. so graciously wrote for me, it's in God's hands. All I've got to do is shoot you guys in order. One, two, three. And it's all over."

Ralphie, wearing latex gloves, removes the gun from the plastic bag. It has a silencer. "I'll do this quick. Dominic, you're going to be first, then the neighbor, then Father B. And hopefully, I'll be halfway across the desert by the time the bodies are discovered," Judge Ralphie says, smiling slightly.

"I ain't ready to die!" Benny says, pleading. "I can't. I'll . . . go to hell. I ain't ready." He leaps up from the sofa about as quickly as can be expected of a man in the final stages of cancer.

Ralphie pushes him back down almost playfully, delighting in the fact that he can overpower Benny so easily.

"We're all going to hell. You're just going sooner than I am," Ralphie says, extending his arm, pushing the gun just inches from Benny's face.

I ponder my options, which at this point seem to be to try and escape and get shot in the back, or to attack Judge Ralphie and get shot in the face. Not exactly favorable odds. Funny what you think about when you're faced with death. I remember I was near a building after a huge explosion, and a guy came walking out of the inferno with his clothes blown off of him like a scene from a Laurel and Hardy movie, his skin hanging from him in gooey sheets. His face didn't even look human, being just a blob of exposed raw muscle and bone, but somehow, through a slit that was his mouth, he was saying, "My wallet. Where's my wallet?"

As Judge Ralphie pushed the barrel of the gun closer to Benny, I flashed on whether or not I was wearing clean underwear . . .

I've thought about death a lot. I've read Sartre and Camus and Kafka while listening to the Doors, stoned on pot. I've cried over beloved aunts and uncles all dressed up in their Sunday best, lying in caskets from Prospect Park to New Rochelle. I saw a friend's brother die in a pool of blood after accidentally falling off the roof of his building. I've smelled death in my own apartment building, where an old Chinese bachelor died in his bed one steamy July and was found after four days by the stench. But now I finally know, nothing prepares you for *the* moment when the death you contemplate is your own. Not the countless stations of the cross or the thousands of acts of contrition or the millions of Hail Marys. I close my eyes and start what is probably the last Hail Mary of my life.

"Freeze, motherfucker!" A voice booms from the dark hallway as a blur of black flies through the room, headfirst, crashing into Ralphie and sending them both across the room.

In a split second, the dark figure has Ralphie facedown with a knee pressing his neck into the carpet. He pulls the judge's arms behind his back and slaps on a pair of chrome handcuffs using just one hand. He's wearing a black leather motorcycle jacket and a salt-and-pepper ponytail down his back, and he has a gun the size of a howitzer jammed into the judge's ear. Father B.'s head hits my shoulder as he collapses to the floor. He may have dropped dead, but I think he just fainted. I glance over at Benny, who looks like he's turned into a wax museum dummy, with his jaw pointing to the floor and his tongue not far behind.

"You fuckin' mutt. I knew you'd try and pull some shit like this. I've been following you for days, you stupid prick. All the way from Arthur Avenue," the ponytailed savior spits at Ralphie.

"Willie?" I ask, stunned at the sight of Benny's brother, who knees Ralphie in the kidneys just before turning him over.

"Yup. Like the saying goes, when the going gets weird, the weird turn pro. Hey, Dominic, it's me. Willie," the man says, turning his head toward Benny.

Benny snaps out of his trance and starts shaking like a bobble-head doll on a diesel truck's dashboard. "What . . . is . . . going . . . on?" he stutters. "Willie? Willie? Oh my God. Thank you, God. Willie . . . my Willie. My baby brother. Oh, Willie." Benny falls to his knees, then collapses forward into a fetal lump of quivering and heaving bony flesh.

Willie stands, never taking his eye off the judge. "I'm here for you, Dominic. Don't worry. Here," he says as he helps get Benny back on the couch. Father B. is still either out cold or dead.

"Now, you, Judge fucking Ralph Bonifazio," Willie says, inching toward him, "it's time for a little instant fucking karma!" He grabs the judge's neck, shoving his face deep into the carpet. "Do you have any fucking idea how many families you destroyed? Do you?" Willie pushes his gun deep into the judge's cheek. "Now it's time for your judgment day."

"Do you know who I am?" the prostrated judge snarls. "Nobody's going to believe you. Who the hell do you think you are? You're nothing but a street punk."

"You want to know who I am? I'll tell you. I'm only one of thousands. We roam the streets at night. We're in urine-soaked subway cars and shitty roach-infested apartments from Kingsbridge to Bay Ridge. We're in the bars from the Upper East Side to the Bowery, trying to forget what we gave to save the city from scum like you: rich, corrupt assholes lining their pockets while we fight your dirty little wars on the streets, in the tenements, in the alleys and sewers." Willie's teeth are almost sparking from grinding together in his clenched jaw. His hands are tense with rage, and I'm surprised he hasn't pulled the trigger already. "We're out there day and night, just hoping one day we can bag scrotes like you. Who am I? I'm the most crazed, dangerous, ready-to-blow-at-any-minute fucking lunatic going to rid the world of unknowing, uncaring, selfish bastards like you." Willie's words are like a cyclone rattling through the room, even making

Father B. appear to come to. Benny, Father B., and I sit frozen in silence, just waiting to see the judge's brains get blown across the room.

"Please, no . . . no . . . don't hurt me," the judge whimpers weakly.

"You wanna know who I am? I'll tell you." Willie moves the gun to the judge's mouth and shoves it in. He puts his lips right next to the judge's ear and says, "NYPD *Retired*."

Willie pulls the gun out of the judge's mouth and grabs him by his turtleneck. "Get up, you sack of shit. You're under arrest. It's nice we've got three witnesses for your confession. As I'm sure you know, even though you're nothing but a fuckin' parking-ticket hall monitor, there's no statute of limitations on murder. Your Honor."

"Benny, call 911, and give me the phone when you get 'em," Willie continues, shoving the judge into a chair. "Yo, you," he says to me, reaching into the judge's pocket and pulling out car keys. "There's a Lincoln on the side street over here. See if there's anything in it and come right back." He tosses me the keys.

I take the keys and go around to the side street, where there's a black Lincoln Town Car with New York plates parked at the end of the block. I'm shaking like a leaf and have a hard time putting the key in the trunk lock. I pray to God it doesn't explode when I open it. I turn the key, and the hood pops open. There are three black canvas bags in the trunk. I rifle through one, and it's mostly clothes. The second one is loaded with cigar-box-size cardboard boxes. I open one of the boxes and find dozens of prescription pill bottles, each with RALPH BONIFAZIO on the label. Checking a few of the other boxes, I discover the contents are the same: pill bottles. I open the third bag to find a dozen or so porno videos, some with girls on the cover, others with boys, but all featuring naked minors. Also in the bag are rolls of silver duct tape and what looks to be the contents of the clearance table in your local sex shop: whips, leather masks, leather crotchless panties, dildos of every shape and color, and a few odd-shaped things with tubes and orbs. I have no idea what they could be. I leave the clothes bag, grab the other two, and head back to the apartment.

I enter Benny's with the bags. Willie is on the phone giving details to the police.

"Yeah, and send an ambulance. We've got a perp here who might need attention. Thanks. Bye," Willie says, hanging up the phone.

"These were in the trunk," I say, dropping both bags a couple of feet in front of the judge, who's now tied to a chair with his hands cuffed behind him.

Willie bends down and begins inspecting the contents. "Oh, you must have some freaking allergies, there, Ralphie boy," Willie says, shaking a pill bottle. "These couldn't be quaaludes or ruffies, now, could they?"

"Ruffies?" I ask.

"Rohypnol. Date-rape candies. Ruffies. Real popular with the sexual-predator set." Willie drops the bottle and unzips the other bag. "Bingo! A predator's starter kit! So, even while you're on a business trip, you've got to have a little recreation, huh, Judge?"

"Everything you see there is legal, asshole," the judge snarls.

Willie walks behind Ralphie's chair, winds up, and gives him a rabbit punch in the kidneys that would have knocked Sonny Liston from here to Barstow.

The judge's chair moves about three feet forward, and the judge winces in agony.

"Fucker," Willie whispers.

"Willie, the hot water's ready," Benny says from the kitchen, unfazed by the judge gasping for air in agony. Uh, oh. I wonder if that's for a little hot-water torture on the judge.

"You want decaf or regular?" Benny asks.

"Regular."

I can hear the sirens coming down the street. Father B. is breathing as he lies across the sofa, but barely. The shithead judge is staring straight ahead. I walk into the kitchen, and Willie is showing Benny some photographs.

"What's that? Old family photos?" I ask the long-lost brothers sitting next to each other at the tiny table jammed into a corner of the kitchenette.

"Nah. These are Willie's crime-scene photos," Benny announces with glee. "Hey, General, ever see a body cut in two by a freight train?"

"You're not serious," I say, peeking over Benny's shoulder to see the most gruesome thing I've ever laid eyes on in my life: a body cut clean in two next to a railroad track, which I recognize as being alongside the Hudson River. "Why, do tell, do you carry such photos with you, Willie?"

Willie gets a devilish grin across his face and says, "If anybody ever asks what I did before I retired, I just whip these out." He begins to laugh with Benny.

"Benny, you've got—" I start, but am interrupted by Benny.

"Whoa! Stop right there, General! It's Dominic. Benny's dead." He looks at Willie, who has just stopped snickering, and the two begin to drop their facades. No more tough-guy cop. No more Benny the porno king. Like two little kids, they embrace while sitting, and the waterworks begin. Just then there's a knock on the door.

"Police!" a cop says through the door.

Willie takes his gun off the table and sticks it in his shoulder holster. He pulls out his badge, stands, and turns on all the lights in the living room. He opens the door, and standing on the front stoop are two LAPD cops with their guns drawn, both with crew cuts, one a blonde, the other an Asian, both looking as if they got out of the academy yesterday. Willie holds his badge up high and says, "Willie Benedetto, NYPD. Retired. Come on in, boys."

More sirens can be heard on the street as ambulances and more cops arrive. From one end of the courtyard to the other, everyone is pouring out of apartments and craning their necks to get a bird's-eye view of the activity at Benny's—I mean Dominic's. Harriet, the old ladies next door, and some people I don't even recognize stand a safe distance away, gazing at us in disbelief. Nina, in a sexy silk robe and pink mules, saunters right over to the bottom of the front step and gets my attention through the open front door, which is not hard to do in light of her outfit. I walk over to her, and she whispers, "Is he okay?"

"You mean Benny?"

"No, Willie. Is he okay?"

"You know Willie?"

"Yes. He has been stopping by with me sometimes."

"Oh. Yes. Willie is fine. Did he tell you everything? Why he was here and all that?"

"Certainly. Unfinished police work, he said. On the sly. Covert. Like KGB."

"Yes, very much like the KGB. I'm sure he'll be out as soon as he has a spare moment."

The inside of Dominic's is buzzing with cops and medics. Willie is on the phone, apparently talking to the LAPD, judging by the conversation. He hangs up and turns to me. "Anything up?"

"Oh, no. Nothing at all. Just another day at Hollywood View Court. By the way, Nina is outside when you have a minute."

"Nina! What a doll. I saw her here when I was casing the joint, then, wouldn't you know it, she's a stripper! I love strippers! And what a sweet kid she's got. She's studying at UCLA, you know. Graduates this spring. Getting a B.S. in, guess what? Criminology! What a kick! Excuse me a minute."

Willie steps out the door, hops down the three steps, and lands in Nina's outstretched arms, immediately beginning a necking session. Harriet and the old ladies watch, their eyes looking like they're going to pop out of their sockets.

The judge is led out in cuffs, followed by the old priest on a gurney. And just like that, the commotion is gone, out the front entryway and onto the street, leaving us behind.

Nina and Willie are still making out. I tap Willie on the shoulder and ask him, "How did you get into the apartment, anyway?"

"Whaddya think? I came in through the bathroom window," he says with a wink. "Do me a favor, the detective said Dom's got to go downtown with me in the morning, to file all the official reports. I'm going to try and, er, sleep for a while over at Nina's. I'll knock on your door around eight."

"Do you know which place is mine?"

"Are you kidding?"

I step into Dominic's and find him laid out on the sofa with his hands folded on his chest.

"You better get some rest, Dominic," I say, patting his hands.

"Yeah. I'll just stay here."

"We've got to go downtown tomorrow to file all the reports at LAPD headquarters."

"Okay. See you in the morning, General." I turn to leave, and as I pull the door open, he says, "Thanks, General. It's nice to be alive."

"Yeah. It is."

Chapter Fourteen

THE NEXT COUPLE of days are spent in and out of meetings with detectives, lawyers, and district attorneys. Willie tells me the D.A. wants to make sure Dominic files a video deposition, since it was obvious that if a trial drags on, he might not be around to testify in person. But a trial is unlikely. The judge and his team of lawyers are trying to cop a plea, which probably means Ralphie will spend the rest of his life in the joint, if he's lucky. Father B. sang like a bird and ratted out Judge Ralphie for killing poor little Louie. And as luck would have it, Ralph had just turned eighteen when he held poor little Louie under the raft. The Honorable Ralphie is in the process of being extradited to New York, where I'm sure some family members from Little Italy in the Bronx will be anxiously awaiting his arrival. Father B. also admitted to being an accessory to Ralph grinding off Dominic's fingers. So it looks like Father B. will be going back to jail for the little time he has left on the planet.

Joan shed some light on the judge for the cops. Turns out a couple of boys staying at Safe Haven fingered Ralphie for cruising the boulevard. Fortunately, they both bailed before Ralph had an opportunity to slip them a mickey. When Joan asked them why they ran off, they said it was because he reeked of garlic. Yet another reason why eating garlic is good for your health! I wouldn't be surprised if, once Judge Ralphie's mug shot is plastered all over the *New York Post*, the *Daily News*, and the local TV news, other New York victims start squawking like seagulls around a garbage scow.

With each passing hour, Dominic's body seems to be deteriorating. Willie, on the other hand, is a new man. He's staying with Nina full-time; he cut off his long greasy ponytail and got a stylish short cut. He's in and out of the swimming pool all day long, and his barroom pallor is transforming into a Coppertone tan. His sinewy frame is beefing up, thanks, I'm sure, to plates of Nina's potatoes, borscht, and pierogies.

Production on the Nostradamus show is still several days away, so I've been spending even more time with Dominic. I bring him the newspaper in the morning, and since his vision is failing, I even read it to him. This morning I noticed something in the paper that I'm going to bring to Dominic's attention, with great apprehension: The Giants are coming to town.

I know Dominic will never fully forgive his beloved Giants for abandoning him, but I figure it's worth a shot. He never asked me to read him anything about baseball from the sports section, but today I discovered his magnifying glass resting right on top of the Giants' box score in yesterday's paper.

Dominic is sitting in his tattered terry-cloth robe this morning, sipping tea in a folding wooden chair placed in front of his door, giving him a view of the pool, drenched in the southern California sunshine. The room is also bathed in more daylight than it has been in years, because Dominic finally opened his drapes.

"I see you've been reading the box scores," I say to Dominic, placing today's *Los Angeles Times* on the small TV snack table set up next to his chair.

"What makes you think that?" Dominic asks with his teacup halted in midair.

"I see your magnifying glass over on the coffee table, right on top of the Giants' box score."

"That's just an accident."

"Come on, Ben—I mean Dominic. Listen, you know who's coming to town tomorrow night?"

"Don't even say it."

"The Giants."

"I told you not to say it," Dominic says, putting his hands over his ears.

"Let's go!"

"I can't hear a word you're saying," Dominic says, his hands still covering his ears and his eyes scrunched closed.

"I'm going right now to the Dodger Stadium box office. I'll get two tickets—"

"No!" Dominic yells, his eyes popping open and both index fingers pointed at me. "Get five! You, Joan, Willie, Nina, and me!"

"Five it is," I say, walking over to Dominic's chair. "Listen, it could be a long walk from the parking lot to the seats, and I don't want you to feel embarrassed, but . . ."

"A wheelchair would be just the ticket. Maybe the gimp section is better than where they stick the regular stiffs," Dominic says, toasting me with a weak sip of tea.

Dominic was right. The wheelchair section isn't bad, and it's certainly better than the regular seats that were available for tonight's opener against the hated Giants. I was able to get four seats in the last row of the field-level seats behind third base, which is right in front of the place where they put the wheelchairs. The excitement in the ballpark reminds me of a slightly tamer version of Yankee Stadium when the Red Sox visit. The only reason the crowd is somewhat tamer is because of one thing: beer vendors. In California they don't allow beer vendors to work the stands, unlike Yankee Stadium, where the brewski sellers are so ubiquitous that they seem to outnumber fans on some nights. It's a cool evening, and Dominic looks like he's prepared for a Packers game in Green Bay, rather than a baseball game in southern California on a spring night. He's sitting with a thick blanket over his lap, a black knit cap pulled down to his ears, and a scarf tied tight around his neck.

"Hey, these seats are great!" he says, patting me on both shoulders from behind.

I turn around to acknowledge Dominic in his wheelchair and am startled by what I see: With his winter outfit, ghostly pallor, and sunken features, he appears to be, by far, the worst off of all his fellow wheelchair-section sitters, who include a chubby forty-ish man with a foot in a cast and a large blue foam Dodger finger; a ten-year-old with an arm in a sling; and a muscular twenty-something black man wearing a tank top, in a racing wheelchair. "Yeah, this is nice. A little chilly for you, Dominic?"

"Not yet. I'll let you know."

Dominic has a scorecard in his lap, and he's written across the top: *Me, Johnny, Joan, Willie, and Nina—N.Y Giants vs. Brooklyn Dodgers—May 11, 1992.* Some forms of denial are stronger than others.

First inning. The Giants are up. There's a leadoff walk, and two strikeouts, which brings Will Clark to the plate. He's probably the best hitter in the lineup, and a leftie. With two strikes on him, he takes a wicked cut, and uh-oh! Here it comes! A screaming line-drive foul ball, hit toward us off of Clark's bat, late on a fast ball. It's not one of those pop fouls where everyone is pushing one another out of the way to get under it as it floats into the stands. Folks are ducking, diving, and fathers are throwing themselves in front of small children in anticipation of this missile hurling at our section. Lucky for us, we're so far in the rear that the chances of it landing anywhere nearby are slim. The ball hits a railing, ricochets up, hits the overhang, continues on its path, hits an armrest, and although it's slowed down substantially, it's amazingly headed straight for us. It bounces one more time off a backrest, goes over my head, and lands harmlessly right in the middle of Dominic's blanket on his lap. The entire section jumps up and gives him a standing ovation when Dominic grabs the ball and lifts it high over his head for all to admire.

Joan, Willie, Nina, and I are standing and applauding with the rest of the crowd, even though Clark has already struck out and the Dodgers are leaving the field. Dominic has been holding the ball up for so long that his arm is growing tired, so he switches hands, and as one hand grabs the ball from the other, the free hand begins wiping the tears as they stream from his eyes, over a wide grin. And he's not alone. As our section finally sits and I turn to Joan, she's deep into her purse, pulling out tissues for herself and Nina.

"That was something else, Dominic," Willie says, punctuating his words by hitting a fist into his chest.

"Sure was. Sure was something," Dominic says, examining the ball. "*Official Ball—National League*. You know what? I think I'm getting a chill. I'm ready."

"It's only the first inning. Even Dodger fans usually stay until the fifth inning," I say, turning to Dominic.

Joan looks at Dominic's worn face, his deformed hand holding the ball, then turns to me with her eyes still wet with tears. "I think I'd like to go, too."

"Willie, you and Nina stay!" Dominic says, handing Willie his scorecard. "You've got to keep score. Please?"

"Are you sure, Dominic?" Willie asks. "You're okay?"

"Yeah, but first sign my ball," Dominic says, handing Willie the baseball. "Everybody signs my ball."

Willie signs the ball, as do Nina, Joan, and I. I hand Dominic the ball, and he looks at each signature carefully. "Oh, this is great. And hit by a Giant, yet."

I decide to take surface streets home rather than going on the freeway. Dominic sits in the back, and Joan and I are in front. We drive along Sunset Boulevard, winding from the stadium through residential neighborhoods and busy shopping districts. This part of Sunset is much different from the tony west end of the boulevard, where Hollywood's elite wine and dine. The eastern end of Sunset, where we are, is teeming with the hardworking Latin immigrants who take the Sunset Boulevard bus to clean the homes, mow the lawns, and change the diapers of the affluent white westsiders. Block after block is busy with mostly Mexican families shopping, selling, and heading home. I thought Dominic was sleeping, but he suddenly yells out loud. "Stop the car. Stop!"

"Christ, what is it, Dominic?"

"Pull over. Pull over."

As I stop and pull into a parking spot, Joan is halfway over the backseat, reaching to feel a pulse on Dominic's neck under his scarf. "Can you breathe? Are you okay?" she asks calmly.

"Back up. I want to go in there," Dominic says, rolling down his window, and craning his neck out to look behind us.

"What the hell are you talking about?" I ask Dominic, throwing the car into park.

"Did you see that sign?" Dominic asks, pulling his head in from the window.

"What sign?" I ask.

"That church. We just passed it. It's what I've been waiting for. A sign. Look at it. The Less Catholic Church," Dominic says, pulling his arms together tightly.

"I'll back up," I say, backing up the car until we're in front of a small stucco church, just a few feet from the curb.

"St. James. The Less. Catholic Church. The Less Catholic Church. He's right," Joan says, reading the sign next to the front door.

"That's it! I want to go in there! The *Less* Catholic Church. That's what I've been looking for," Dominic says, pushing the blanket aside and opening the car door.

"Whatever you say, Dominic. Do you want the wheelchair?"

"Nope. No chair. Just go in there and tell the priest there's somebody who wants confession. Please," Dominic whispers.

"You stay here with Joan. I'll be right back," I say, closing his car door and walking down a narrow alley next to the church. I ring a small buzzer on an intercom box, and a male voice answers, "How may I help you?"

"May I talk to you? Someone here needs . . . a confession," I say into the dusty plastic box, fully expecting to be told to come back during business hours.

"Come in," the voice says as the door buzzes, allowing me to push the door open and enter.

The room is tiny, with a wooden desk next to a doorway. A very short man, probably no older than I am, wearing a long priest's robe and sporting a full beard with an earring in his right ear, appears. He extends his hand to me. "How may I help you?" he asks in a slight Mexican accent. "I am Father Noriega. Call me Father Rick."

"Father Rick, we were driving home from the Dodgers game, and I have a very sick friend. He's dying of cancer. I know this sounds nuts. He's going through some very, very difficult things right now, and we passed your church and he felt he had to . . . make a confession. Here. Now."

"Most certainly. Bring him in through the main entrance. I'll be there in three minutes," the priest says, smiling, folding his hands together, as if praying. "No problem. See you in three."

"Thank you, Father," I say, exiting.

Joan and Dominic are sitting silently in the backseat together. "What happened?" Joan asks.

"The priest said come on in," I tell them, opening the car door.

"I knew it. I just knew it. I'm ready. Let's hit it." Dominic grunts as Joan helps him out of the car and onto the sidewalk.

The front door to the church is unlocked. We push it open and enter the dimly lit, small church, which seems more like a chapel. Dominic, Joan, and I sit in a pew next to the confessionals, which are about halfway back. The priest, now with a purple scarf around his neck, comes from a door behind the altar and briskly approaches. "I'm Father Rick. You are here for confession?" he asks Dominic.

"Yes, Father," Dominic says with comfort in his voice.

"Let me help you up," Father Rick says, extending his hand, which Dominic grabs with his deformed right hand.

"Oh, excuse me a second, Father," Dominic says as he stands. He pulls Joan and me a few feet aside from the priest and whispers, "I need a pen and paper. When I was a kid and I got penance, it was usually just ten Hail Marys. I have a feeling that this penance will need some serious note-taking."

Joan reaches into her purse and hands Dominic a pen and a piece of paper. Dominic takes them, smiles, winks, turns, and opens the door to the confessional.

"I'm going to make sure I write down everything. I don't want there to be any misunderstanding. My mother always told me that if you want to make sure you remember something, write it down," Dominic says, dangling the pen in one hand and the paper in the other.

Just before he shuts the door, he pops his head back out and says, "It won't be long. I am ready. Really. See ya. And thanks."

Dominic pulls the door closed. Joan and I hold hands, go to the last row of pews, and sit in silence. I pull the kneeler down and kneel on it. Joan joins me. I try to empty my mind in prayer, but it's filled with images of Dominic. I can't imagine what he's saying at this moment in that wooden box to that total stranger, but I hope it brings him peace.

I look to the front of the church, where a realistic figure of Christ on the cross hangs on the wall, complete with deep blood-red wounds. I concentrate on that and begin a rosary, using my fingers: starting with an Our Father, then ten Hail Marys, and repeat ten times. Our Father who art in heaven . . .

Just as I reach my fourth cycle of silent prayers, the door to the confessional bursts open.

"Come quickly. Please!" Father Rick says to us, his words echoing through the stillness of the church as he bounds from his side of the confessional booth. Joan and I run down the aisle, arriving just after Father Rick has opened the door to Dominic's booth. Dominic is slumped forward, his head against the wooden shelf in front of the confessional screen. The three of us pull Dominic out of the confessional and lay him out on the church floor.

"Do you know CPR?" Father Rick asks us.

"I do," Joan says as she begins to undo Dominic's shirt. His mouth is opening and shutting as if he's trying to speak, but only undecipherable moans and groans are coming out, as though he's speaking in tongues. The guttural sounds are punctuated by what I've heard my mom call a death rattle. His limbs twitch slightly, but he finds the strength to hold up his deformed hand, clutching the paper Joan gave him.

"Wait. The paper!" I say, taking it from his hand and reading it, "*No resus. Ball and cross in box*. What's *No resus*?" I ask, looking at Joan, fearing her answer.

Joan looks at the note in my hand, then reaches down to Dominic's face and strokes it. "Let go, Dominic. Let go. You're ready now. You're ready . . ."

Dominic's head jerks to the left, and he gives one final short gasp that makes his chest heave slightly.

"It means *Do not resuscitate*," Joan says, taking her right index finger and closing Dominic's eyes. He looks incredibly peaceful. I feel like a jerk for thinking of this, but the first thing that pops into my mind is the scene at the end of the classic horror film *The Wolf Man*, when the werewolf is killed and the tormented beast is transformed before our eyes into the smiling Larry Talbot, at peace at last.

Father Rick kneels on the hard granite floor and begins praying silently over Dominic.

"Is that the extra munchkin?" Joan whispers into my ear.

I nod and can feel Joan collapse against me with soft puffs of sobs. We both sit on the church floor and watch Father Rick perform Extreme Unction over Dominic's lifeless body.

Finally, Father Rick rises and walks toward the altar, leaving Joan and me alone with Dominic. Joan places Dominic's hands on his chest and reaches for my hand. She then slowly places our hands on top of Dominic's. His hands are already shockingly cold underneath mine, but Joan's hands actually feel hot.

Father Rick returns with a small ornate pillow and puts it under Dominic's head. He then takes a purple satin cloth with gold trim and places it over Dominic's face.

"I called the police. They're sending the coroner over. Would you like to pray with me?"

Joan and I turn toward each other and say simultaneously, "Yes."

"Is there a prayer you'd like to start with?" Father Rick says, eyes closed.

"Um, the Hail Mary?" I suggest awkwardly.

"Certainly," Father Rick says, taking hold of our hands. " 'Hail Mary . . .' "

Joan and I pray together with Dominic for the very first time.

Chapter Fifteen

THE SERVICE AT FOREST LAWN is a simple one. In attendance are Joan, Willie, Nina, Dominic's old porno partner Larry, and Father Rick. Dominic's ex-wife and son never showed. In a short ceremony before the burial, we pay our last respects to Dominic in an open coffin. He lies there with the baseball he caught at the game, signed by each of us, in his right hand, and the crucifix that Joan bought him wrapped around his left hand. After the coffin is closed, we follow it as it is rolled by several workers about thirty yards away to an open grave, surrounded temporarily by a carpet of bright green artificial turf. I'm sure Dominic would've preferred natural grass.

We watch as the copper box is lowered into the earth. Father Rick sprinkles holy water from an ornate stick over the coffin as it sits at the bottom of the grave and says, "Deliver us from evil. From the gate of hell. Deliver his soul, O

Lord. May his soul and the souls of all the faithful departed, through the mercy of God, rest in peace."

"Amen," we say in unison.

Willie and Nina, walking hand in hand in the bright morning sun, approach Joan and me as we are getting into my car.

"Thanks for everything. Dominic told me how much the two of you did for him," Willie says, his eyes still moist. "Oh, and by the way. If you want to get in touch, here's my number." He hands me a slip of paper with a phone number scribbled on it.

"You're going back home?"

"I am home," Willie says as he and Nina exchange warm smiles. "We're renting a house in Glendale. We're moving this week. Keep in touch." They walk over to his motorcycle, put on their helmets, and take off. Joan and I watch them roll down the tree-lined cemetery road.

"You know what we need?" I ask Joan as we walk toward my Woody.

"What's that?"

"A dog."

"We do?"

"Yeah."

"I know how to get to the Humane Society," Joan says, opening the driver's-side door and hopping in.

"I can't have a dog at my place," I say, getting into the passenger side.

"Well, maybe the dog will have to live with me," Joan says, putting the key in the ignition.

"And what about me?"

As Joan turns the key, she gets a shock that makes a crackling sound loud enough for me to hear. "Did that hurt?" I ask.

A crooked smile comes across her face and she says, "Felt great."

"Are you sure?" I ask.

"About what?" Joan asks, both hands on the wheel as the engine rumbles.

"About me and the dog moving in with you."

"Let's hit it," Joan says as she puts the old Woody into gear and we roll down the road.

I look into the rearview mirror on my side. The chapel is getting smaller and smaller in the distance until it finally disappears behind a lush green hillside as Joan steers us out of the cemetery and onto the road that leads back to Hollywood. But just before our right turn onto Los Feliz Boulevard, Joan makes a left instead.

"You know, my place is a little small for two people, a cat, and a dog," Joan says, watching the road. "I hear there are some good deals on houses in the areas adjacent to the burnt-out riot areas in Hollywood. The animal shelter is this way," she says, smiling at me.

I place my hand gently on Joan's thigh, which brings a soft smile to her face, and say, "Let's name him Benny."

Printed in the United States
By Bookmasters